Today's Desire

by

Cassandra Bella

*The Grady Brothers Trilogy,
Book Two*

This is a work of fiction. Names, characters, places, and incidents are either the product of the author's imagination or are used fictitiously, and any resemblance to actual persons living or dead, business establishments, events, or locales, is entirely coincidental.

Today's Desire

COPYRIGHT © 2020 by Cassandra Bella

Cover Art by *The Wild Rose Press, Inc.*

The Wild Rose Press, Inc.
PO Box 708
Adams Basin, NY 14410-0708
Visit us at www.thewildrosepress.com

Publishing History
First Crimson Rose Edition, 2020
Print ISBN 978-1-5092-3118-8
Digital ISBN 978-1-5092-3119-5

The Grady Brothers Trilogy, Book 2
Published in the United States of America

He'd felt the tug deep in his gut. The one promising to stretch further, leaving him wanting even as he was satisfied.

Backing Tori against the wall as soon as he had her inside her bedroom, he took with all he had, needing every bit of her. A full surrender, giving in to the needs swirling so hot, so desperate, between them.

He should have gone. He'd admit it. When she tried brushing him back to the ranch, he should have turned on his heels and walked away without a look back.

But…damn. He couldn't do it. Not with her.

There was something there. Something dragging at him and pulling him under. Everything that was right and sensible around her became nonexistent. And it became nothing more than needing to feel and know the beauty, the fiery mystery she promised with no more than a look from her intoxicating, emerald eyes.

Dedication

to Darren McGowan

~

Whenever I think of you, I always think
of jean jackets and Ram Chargers.
I'm so thankful my life has been blessed
with your friendship!

Prologue

He'd hoped against it but she'd searched. She'd found.

Ice cubes hit the sides of his crystal tumbler as Filip Pavenco took a long, slow drink from his scotch, watching the lazy flow of the river far below. The life that was Chicago buzzed along the streets and sidewalks yet failed to match the constant rush running through his own mind.

He'd always known, feared, this day might come. Though he'd done all he could to prevent it, there had never been a guarantee.

She had stubborn in her blood.

Turning away from the window, he set his scotch on the desk and glanced at the simple silver frame in the corner. She'd come by her stubbornness at birth, inheriting it from her mother.

They smiled back at him through the picture. The small child she'd once been cuddled in her mother's lap. So young. So innocent. And her mother—

It wasn't a road he needed to travel. That was done...over.

Picking up his scotch, sipping on it, he accepted there were things needing to be done. She'd make contact. There was no stopping it. But she must be discouraged from staying.

There was no other way.

To give them time together would be to expose the truth he'd worked so hard to keep hidden. He couldn't allow it. *Wouldn't allow it.*

She may have sought. She may have found. But he remained a step ahead. He'd use it, as he always had, to his advantage, bringing an end to the threat before it had a chance to take root.

Chapter One

A September blizzard. *Really?*

Narrowing her eyes, Victoria Mundola strained to see through the heavy sheet of white. Fought to keep all four tires on the slick, mountain road.

"Come on, Tori," she hissed through her teeth. "You can do this."

She knew snow. You didn't grow up in Chicago without knowing how to drive through the storms.

But this...it was different. The flakes so thick. So full.

She'd never known such snow existed.

It was meant to be wet. And sticky. And annoying.

It shouldn't be this big fluff of white, pretending such innocence while grabbing at your tires and threatening to toss you over the edge.

She'd barely seen a thing since turning off the interstate onto this pitiful stretch of road they called a highway.

She couldn't even tell if Snow Ridge was close, though the irritating voice of her GPS kept insisting it was.

How could anyone know anything in this mess?

Another bright idea turning into a disaster. It shouldn't surprise her. It was the way of her life. She was good at grand thoughts. But carrying them out to success wasn't her thing. Never had been.

And this one was about as foolish as she'd ever come up with. Packing it all up, leaving behind everything she knew for a brother who obviously hadn't given a damn about her in over two decades.

Yeah. Great idea.

Hands curled tight over the steering wheel, she inched along, praying her small compact wouldn't let her down. It had to be a bad sign she was the only car on the road. Only someone foolish pushed on in such weather.

But what choice did she have? If there was a place to pull over and wait out the storm, she couldn't see it through the thick sheet of white. She could pass by a dozen hotels and have no clue.

So, she'd go on and count this as another adventure in life. Not that she needed any more. But, sometimes, there wasn't much choice.

Her GPS chirped, warning a turn was coming up.

She slowed, having no idea how she'd see the road. There were no tire tracks to follow. No hint of where a turn lane might be or a new street began.

There was only white. So thick she was sure she'd pass right by and drive herself off into who knew where.

Inching along, she kept one eye on the road and the other on the digital map from her GPS, counting down the miles, then the feet, until her turn.

She could do nothing more than trust when it told her to turn and hope it was road she hit.

Though she was cautious, the back end of her tiny car slid. She turned into it and prayed she gained control.

It did no good. There was nothing but slick ground

beneath her tires, pushing her back the other way. Catching a groove, she slid through the turn and down an embankment she didn't see and could only feel through the snow.

She knew it was useless, still she pushed on the gas and yanked on the wheel.

Nothing. Her little car rested at an odd angle. Not quite tilted but close. And she was stuck there. For who knew how long.

"Damn." She slammed an open palm against the steering wheel. A half tank of gas was what she had left to keep her protected from the biting cold. After that, she was out of luck.

Yeah, she could see the story now…crazy, irrational woman freezes to death on the side of the road. Missed by no one.

It would be the way of it. What she'd known, lived by, for most of her life. This trip to Snow Ridge was the chance to change it. But it didn't appear she'd be making it or changing anything.

Just to say she'd done it, she tried once more, tires spinning while her car refused to move an inch.

She was stuck. There was no getting around it. And she didn't even have a clue if she was near the road she'd hoped to reach. For all she knew, she'd driven into the middle of a field. Lost and forgotten.

****

It was one hell of a night.

A native to these parts, Luke Grady worked his police-issued four-wheel drive down the road without worry. The storm had come in quick, hard and heavy, especially for September. But it was a snow they knew well in these parts and would have plenty more of as the season carried on.

He passed by the Double G Ranch, wishing for home.

He'd be there soon enough. One pass along this stretch of road leading into town and his duty would be done.

The residents of Snow Ridge had hunkered down early. State Patrol was out in force, handling the Interstate. He'd left good officers in charge and was easy to reach.

There was nothing keeping him from closing himself away at the ranch and taking a few hours of much-needed sleep before heading out again.

It wasn't far—down one way and back the other. Then it would be some of Hattie's famous Irish Stew and a blazing fire for him.

The headlights did so little to break through the thick sheet of snow he almost missed the reflection bouncing back from the opposite side of the road.

It was probably nothing. Still, he needed to check.

With no other cars to worry about, he cut across the lanes and inched along the edge of the road. Surprise caught when he realized it was a car awkwardly caught at the edge of the drainage ditch.

He thought it abandoned until he drew closer, headlights catching the shadow of someone inside. A puff of smoke spiraled from behind.

Flipping the lights, he brought his vehicle to the front bumper of the other car, calling in his stop to the station. A blast of frigid cold hit as he opened the door, leaving the warmth inside.

Turning on his flashlight, he used it to guide his way and bring shape to the shadow inside the car.

Chestnut hair tumbled over slender shoulders, shadowing deep emerald eyes, uncertain as they watched him come around the front and stop at the driver's door.

He readied his badge to reassure any fears she might have while he waited for her to roll down the window. "I'm Chief Grady with the Snow Ridge police department. Looks like you could use some help."

Though a flash of relief sparked in her gaze, it quickly disappeared. Again she looked at him with uncertain, almost fearful, eyes. The badge and flashing lights obviously did little to soothe whatever worries she had.

"I was turning off the highway." She looked behind her, waving her hands. "And I slid. Couldn't get my car out."

But Tori actually hit road. Somehow, even in all this, it was a relief to know. She released the breath she held tight in her chest and forced her nerves to calm.

Even knowing he was there for good, the sight of the uniform pulled at old memories, bringing back fear. Heartache. A reminder of all she'd lost so long ago.

"I didn't know there'd be a blizzard. I was headed into Snow Ridge for an interview and thought I'd get here a day ahead to give myself time to prepare." She heard the frantic rush of her words and knew she needed to settle down or risk looking like a fool.

He merely looked at her, thoughts unreadable in his expression. He was a sight to see on the side of the road, surrounded by the heavy snow. His face was carved to stone perfection. Every line, every curve, hinted at a strength lingering inside.

Black hair, cut short, added charm to the sun-kissed tone of his skin, deepening the hazel color of his eyes.

As a Chief of Police, he was a handsome one. And a suspicious one, she realized, as he stared at her, saying nothing while using his piercing gaze to determine what he could.

"I'm sorry." She sucked in a harsh breath, forcing old fears down where they belonged. She had nothing to worry about. "It hasn't been a pleasant time, trying to drive through this. I've been sitting here for hours, afraid of what I'd do when the gas ran out."

That seemed to do the trick. His gaze softened. A smile hinted on his lips. "It's not the time to be out driving in this. The warnings were to keep off the roads."

"I've been driving since Nebraska early this morning. Wasn't aware of any warnings, or even snow, till I headed into the mountains and found myself stuck in this."

He lowered his flashlight and stuck his badge back at his waist. "Storm's too thick to try pulling you out. Is there somewhere I can take you? Somewhere you're expected?"

"I'm not expected anywhere until tomorrow afternoon. I have an interview at Precious Gems." She hadn't even bothered to book a hotel, figuring she'd wait till she got to town to find one she liked.

"You must be Victoria Mundola."

"Tori," she corrected, hating her full name. "How would you know?"

What kind of town was this? She knew it was small but now she worried. There were limits. And a Chief of Police knowing so much definitely pushed them.

"Your interview is with an old friend and soon to be sister-in-law." He looked at her, seeing more than she was comfortable with. "I ran background checks on the ones she chose to see."

"You ran a background check on me?" The idea was unsettling. Not that he would have found anything. Not even a parking ticket. But she didn't like cops, hadn't since she was a tiny girl. Knowing one had dug into her past unsettled her.

His eyes narrowed. She'd piqued his suspicion. Something she didn't want to do. She forced a smile, silently cursing her fate. Maybe she'd have been better freezing inside her car as she'd first imagined.

"It was my own doing." He watched her, his gaze heavy as if searching for the secrets she kept carefully buried inside.

The snow thickened, swirling around him. "Storm's getting worse. I'll take you to the ranch and get you out of the cold."

"The ranch?" She hesitated as she looked back inside her car and considered staying there, stuck, on the side of the road.

"My family's place." Impatience touched the deep timbre of his voice. "The Double G. It's just up the road."

He pointed a hand as if she had any clue where she was. "You'll have some food, get warm, and have a chance to meet Cara."

She was having a hell of a time keeping up with him. Tori shook her head and tried to make sense of everything he said. "Who's Cara?"

"The owner of Precious Gems. The one you came all this way in the middle of a blizzard to meet."

Yeah, she was lost, mentally and physically. This had been some kind of screwed up day she couldn't make sense of. "Maybe it would be better if you took me into town."

"In this storm, even in my vehicle, it would be a crazy risk. The ranch is much closer." Obviously done with trying to convince her, he grabbed the handle and opened the door. "You'll feel right at home. I promise."

She looked at him, a trace of fear riding up her spine. She chased it away. He was the Chief of Police after all. There were no threats. No reason to worry. She was never one to trust, but she could at least give the benefit of the doubt.

"Okay." She rolled up the window and turned the key in the ignition. Reaching in the back, she grabbed her bag which he took from her as she stepped out into the snow.

He waited while she locked the doors before turning to follow.

She'd go to this ranch of his and wait out the storm. She could handle that much. It wasn't a great commitment he asked for, only a short time for the blizzard to end. Then she'd be back on her own. Just as she preferred.

Chapter Two

There was something about her. Good or bad, Luke hadn't decided yet.

Turning onto the ranch, he stole a glance, her silhouette a shadow in the dark. There was no denying she pleased the eyes. The long stream of hair flowing over her shoulders, down her slender back, nearly screamed for a man to run his hand through the silky strands. And her eyes, such a deep emerald, it felt like you could drown in them.

But there was something else. Something he couldn't put a finger on but itched in the back of his mind. It was in the nerves darkening her gaze. The fear shaking in her voice.

He'd made her uncomfortable when he'd appeared at her window. But it wasn't the discomfort he knew or had experienced many times as an officer of the law when those he'd come across had a crime or two to hide.

This was different. And he wanted to know why.

"It looks so…warm." Uttering her first words since climbing into his truck, Tori stared out the window as he stopped in front of a beautiful, sprawling house.

Through the dark and snow, it glistened. Light shimmered from the porch lights and through the large front windows. Smoke spiraled from the chimney, tangling with the thick flakes.

There was beauty here. Though she couldn't see it through the heavy white, she knew it. Sensed it. Through the snow, she saw the outline where someone had shoveled the path leading to the grand porch twisting around both sides of the house.

An old oak stood like a protector, branches drooping from the weight of the flakes. Rockers tucked into a corner of the porch moved with the cold wind. A blanket of white covered the flowers peeking from pots at their sides.

The size of it, rising high, stretching long, only added to the comforting look and welcomed those who came. Promising not just a house but a home.

Luke grabbed her bag and climbed out. Coming around the front of the truck, he opened her door. "Wait till you get inside." He waited for her feet to hit the ground before starting up the path beside her.

She didn't understand until he opened the door and stepped back so she could enter ahead of him.

A red-brick fireplace greeted them, fire blazing. The crisp scent of burning wood curled around them. Soft leather couches and matching chairs took up the large space in the front room, encouraging a sit and a discussion in front of the fire's warmth.

Luke dropped her bag in the foyer and waved her on.

She followed through a dining room big enough to sit an army. Wood glistened and the scent of lemon polish hovered in the air.

And then it hit her. A rich, meaty aroma mixing with the unmistakable smell of fresh-baked bread. It teased, taunted, and brought forth a hunger she hadn't been aware she carried.

Then the voices. They drifted, like a song, rising one over the other. And laughter, so deep, so true, it tugged a smile from the corners of her mouth, growing stronger as Luke led her from the dining room into a large, bright kitchen.

The voices, she guessed, came from the three women gathered at the long counter beneath the wall of windows. They turned as one, eyes trailing over her and Luke while smiles spread across their faces.

"There you are." The oldest of the three broke away. Arms stretched, Tori expected her to reach for Luke. Instead, she grabbed Tori's hands and looked her over, concern heavy in her gaze. "You must be cold to the bone."

"I'm...uh—"

"Get her a bowl." She waved a hand at the two still at the counter while draping an arm around Tori's shoulders.

"You'll sit." She eased her down in one of the many chairs lining the well-worn kitchen table claiming the far corner of the kitchen. "You'll eat. And you'll feel better."

Was she sick? Tori shook her head, fighting off the confusion taking hold since Luke appeared at her window and brought all this her way.

It was so far out of her comfort zone her head was spinning.

A bowl in one hand and a plate of sliced bread in the other, the youngest of the three approached. There was understanding in her deep blue eyes and a knowing smile on her lips.

She nudged the older woman out of the way, settling in the chair next to Tori and placing the bowl

13

and plate in front of her. "Bit overwhelming, isn't it?"

She shook her head at Luke, still standing at the curved entrance to the kitchen. "The Gradys tend to be that way. They come on strong and leave your head spinning."

Yes. That explained it. At least someone understood.

"You're Tori." She pushed the bowl closer. "We know because Luke had dispatch call to let us know you were coming."

When? She pushed back through her memory, trying to pinpoint the moment when he'd had the chance to do so. Nothing came, leaving her even more frustrated and confused.

"And I'm Cara." She offered a hand and a soft, comforting smile. "We were supposed to meet tomorrow. But it looks like the snow changed that."

It did. It changed so much.

"I'm—"

She struggled for a sense of balance. If she didn't find a way to manage more than a word or two, she'd leave them thinking she was crazy.

"She's not even sure she wants to be here." Luke's deep voice broke through. Though he winked at her, it didn't ease the kick of anger pushing through.

She narrowed her eyes, tempted to let him have it.

"Don't you let him bother you." The older woman pushed between her and Cara, patting a hand over hers. "He's just poking like he does best."

"I *am* grateful for this." Tori found her voice, forcing words through her confusion. "I don't want you to think otherwise."

"Don't you worry about that. Must be something, a

stranger to these parts caught in that storm." Hattie's smile, so soft and gentle, tugged at a longing Tori thought she'd done away with years ago.

"Thank you, ma'am."

Her answering laugh was quick, reaching up to her dark brown eyes. "No ma'ams around here, just Hattie." She urged Tori back to the food in front of her. "You eat then we'll see about a room for you."

"Penny." She turned back to the only one left at the counter. "Dish Cara up some of that stew. She can eat with our guest while we wait for the men to return."

The men. There were more?

She didn't do crowds. Didn't do people. Her life was a solitary one. The way she liked it.

A step ahead of Penny, Luke met her at the table. Grabbing the bowl, he took his own bite before placing it in front of Cara. "Where are the others?"

"Your dad, brothers, and Joe are walking the barns, checking on the horses." Hattie waved a hand at him as he came up behind her and grabbed a slice of bread from the counter.

"Joe?" He looked at Cara, eyebrows raised.

"He's stubborn." Though she shrugged, Tori caught the shadow of worry in her blue eyes.

She couldn't keep up. Deciding she really didn't want to know what they talked about, she gave in to the enticing scents teasing her. Taking a bite from the stew, flavor exploded against her tongue.

It was…heaven. There was no other word she could think of.

She knew Lean Cuisine from the freezer. An occasional splurge on pizza from Gittano's. But this— her taste buds sang for joy as she took another bite before tearing off a corner of fresh-baked bread—was an experience she'd never forget.

*****

Watching her wasn't easy.

As the hours passed, Luke reminded himself he was a well-trained officer of the law. He knew to observe, catalog facts, make decisions, and go on from there.

This woman he'd found stranded on the side of the road turned it all upside down.

Tori was—

He didn't know. Couldn't figure her out. And it was driving him crazy.

She was like a switch flickering hot and cold. The tense shyness she'd entered with had eased. She smiled more, even laughed when meeting his brothers as they'd come in from the storm.

But there was still something. A barrier in place, protecting her from whatever risk she found surrounded by his family.

"So you're here with hopes to work for Cara." His dad, Patrick, set his spoon next to his empty bowl and rested back in his chair. "It's a good place she has."

Her food long ago finished, Tori rested her hands on the table. She honestly didn't know much about Precious Gems. Only that they were in need of a retail clerk and she was in need of a job. "I look forward to seeing it."

"You will. As soon as the snow clears." Beside her, Cara smiled. She sat tucked close to one of the brothers Luke had introduced her to. Cade...Tori was pretty sure that was his name. There was no mistaking the family resemblance. While Luke's hair was darker than his brothers, they shared the same hard sculpted features, handsome as well as dangerous. Standing tall, Irish pride giving a swagger to their steps, there was an arrogance to the smiles they gave freely and often.

But it was the eyes. Those deep, hazel eyes, leaving no doubt they were related. They held the power to reach into your soul and pull out your darkest secrets.

Which is what frightened her the most.

"Might as well give her the job." The other brother, Jake, popped the last bite of bread into his mouth. "She did brave a blizzard for you."

Cara shot him a look. Though Tori expected anger, there was more amusement than anything else. "Though I'm leaning that way, I still think it's best to have a proper interview first."

"We could do it in the morning." She turned to Tori. "There's nothing demanding we have it at the store. If we could find a private moment." She shot a look around the table. "We should be fine."

"I do believe that's a hint." Cade looked at Luke across the table, a smile teasing the corners of his mouth.

"A not so subtle one." Luke looked at Tori and caught the hope brimming in her emerald eyes before she shoved it back down.

What brought her here? Relocating to a place like Snow Ridge from Chicago was a big step. As much as he loved Cara and what she'd done with Precious Gems, he didn't believe for a moment the chance to work for her was enough for someone to give up the life they knew for such a drastic change.

Maybe he should dig a little further. Not that he

figured it would get him anywhere. There wasn't anything he'd found the first time around giving red flags. Nothing suggested a second look.

Still, it couldn't hurt. Especially if Cara was leaning toward hiring her.

It didn't, he reassured himself, have anything to do with his own draw toward her. She was a beautiful woman. But he'd seen plenty of them. Enjoyed a fair few.

There was something about her leaving him curious, wondering what secrets she held behind her shadowy gaze.

But none of that played into his urge to learn more and discover what he could about this woman from the side of the road. He just wanted to make sure she was a good fit for Cara. Especially after what she'd gone through only a few months before.

That was all it was. He was sure of it.

"I have a room ready for you." Hattie rested a hand on Tori's shoulder as she pushed a platter of warm brownies into the center of the table. She barely had her hand away before Luke grabbed one seconds before his brothers did the same.

Shaking her head, clucking her tongue, Hattie turned back for the counter, grabbing a fresh pot of coffee and setting it next to the brownies. "Tori will think I never taught you a lick of manners with the way you're acting."

Mouths full, they smiled at her, earning another shake of the head.

"They're grownups," Cara grabbed the edge of the platter and offered one to Tori, "until Hattie brings out her homemade brownies."

Though she knew she'd have to pay for it later, Tori took one, unable to resist the sweet smell teasing her. So much food. So many people inside the house while a blizzard raged outside. It was odd, the comfort existing between them. The simple feeling of home that seemed to pour from the walls, surrounding them.

A storm like this in Chicago would have isolated her in her little, one-bedroom apartment with a bottle of wine, a microwaved dinner, and a movie-on-demand. And it would have been good for her. All she'd known. Never needing more.

Is this what families did? Come together to eat, laugh and make it through the storm.

"Cade, get my daughter to pass those brownies, would you?" From across the table, Cara's dad grabbed the pot of coffee and poured a cup.

He'd come in with the others, cane in hand, limping painfully to a chair while ignoring the worry in his daughter's eyes. Penny had fussed over him while scolding him for going out.

There were so many of them. All smiles and laughter. Teasing while they ate. Voices rising and falling through the kitchen. A constant clatter of noise making Tori's head spin.

And yet, somehow, they all fit. All seemed right.

"So, Tori, do you know anybody here in Snow Ridge." Passing the brownies down the table, Cade slung an easy arm around Cara's shoulders.

She paused, the brownie halfway to her mouth, not knowing how to answer. She did have family here. Just like them. But it wasn't the same. Was nowhere close to it.

Luke's heavy gaze burned into her side as she

hesitated. Glancing over her shoulder, she caught the intense look in his hazel eyes, felt it reach deep inside.

"I don't." She found the words, reasoning they weren't lies. She didn't know her brother anymore. Hadn't for a very long time.

While the others turned away, satisfied, Luke's heavy gaze continued to burn. She didn't want to look at him. Didn't dare.

Something about him frightened her even as it excited her. Concentrating on her brownie, she wished he'd go away and leave her alone. Everything about him made her uncomfortable. He sparked an uneasiness she didn't like. Had no clue how to handle.

She did her best to ignore him, finishing her brownie and following the constant flow of conversation around the table.

They talked as one, understanding on a level she was foreign to. There was the ease and care, reserved only for those who knew one another intimately. In ways others could only hope for.

She'd been one who'd once hoped for that. *Family.* The closeness of it. Her life had started that way. She still remembered the love just as she felt around this table.

She'd only been a small girl of three when she'd lost it. And though she'd kept hope for the years following, it took a string of heartbreaks and backs turned for her to realize it was not for her. Would never be.

"I have to go back on duty for a bit." Luke pushed his chair back from the table, grabbing his empty coffee cup. Standing over Tori, he looked down on her, an expression glowing in his eyes she didn't dare try to decipher. "I'll show you to your room before I go."

"Oh. That's not necessary." She fumbled with the handle of her cup, doing all she could not to meet his stare.

Shock shot through as his finger caught under her chin, lifting her eyes to his. "It is. I brought you here. I'll make sure you're settled before I go."

He grabbed her cup and added it to his own.

She couldn't speak. Couldn't respond. She could only stare like a foolish girl as he turned for the sink.

Heat flushed her cheeks. The tingle of his touch lingered against her skin. Grabbing desperately for control, she pulled back to functioning thought.

"Cara's old room is ready." Hattie grabbed the cups, pushing him aside as she set them on the top rack of the dishwasher. "You make sure she has everything she needs before you go."

More time with Luke was the last thing Tori wanted. She wanted a bed. Some sleep. And to forget this day ever happened. Forget about the dark, handsome man who'd come to save her and had irritated her ever since.

He stood at the edge of her chair, waiting.

Reluctant, she pushed from her seat. "Thank you." She smiled at Hattie. "The food was wonderful."

Flicking a kitchen towel at her side, Hattie came to her, resting a gentle hand on her shoulder. "You've had quite a day. Get some sleep. Tomorrow will be better."

Luke stepped aside and held out his hand, inviting her to go ahead of him. Clinging to the fact she'd soon be rid of him, she stepped out into the hall and waited for him to grab her bag.

"This way." He pointed to the stairs, falling into

step behind her.

At the top, she moved aside, letting him lead her down the hall to an open door on the right. He stepped in ahead of her, dropping her bag by the bed. "The bathroom is there." He pointed over his shoulder.

It was a beautiful room, so much more than she'd expected. A soft teal claimed the color, from the comforter to the curtains draped over the windows.

She moved to the dark oak vanity pushed against the wall, running her fingers along the edge. She'd dreamed of such a thing as a little girl. Had played with images of sitting in front of the mirror and feeling like a movie star as she prepared for the day.

"This was Cara's room?" Remembering Hattie's words, she turned to where Luke stood between the bed and the door.

He nodded. "She grew up here on the Double G. This was her room when she stayed at the big house rather than her place with her dad just down the way."

"Her dad...Joe?"

"He's been our foreman for over thirty years. He's family."

There it was again—*family*. Something she'd lost so early in life, been denied for so much of her childhood, and had given up on by the time she became an adult.

She didn't know this, the connection and love holding these people together. Hell, she was here not even sure her own brother would give her the time of day. What they shared wasn't something she could hope for. It was too far out of reach.

"I'll be staying here tonight instead of my place." Luke gave her one last look before turning for the door.

"I shouldn't be longer than a few hours. If you need anything, my room is only a couple doors down."

"Your room? You'll be that close?"

"I will. For the night. So will Cade and Cara, my dad and Hattie. And I'm guessing Jake will be staying instead of daring the ride back to his pub."

"Maybe I should sleep on the couch so there are enough rooms for everyone." She stepped away from the vanity and made a move for her bag.

He wrapped a hand around her wrist, stopping her. "This big house has enough room for everyone." Heat curled where he held her, lingering even after he let go.

"Get some sleep." He looked down on her, and her breath caught hard in her chest. "You've had a busy day."

He didn't give her a chance to respond. Turning his back, he stepped into the hall and quietly closed the door behind him.

****

Only by the best of luck, he'd made it to Snow Ridge.

So many times, he'd wanted to pull over, give up, and wait for the storm to take him. But he was stronger than that, known for his guts. His stubbornness pushed him on in the worst of circumstances. The last thing he needed was to be remembered as the one who lost it all in a blizzard in the middle of the Rocky Mountains.

Dropping his wet, snow-covered coat over the back of the chair, Anton moved to the window, staring out over the dark night and the heavy blanket of snow refusing to ease.

He was one of the best. He'd worked hard, clawing his way into a place of respect and sometimes fear. The

Pavenco Family had much to thank him for. He'd brought many successes to them.

But this—he couldn't help but feel it was beneath him.

Cursing as he turned away from the window, he checked out the minibar provided by the hotel. There wasn't much. It was the limited selection he expected to find in a small town. But the small bottles in the door were enough. Choosing a whiskey, he closed the door while reaching for the small glasses settled on a tray above.

He should have ice but didn't have the energy to fetch some. Twisting off the top, tossing it in the trash can, he poured a hefty share into the glass and enjoyed the first, slow sip.

This job…it didn't feel right. Not by the standards he knew the family operated under. He was to follow, discourage when he was told, but nothing more. Not without permission first.

And who in the hell was this Victoria Mundola anyhow?

In the years he'd worked for the family, he'd never heard the name.

But she obviously meant something. The request sending him here had come personally from the top, something that didn't happen often.

He'd been called in, served the finest scotch, and asked to do this. As a favor. One that would be repaid greatly.

So here he was, in the middle of a blizzard, stuck in a small mountain town and acting as a babysitter for some unknown woman who was important enough to draw out the best of the best.

Chapter Three

The snow slowed but continued to linger with the morning hours.

Luke's only thought as he stumbled into the kitchen was coffee. The savior she always was, Hattie shoved a cup in his hand and pushed him toward the table where his dad and brothers sat.

"Heard the storm's closed down most of the town." His dad took his own slow sip of coffee while reaching for one of Hattie's homemade blueberry muffins centering the table.

Luke nodded, not yet ready to speak. The time before the ski resorts opened and tourists poured in, the owners of the shops and restaurants scattering the town were quicker to call a snow day, staying safe and sound in their warm houses. Had it been a couple of months later, the result would have been different. Though some may have still chosen to close due to the weather, many more would have done all they could to keep their doors open.

It was the two tales of Snow Ridge. Founded as a small, ranching community in the Rocky Mountains, it held on to its roots during the late Spring to early Fall. But once the snow started flying, accumulation adding up, the changes came. Sandwiched by two popular ski resorts, it turned to a busy, vibrant tourist town. A constant rush of people and the life they brought with them.

Year after year, it was the same. From slow and easy to frantic and rushed. That was the town they called home. One his own ancestors had a hand in bringing to life. Never anticipating what it would become.

"I'm thankful for it." Cade grabbed his own muffin and ripped a chunk from the side. "I don't want Cara out in this mess. It's better having her home where I know she's safe."

"You'd keep me home and safe forever if you could." Cara stepped into the kitchen, pouring her own cup of coffee before settling beside Cade at the table.

"Careful, honey." She leaned over, dropping a soft kiss on his cheek. "Your protective streak is showing."

Cade scowled then smiled, leaving his own kiss on her lips, lingering for a moment before pulling away.

Luke enjoyed watching them, knowing and understanding how far they had come to be able to joke about Cade's over-protective ways. "Storm's supposed to clear by afternoon. Snow Ridge will be back to life tomorrow."

"Tori won't want to be here another night." Carrying the wisdom of many years, Hattie moved around the table, refilling coffee cups. "No matter what the storm's doing."

"She's a frightened one. Though I can't figure out why." The maternal love, known by them all, swelled in Hattie's eyes and drifted softly through her voice.

She'd been part of raising them all—Luke, his brothers, Cara. Ireland had been home but here, on the Double G, was her family.

"I like her." Cara stole a bite of muffin from

Cade's plate before wrapping her hands around her cup. "She was overwhelmed last night. But who can blame her? You Gradys do tend to bring out such a reaction in strangers."

She eased her words with a soft smile. "I'll do the interview when she gets up. But I'm already pretty set on hiring her. And if I do, part of the benefits of the job is free rent in the apartment above the shop. She could stay there tonight if it makes her feel more comfortable."

Cade looked past Cara, catching Luke's gaze. He understood, without words, the questions in his younger brother's expression. Though he wouldn't put it to words, he needed reassurance there were no worries with Cara putting her trust in Tori.

And there weren't. Not really. Luke had his own questions. But none of that played a part in Cara's trust in her. "I think that would be a good idea." He looked at Cade, giving the answer he sought.

****

They were back at the kitchen table.

Tori shook her head and wondered about this family that had taken her in. The Grady brothers were a sight. A handsome trio. They each held a power. An air that spoke of strength and loyalty. Looking at them, their dad, there was no doubting the ties—physical and beyond—between them. They held a connection, a bond, she couldn't begin to understand.

And then there was Cara, so soft in beauty. Yet there was a sense of strength simmering below the surface. And she was one of them. There was no question. She was just as much a part of the family as the others sitting around the table.

27

As if brought aware by her thoughts, Cara looked up, smiling as her glance fell on Tori standing hesitantly in the entry to the kitchen.

"Good morning." She rose, wrapping an arm around Tori's waist as if sensing her hesitation. As if she knew the uncertainty and understood how hard it was to be in a new place and a new life where everything was foreign. "You sit. I'll get you a cup of coffee."

Hattie was already a step ahead of her, placing a steaming cup in front of Tori as she took the empty chair between Cara and Luke. "You'll have a muffin." Hattie placed one on a plate in front of her. "We don't want you going hungry."

She wasn't a breakfast eater but didn't argue. Had a feeling, with Hattie, it would be pointless. She picked off a small pinch of the muffin and felt as if all eyes around the table settled on her.

"Did you sleep all right?" She nearly jumped in her seat as Luke's deep voice washed over her. He stared at her, drawing her in. Tempting her to places she didn't want to go.

"I did." She pushed past the nervous knot in her throat. "Thank you."

Tori felt the tension between them and couldn't help but wonder if the others sensed it too.

"How about a walk after breakfast?" Cara looked at her with a knowledge that made Tori uncomfortable. "It will be through the snow. But it will be a nice one. Get us out for a bit in the fresh air."

"A walk?" Tori stared at her over the rim of her cup.

Cara nodded. "To the main barn. I thought we'd

have the best privacy if we held the interview in Cade's office rather than trying to find a quiet place in the house."

Though the flakes still fell and the cold lingered, Tori liked the idea. Getting out and about, away from Luke's hovering presence, was just what she needed. "I'll finish this." She swept her hand over her muffin and half-finished coffee. "And I'll be ready."

It would be good to get out and away from this family that left her with odd feelings mixing with strange desires.

And away from the one who'd come to her in the worst of the storm. Remained a part of her thoughts ever since.

****

The flakes were nowhere near what they had been.

Someone had shoveled a path through the thick white blanket. It was cold but not bitterly so. As Luke had said, the worst had passed.

Hope rose as Tori walked side by side with Cara away from the house toward the large barn ahead.

There was comfort here she hadn't felt inside the house. Maybe it was because she was better with one on one interaction. Or because she sensed an understanding in the other woman. A knowledge of the struggle to settle in a home so rich with family, love, and loyalty.

"I'll brew us a fresh pot of coffee and we'll get started." Cara pulled on the big, heavy doors. They slid effortlessly in their tracks, washing warmth over them as they opened.

Stepping inside, the strong scents of well-worn leather and fresh hay surrounded Tori. Looking around, she was surprised at what she saw.

As a big city girl, knowing ranch life only through the movies she watched and books she read, it wasn't what she expected. Where she imagined a wild-west version of boots thrown, saddles leaning against stalls, hay littering the ground, she found a much different reality.

Gray rubber created the floor beneath her feet, softening her steps. To her left, a large opening gave view to a room full of so much gear and equipment she was caught by all of it, unable to recognize anything past the saddles, halters, and ropes.

To her right, an open door led way to what she assumed was Cade's office, where they were to have their interview.

Beyond that, long rows of windows followed the path of the roof on both sides, allowing in what limited sun there was to be found through the snow. Beneath, pale-wood stalls, fronted by white gates, stretched on. Each one perfectly centered underneath a window, giving light and life to the horses closed within.

"It's a sight to see, isn't it?" Cara smiled at her. "The Grady's are long known for this ranch and the prize-winning Quarter horses they breed. Their family goes back generations around here." She waved a hand at the open office door, waiting for Tori to enter ahead of her.

Inside was cozy, comfortable. Not in any way what Tori had imagined when Cara made her suggestion. A large desk centered the spacious room, a plush leather chair matching the two on the opposite side.

Along the back wall, long deep bookshelves stretched from one corner to the other. The titles lining them were a varied collection of everything from horse care to local lore.

"Make yourself comfortable." Cara moved around Tori, tapping the chairs on the other side of the desk. "I'll get the coffee started."

In the opposite corner of the room, she made quick work of the coffee pot stuffed by the small sink and make-shift bar. "It won't be Hattie's specialty, but it will be better than the tar they usually make out here."

Turning, two full cups in her hands, she offered one to Tori, wrapping her fingers around the other as she took the seat across from her.

It was a surprise. Tori had expected her to take a place behind the desk. Instead, Cara pulled the chair even closer and relaxed back in its comfort. "I think we've passed the point of needing a formal interview. Not that I'm much for formal in anything I do." She smiled before sipping from her cup. "So, remind me, what it was you were doing back in Chicago."

"I was the manager of a rare and vintage book store." The pang of loss hit hard. She'd loved her job. Every day surrounded by old books. The feel of them. The scent of them.

She could walk to work. Often did. Stopping for a cup of coffee at Francine's, she'd take in the morning air, letting it clear her thoughts. She'd loved those moments. Would miss them desperately. "I worked there for six years."

The day she'd resigned had broken her heart. Left her second-guessing her decision to leave it behind in her search for something she had no guarantee of.

Cara looked at her with a curiosity carrying more questions than Tori could answer. "So, what made you decide on Snow Ridge?"

Tori held off her answer with a sip of coffee. She was quickly finding she liked Cara. The idea of lying to her didn't sit well. But the truth wasn't something she wanted to share. It was hard enough accepting it herself.

"It felt like time for a change. Other than my job, there was nothing to be missed in Chicago." It was close enough to the truth it couldn't really be counted as lying.

"What about your family?"

"I don't have any." She chased away the catch in her heart. "My parents died when I was only three. I passed through foster homes after that. Once I hit eighteen, it was only me. It's been that way ever since."

Her voice was matter-of-fact, accepting what was her reality. She'd had her struggles. Her realization she'd never be the chosen one for the foster families who'd taken her in. She'd been too difficult of a child. Too much work for those wanting to pretend her life only began once she came into their lives.

"I'm sorry." Cara reached over, dropping a soft hand on her arm. "I lost my mom when I was young. I've always had my dad but it still hurts to this day. I can't imagine what it must have been like for you, losing both your parents."

As she'd learned to do with her loss, Tori shrugged away Cara's kind words. Those emotions that hurt, could stab a knife straight through her heart, were the first ones she'd learned as a child to bury away. "I've done okay."

"Of course you have." Pushing from her chair, Cara grabbed the coffee pot and refilled both their cups.

She sat back down, looking at Tori over the rim of her cup. "I like you. I know the guts it takes to leave everything and start over somewhere new."

Something in her words, her understanding, tugged at Tori, punching a hole in her defensive wall. "I'm terrified." She sank into her chair, using the warmth of her coffee cup to chase away the chill building inside.

"I've only ever known my life in Chicago. This isn't me, making such a big change. I'm still not sure it's for the best." She turned to stare out the window at the snow continuing to fall.

The fear she'd tried denying beat steady in her heart. Surged forward what she wouldn't let herself feel in the moment she'd closed the door on her old life and set out for this new, uncertain one.

The warmth of Cara's hand on her arm drew her back. She'd shared more than she intended or felt comfortable with. She knew better. Forming the kind of relationship encouraging such sharing wasn't her way. She relied on herself. On the day she faced. Nothing more. Nobody else.

"Sorry." She flashed what she hoped was a convincing smile, hiding the true emotion underneath.

Cara shook her head. "Nothing to be sorry about." She pulled her chair closer, grabbing Tori's hand. "I've been in that fear. Known it better than I like."

"I left here over a decade ago." She stared hard into Tori's eyes, creating a connection Tori wasn't sure she was comfortable with but was comforted by just the same. "And I was terrified, too. I called myself a fool a thousand times. Wondered what the hell I was thinking. How I could possibly imagine it was a good idea, leaving behind everything I knew for things I had no guarantee over."

Her words hit so close to Tori's own struggles. She wasn't one to trust. Wasn't one to give. But there had been something about Cara from the moment she met her. A knowledge that she understood and cared in a way most others never did.

"Do you regret it?"

"No. Not any part of it." Cara looked over at the picture of her and Cade centered on the desk. "I'm where I should be today. I don't question that. But it doesn't change my belief I did the right thing. I wouldn't be who I am today if I hadn't taken such a risk."

"I hope I don't regret it." Tori sipped slowly from her coffee, lost in thought. She battled the fear of making a mistake. Fought against the suggestion she'd screwed up, giving everything she'd always known up for a fleeting chance to meet a brother who may only turn his back on her and walk away as he'd done twenty-five years earlier after their parents' death.

Cara watched her and Tori resisted the urge to turn away.

"I hope the same for you." Her voice was soft, comforting. "Especially since I believe you'll be the perfect fit for Precious Gems."

Relief rose, settling some of the nerves Tori fought. "Thank you. I was hoping for the chance."

"You have it." Cara finished up the last of her coffee and rested back in her chair, easing the mood inside the office. "My partner, Jackie, will want to meet you, of course. But I have no doubt, she'll feel the same way."

It helped, more than she thought it would, to have

the promise of a job. The offer of some sort of stability in what was still so new and unknown.

****

"She's caught your interest." From the passenger seat, Jake smiled at his brother. "No wonder you picked her up from the side of the road."

Luke looked his way long enough to send a scowl. "The only interest I have is trying to figure out her story."

The county plows had been out, clearing snow. The conditions were far from good but they were better than they'd been in the worst of the blizzard the day before. And the four-wheel-drive he maneuvered through the deep drifts made it even better.

"Tell me you trust her or we're turning around and going back for Cara." From the backseat, a hint of worry flashed in Cade's eyes, reflecting back at Luke through the rearview mirror.

"She isn't a threat. That much I'm sure of." He slowed to flip the same turn he'd made the night before, pulling up in front of Tori's car.

He figured it'd be a nice surprise, towing her car back to the ranch. And it'd be safer there than sitting on the side of the road, buried in a foot of snow.

"Then what bothers you?" Jake pushed out the passenger door, sinking into the deep, soft snow along the side of the road.

The gentle look of her. The sweet scent of wildflowers that seemed to surround her. The soft, tempting glimmer in her emerald eyes.

Luke shook his head, chasing away such thoughts. With Cade, he climbed out of the truck and joined Jake. "Tell me why a young, pretty woman such as Tori would uproot everything to come to a place like Snow Ridge."

He dug into the storage compartment at the side of the truck, pulling out the tow chains. "And why, with no criminal history, not even a traffic ticket, she'd have a fear of law enforcement."

"Maybe it's just you she fears." Cade took the chains and circled around to the back of the truck. "You are a bit terrifying."

He hooked an end to the long, black trailer hitch pushing out from beneath the bumper. "And don't forget, Cara herself uprooted everything to start over in Denver."

"She was trying to get away from you." Jake nudged his younger brother with an elbow before grabbing the other end of the chain.

Cade shot him a look, yanking harder than he needed to on the chain.

"But Cara ran to Denver where there was hope and opportunity for her paintings." Luke stepped between his brothers, taking the chain from Jake, wrapping it tight around the front of Tori's car. "What was the reason for Tori to come here?"

And what did it matter to him? He believed in what he'd said…she wasn't a threat. On the surface, her story rang true. Her intentions showed only good.

It was what she kept hidden deeper inside gnawing at him. Though there was no reason to justify it. She was just another traveler, finding her way into Snow Ridge. Another face he'd see on the streets. Another person he'd follow his duty to serve and protect.

He went back to the truck to grab the shovels, missing the knowing looks his brothers passed over him.

"Like I said, she's caught your interest." Jake grabbed a shovel from his hand and tossed another to Cade.

Luke knew arguing would be worthless. He was a cop. He wanted answers. That was all it was. But he also knew, since he struggled to convince himself of such a truth, trying to convince his brothers would be close to impossible.

They worked quick, shoveling through thick snow, clearing a path good enough to free the car from the drifts collecting overnight.

He was thankful they said nothing more about Tori as they pulled her car free and started back for the ranch. He'd quickly grown tired of defending himself and his interest in her.

The fact her sweet, feminine scent seemed to surround him and his mind played games with her full, pouty lips, and the soft sway of her hips meant nothing more than a grown man's attraction to a beautiful woman.

It wasn't what fueled his interest. He was sure of it. Or at least, wanted to believe he was. Because the alternative was not something he was ready or willing to deal with.

Chapter Four

She had a place of her own.

Tori stood in the center of the small comfortable apartment above Precious Gems, taking it in. Late morning sun sifted through the windows, dancing over the soft green couches and thick oak coffee table.

She'd been tempted to dare the drive into town the night before. As soon as the snow stopped falling, she'd craved the chance for her own personal space. But she knew it wasn't wise. Didn't want to end up stranded on the side of the road all over again.

Luke had offered to take her in but the thought of being so close to him, for any amount of time, was unsettling.

So she'd spent one more night at the ranch only to be up early and ready to go the next morning. Thrilled to see the sun peeking through the clouds, she felt the hint of warmth slowly finding its way back.

Cara rode with her. The brothers followed. Tori wondered, as Cara directed her down Main Street, if they ever traveled apart. She'd known them only together. Wondered at the relationship they shared while unable to stop thinking of her own brother.

She'd contact him soon, she thought as she turned back to Cara standing between the kitchen and the front room. "This is great. More than I would have ever expected."

"The furniture might be a bit old but it's comfortable." Cara moved into the room with her, fussing with the outdated magazines piled on the coffee table. "The linens and towels though are all brand new."

"And this is all a perk of the job?" Tori shook her head, unable to believe it.

"It is. I'd rather have someone living here than it sitting empty. I thought about listing it for rent but decided I'd rather offer it first to whoever became a part of Precious Gems."

With a smile, Cara inched her way to the door. "I'm going downstairs to see about getting Precious Gems ready to open after the storm. You take your time. We'll get everything else taken care of later."

And then Tori was alone for the first time since getting herself stuck on the side of the road. It felt amazing. Freeing. Bringing her right back to where she knew she belonged.

****

She'd taken longer than she'd planned.

Close to three hours passed before Tori took the stairs leading her to the back room of Precious Gems. Voices drifted her way. One she recognized as Cara. The other wasn't one she'd heard before but there was laughter in it and a pitch of excitement drawing a smile.

"There she is." Cara turned and smiled as Tori stepped into the heart of Precious Gems.

It was amazing, taking her breath away. Delicate glass shelves lined the walls, giving home to everything from intricate marble statues to simple, hand-carved wood figurines.

One corner gave room to a large fountain. Water

ran smoothly from the paws of the copper-carved Grizzly proudly centering it before falling into a round tub etched with intricate leaves twisting through delicate petals.

The opposite corner was home to a large canvas. Bold and brilliant strikes of black and red merged beautifully with the flow of vibrant yellow lingering in the background. The abstract scene came to life, pulling Tori in, sucking the breath from her lungs as the painting seemed to move with her every step.

"That's one of mine." Cara joined her where she stood rooted in the center of the shop.

Tori looked at her, putting in to place the woman she was coming to know with the amazing work of art she created. "It's beautiful. I didn't realize you were an artist as well."

"I like my secrets," Cara teased, tossing an arm around her shoulders. "Come. Meet Jackie."

Caught by the beauty surrounding her, she'd forgotten there was another voice she'd heard when she first entered the store. This was the part she didn't like—meeting new people. It had never been her comfort zone.

And yet she'd had an overdose of it since Luke first appeared at her car window. More than she'd been prepared to handle.

They came around a delicate display of turquoise and found their way to the counter on the other side.

"You must be Tori." A smile dancing on her lips, reaching up to her deep, brown eyes, the woman behind the counter came around and stuck out a hand. "I'm Jackie. Cara's partner."

There was a spark about her. An energy so fitting

to the red curls tumbling over her shoulders and the small but vibrant look of her.

She took Tori's hand and held on, smiling over her shoulder at Cara. "We should go to the pub."

"We're supposed to be working." Cara moved around Tori, stopping at her side. "There's no reason not to open the shop for the afternoon."

Jackie looked back at Tori and winked. "Sure there is. We need to get to know each other." She held up their still joined hands.

"You're always a bad influence." Though Cara shook her head, a smile teased the corners of her mouth. She moved behind the counter to grab her purse, a silent acceptance to Jackie's request.

"You will quickly learn." She threaded an arm through Tori's and turned her toward the door. "Jackie has a terrible weakness for the pub. If she can find a reason to go, she'll take it."

"The pub?" Again confused, Tori wondered if she should just accept it as a normal reaction for her time in Snow Ridge. All these relationships, connections. They left her head spinning. Made her aware of how far she was from what she knew and accepted as her life.

"Jake's place." Cara held the door open for her, waiting for Jackie to follow before locking it behind them. "Grady's Pub. It's a favorite around here."

With Jackie on one side, Cara on the other, she was led along the snow-covered sidewalk to the far corner of Main Street. There wasn't a sign of traffic to stop them as they crossed and stepped up in front of an old wooden building rising high from its perch on the corner.

"It used to be the old firehouse from back in the

day when they still used horses to pull the water wagons." Pride was clear in Cara's voice as she pushed open one of the heavy wooden doors. "The place was deserted for years and falling apart before Jake brought it back to life."

A gentle, welcoming warmth surrounded Tori with her first step inside. From the gray-stone hearth centered on the wall, a smoky, earthy scent drifted from the flames burning bright.

"It's a traditional peat fire." Jackie hooked an arm through hers and Cara's, guiding them past the long mahogany bar and around the whiskey barrel tables. "It's a smell you will never forget once you've had the chance to experience it."

Curling around the corner of a small stage, she settled at a table tucked away in the corner. "This will be a much better place to get to know one another."

Tori took a chair and looked around. The pub held only a few gathered around the interesting tables. The snow, she was sure, kept many safe inside.

She recognized Jake coming out from behind the bar, couldn't stop her smile in response to the one he shot her way.

"Where's the baby?" He looked at Jackie as he laid menus in front of them.

"At home with his dad. I didn't want him out in this cold." She pushed her menu out of the way without giving it a look.

Cara did the same, leaving Tori self-conscious as she opened her own to look over the choices. It was odd, feeling so out of place and yet so accepted all in one sweep.

Jackie leaned close. "The wings here are the best."

She gave a confident nod before looking at Jake, ordering the wings and a beer.

Cara narrowed her eyes at Jackie. "A beer? I take it that means we are officially done with work for the day."

"We were the minute we walked out the door." A mischievous glint danced in her brown eyes before spreading through the smile on her face.

Watching them, Tori felt a longing inside. There was no missing the closeness they shared. The friendship holding them so tight together. They seemed to know what the other was thinking and shared a smile, a look, with a secret message outsiders had no hope of understanding.

She'd never known that. Never had such a closeness with another person. At least not since that fateful night when she'd lost everything she'd ever known and loved.

It had always been too much of a risk, forming such a tight relationship with anyone. She'd known so much denial. So much heartbreak during her years in the foster system. There was no choice left but to find her own way to survive without taking the risk of commitment.

Her life in Chicago was easy. Simple. She lived for the day she survived in. That was all. Building friendships, like the one between Cara and Jackie, wasn't for her. Too risky. Too threatening to bring her back to the loss she'd experienced so many times as a child.

It was easier living for today rather than putting trust in what tomorrow might bring.

"All right." Cara's quick laugh brought her back to

the table. "I guess I'll be having the same then."

Jake looked at her, waiting. Deciding to trust them, Tori closed the menu. "Make it three."

****

It was hell to concentrate.

Frustrated, Luke read through the reports piled on his desk, trying to make the words stick.

But there was no use to it. He was wasting time and accomplishing nothing more than a fevered pitch of curse words Hattie would have him washing his mouth with soap for.

It was Tori.

He knew it was useless denying the reason for his distraction. Getting her out of his mind proved impossible. Something about her struck him, refusing to let go.

He'd spent his morning at the station digging further, trying to satisfy his questions. And he'd gotten answers. Not that he liked them.

There was a vague report of her parents' death when she was only three. A suspected robbery gone bad. And then a spotted history of her being passed from one foster home to the next, passed around until she'd aged out of the system at eighteen.

But there wasn't more. Nothing explaining the fear he sensed with the knowledge he was a police officer. The decision to give up the life she'd known in Chicago to come to Snow Ridge.

What he learned only brought to life more questions rather than satisfying the ones he had. And the frustration was enough to leave him desperately needing a break.

Shoving the reports out of sight, he pushed away

44

from his desk. What he needed was some time away from work. Away from the torturing thoughts Tori brought.

Grabbing his coat from the hook by the door and closing his office up for the day, he waved his way out of the station. He'd go to the pub and relax a bit before heading home to the ranch. With any luck, after a couple of beers and one of Jake's famous Reubens filling his appetite, he'd find the ease he needed to work Tori from his mind and concentrate on more important matters.

Chapter Five

Luke recognized the seductive rise and fall of her voice the minute he walked through the door.

Sure he was cursed by the emerald-eyed beauty, he made his way through the pub and past the musician's stage where two tables had been pushed together. Baskets of wings fought for space among the empty and half full beer mugs spread out along the tops.

His younger brothers took up the far end of the tables, sitting across from one another. Cade at Cara's side where he tended to be more often than not.

Jackie was there, her vibrant laughter filling the air.

But it was only one who truly caught his attention, drawing him to the lively table.

There was such an elegant beauty around Tori. It was no wonder he couldn't pull his mind away. Any single, healthy male would suffer the same by just a simple look.

Drawn to her, he couldn't get his feet to move quick enough. She caught sight of him as he drew close. Her emerald eyes held ease in the moment before they clouded over with uncertainty.

Yeah. She didn't like him around. He'd figured that out from the start. It didn't work in persuading him to stay away. If anything, it pushed him to be around her more.

"Looks like I'm late to the party." Though he was

tempted to kick Jake out of his place and claim the chair next to Tori, he settled with the chair on the end.

"The ladies came in for lunch and never left." Jake waved at the bartender, holding up his beer in a silent request for another one for his brother. "They were having entirely too much fun on their own so Cade and I decided to join them."

Luke grabbed a wing from the basket in front of him while watching Tori struggle not to look at him. "What happened to getting Precious Gems opened up after the storm?" He shot Tori a knowing smile before turning his attention to Cara.

"Jackie happened." It was all the explanation needed.

"We had to get to know one another." Jackie shrugged, unconcerned. "And we've been having a great time doing it."

Luke was surprised to see the comfort in the smile Tori shared with Cara and Jackie. As the bartender approached, setting a beer in front of him, he watched her over the rim as he raised it to his mouth.

She'd let her guard slip around them. Not that it should surprise him. Cara and Jackie were a force to be reckoned with. There was no protecting yourself once they were around. The two could charm the coldest heart if given long enough.

But she was still wary with his brothers, and especially him. The thought made her even more compelling. The questions only continued to grow. He'd done what research he could through the ordinary channels. Now it was time to change tactics and find out what more he could learn from her.

It would be a pleasure. Something about Tori left

little doubt to the enjoyment he'd find in being close to her, for whatever reason.

****

She'd actually started to relax and enjoy herself until Luke came through the door. There was such power about him. A strength to his presence. She couldn't forget him no matter how desperately she tried.

Grabbing her beer, Tori did her best to ignore his hard stare weighing heavy across the table. She wanted to think of things other than the heat in his hazel eyes. Like the enjoyable afternoon she'd spent with the two ladies she'd soon be working with.

Their lunch had turned into an afternoon snack trailing right into the dinner hours. And though she'd been cautious and unsure to start, Jackie and Cara quickly chased away the reservations she carried. There was something about them. The kindness they offered. The easy affection they gave. She'd had no choice but to find herself more comfortable and at ease as the hours passed, the conversation flowed, and the laughter came.

"Snow will be melting by tomorrow." Jackie grabbed a wing and pushed the basket at Tori. "It'll be a better day to open, anyhow."

"She's been using that same excuse since they got here." Jake flashed her a teasing smile.

Easy laughter rose over the table, easing some of the tension Tori had found since Luke joined them. It had turned out to be a really good day. She wasn't willing to let Luke and his overpowering presence take that away.

And Jackie had been right, she admitted as she

reached into the basket in front of her, the wings were some of the best she'd had.

"Looks like we're not the only ones taking advantage of another snow day." Jake lifted his mug.

Tori followed the line of his gaze.

There was an air of confidence in the man making his way around the tables. Something in the way he moved with a firm step and a stubborn tilt to his chin stirred a strange sensation inside.

He flashed a bright smile as he headed for their table, his gaze passing over those who sat there. His pale blue eyes landed on her and her breath caught in her lungs, her chest burning with the need to breathe.

She knew him. Deep inside, on a primal level, there was a connection.

Of blood. Of family. Of recognizing a soul so much like her own.

His smile faltered, confusion dancing in his eyes as their gazes locked. For a moment she wondered if he felt it too.

Recovering quickly, he held out a hand as Jake stood to greet him. "Good to see at least the pub has some life." He grabbed a chair from an empty table, settling between Luke and Jake.

Tori couldn't take her eyes off him. She was sure…so sure. Though hair that once matched hers was now darker, and he'd aged to a point she no longer recognized him as the boy in her memories, her heart knew she was looking down the table at her brother. The very reason she'd come to Snow Ridge.

"The ladies are responsible for that." Jake again waved at the bartender for another beer. "They decided to take another snow day rather than getting to work."

His pale blue eyes again caught Tori's. She wished she could read his thoughts. Know if he felt anything close to what was simmering inside her.

"Her name's Tori." Luke's voice was rougher than he intended. But it was a damn thing, sitting there watching the two staring at each other. "She'll be working with Cara and Jackie over at Precious Gems."

"And that's Seth," Cara picked up from her side of the table, a curious look in her eyes. "He helps his aunt and uncle run Moonshine Ranch."

For a moment, an odd silence fell over the table. Tori grew ghostly pale and looked like she might pass out. Luke pushed up from his seat, pausing as she fought off whatever gripped her. She looked at him and shook her head. And though he had no clue what was going on, he lowered back down, grabbing a long draw from his beer.

"Can't think of a better way to welcome a newcomer to these parts." Though he smiled wide, Luke noticed the slight shake in Seth's hand as he wrapped long fingers around the mug the bartender set down in front of him.

What the hell was going on?

There was something between Tori and Seth. But for the life of him, he couldn't figure out what it was.

He looked again at Tori and caught the slight tremor in her bottom lip as she stared at Seth, a look of caution mixing with anticipation.

He'd thought there couldn't possibly be more questions to have when it came to her. But he was quickly learning he was wrong.

****

Tori struggled to act normal. It was a fight she was

quickly losing as the night dragged on.

How was one supposed to handle it when they learned they were sitting at the same table with the brother they hadn't seen in twenty-five years?

Seth Mundy.

She didn't need to be told he'd changed his last name. She already knew from the information her Search Angel had provided. It had included Moonshine Ranch and the couple he claimed were his aunt and uncle.

There was no doubt left. Sooner than she'd planned, she'd come face to face with her brother.

And she was having a hell of a time dealing with it.

But her brother didn't seem to be facing the same struggles. She couldn't even be sure he realized the connection between them. Other than his brief, strange reaction when they were introduced, he showed no signs of being affected.

She was thankful when everyone began pushing their empty beer mugs out of the way without bothering to order another. The night was coming to an end and she was more than grateful for it.

Her knees weak and wobbly, she pushed to her feet with the others. The goodbyes began, working around the table. She made it through until the moment she turned and came face to face with her brother standing only inches away.

There was a look in his eyes she couldn't figure out. She wanted so desperately to grab him and pull him away so they could talk. So she could tell him she was his sister. The one he'd walked away from so long ago.

"It was nice to meet you." There was nothing but a

smooth drawl to his voice. A look of calm in his expression.

She accepted his hand, holding on a moment longer than she should, praying he'd feel the connection.

There was nothing. Her heart ached with the truth of it.

"Cade, you and Cara take Jackie home. I'll make sure Tori gets back to her place." Luke stepped up beside her, adding another layer to her already jumbled emotions.

"That's not necessary." She took a step back, putting some much-needed space between them. "I know where I'm going. I can walk."

"So can I." His hazel eyes burned against her skin. "And I'll be walking you back to your place to make sure you get there safely."

Silently, she cursed him but knew better than to argue.

He turned, leading the way out the door. Everyone except Jake followed, stepping into the dark, chilly air.

"You didn't get much of a chance to get settled." Caught tight in Cade's arms, Cara turned Tori's way on the snowy sidewalk. "Take some time in the morning. Jackie and I will get the store opened up. You can join us later."

She really didn't have anything to get settled but she thanked Cara before waving her and Jackie off to where Cade's truck waited.

Seth lingered for a moment at the curb, looking at her one last time. There was a shadow in his gaze she couldn't read. A pull to his lips that hadn't been there before. "I'm off. Take care."

Tori watched him turn on his heels and walk away.

She couldn't pull her eyes away as he disappeared around the side of the pub. The more she saw, the more she found the finer points leaving little doubt who he was.

Memories surged at the sight of his confident stride. It was so like their father's. Powerful yet graceful, all in one. Images from the little girl she was pushed forward. Watching her dad walk through the front door, running into his arms. Seeing him through the darkness as he'd come in to soothe her from a nightmare.

Feeling Luke's heavy gaze, she shook off the memories, forcing a smile as she turned back. "I really can get back on my own. It's just down the street."

"I know where it is." He curled a firm hand around her elbow, turning her in the right direction.

Luke wanted to know, demand she tell him, what was going on between her and Seth. He'd been on the force too damn long not to notice the strange reaction they both carried. There was a desperation to hide things. An uncertainty crackling between them.

He wanted to know why. Was tempted to push until she gave up the answers he sought. But something about the look of her stopped him. He sensed there was more to her emotions than she was letting on. A deeper cut she fought to keep hidden.

So instead he remained silent, walking her down the sidewalk toward Precious Gems. Her delicate, sweet scent surrounded him. The curve of her elbow, cradled in his hand, sent a shot of awareness up his arm.

Forced to let go to make it through the small space between Precious Gems and the coffee shop, he enjoyed the soft sway of her backside as she led the way. Found the awareness growing stronger as they stepped out into the alley.

"I think I can make it from here." She stopped at the bottom of the stairs. Cast in shadows, her emerald eyes burned through the dark, reaching deep inside and pushing him to want more, satisfying the growing need.

He knew better, calling himself a fool even as he took a step closer. Uncertainty danced in her gaze but she stayed where she was as he curled his hands over her slender shoulders.

He wanted a taste—just a taste—to satisfy the hunger, then he'd go. "You should go up," he suggested as a last chance to run.

She nodded but made no move to start up the stairs.

He shouldn't be here, tempted to cross over a line he knew would only bring more problems. But logic wasn't his friend at the moment. Only desire, sharp and piercing.

Pushing closer, his hands over her shoulders held her captive. Her eyes widened, brilliant emerald calling to him. He dipped, brushing a quick kiss across her soft lips.

It wasn't enough. Not even close. Pulling her tighter, he found her tempting mouth again, taking what he so desperately desired.

Tori knew there was so much wrong. Yet she couldn't pull away, though the sensible part of her mind screamed at her to do so.

She didn't even like him. What in the world was she doing kissing him?

He curled his hands together behind her back, pressing her to him. The feel of his hard chest pushing against her softer curves sent a tantalizing chill running through her veins. Pushing up on her toes, she gave more. Sought more. Needing to satisfy the hunger growing inside.

As much as she knew it wasn't right, she couldn't stop it. She moaned in protest when he placed large hands over her shoulders, stepping back and breaking the kiss.

He waited a moment for her gaze to clear. "I should be going. Make sure you lock up once you're inside."

He backed further away before stopping to watch. Shaking her head, fighting back confusion and disappointment, she was careful not to meet his eyes as she turned and headed up the stairs.

By the time she reached the top, sensible thought began its return, bringing with it a feeling of foolishness and the first sparks of anger.

She refused to acknowledge Luke hovering in the alley, keeping an eye on her. With a wave of disgust, she shoved the door open, slamming it behind her.

Hitting the lock into place, she tossed her purse on the counter, cursing Luke's very existence as she stormed down the hall to her bedroom.

She hadn't wanted to kiss him to start with. His cool break from their embrace just added fuel to such a humiliating thought. She'd known it was wrong. Knew it would bring no good. Yet she'd been weak and given in, like a poor, lost school girl with a crush.

And all she got in return was a flash of embarrassment as he sent her on her way.

Stripping her clothes, throwing them on the chair in the corner, she yanked her cotton nightshirt from the hook on the bathroom door.

The kiss might have stirred a hunger she'd been unaware of but it wouldn't be something she'd allow to happen again. It wasn't like she'd be missing it. She'd had her experience and now she'd move on, happy to say she didn't care for a repeat.

Yanking the nightshirt over her head, she caught a glance of the flushed, fully-kissed woman staring back at her through the mirror and knew she was lying to herself.

****

Though he detested conducting business late at night, he understood, at times, there was no choice.

Easing out of the bedroom, where he refused to let business intrude, Filip waited until he was safely down the hall before answering the call.

"You have news?" He didn't bother with customary greetings. They were a waste of time, leading him nowhere with the information he hoped to gather.

Pausing at his office door, he considered a scotch but thought better of it with the late hour. With his age, certain enjoyments now had to be limited.

"She's been given the job." Anton's voice carried static as it broke through the line. "And she's been given a place to live."

He didn't like the news but wasn't surprised by it. "Perhaps a visit is in order. With the one who is now her employer."

"That would be Cara Bennett. Seems she moved back to Snow Ridge not too long ago. Opened up Precious Gems on her return."

Stepping into his office and finding his way to the floor to ceilings windows he so loved, Filip stared out over the dark of night settled over the city. "Is there anything we can use on her? Perhaps some leverage to convince her that her new employee is not a wise choice."

"I've checked. There's nothing." A trace of frustration jumped in Anton's voice. "She has a sorry past…a teenage boyfriend who died in a drunk driving accident. And not too long ago she had a crazed killer with his sights on her and barely escaped with her life. But there's nothing questionable, or even hints at questionable, that I could possibly use."

He didn't like the answer. Was never happy when those he wanted to persuade left him little to work with. "Perhaps money is the answer." He turned from the windows and caught the picture on his desk. The smiling faces hit harder than usual.

"A good enough offer might convince her," Anton agreed. "Small business owners often struggle. A bit of security could be the answer."

Optimism wasn't in his nature though Filip desperately wished for different at the moment. He wanted a quick and easy solution. One that would cause the least damage.

In the past, it had taken a few phone calls and some meager checks written to deter her search. This one had gotten away from him. He admitted it though he was loath to. But it didn't mean he was unable to regain control of the situation.

For twenty-five years he'd held the secret. Kept hidden what only him and a select few were aware of. This would not be the time to change that. He'd make sure of it.

Chapter Six

She loved watching her mother pretty up for a night out.

Sitting on the corner of the bed, small legs dangling over the edge, Tori watched her mother at the vanity table. The red gown she wore reminded Tori of the popsicles she and her brother enjoyed when the days were hot.

"Will I be as pretty as you mommy?"

Her mother turned, her smile soft and loving. "You're already prettier than I could ever be." Pushing up from the padded bench, she came to the side of the bed. Reaching up, she pulled the golden clip from her hair, thick chestnut curls tumbling over her shoulders.

Gathering Tori's own shorter chestnut curls into her hands, she caught them with the glimmering clip at the back of her head. "See." She moved, giving her a clear view of the mirror above the vanity table. "You're beautiful."

She dropped low, leaving a kiss on the tip of her nose. "The most beautiful little girl in the world."

Tori smiled at her reflection in the mirror. "I like—
"

A strange pop echoed from downstairs, stopping her words. Wide-eyed, she looked at her mother.

Though she tried to hide it, Tori caught the quick slice of fear in her eyes. "Stay here, sweetheart." She dropped a gentle hand over her shoulder and squeezed softly.

She waited for her mother to leave the bedroom then slipped from the edge of the bed and tip-toed to the open door. Daring a step into the long hallway, she jumped back into the room as her mother's scream burst through the quiet.

Hovering at the edge, just able to peer around the door frame, she heard her father's voice. Though she couldn't make out the words, she heard the anger.

Another pop echoed. Frantic footsteps.

Tori was afraid...so afraid. Her heart hurt where it beat against her chest. She wanted her mother, her father, even her annoying big brother. She wanted them with her, keeping her safe.

But Seth was playing with his cars in his room and she couldn't see her mother or father from where she hid inside the door. It was just her. Alone and terrified.

"Don't do this." Her mother's voice sounded close. "Please, don't do this."

Tori needed to see her. Be near her.

Forcing herself around the door frame, she dared first one step then another into the hallway. An eerie presence settled. With only the light from her parents' bedroom offering any kind of sight, shadows danced and played along the dark painted walls.

Sucking in a harsh breath, she turned and saw her father standing at the top of the stairs, her mother at his side. Two others stood across from them. One was nothing more than a dark shape, hovering a few steps down.

The other stood only a few feet between him and her parents. The gleam of his teeth flashed back at her as he smiled, though it wasn't a happy smile. The look of it sent shivers over Tori's skin, making her feel sick to her stomach.

Fear made it hard to breathe. Hard to do anything but stand and stare. A chill ran through the air. A strange silence hovered, dark and ugly, through the house.

The man standing in front of her parents raised his arm, a strange bulk clasped in his hand. He spoke but his words made no sense. He looked from her mother back to her father, the evil smile on his face growing wider.

"No." Her mother's scream pierced through the hallway as she lunged in front of her father. Another pop broke through. Then there was blood. So much blood, splattering over her father and the carpet around him as her mother fell limp at his feet.

Time froze. Tori fought to deny what she'd seen. But she couldn't. She might not understand all that was happening. But she knew none of it was good. And she understood, with the most pain she'd ever known, her mother had been hurt in ways worse than she could imagine.

A sharp angry growl escaped the dark shape hovering on the stairs. He moved quickly up the remaining stairs, light catching his face. For a moment there was recognition then it was gone as the other man raised his arm again.

"Daddy," Tori screamed. No longer frozen in place, she was frantic to get to her father.

He turned at the sound of her voice. "Tori, run." He came toward her. "Go back—"

The loud pop hurt her ears. Her father froze in

place, eyes wide, mouth open. A dark red bloomed over his shirt. "Tori..." His voice barely a whisper, he stumbled forward, his gaze holding hers as he fell.

His outstretched hand brushed against her ankle. Screaming, she jumped back, tripping over her own feet, falling to the carpet only inches from her father's lifeless form.

"What's happening?" The familiar sound of her brother's voice broke through her screams. She couldn't stop, the terror too strong to fight against. It echoed inside her head, pounding with the harsh beat of her heart.

The world was spinning. Nothing seemed real. She wanted to close her eyes and chase it all away. But she couldn't. She could only sit there and stare at the man slowly inching closer.

"Tori, come on." Her brother curved his hands beneath her shoulders, doing all he could to drag her back. "You have to get up. You have to run."

Though she heard Seth's desperation, she couldn't do it. She suddenly felt so sleepy. A strange fog settled, urging her down. Even her brother's frantic demands became a slow, mumbled growl she barely heard.

Standing over her father's body, the man stopped and looked her right in the eye. Cold grabbed her, racing through her veins. He was going to do to her what he'd done to her parents. The truth made her stomach roll.

"Not the children." Cloaked by the shadows, the dark shape from the stairs bit out the order. "Leave them be."

The man took a step closer. Seth stopped dragging her back. Time froze as he stared at them. For several *long seconds, the only sound she heard was the push of breath through her lungs.*

The man shook his head before turning on his heels. The dark figure hovered as the other man started down the stairs. He looked back, light again catching his face.

Seeing him, she screamed again.

Bolting up in bed, Tori's screams echoed through the apartment. Heart beating painfully against her chest, every breath was a fight to drag through her lungs.

It had been years since she'd been haunted by the nightmare of her parents' murder. But tonight, it had come back with force, leaving her shaking in bed, covered in the sticky sweat brought by fear.

Tori forced deep, calming breaths, waiting for the worst to slip away. Even as her heart slowed, a pounding kicked up behind her right temple, bringing on the headache that always followed.

Waiting until she was sure her legs would support her, she slipped from the side of the bed. She knew the routine—a couple of aspirin to chase away the headache and a cup of tea to calm the nerves—if she wanted any hope of getting back to sleep.

She'd left the hallway light on. It guided her from her bedroom to the kitchen. It was so quiet inside the apartment. She was tempted to turn on the television for some background noise but decided against it.

She'd done this, lived in the aftermath of her nightmares for most of her life. Though some noise would be a nice distraction, it wouldn't help her work her way back down from the fear and terror raging inside.

She found a bright-red tea kettle in the cupboard by

the stove. Filling it with water and setting it on a burner to warm, she dug in her purse for the bottle of aspirin she always kept handy.

This one hadn't been as bad as some in the past. For that she was thankful. When she'd been a small child, she'd seen the devil's face in the dark figure. The terror of it used to wake her up with heart-wrenching screams and tears that would last for hours.

She couldn't be held, couldn't be touched, for days after. The pain was too much. The loss of her mother and father too great to function as she was expected to.

The struggle earned her the title of a troubled child. She'd heard it often enough, whispered from the social workers to the next foster family taking her in. And as she'd grown older, past the acceptable years for couples looking to adopt, troubled became hard to place.

Until she'd turned fourteen. Until it had been decided her needs would be better served in a group home.

The whistle of the kettle brought her back from that painful part of her past. It took some searching to find the mugs. And longer to discover the tea bags stored in a small wooden holder at the far end of the counter.

Thankful to find Chamomile, she dropped the small bag into her mug. Steam rose as she poured water over it. The sweet, earthy scent pushed up, helping to calm her nerves.

She settled at the small kitchen table, hoping it would only take her one mug of tea and some time for the aspirin to kick in. The glowing numbers above the stove told her it was only three in the morning. Much too early to be staying up and starting the day.

It was Seth. He was why the nightmare had come

tonight. Seeing him again opened the door for the painful memories of that night. Memories she held only in her dreams.

That was all she knew of the night her parents were killed. She had nothing to look back and hold on to from the actual experience. All she had was what the nightmares gave her.

Which was more than enough.

As she'd grown older, she'd accepted that what existed in her dreams was as close to the truth as she'd ever get. And in that truth, she knew and understood the face of the dark figure was one she knew. For the many terrifying shapes it had taken, the countless nights she'd woken up screaming from the sight, there was always the realization that somewhere buried deep in her mind, was a name to go with the face haunting her for twenty-five years.

But now was not the time to try and dig for it. She'd gone that route countless times in her past only to come up empty and disappointed.

She didn't want to face that battle tonight.

The aspirin and tea working their magic, she pushed up from the table. For a moment she was caught by the darkness out the window as she rinsed out her mug. She saw the shadows from her nightmare. The dark figure lingering there.

Something existed. A knowledge she sensed had the power to answer so much. But it wouldn't come to her. It never did.

****

He'd dressed in hopes of blending in as a casual tourist, discovering all that Snow Ridge had to offer.

He was good at what he did because of his ability

to adapt. Whatever the situation called for, Anton had the look and ability to become one who belonged. From the darker streets of Chicago to high-end business meetings to this tiny place stuck in the mountains, he was whoever he needed to be to get the job done.

Not that this was much of a job.

Taking one final sip from his coffee, he bit back his impatience. It would do him no good for the task ahead.

He did what was asked of him by the family. The reasons why were not his concern. Whatever the story was with Victoria Mundola, it wasn't his to worry about. He'd get the job done, head back to Chicago, and not give her another thought.

Turning off the morning news before grabbing his keys, he left the hotel room with the hope he'd soon be walking out the door for good.

Money had power. And for the right people, it could be a great persuader. If his luck was with him, the offer would be accepted, and he'd be on his way, never looking back.

Chapter Seven

For the past four months, her heart had been stolen.

Hitching Baby Evan higher on her hip, Cara smiled down on his sweet face, falling in love even more.

She loved the days when Jackie brought her son to work. She may be an only child but Jackie was everything she could have for a sister. Which gave her all the permission she needed to be an over-indulgent aunt to the bundle of wonder she held in her arms.

"I think he's teething." Jackie dumped the bulging diaper bag behind the counter. "Peter was up with him all night. Thought I'd be the good wife this morning and bring Evan with me so he could sleep."

She came around to stop in front of Cara, dropping a soft kiss on her son's chubby cheek. "Is Tori getting settled?"

"I'm guessing so. I haven't seen her since leaving the pub last night." Reluctantly, Cara gave Evan up to his mother's waiting arms. "I told her to take the time. She needed it."

Jackie cradled Evan close. "Not like we'll have a rush of customers this morning."

No. They wouldn't. This lull before the slopes opened was the hardest time for a business owner in Snow Ridge. The summer boost ending while the heart of the town's existence—ski season—not yet beginning.

It was quiet. It was slow. And it was far from profitable.

The bell on the door rang as Jackie took Evan behind the counter, searching in the diaper bag for his teething ring.

Cara turned, expecting a familiar face. The man coming through the door though wasn't someone she knew or had seen before.

Still on the younger side, wearing khakis and a blue polo shirt, he looked like the many others who visited Snow Ridge. Yet there was something about him. Something she couldn't explain or make sense of. He gave her an odd feeling. One setting her on alert as she offered a polite, professional smile.

"May I help you?" She kept her gaze steady as he pretended an interest in a display of crystal wind chimes.

He was slow, unconcerned, as he looked at her, piercing gray eyes making her even more uncomfortable. "I was hoping to speak to the owner. A Miss Cara Bennett, I believe it is."

She felt Jackie press closer. "That would be me. What can I do for you?"

"It's actually more about what I can do for you." He stepped up to the counter, leaving only a few feet between them. She resisted the urge to take a step back.

He smiled at her but it did nothing to settle her unease. "I'm here to make you a very generous offer."

She wasn't liking this. "What kind of offer?"

"One that could be very profitable for a small business owner, such as yourself." He looked around her store as if rating its worth. "I'm aware what a struggle it can be for someone in your situation. A little place like this, surviving on the tourist trade."

Though there was no bite to his words, she was still insulted. "I do just fine, thank you. And I have a feeling, whatever offer you have, you'll be wasting your time."

From behind, she heard Jackie's quick take of breath and knew she suffered the same insult.

"I wouldn't be so quick to rush to judgment. The man I work for is prepared to write you a very generous check." His look was smug. Almost arrogant.

Jackie stepped up beside Cara, bouncing Evan on her hip. "And why exactly would he do that? There's no reason for some stranger to be writing us a check for anything."

He flashed her an uninterested glance. "He's hoping there will be a reason. He's willing to offer you two hundred and fifty thousand for nothing more than a small favor."

Quarter of a million dollars. Cara had to hold herself up at the edge of the counter. "Who would be crazy enough to offer that kind of money?"

"Not crazy." He gave a small shake to his head. "Just very set in his belief the favor is worth it."

"And what *exactly* is the favor?" Though she had no firm reason to believe so, Cara was sure she wasn't going to like the answer. He was too smooth, the offer too outrageous, for it to be anything else.

"You've recently taken on a new employee. A Victoria Mundola." He looked around the store as if searching for her. He hesitated at the back door where the stairs leading to her apartment were located.

Jackie moved, diverting his gaze. "What does she have to do with this?"

"She'd be the favor." He turned back to the two of them. "All that is asked is that you let her go. If that's done, the money is yours."

Of all things, that was not what Cara expected. Taking a moment, she fought back the anger at such a request. Though she knew her answer, she wanted to know why it was even asked. "What does Tori working here matter to anyone?"

"That I cannot tell you." His smile was back though it never reached his dark eyes. "But only a fool would turn down such a generous offer. She's only just begun here. You won't suffer a loss by letting her go. But the gain will be something that can't be matched."

"Then consider me a fool." She looked directly in his piercing eyes, leaving no doubt to be found in her response. "I'm not interested. And I see no gain in being paid off to unfairly fire one of my employees."

He raised his dark brows and shook his head. "Surely you realize how far such money can take you. You'd give up financial security for someone who is a stranger to you? Somebody who can be replaced by the end of the day."

Anger growing, Cara looked back at the door, tempted to throw him out it. She didn't understand any of this and couldn't imagine a reason why anyone would discourage Tori from working for her. Would actually be crazy enough to pay such a ridiculous amount for the act of firing her.

Something wasn't right. With the man or his offer. It was time for him to go. "My answer won't change. You're only wasting your time."

"I had hoped you'd be wiser. More apt to see the advantage of accepting such a generous offer." He shrugged, moving around them for the door. "I can give you a few days to think it over."

Cara stepped for the door herself, more than ready to help him out, if that's what it took. "It would be a waste. My answer will still be the same."

"And I see no reason for you to bother coming back," Jackie added from behind the counter, her narrowed gaze leaving little doubt to her feelings for the man. "While Tori is, and will continue to be, welcome here, you no longer are."

His smug look returned as he flashed a smile at Jackie. It was all Cara could do not to shove him out the door. Thankfully, he found his own way, never looking back as he hit the sidewalk.

Cara watched him. He didn't climb into a car as she expected. Instead, he continued down the street, disappearing around the corner.

"What in the hell was that?" Jackie came out from behind the counter, cradling Evan close.

Cara resisted the urge to lock the door and keep them safe inside in case he returned. "I don't know but I don't like it. Something is definitely wrong."

Stopping long enough to press a gentle hand to Evan's back, she grabbed her purse and dug inside. "I'm calling Luke," she answered Jackie's curious glance. "I think he should know about our unwelcome visitor."

****

She'd overslept.

Tori stared at her tired-stained eyes in the mirror. Though she'd done all she could to come back from the terror of her nightmare, it had still taken close to two hours before sleep returned. And even then, she'd tossed and turned through most of it.

Two cups of strong, black coffee, a long, hot shower, and she hadn't been able to erase the proof of her troubled night. She did what she could with make-up but still caught the hint of dark shadows under her eyes.

It would have to be enough. She couldn't be any later. Cara had told her to take time in the morning. But she was already close to two hours past opening. There was no justifying taking any longer.

Deciding she'd use the excuse of settling in a new place if asked about the tired look of her, she slipped her shoes on, grabbed her purse, and headed down the stairs.

A mix of voices hit her as she entered. Coming around the displays that had distracted her the day before, she stopped before she was seen.

Something was going on. That much she could figure out. Dreading what it might be, she was tempted to turn, go back, and hide inside her apartment.

But before she could decide if it was a wise decision or not, Luke turned, catching her in his hard gaze. The smile he offered was forced. The shadows filtering through his expression left little doubt she wasn't going to like whatever it was that brought him here.

Cara saw her too and nudged in front of Luke before he could approach. Her look was long and searching as she reached Tori, grabbing her hands and holding tight. "Are you okay?"

It wasn't a question she expected. Looking from her to Luke, she had a sick feeling in the pit of her stomach. "I'm fine. Why wouldn't I be? What's happened?"

Before Cara could respond, the bell above the door echoed through the store. Cade rushed in, bringing the morning chill with him. He searched frantically through the store, finding Cara with a loud sigh of relief.

"What in the hell is going on?" He rushed to her, curling his arms around her shoulders and yanking her against him. He held her there, reassuring himself she was okay.

"I'll tell you both." She looked from him to Tori, uneasiness shimmering in her blue eyes. "It hasn't been a pleasant morning."

Easing from Cade's firm hold, she reached a hand out for Tori. Guiding them to the counter, she led Tori to exactly where she didn't want to be, closer to Luke.

A look at his sharp gaze and she was back to the moment when his lips first brushed against hers. Heat simmered again, as if it had never died. The remembered feel of him burned against her skin.

"I'm okay, really." Cara brushed a soft kiss against Cade's cheek as he continued fussing over her. "We just had a very strange visitor this morning."

"One, it seems, who was very interested in the fact you work here." Luke's hard gaze fell on Tori. So different from the heat burning in the hazel depths the night before.

"Why would anyone care where I work?" She looked from him to Cara, thankful to find a gentler set to her expression. "I'm not close enough to anybody for them to know, or even care, that I'm here."

"Someone cares." Luke took a step closer. Gone was the man who'd kissed her senseless. In his place was the cop he was. He stood stiff, raking suspicious eyes over her from head to toe. "Enough they were willing to offer an outrageous amount of money for your job here to end."

Tori's mind raced. It sounded too ridiculous to be real. "I don't understand." She looked at the others around her, catching the questions brewing in the gazes settled on her. "This doesn't make sense."

Luke's hard look didn't ease. Hands clasped tight behind his back, he stared down on her. She took a step back, feeling like a suspect being prepped for interrogation. "You don't have any idea who'd come all the way here to try and buy off Cara so she'd fire you?"

"I told you I didn't." She steeled her spine, refusing to be intimidated by his cold glare and accusing tone. "You can ask all the questions you want. I don't have the answers for you."

"And I'm sorry." She turned on her heels, facing Cara. "I didn't mean to cause any problems with you hiring me. If you prefer I go, I understand."

She was thankful for Cara's answering smile. "Don't be silly." She came out of Cade's protective hold, placing herself firmly between Tori and Luke. "As I made perfectly clear earlier this morning, I have no intention of letting you go anywhere."

It sank in then…what Cara had been offered and turned down. "You barely know me. You could have taken the money and gone on to hire somebody else."

"I could have." Cara looked thoughtful. "And then I would have had to live with the fact I'd done something like that to someone I've come to know and like."

Tori didn't have words. She could only stare, not sure how to react. In her life, people didn't do such things. Especially not for her.

"So who was that guy then?" Jackie came around the counter, juggling a chubby-cheeked baby on her hip. "And who, exactly, was he making the offer for?"

"I honestly don't know." Doing all she could to ignore Luke, Tori reached for the baby, smiling as he wrapped pudgy fingers around hers. "It doesn't seem possible anybody would even do such a thing. Other than my former boss, and a couple co-workers, nobody knew I was coming to Snow Ridge."

Luke moved around Cara and Jackie, refusing to allow Tori the chance to avoid him. It was time to get answers to the questions he had. He couldn't be sure if she was telling the truth or not. But he did know she was hiding something. Had been since the moment he'd found her on the side of the road.

"Why did you come to Snow Ridge?" He held her gaze, refusing to let her look away.

The others grew silent as she stared at him, anger clear in the depths of her emerald eyes. A hint of guilt crept up. He chased it away. He may have kissed her senseless the night before. But he was, always would be, a cop first.

And, right now, he was a cop who wanted answers. "I don't—"

Tori looked around at the faces staring back at her. She wanted to lie. Wanted to tell him it was none of his business and pretend like the job was the only reason she was there. But she caught the soft smile Jackie offered. The kindness in Cara's blue eyes. They both could have turned her out on the streets. Taken the money and come up with an excuse to let her go.

She was almost thirty years old and they'd offered

something she hadn't known, hadn't allowed herself to know, through all her years. They'd given immediate friendship. Refused to let her back into her protective shell where commitment could be avoided.

Instinct demanded she share nothing and keep her personal life to herself where she wouldn't be vulnerable to the pain that came with letting others close, giving them a part of her she could never get back. A trust she knew could so easily be shattered.

But it didn't feel right. Not now. Not after what had happened in the short time she'd been in Snow Ridge. "I came to Snow Ridge to find my brother." She sucked in a stabilizing breath, fighting back the unease creeping up her spine. "I haven't seen or talked to him since I was three and he was eight."

She looked straight at Luke, wishing she could read something in his hard expression. "The last time I saw him was the night our parents were murdered."

"Oh, Tori." Cara was there, grabbing her hands, pulling her close. "I'm so sorry. How can it be possible to be separated from your brother for so long? Especially after the tragedy you both suffered."

"I don't know." Tori shook her head, fighting off the threat of tears. "I don't remember much of anything from that time."

She remembered the looks though. The strange silence that would come when she'd ask for her brother. There was pity at times. Frustration other times. But never the answers she needed. And after so many years she'd simply quit asking.

"How do you know your brother is here?" Luke came around Cara, his hazel eyes still cold.

Cara looked at him, jabbing an elbow in his side.

"Enough cop mode," she scowled, moving so she stood directly between them. "She doesn't need that right now."

"No, she doesn't." Jackie was there, side by side with Cara, a protective wall between her and Luke. Between them, the baby on her hip gave a wide, toothless smile.

Tori wanted to laugh, cry, and hug them all in one big swoop.

"Enough." Luke came around as he shot a harsh look at Cara and Jackie though he made a point of softening his gaze before turning for Tori. "No use in telling me not to be a cop as I'm standing here in my uniform, answering a call you made." He shot Cara a knowing look.

She shrugged, unaffected by his sharp tone.

Luke scowled as he looked over her to Cade, receiving nothing but a shrug of the shoulders and a hint of a smile.

He should put them all in their place. Flash his badge to remind them he was only doing as his job required. He might not have felt so good, treating Tori as a suspect. But damn, he *did* have a job to do. Even when it was unpleasant.

And there was no question there was something very wrong with what had happened here this morning. And Tori was the center of it, whether she knew the reasons why or not.

"I shouldn't have to remind you, somebody wanted Tori gone enough they were willing to pay dearly for it." He met every set of eyes looking back at him. "There's a reason for it. It's my job to figure out what that is."

But, it was looking more and more like Tori was a victim to it, not a suspect. Not that it meant he could ease off. Not until he had some sort of answer. "And part of that figuring out is needing to know how she's so sure her brother is here in Snow Ridge."

If he'd been expecting an ease in the accusing gazes bearing down on him, he'd been wrong. At least from the ladies around him. Cara and Jackie took a place on each side of Tori and looked ready for a fight if that's what it came to.

And Tori—

There'd be no repeat of the night before. Of that he was sure. Still, she sucked in a deep breath before giving him a hesitant look. "I was twenty-one when I started searching for my brother. Twice I paid out more than I could afford for a personal investigator to make promises of coming close to finding him only to suddenly change their tune at the end and claim there was nothing they could do for me."

The same old frustration and anger rolled through Tori as she remembered. She was like so many, living paycheck to paycheck. She'd lived on the bare minimum, going hungry when needed, to save up the money she needed. And all she'd received from both was an apology and a request to not contact them again.

She'd been an absolute mess after the second failure. Had lost her usual restrictions when it came to talking about her life, grief taking over sensible thought. "I'd given up ever thinking I'd see my brother again. But there was a long-time customer, Prissy, who made monthly trips to the bookstore where I worked. And she became my miracle."

She sucked in a deep breath, calming the emotions

battling inside. Though she felt the burn of Luke's gaze, she couldn't look at him. Instead, she turned to Cara, finding comfort there. "Prissy is a Search Angel. I'd never heard of them until she told me. They help people who have been separated, usually in situations like adoption, find their loved ones. And they do it to help others, never charging a penny for all they do."

"And she was my angel, in every way." Tori found the courage to turn back to Luke. "After seven years of searching, she had the answers I so desperately needed. Answers that led me here."

"You're sure her information was correct?" Though his tone softened, Luke still remained firm and strong in front of her.

She nodded. "After last night, I know it was."

"Last night?" It was Jackie who jumped in, pulling Tori's attention away. "We were at the pub last night. How did that make you sure?"

"Because my brother was there." She couldn't stop the hesitant smile.

Silence fell as they looked at her, confusion and wonder weighing heavy in the air.

Cara took her hand. "Who's your brother?"

She hesitated, cautious to share what was still so much for her to take in. But a look at them and she knew there would be no holding back the name they so desperately wanted to know. "Seth Mundy."

Shock kept the words from coming. She saw it in their eyes…disbelief so strong they didn't know what to say.

Luke stepped closer, taking her free hand. "Are you sure?"

Before she could answer, the bell above the door

chimed through the store. All heads turned as one. And there he stood, as if called by their very conversation.

Seth Mundy.

Chapter Eight

Well…hell. This wasn't what he expected.

Standing inside the door of Precious Gems, Seth did his best not to turn and run as five sets of eyes bore down on him. Whatever he'd walked in to, he had a feeling it wasn't good. Or anything he wanted to be part of.

"I'm sorry." He reached behind him for the door. "I didn't mean to interrupt. I can come back at a better time."

Luke stepped away from the others and headed right for him. "Actually, you're here at just the right time."

"Though it's a bit odd," he looked back over his shoulder before stopping with only a few feet separating them, "you showing up now."

Seth didn't like the look in his eyes but remained firm where he was. He'd done nothing wrong. Though every inch of him crawled with the feeling he had.

She'll be safe, boy. As long as you stay away from her.

The words, uttered by another officer in uniform, crept back. He shook free of them, refusing to let them control him as they had for so long.

"I see nothing odd about it." He looked past Luke, clashing with a set of emerald eyes bringing back memories. Some he wished to forget. Others he held on to desperately.

"So, you just happened to come by," Luke paused, looking down at his watch, "before noon for some casual shopping?"

He heard it. Knew he was being walked into a trap. Seth looked from Luke to those standing behind him, wondering what he'd come in to. How much they knew.

"Enough, please." Tori broke away from the others, hating how things were playing out. This wasn't what she expected. What she wanted when it came to thoughts of reuniting with a brother she wasn't even sure wanted her in his life.

Luke spared her a glance as she stopped beside him. He looked as if he wanted to say more but chose instead to step back, leaving her acutely aware of his presence behind her while she stared, again, into a face she knew in her heart, if not in her memory.

She knew everyone watched…waited. In that moment, she regretted ever saying a word.

"Why are you here?" She looked hard into his eyes, fearing what his answer might be.

His deep, intent look made all the others fade away. She saw only her brother while reliving the few memories she carried of him. If asked, she couldn't explain how it felt, standing there, looking into a face that was a part of her. Into a person who mirrored back everything she was.

Even if he wanted nothing to do with her, she'd never regret the chance to see him again. To know what it was like to be close to her brother, stealing a few stolen moments she'd dreamed of for so long.

"I was hoping we could talk." He looked around

the store. "Privately."

She wanted that more than anything.

"I think you need a cup of coffee." Cara was there, pressing a soft hand to her back. "And, luckily, we have a great place right next door. They even have tables where you can sit and have a nice conversation."

Tori shook her head. "I can't. It wouldn't be right. Not after what's happened. And with my being so late already this morning."

"You'll go without argument." Cara urged her forward. "We aren't exactly swimming in customers, just yet. Now's the time, if any, to get those things that brought you here settled."

"I'll have questions when you're done." Luke stepped up, looking between her and Seth. "I have to head to the station but I will be expecting a chance to talk to you."

Tori didn't answer. Didn't have a desire to. The Chief she'd come to know today was nothing like the man she'd kissed the night before. She'd needed an excuse not to repeat her mistake and he handed it right to her.

As far as she was concerned, he was nothing more than a reminder of why she didn't bother with relationships. With commitments that would only fall apart with time.

Her life was and always had been about today. About the moment she currently lived in. And right now that moment was giving her a chance to know the brother she'd come so far to see.

Nothing else mattered.

****

The silence was killing her.

Sitting across from her brother at a small table in the back corner of the coffee shop, Tori bit down her impatience. They'd ordered coffee, a pastry to go with it, and settled with only a few words spoken.

"I know who you are." Seth's voice broke through, drawing her attention away from the croissant she picked at. "I knew last night but wasn't ready to admit it."

She looked at him, into his pale blue eyes, seeing the battle raging there. "And that doesn't make you happy?" She picked up her coffee and took a slow sip.

"I don't know what it makes me. Damnit, Tori." He hit an open palm against the table, pulling curious glances from those around them. "I figured I'd never see you again. Accepted it long ago. And then, suddenly, here you are. Far from home. In some small mountain town you shouldn't even know exists."

He looked at her, long and hard. "I don't even know how this is possible."

"It's possible because I've spent the last seven years searching for you. Unlike you, I refused to accept I'd never see you again." She bit back the pain. Didn't want him to know the bite his words left behind.

Seth looked at her, not sure how to react. She'd searched for him. Wanted to see him. The thought warmed him even as it frightened him.

As long as you stay away from her.

The warning echoed again, the deep, thick voice one he'd never forget. But that had been so long ago. The fear may have never left him, the words as strong now as they had ever been, but what could happen? Now? In this time when she was all grown up.

"I'm sorry." He reached over the table and took her

hand in his. "I'm handling this like a fool, carrying on as if you've done something wrong by me. And that's far from the truth."

He looked into her emerald eyes, saw a glimmer of the little sister he'd never forgotten. She'd never been far from his thoughts. Had remained in his dreams even to this day. "I'm glad you searched. Even happier you found me."

"Are you?" A hint of tears shimmered in her eyes. "I was afraid you wouldn't want anything to do with me. Would turn me away the minute I found you."

"It's a shock, I won't deny it. I was sure I'd never see you again. And when I realized who you were at the pub, I didn't know how to handle it."

He offered a hint of a smile, hoping to ease some of the tension. "And I've done a pretty lousy job handling it, even now." His hold on her hand tightened. "Not exactly the best kind of greeting for my baby sister."

She didn't say a word, only stared at him from across the table. The first of the tears he'd seen hints of only a second before slowly slid down her cheek.

Leaning over the table, he swiped at one with the pad of his thumb. "I'll get better at this, I promise."

She laughed a small, quick sound through her tears. "You'll have time since I'm hoping to be around for a while."

"You're working for Cara now." He let go of her hand and reached for his coffee.

"I am. At least for now." She picked up her own cup for a long, slow sip.

He shot her a curious glance over the rim of his cup. "What does that mean? You just started there, didn't you?"

"Yes." She went back to picking at her croissant. "And somebody already wants me fired."

"What?" The single word was loud, too loud. Remembering they were in public, he fought to lower his voice. "Who would want you fired? *Why* would they want you fired?"

"I don't know." She looked lost and confused staring back at him. "This morning, before I came down, someone came into the shop and offered money if Cara was willing to let me go."

She stuffed a bit of croissant in her mouth though he doubted she was even aware of it. "It makes no sense. There's nobody in my life to care where I'm working or why I'm here in Snow Ridge."

The warning echoed again inside his head, louder this time. "Maybe you shouldn't stay. Snow Ridge might not be the place for you."

He saw the hurt on his sister's face, felt it like a firm punch to the gut. She looked down at the table while running a finger around the rim of her coffee cup. "What is it with you men and finding out someone was willing to pay to have me fired? First Luke, now you?"

"Chief Grady?" He waited until she looked up at him. "What does he have to do with any of it?"

"Nothing really, other than kissing me senseless last night only to flip the switch and become a cold, interrogating cop this morning."

Over the length of the table, her eyes widened and red stained her cheeks. "I'm sorry. I don't even know why I told you that. Him kissing me has nothing to do with anything."

It might have been twenty-five years since he'd last

seen her but Seth found himself rolling around the idea of Luke kissing his little sister, not sure he liked it. "You can barely know him. What were you doing kissing him? And what the hell was he doing kissing you?"

She stared at him for a moment. "Doesn't matter." She shook her head. "He made it clear today where he stands. Just as it seems you're trying to do since learning about what's happened."

"It's not how it sounds." And it might be nothing at all. But still—"

He saw the confusion tightening the lines between her eyes. He wasn't handling this right. Was stumbling his way through his first real conversation with his sister.

He sucked in a deep breath, knowing he had to do better. "That night, when Mom and Dad...when they were shot...what do you remember?"

"Only what's haunted me in my dreams." She crossed her fingers tight over the edge of the table. "I see myself in their bedroom, watching Mom get ready for a night out. And then I'm in the hallway, watching as they're killed in front of me. Then you're there, trying to pull me away."

He reached over, held his palm out, and waited for her to lay her hand in his. "Do you remember after that, when we were taken to the police station? When they literally had to pull you off me and drag you away."

There was sadness in the shake of her head. "I can't...I don't remember anything other than the nightmares haunting me since that night."

"You were so little. So small." For a moment he drifted away, seeing her in the hallway, their father dead at her feet, his blood staining her clothes. And there was their mother, already dead, at the stairs.

No matter how hard, how far, he'd run, he'd never been able to escape that terror. "They took you away when we reached the station. Refused, for hours, to let me see you though I could hear you calling for me."

He was still there, even now. So small himself and surrounded by big, frightening men in uniform while being kept away from her desperate pleas. Told it was for the best. His parents were dead, his sister called for him through her tears, and nobody around him seemed to care.

"They finally let me see you, though only through the window of the room where they kept you." His fingers tightened with hers.

There was something good, sitting here, sharing this with her. As horrifying as it was, there was comfort in finally giving his sister the truth. "I'll never forget seeing you sitting there inside that room. It's an image that has stayed with me ever since."

Tori clung to every word, understanding there was so much in what he said. So much in what she'd searched for and needed to know.

"You'd stopped crying by then. But you still looked so fragile. And I kept seeing you as I had back in the hallway, screaming like you were and so terrified."

There was such sadness in his eyes. She wanted to go to him and throw her arms around him.

"Damnit." He curled his free hand into a fist. "I was only eight. And yet all I wanted to do was go to you. To protect you. But they wouldn't let me. There was an older, pudgy officer I'll never forget. He held me back, pulling me aside when the others wanted to let me in the room with you."

"Why?" The chill of her nightmares raced up her spine. "Why wouldn't he let you come to me?"

He shoved a frustrated hand through his hair. "I don't know. I'll never know. But he made it very clear there was danger. And the only way to keep you safe from that danger was to stay away from you."

"And I did. I have." There was defeat in his voice, reaching over and falling heavy on Tori. "For every time I missed you. Every night I had a dream with you. Every thought I had about you. I'd hear him again. Hear his voice, warning me, if I wanted you safe, I had to stay away."

"That's why." She choked back the tears caught in her throat. "After all these years, that's why you never found me. Never did so much as give me a hint you were there, were still my brother, wanting me as part of your life."

"I couldn't." His own pain echoed in his voice. "I believed him. Still believe him. For whatever reason, you're at risk if you're around me."

"That's ridiculous." She was too loud, drawing the looks of others.

"Is it?" His look was hard, probing. "How long have you been here? And already somebody is doing what they can to get rid of you."

The connection she hadn't thought of hit, settling painfully in the pit of her stomach. "It can't be because of that. It just can't."

Her mind didn't want to go there. Didn't want to think of such a possibility. She looked at her brother, thought to argue, but she couldn't do it. Couldn't chase down the fear enough to try and believe none of it was related.

So she only nodded. Left with nothing else.

****

Though they had their fair share of curious glances, Jackie and Cara asked no questions when she returned.

Tori was thankful for it, still unsure of everything she'd learned in such a short amount of time. She hadn't packed up her life, come to Snow Ridge, and expected it to be easy.

But nothing could have prepared her for what she'd found since the moment the blizzard welcomed her. There was too much to think about and work through.

Needing a break from it, no matter how short, she concentrated on learning everything she could about Precious Gems and all it had to offer.

It felt good to throw herself in, worrying about nothing but the work in front of her. The customers had been slow, but they'd been enough, giving her a sense of what to expect once Ski Season settled in.

With Luke and Cade gone, it had just been the three of them and Baby Evan until late afternoon when his dad came to pick him up.

It was easy to like Jackie and Cara. They had a way about them. A kindness they showed over and over again in the time she'd spent with them.

While the rest of her life felt as if it had landed in the midst of chaos, the time she spent with them gave her the comfort she needed.

By the time the day began to wear down, she was feeling better and more like herself. The setting sun danced rays through the big front windows, warming the insides even as it continued to melt off the snow.

Settling on a stool behind the counter, she took a moment to just look. At what was around her. The place she worked. The two women she was thankful had come into her life.

On one side, she had so many things she couldn't even begin to understand, but on the other side, where she sat now, things felt good, giving her reason to smile.

"You're looking better." Cara came to stand beside her, resting a gentle hand on her shoulder.

"Feeling better, too." She swept stray strands of chestnut hair from her face. "Though I'm not sure how long that will last."

"Want to talk about it? Jackie and I are great listeners. Once we lock the doors for the night, we could open a bottle of wine and have a good chat." Cara looked across the counter at Jackie, receiving a nod in agreement.

It was strange realizing she wanted what they offered. It wasn't her. Never had been. "I wish we could but I'll have to take a raincheck. Seth is coming back once we're closed. He seems to think we need to have that talk with Luke I was hoping to avoid."

She didn't agree. The last thing Tori wanted was another second with the man who sent her emotions on such a rollercoaster.

"There's more to the story, isn't there?" Jackie came around the counter, finding a place on the other side of Tori.

"Might be. Though I'm not fully convinced of it." She released a long, deep breath, feeling the fear creep back. "It's enough to warrant letting Luke know. I'll agree with that. Though I figure Seth should be able to handle that on his own. Don't see why I need to be there."

Cara's quick laugh snapped her attention up. There was knowledge in her eyes Tori wasn't sure she liked. "I used to feel the same about Cade when I first moved back to town. Saw no reason why I needed to be around him."

Surprised, Tori looked at her with wide eyes. "But you're engaged to him?"

"Uh, huh." Cara let that one sit until understanding struck.

"Oh, no," Tori was quick to deny, shaking her head. "This isn't the same. The only feeling I have for Luke is disgust. He irritates me to the point of craziness."

"Carrying on like he was in here." She swept her arms out and blew out a frustrated breath. "Any man who'd kiss a woman silly only to treat her in such a way the next day isn't a man I want to know."

"I knew it." Jackie threw an arm around Tori's shoulders, squeezing hard. "I told Cara something had happened. Nobody gets those kind of sparks for nothing."

"Doesn't matter now." Tori pushed up from the stool, resisting the urge to pace the floor. Instead, she fussed with the display of polished gems at the edge of the counter.

Cara came up behind her and wrapped an arm around her slender waist. "He's a Grady which means Luke can be a hard man at times. But he's a good man. That much I know. And he's not one to kiss a woman unless there was some meaning there."

It wasn't what she wanted to hear. She preferred to

be told he'd kissed his way through Snow Ridge, never giving a second thought about it.

Not that it mattered. Whatever had been the reason or meaning for the kiss, it was done. And she didn't see a chance of a repeat.

Chapter Nine

No. She was not doing this.

Scowling at the clothes she'd unpacked, Tori grabbed an old sweatshirt and threw it over her jeans. Looking over her nicer shirts and thinking of Luke was absolutely ridiculous. She didn't care a thing about him. Wasn't about to do with anything but comfort when she saw him.

With that in mind, she ran a brush through her hair, sweeping it up in a ponytail at the back of her head. She added a light tint of lipstick. But it had nothing to do with Luke. *Nothing at all.*

She threw on her tennis shoes, grabbed her jacket, and was ready when the knock came.

The smile on her face fell away as she swung open the door. Luke stood at the top of the back stairs, shadows dancing over the hard-carved lines of his face.

"What are you doing here?" She scowled, folding her arms firmly over her breasts. "Seth was supposed to pick me up and take me to the station."

She wanted to smack him as he pushed his way through the door and into the tiny kitchen. "Change of plans. We're meeting at the Double G. And since Seth is already at the Moonshine, I told him I'd pick you up so he didn't have to come back into town."

Cursing her brother, she was tempted to refuse, turn back, and bury in the comfort of her bed. But she wouldn't. She'd be the adult she was and go and get it over with.

"Had I known," she grabbed her purse from the back of the chair, "I could have driven myself."

"That wouldn't have worked." He held open the door for her, waiting until she turned to lock it. "'Cause I wouldn't have had the chance to try and convince you, all over again, that I'm a good guy."

She stopped at the bottom of the stairs, shooting him a look. "I don't think you should waste your time. I'm flattered, but I don't see how it will be worth it."

Before he could answer, she turned on her heels, disappearing through the small space between Precious Gems and the coffee shop.

Luke resisted the urge to grab her and pull her back. He was a cop first. Had acted in the line of that duty and wouldn't apologize for it.

But he did regret the way things fell together. Wished for better.

But, obviously, for Tori, what was done was done.

She waited for him at his truck, climbing in quickly the second he disengaged the locks, giving him no time to come around and open the door for her. Sitting stiff and straight in her seat, she didn't spare him a single look as he climbed in and started the engine.

He wasn't exactly a patient man. The silence wore thin by the time he reached the edge of town. Sparing her a glance, he caught her insisting on her blank, intent stare out the front windshield.

By the time he reached the ranch and turned off the main drive, he was tested to his limits.

"Where are we going?" She finally broke her silence, glancing his way when the main house drifted off in the background.

"My place." He didn't look at her as he continued down the road, passing the barn and a white-fenced corral where a young girl sat across a black-spotted horse, twisting around barrels set into the ground.

"You said we were meeting at the ranch." She looked back where the main house was barely a speck now.

"We are." He spared her a glance, turning off the road and cutting through a tumble of Thistlewood edging the dirt drive. "We're meeting at my place."

Tori saw it then, backed up against a lush wall of green, still carrying the hint of snow. A beautiful contrast under the rays of the slowly setting sun.

Dark logs stretched high and long, creating a breath-taking two-story cabin blending with the rise and fall of the mountains in the background. A peaked roof and long wide porch completed the rustic look, giving the sense of comfort before ever reaching the front door.

"I didn't know your place was here on the ranch." The idea of it would have made her much more hesitant to leave with him. It was one thing, being at the main house, surrounded by the constant flutter of activity. It was another to be inside his own personal space, just the two of them until Seth arrived.

He pulled to a stop next to a thick growth of Chokeberry. "Built it years ago. Jake's working on his own place a bit further since he figured it was time he moved out from above the pub."

"And you're all fine living here on the ranch together?" She opened her door, stepping out on to the pebble path leading toward the house.

Luke came around the front to join her. "Why wouldn't we be? We all grew up on this ranch. It's home."

Tori couldn't imagine the connection they had. To each other and to the ranch.

She thought of Seth. Couldn't help but wonder if they'd ever know what the Grady brothers shared. Even just part of it. She couldn't imagine what it was like. How it felt. Too many years she'd spent alone. There was hardly a memory of being part of a family. Of sharing something unique with those who were so much a part of you.

Following Luke up the path, she shook off the wonder. It would do her no good. Especially not now when she needed all her concentration on ignoring the hot spikes finding life as his arm brushed against hers.

Columbines, tangling with Bluebells, arched around the porch, their color revived with the melting snow. Softening the look, they led the way up the wide stairs to a porch that took her breath away.

Nearly as wide as a room itself, it was lined by terra cotta pots, overflowing with the last of the summer flowers. Bursting color mixed with the deep green cushions lining the many chairs centered around a horseshoe-shaped table.

"It's amazing." She couldn't stop herself, forgetting for a minute she was determined to remain distant.

He smiled at her, pride clear in his hazel eyes. "Wait till you see the one out back." He put a key in the door then swung it open.

And again she lost her breath.

Stretching both levels of the house, the front room

was an amazing play of light and wood. Windows, uncovered and bright, curved around the walls, bringing in the last of the daylight. The muted, beige colors of the overstuffed couch and matching chairs added to the beauty of a large stone fireplace centering the far wall.

Luke took off his coat and hung it over the thick banister edging the winding staircase butting against the opposite wall before holding his hand out for hers. "I'm not too formal around here," he explained, draping hers over the top of his.

She could only nod, too taken by the beauty surrounding her. So caught up she didn't protest when he took her elbow, guiding her down the wide hallway.

"This is one of Cara's." She was struck by the bold strokes of yellow and orange covering the painting hanging on the wall.

He stopped with her as she admired the power it held. "I didn't think there was a place for something so modern. Didn't think it would fit. But she proved me wrong the minute she hung it."

"It's perfect." She nodded her approval before falling back into step with him as he led her further down the hallway. Past an office done in soft leather and lined with floor to ceiling bookshelves, to a kitchen as powerful and modern as the painting they'd passed.

"Oh, wow." She couldn't take her eyes away from the gleaming stainless-steel appliances. The granite countertops shimmered in different tones of gray, from the lightest to nearly black in the depth of it.

"You don't grow up with Hattie and not understand the importance of a good kitchen." Letting go of her elbow, he crossed over the black slate floor and pulled open one of the two refrigerator doors. He held up a beer, grabbing a second one at her nod. Popping the tops, he handed one to her as he took a long swallow from the other.

Turning in a long, slow circle, she took a drink of her own. "How did you—"

Her gaze rested on a room off the kitchen, surrounded by nothing but glass. "How did you afford a place like this? I mean—"

She broke off, embarrassed by the line her questions were heading.

"You mean how does a Chief in a small mountain town have the money for this," he finished for her, his smile easing her embarrassment.

He waved a hand, leading her toward the glass-covered room still holding her attention. "The land was free, of course. And us Grady men are handy with our building skills. My dad and brothers, and even Old Joe helped. I did what I could with both time and money. Took me nearly three years to be done. But it was worth it."

Yes. She agreed.

"This is my favorite room." He moved around the large table centering the room with thick cushions topping the long benches edging the sides. Stepping between the matching chairs tucked in a corner, he flipped a switch high on the wall.

Tori watched in wonder as the floor to ceiling windows spread apart, opening the room to the outdoors and the porch beyond.

Luke turned back, watching her, enjoying the look on her face. It meant something to him, knowing she liked his place. Gave him a warm feeling inside to be able to share it with her.

She moved up beside him, stepping out onto the porch.

This was his sanctuary. His place to escape the stress and harsh reality of his job. And always a ranch boy at heart, the outdoors, so often, offered exactly what he needed. Especially here on the Double G where the air he breathed, the ground he walked, was so much a part of who he was.

"It's amazing." She ran a soft hand over the tops of the outdoor couches circled around a large redbrick fire pit. Potted miniature fir trees graced the sides, creating the perfect place to simply sit back, relax, and enjoy the beauty stretching as far as the eye could see.

He watched as she moved over for a closer look at the built-in grill. "See, there is more to me than the hard-nosed cop you came to know this morning."

She shot him a look over the bend of her shoulder. One he couldn't read. But there was a hint of something in her emerald eyes. A softening to the hard stare she'd used on him since he'd picked her up.

He'd take that as a good thing. Take every small step that might give him another chance at kissing those luscious lips of hers. Another chance to feel her soft curves fold into his, taking what he had to offer.

Such thoughts had him taking a step forward, closer to what he craved. Her gaze lifted and landed on him, widening as he took another step.

Just a bit more and he'd have her in his arms again. Know that pleasure that had burned through him the night before. He didn't know if she'd stay or turn and run. But it was a risk he was willing to take.

He was nearly there, ready to reach out, when the doorbell caught them both off guard.

Cursing under his breath, he turned, swearing he'd try again before the night was over.

****

"I know it's a longshot but I still don't like the idea of what's happened." Seth took a long draw from his beer, looking from Luke to Tori sitting across from him at the table.

He sensed the tension, caught the spark of anger still lingering in his sister's eyes, and wondered how, or even if, he should handle it.

There was no handbook for this sort of thing. Nothing to give guidance on what to expect after being reunited with your sister after twenty-five years apart. He felt like a stranger, with no right to worry or care. Yet he did worry. He did care. And he couldn't stop the protective streak kicking to life, making him watch and judge every movement, every word, Luke made when it came to Tori.

"You don't know what danger he talked about?" Luke looked at him, hard and questioning like the cop he was. "And you're sure the one who talked to you was a police officer?"

Seth drifted back, saw the night as if it was still happening. "He came in after the first round of cops. Him and a few others. By then I could no longer hear Tori's cries echoing through the station."

He looked at his sister while his heart pulled painfully. "I'll never forget the look of them standing there inside that room. I was afraid of them at first sight."

He still saw them, as clear as if it was yesterday. "They had so many questions. I remember wanting to run away. They pushed and pushed, as if they didn't believe me when I told them I didn't recognize the two men who had killed our parents."

Tori moved over a chair and grabbed his hand in hers. Her eyes were wet…sad. Of all things to find a connection between them, this was it. The terrible death of their parents.

It tore at his heart to know it. Made him wish, for a fleeting moment, he'd never walked into the pub the night before. "They never mentioned any kind of danger during the questions. Never hinted at it. Not until they took me to see her through that damn window where I couldn't even let her know I was there."

He should have done more. The thought he'd battled for so many years returned with a vengeance. He should have demanded they let him inside the room. Should have never allowed them to take away the chance to at least say goodbye.

Luke's gaze was thoughtful, staring at him over his beer bottle. "I'd say I'm sorry. But I'm not sure that's appropriate after all this time."

He turned for Tori, his gaze softening even more. "I didn't know, didn't realize, all this when it came down this morning. If I had, I would have handled it in a different manner."

Tori wondered if that was his attempt at some kind of apology. Not that it mattered, she reminded herself, turning her attention back to her brother. "I didn't, have never known, any of that. My memories are only what I have in my nightmares. My last memory of you is in the hallway, with our parents dead."

It was a hell of a thing to realize. She shook her head, not wanting to dwell on it. Needing the distraction, she picked up her beer bottle and took a drink.

"Do you remember the names of the officers?" Though he questioned Seth, Luke kept his attention on her. She didn't like it. Didn't like the uncomfortable feeling he created with his gaze peering deep, searching for something she couldn't understand.

"No. Not a one of them." Seth finished off his own beer, pushing the empty bottle out of the way. "It was a long time ago. And I was still a kid."

"And the ones who killed your parents." Luke looked from her to Seth. "They were never caught?"

Seth glanced at her, his own sadness clear in his eyes. "No. As far as I know, the ones who killed our parents never faced any sort of justice for what they did."

It hurt to know. Dug deep to think they were still out there. Tori had never thought to ask or find out for herself. From foster home to foster home, she'd learned to do her best to push any such thoughts from her mind while pretending her life started and ended with the new family taking her in.

If the nightmares hadn't haunted her she might have been successful at it.

Luke finished off his beer, grabbing his empty bottle and Seth's as he pushed up from his chair. "I'm going to do some checking." He pulled open a door beneath the sink, dumping them in a bin. "It does seem a stretch, thinking what happened all those years ago has anything to do with what happened this morning. But, I'm not going to discount anything until I get more information."

Tori was numb. Of all things she'd imagined, come to think of when it came to moving to Snow Ridge, she'd never thought she'd find herself caught so heavily in the mystery surrounding her parents' deaths.

"I don't like the idea there might be some kind of threat against my sister." Seth stood and came around behind her, resting a hand over her shoulder.

Luke turned from his place at the sink, looking at them both. "I don't either. We don't have anything to warrant official protection. But, between the two of us, we should be able to keep a pretty good eye on her until we have some answers."

She looked at her brother, at Luke, and did what she could to push down the anger building as they talked around her. "I don't need any sort of protection," she put in her own opinion. The one she figured should count most. "I live and take care of myself just fine."

Though she couldn't pinpoint why, she didn't like the look exchanged between them. There was more there than they were letting her know. More, she was sure, she wouldn't like.

But they dropped the subject which was good enough for her at the moment. She was getting tired, worn from the excitement she couldn't seem to escape since arriving in Snow Ridge. The privacy of her apartment and the comfort of her bed began calling her.

As if reading her thoughts, Seth moved away from her, holding out a hand for Luke. "I need to be getting back. I have an early morning ahead of me."

"I'll let you know if I learn anything." Luke accepted his hand.

"I'd appreciate it." Seth turned to Tori, waiting for her to push up from her chair.

The minute she stood, he wrapped her in a hug, catching her unprepared. "I might be a bit rusty at this big brother thing but it doesn't mean I've forgotten how to worry about you."

He pulled back enough to look her in the eye. "Just watch yourself and be careful, okay."

Shocked from the unexpected hug and his words it took a second for her to find her voice. "I will. I promise." She managed a smile. Pushing on to her toes, she dropped a soft kiss on his cheek.

He smiled, one that reached his eyes. With one last nod of his head to Luke, he turned on his heels and headed down the hall for the front door.

Tori listened to his footsteps fading as he let himself out.

So many changes. Some good. And some so very bad.

****

"You don't need to walk me to my door." Tori hesitated as Luke swung the driver's door open. She'd been so eager to be back at her apartment. Eager to be alone and escape it all for a while.

And she was so close. If only Luke would go and let her take care of getting to her door on her own.

"Don't need to means nothing when it battles against wanting to." He sent her a smile, full of so much confidence, she was helpless to the flutters gathering in her stomach.

"Fine." Knowing a useless argument when she came to one, she climbed out of the truck, waiting for him to join her on the sidewalk. "But, if you're expecting a repeat from last night, you'll only be disappointing yourself."

He didn't answer, only flashed her that damn confident smile again.

So cocky. She turned her back, starting out ahead of him. If he thought he had a chance at another kiss, he was only fooling himself.

In two long strides he caught up with her, his arm brushing against hers. She cursed the surge of heat rising to her shoulder. Knew it wouldn't play good into her determination to turn him away at the door with nothing more than a simple and short thank you.

Left no choice, he fell behind her through the tiny cut between the coffee shop and Precious Gems, finding his place back by her side as soon as they reached the alley.

She stopped at the bottom of the stairs, fully expecting him to say his goodbyes there. Instead, he looked at her before pushing past, making his way to the door.

"I don't know what you're thinking," she called up to him as she started up the stairs. "But I do know, whatever it is, you're only wasting your time."

"Who says I have to be thinking anything but walking a pretty lady to the door." He smiled at her as she joined him, moving aside as she pulled her key from her purse and aimed it for the door.

She stopped before putting the key into the lock. "I can't decide if you're trying to be smooth, irritating, or both." Daring a full look in his hazel eyes, she regretted it as the heat simmering there drew her in, pulling the breath from her lungs.

He said nothing. Only stared until she felt she'd go crazy from the force of it. With a step, he forced her back until she pressed against the railing behind her. "Tell me again about that kiss you're denying."

Her heart pounded against her ribs. She wanted to

shove at him. Insist he leave. But she couldn't do it. There was nothing left in her to fight against the need he stirred inside.

Still he did nothing but stand there and stare at her.

Seconds passed slow, fueling the heat spreading through. He didn't touch her. Didn't make a move to get closer. She felt every inch of him, burning against her. Teasing and taunting until she was sure she could take no more.

Then he was there. Just his lips, brushing over hers.

Only a hint to start. A question to her reaction after she'd been so determined to keep him away.

And she had been. Until that first touch. Until the reminder of how perfectly his lips molded with hers. How her own heart seemed to catch, picking up the beat with his as he drew her in.

He pulled back, looking hard into her eyes.

She said nothing. Didn't have to. What he saw there gave him the permission he needed. Still without laying a hand on her, he pulled her in with the simple touch of his mouth against hers.

She didn't reach for him. Couldn't form the thought to as every part of her was frozen in the moment of his kiss.

He deepened it. Sighing, she forgot about every promise she'd made to herself. There was nothing but sensation and need drawing on her, pulling her deeper and deeper under the careful seduction he brought with nothing more than his lips. Seeking, giving more than she knew to take.

And still he went on until she was sure she'd melt right there at the door. Knees weak, heart pounding against her ribs, she wasn't sure she'd ever be able to pull back from the places he took her.

He groaned, low and deep, before pulling away. "I'd take you in if I thought it was a good idea and continue this in the proper place."

But it wasn't a good idea. She understood it even as dread took a grip. Shaking her head, trying to find her bearings, she looked up at him. "Goodnight, Luke."

He dropped one final, quick kiss to her lips. Stepping back, he waited until she had the door open and was safely tucked away inside, locks firmly set.

Falling back against the door, still desperate to catch her breath, she heard the echo of his steps down the stairs. Thought for a moment to call after him and invite him inside after all.

But she knew better. And with one final hard draw of air through her lungs, she started for her bedroom on legs barely able to carry her.

Chapter Ten

He'd waited a few days before making the call.

Not that he believed any minds would be changed or checks written. But it didn't sit well with him, calling so soon to report something he knew would be viewed as a failure, regardless of his lack of control over the situation.

Phone in one hand, a glass of whiskey in the other, Anton settled at the small table by the window. The snow had all but melted. The late afternoon sun shimmered in the clear, blue sky. If he was the sort of man to have more appreciation for such things, he'd sit there all day, staring out at the beauty surrounding this small, mountain town.

But for him, all he saw was the prison he was confined to until the job was done.

The phone seemed to ring forever on the other end. Perhaps he'd get lucky and be given one more day before having to report the latest.

Unfortunately, that was not to be.

"I presume you have news." Filip's heavy, Romanian accent drifted through the line. He didn't bother with a greeting. Which was no surprise. The man was, always had been, all business for as long as Anton had worked for him. For the family.

"There's no chance with the money." Anton followed the same directive, keeping business clear and present. "It was turned down without any chance of consideration."

There was a pause. A long draw of breath. "Shouldn't be surprised. Tori is one who comes by it naturally…inviting loyalty from others. Just another part of her that can't ever be changed."

Was there a bit of emotion in his words? Anton couldn't be sure. But he did know, the tone he heard wasn't the normal used in discussing business. There was something deeper to it. A hint of feeling he'd never known in his many years dealing with Filip.

"There's more." He almost dreaded having to continue. "She's not only made contact with but has spent time with this Seth Mundy you advised I be aware of. They had some kind of rendezvous with the Chief of Police the other night which doesn't sit well with me. Never been one to like the badges involved."

"Nothing to get worried about. We simply need to change some of our ways."

Yeah. He'd figured that. Though he still wished he knew the full story behind his reason for being here. Not that it had ever been a bother before. But something here felt different. So much different from any other job he'd carried out.

"What do you suggest?" He took a long drag from his whiskey while staring hard at the sun beginning its dip behind the mountains.

"I'm guessing, by now, she's had a hint things aren't as smooth as she thought they might be." There was a touch of regret in Filip's voice. "It's time to play on that. Make her believe staying in Snow Ridge would only bring even more unsettling situations her way."

"A bit of a scare may be what she needs." Though

he couldn't be seen, Anton nodded in agreement.

"Just be sure it's only a scare. Nothing more. There's no reason for any true harm to come to her."

As all else since he'd taken this job, the caution surprised him. Still, he knew there was no problem in handling it. "I'll take care of it."

It was all that needed to be said.

****

"You got a hot date?" Jackie shook her head as Tori checked her watch for the third time in an hour.

"Actually, I do." Tori beamed a smile. "My brother is coming over for dinner."

"Oh, well—"

Jackie shook her head and rolled her eyes. "That wasn't exactly the answer I was expecting, but I'm excited for you. And for Seth. I like the thought of you two getting to know one another."

Tori did too. She'd spent the day not only liking the idea but excited for it.

Since the night at Luke's, she'd only had the chance to talk to Seth by phone. It was nice. But not the same as a face to face.

"But I have to say, I was more hoping you'd tell me you had a hot date with Luke." Jackie's smile was sly, hiding nothing of the way her thoughts drifted.

At the mention of his name, Tori's blood ran hot all over again. Just as it had done for the last few days every time she thought of him. Of the kiss at the top of the stairs.

Her mind had played around it, worked with it, ever since, never finding anything but need and frustration left behind. "Sorry to disappoint." She shrugged, heading for the front door. "Haven't seen or talked to him since the night of all the strangeness that happened."

And she was doing her best not to let that bother her.

She flipped the lock on the door, officially closing them down for the day. It was up to her and Jackie to tie up the closing duties as Cara had slipped away early to check out a suggested venue for her upcoming wedding.

Though so limited in their time with one another, they worked well together. The store, and all the responsibilities of closing up, finished quickly.

Standing at the edge of the counter, Tori looked at Jackie, juggling her conflicting feelings on the friendship she felt growing. "I don't suppose—"

She swallowed hard over the lump in her throat, uncertainty rising as she took a step she'd never had the chance to before. "I wonder if you have time for a glass of wine before you head home. I could really use some distraction so I don't worry myself to death before my brother shows up."

And there it was—the show of her vulnerability. A step in exposing herself for the hopes of a stronger friendship. Something she'd never dared before. Was terrified of even as the question came.

"As a new mom, it's actually shocking to say, but I do have time for a glass of wine." Jackie glanced at her watch, smiling back at Tori. "My mom is busy spoiling Evan for at least another hour or two. Which means I get to spoil myself, as well."

Tori released the breath she hadn't been aware she was holding until relief set in. "Oh, thank goodness." She laughed with the nerves fluttering around. "If not for you, I wasn't sure what I'd do with the hours yet I have to face."

"Well there you go," Jackie slung an arm through hers and turned them toward the stairs at the back of the store. "We've both got a good reason for that glass of wine."

****

It was exactly what she'd needed. The glass of wine with Jackie had worked miracles, calming nerves pestering her through the day, bringing back down the unease she'd struggled with since she'd invited Seth for dinner.

Tori took care of the final touches for her sweet pepper salad, carefully adding the olives and cheese cubes. It was one of the very few dishes she carried memories of from her mother. Though she didn't have her recipe, a quick internet search provided what she'd needed for the final touch to the meal she'd prepared.

By the time her brother's knock echoed on the door, she had another bottle of wine breathing on the countertop and dinner settling in to place nicely.

She opened the door and stepped back in surprise. "What in the world?"

A small, brown pile of fur wiggling in his arms, Seth smiled at her. "We've come for dinner." He dropped a comforting hand over the puppy's head, drawing back some of his excitement. "If we're still invited, that is."

"Of course." She stepped back, unable to take her eyes off the bundle of energy cradled in her brother's arms. "I just wasn't aware you were bringing along a guest."

Seth stepped into the kitchen, closing the door

behind him. "Smells wonderful." He pushed the puppy into her arms.

Unprepared, she did her best to keep hold of the wiggling mass suddenly left to her care. Seeming not to notice her struggle, Seth pulled on the sleeves of his heavy flannel, tossing it over the back of the chair at his side.

"His name's Derby." He looked from her to the bottle of wine breathing on the counter.

Handing the puppy back, she grabbed two glasses from the cupboard and poured them each some. "Cute name." She handed one to him before taking a sip from her own. "I take it he's yours."

"Actually—"

Seth took a slow steady drink from his glass. "I'm hoping he'll be yours."

She nearly choked on her wine. Carefully, she set it on the table beside her. "Mine? I have no place in my life right now for a dog."

Giving in to the demanding wiggles, Seth set Derby on the floor. He took off, running circles around her legs. Looking up at her with big, brown eyes, his tail whipped a happy beat.

She couldn't resist. Bending down, she gave him a good scratch behind the ears. He nudged her with his short, dark brown nose. A long, excited lick up her face let her know he was happy to meet her.

"He's a Boxer mix. Born on the ranch a couple months ago." Seth bent down, joining them. "He's the last of the litter. The runt. And the only boy of five."

Derby turned his attention, nearly knocking Seth to the floor as he jumped at him. "I was watching him today, following the ranch hands around, and I thought of you."

"Or…more honestly…" He dropped a quick kiss to Derby's nose before looking at her over the small stretch between them. "I thought of a much younger you. The one who begged our parents for months for a puppy."

Tori went back and tried to remember, but nothing came.

Seth waited, shaking his head when she gave him nothing, a touch of sadness in his pale, blue eyes. "You'd finally worn them down. They had friends, right outside Chicago, with a litter ready for families. We were supposed to go the next weekend. Until—"

Until their parents had been murdered.

The truth settled as Derby came back to her, pushing his head beneath her hand, eager for a pet. "I don't remember." She pulled Derby close, giving him the petting he sought.

Still so tiny compared to the growth his large paws promised, he pushed even closer until she fell back, her lap his for the taking. He turned a full circle, gave her face another lick, and turned a circle again before finding his place, settling down on her crossed legs.

She rested a hand over his small back while looking at Seth. "I can't imagine Cara would allow this."

His answering smile was wide and hopeful. "Already talked to her earlier today to make sure. She thought it was a good idea."

A puppy. A constant ball of energy. Needing so much attention. So much time.

She wasn't sure she could do it. Wasn't sure she could take such a responsibility on.

Seth pushed closer, taking her hand. "I don't like to think of you alone here."

She looked up, meeting his eyes. "I've been alone for most of my life. I'm used to it. It's all I know."

"I don't like the thought of it." He gave Derby a scratch behind the ears, his tail beating against Tori's legs. "With this guy, you'll always have someone to welcome you home. He'll love you unconditionally. And give you plenty of reasons to smile."

She looked down on the puppy curled in her lap. As if a part of Seth's reasoning, he set wide brown eyes on her. Looked as if he smiled with the slight tilt to his mouth.

She bent lower, rubbing her nose with his. "I've never had a pet of any kind. I won a goldfish once at a carnival. But the foster family I was with at the time didn't think it would be a good idea taking it home, so I had to give it back."

"You won't have to give Derby back." Seth's smile was slow and soft, the look of a brother who cared. "He needs you as much as you need him. I knew it was right, you two being together."

She'd been fine being alone. Never thought to want or desire more. But since finding her way to this little town in the Rocky Mountains, all she'd known seemed to fly out the window.

Cupping a hand on each side of Derby's sweet face, she gave him another nose rub. "What do you think, boy? Shall we give it a chance?"

He yipped in reply, giving her a good, long lick.

And so it was decided. She and Derby were about to start a brand new life together.

Chapter Eleven

She was far from a gourmet cook. Her dishes stuck more to simple rather than elaborate. But she did enjoy creating the flavors and the taste of a good meal. Hoped she'd succeeded with her first dinner with her brother.

They had spiced chicken and rosemary potatoes to go with the sweet pepper salad. Seth had two helpings before declaring himself full.

Tori cleared the plates, refilled their wine glasses, then decided it was time to take Derby out for a bathroom break. He dashed ahead of them down the stairs, looking back when he reached the alley, making sure they followed.

He ran off when they reached the bottom and found a stick in the stretch of weeds and wildflowers growing on the other side, bringing it to them.

He dropped it at Tori's feet and looked up at her. Laughing, she picked it up, giving him a good scratch behind the ears before tossing it for him to fetch.

"Will you answer a question for me?" She looked a moment at Seth then back to Derby, chasing after the stick, nearly tripping over his long legs.

She saw the hesitation in his eyes but he only smiled, giving a quick nod. "What is it you want to know?"

"Nothing too terrible, I promise." She bent down as Derby returned and tossed the stick again. "I just wondered how you got here, to Snow Ridge."

He took a slow sip from his wine. "The story that is known in town is that I came to help out on my aunt and uncle's ranch. It's not too far from the truth."

"Except we don't have any aunts or uncles still living." She looked at him, seeing her dad in the long lines of his face, the way his eyes creased at the corners when he was lost in thought. "Mom was an only child. And dad's brother died before I was born."

"You remember that?" Surprise danced in his eyes.

"Yeah." She turned her thoughts in, fighting off the touch of sadness coming forth. "I heard it enough growing up. The poor, troubled girl with no family to speak of. Lost her parents, had nobody else able to take her in. Left to the foster system for life."

He reached for her hand, squeezing tight. "I'm so sorry, Tori. I didn't know. The times I was brave enough to ask, I was always told you were young enough you'd be guaranteed to be adopted into a kind, loving family. It's what I held on to for so many years. What got me through during the harder times."

"Yeah...well." She took a needed step away, catching Derby and his stick. "It might have been if I'd been a different, more obedient, kind of child. As it was, I had terrible nightmares that affected me for days, sometimes into a week or more. Those looking to adopt didn't exactly have much patience for a child who took more work than they were expecting when those terrible dreams came around."

"Then I simply got too old to fit the mold of the wanted child." She shrugged, letting the story end itself.

"But none of that," she patted her leg for Derby to follow before heading back up the stairs, "has anything to do with knowing how you ended up here."

Seth pushed up ahead of her, holding the door until she and Derby made their way inside. Grabbing the wine bottle from the counter as he passed, he waved her back to the table and topped off their glasses as he sat across from her.

"At thirteen, the Ritchells became my foster family. They were good people. Really good people." He picked up his glass and took a slow drink as he drifted back

"I stayed with them, officially, until I aged-out of the system. And then, unofficially, for another couple years while I enrolled at the community college and tried my luck with some business courses."

So different, Tori thought, then the group home she'd been placed in until she'd aged-out then left on her eighteenth birthday to find her own way.

But she'd done it. Of that much, she could be proud.

Derby eased over to Seth, resting his front paws on his leg. "It wasn't for me though. I was restless and got myself in some trouble." He reached down and ran a hand over Derby's smooth coat. "Diane and Mark—the Ritchells—told me about Mark's brother. Said the ranch he owned might be a good escape for a while."

"That was thirteen years ago." He lifted his wine glass, holding it out in a mock toast. "I've been here and part of the Moonshine ever since."

Tori couldn't deny the stab of envy before quickly brushing it away. She was happy for her brother. Happy he'd found his place here. "I never would have thought you one to work a ranch."

"Me either." He gave a laugh to that. "But coming

here, doing the work, being a part of the ranch...it fit somehow."

"You should come sometime." He reached over, resting a hand over hers. "See what I do. Meet Corryn and Jeff who own the Moonshine. I know they'd love a chance to meet you."

"You told them about me?" She sipped slowly from her wine and wondered about the strange feeling inside.

"They've always known I had a sister." He glanced over as Derby walked away and headed back for the door. "And this is a small town. There was no hiding you were here."

She hadn't thought of that, the gossip that would come. Growing up in Chicago, a loner in so many rights, it had never been that great of a concern.

But here, where the town was small, where so many seemed to know each other, it made sense rumors would start and pass from one eager mouth to another.

"I think I'd like that. Seeing the ranch. Meeting them."

She turned as Derby scratched at the door. "He was just out."

As if understanding her hesitation, Derby looked back at her, to the door again. He stood at full alert, staring as if he could see through the wood to whatever waited on the other side.

"I don't think it's a bathroom break that's got him anxious." Seth pushed up from his chair.

Tori followed, reaching the door as he did. "What else could it be? There's not much excitement out there." Derby barked as she wrapped her hand around the knob, giving her a nudge in the leg with his nose.

"Something has him worked up." Seth pushed in front of her as she opened the door, Derby racing out ahead.

He dashed down the stairs, reaching the bottom before Seth made it halfway down. His tail high, nose in the air, he paused, sniffed.

Tori right behind him, they took the last step and stood beside Derby as his gaze shifted quickly, side to side. Searching for something neither of them could see.

"Maybe he's not used to life off the ranch." Tori reached down to pet him, surprised at the rigid muscles underneath his fur.

With a low growl, he took a step, then began to bark into the dark.

Seth moved out ahead of him to look around. For several long seconds he said nothing, only stared at the far end of the alley.

"Somebody was out here." He turned back, bending down where Derby remained alert and aware.

"You were a good dog." He stuck his hand between his ears, giving the kind of worthy rub he deserved. The threat gone, Derby rolled over and offered his stomach for a deep scratch.

"It doesn't mean anything." She wasn't sure if she was trying to convince herself or her brother. Probably a little bit of both. "It's a public alley. Anybody could have been walking along back here."

"Close enough to your place to catch Derby's attention?" The same doubt she battled reflected back as Seth looked up and caught her in his heavy gaze.

"How do we know?" She shrugged, not wanting the night with her brother to end with any sort of fear.

The truth was, if it had not been for the strange visitor from a few days earlier and what her brother had shared from over two decades ago, there wouldn't have been a second thought to who might or might not be walking the alley.

Logic said it was nothing more than the situation feeding into something that wasn't really there.

And that is what she relied on. Needed to hold onto in order to keep her own sanity. Enjoy with her brother something she'd never been sure she'd get.

"We don't." Calling Derby, Seth retraced his steps, joining her back at the bottom of the stairs. "Doesn't mean there's not a reason to worry. Not with what's happened."

"I don't want to worry. I just—"

She shook her head and started up the stairs, Derby at her feet. "I want to enjoy a night with my brother. I want to do good at my new job. Find out what all the locals love about Snow Ridge."

She pushed open the door, letting Derby in ahead of her. "I want to be normal. Something it's hard to be when you witness your parents being murdered at three years old."

Seth watched her, emotion fueling her every step, wondering if he should reach for her or let her be.

She turned to him, a desperate look in her emerald eyes. "I don't want to worry about things I have no control over or clue about. I don't want to think about any kind of danger I might have been in all those years ago. Or why someone thought I should be fired from Precious Gems."

Her smile was small but it still held so much behind it. "Can't I have this night, if nothing else. To enjoy my new puppy." She bent down and rubbed the top of Derby's nose. "Be happy my brother wants me in his life. Wants to spend a wonderful night with me, eating dinner and drinking wine."

He wouldn't argue with her. Not now. Not when she needed a bit of happiness. Not the stress of worry. Walking over to her, he slung an easy arm around her shoulders, pulling her close. "You can have this night and any other night you choose."

He dropped a kiss on the tip of her nose and looked into eyes pleading for so much. She didn't have to worry. Not now. He'd keep that from her.

But for him…the worry wasn't going anywhere. Whoever was in the alley, he didn't believe it was for anything good. So he'd keep an eye out. Come around more often. And be thankful he'd brought Derby to her life.

She wouldn't be alone. And she'd be watched.

Of that he'd make sure.

****

His coffee was cold. Bitterly so.

Luke looked down into the black dredges and considered pouring another cup. A look out the window at the dark night then at the clock on the edge of his desk, he decided against it.

He'd spent entirely too much time locked up in his office the last few days. It was time to give himself a break and let the information he'd learned process through.

The case of Tori's parents had long ago grown cold so the details weren't as easily found as he'd hoped. And even as he dug deeper, he found walls popping up at every turn.

Which only made him more curious.

Rinsing out what was left of the coffee and grabbing his jacket off his chair, he flipped the light switch and closed his office door behind him.

The station was quiet. Only a few officers sat at their desks. The usual clatter of the day was long gone. He waved to those that were there before finding his way outside.

Nearly to his truck, his phone rang. Surprised to see Seth's name flash back at him, he put a finger to the screen. "This is Luke."

"Hi. I hope I'm not interrupting anything." Seth's voice was hesitant on the other end.

Luke's curiosity peaked as he climbed inside his truck. "No. Just leaving the station. Is everything all right?" He didn't pull out of the space, waiting until he had a better handle on the reason for the call.

"I'm sure it is. I'm probably worrying for nothing, but I still thought you should know." His voice drifted out, back in, through the crackle over the line. "I just left Tori's place, and I'm pretty damn sure there was somebody poking around while I was there."

"Did you get a look at whoever it was?" Luke pulled out, turning back into town rather than heading for the ranch.

"Nothing but a quick shadow before he disappeared. I can't even say for sure he was there for anything involving Tori. But I don't like the feel of it, somebody back in the alley at that time of night."

Luke didn't like it either. "Thanks for letting me know. I'll check up on it."

"If you're thinking of going by, just know she'll be mad as hell if she knows I told you." Luke recognized the frustration in Seth's words. Understood it more than he liked to admit.

"Thanks for the warning." He turned on to Main Street and headed for Precious Gems. "Nothing wrong with stopping by to see how she's doing and getting a look around while I'm there."

He took Seth's laugh as acceptance before ending the call as he came to the store. Parking out front, he looked down the dark road, seeing nothing to pique his interest. It looked as it did every other night of the week. Restaurants and bars open and lively. The stores closed up, waiting for the next day.

Deciding to bypass his usual route, he strolled further up the street. Past the coffee shop, bank, chocolate shop and cutting into the alley through the small space between the consignment shop and gift store.

There was nothing out of place. Nothing out of the ordinary to be seen. Not that he'd expected different. Seth had said he couldn't even be sure there'd been anyone hanging around. Just a shadow he saw from a distance.

It was a stretch. He admitted to as much as he turned down the alley and headed for the back stairs to Tori's place.

But it was a good reason for him to be here to check on her. He hadn't stopped thinking about her for the past few days. Had hoped for an excuse to see her. And this one was as good as any.

And it did put him on edge, thinking of someone hanging out in the alley, possibly finding his way too close to Tori. So he was killing two birds with one stone. Which worked for him.

He heard the strange yips from halfway up the stairs. Was that a dog? Inside Tori's apartment?

He couldn't imagine it but was sure of it the closer he drew to her door. He lifted his hand to knock, dropping it to his side as the door swung open before he had a chance.

"What are you doing here?" There was an uneasy rush to Tori's words, her emerald eyes a bit too wide.

"I came by to check on you." He looked from her to the brown bundle pushing at her legs, wanting out. "Is something wrong?"

"No. I—"

She stepped aside, grabbing the puppy into her arms as she did, letting him inside. "Derby was barking at the door. It made me nervous. That's all."

"I'm guessing this is Derby." Closing the door behind him, he stepped closer, rubbing his hand between the dog's ears. "I wasn't aware you had a dog."

Her sweet scent surrounded him, reminding him of all he'd missed in the past few days. He wanted to draw her close. Find those full lips of hers and get lost in them.

Tori took a needed step back. "I didn't. Until tonight. Seth seemed to think we belonged together." She set Derby back to the floor, fighting the urge to keep him in her arms as protection between her and Luke.

He took up all breathable space inside the small kitchen. Closing her in. Making her aware, with every breath, of the need still burning inside.

There was so much of him. That was the problem. The size of him alone was enough to make anyone feel closed in. And he carried a strength, beyond physical, refusing to be ignored. Calling to her even as she tried pretending it didn't exist.

"You get nervous every time he barks at the door, you'll be a wreck before too long." Though he offered a smile, there was a prying look in his eyes.

"It's not a worry." She moved past him, grabbing her half-full glass of wine from the counter where she'd left it when Derby began barking. "Just a bit off tonight. That's all."

"That's all?" His look doubtful, he moved in closer, leaving her trapped between him and the counter. Reaching out, he grabbed her wine and took a sip, ignoring the glare she shot his way.

"Yes. That's all." She took her glass back. "There was an incident earlier. It was nothing. But it still caused some nerves when Derby started up."

"What kind of incident?" The knowing shift of his eyes made her uncomfortable. It took all she had not to push him away and get some much-needed air.

Thankful for Derby pressing against her legs, she used him as a distraction, bending down, pulling him into her arms. He'd be good protection, after all. "It was just someone in the alley. Derby reacted. I'm guessing he needs some adjustment to life off the ranch. Seth seemed to think it was more."

Luke turned thoughtful, setting her on edge. "Derby didn't start his barking till I was halfway up the stairs. Seems, me being in the alley didn't bother him. It was only when I was on the stairs he became alert to my presence."

She didn't like the route his mind was taking. "Whoever it was could have walked close enough to the stairs to grab Derby's attention. It doesn't mean it had anything to do with me."

"You're right. It doesn't." Surprised by his comment, she didn't protest when he took Derby from her arms.

With a quick pet, he set him on the floor before pressing close. "Doesn't mean I feel good about it."

Trapped, her back pressed tight to the edge of the counter, she looked up at him. "You're a cop. You're not supposed to feel good about anything."

She cursed the flutter in her stomach. The coil of heat climbing up her spine. Even as she told herself she didn't want another kiss, her traitorous body claimed otherwise, pressing closer, seeking the heat he offered.

"I feel good about this." His smile was slow, seductive, tugging at all the right places. He bent, took a nip from her bottom lip. "Have found it hard to think about anything else."

She nearly melted. His eyes held hers, reaching deep. It was hard to take a breath. Hard to do anything but feel the force of the man pushing against her.

When she didn't move, he lifted his hands, spearing fingers through her long chestnut curls, holding her there, still and stunned.

She was dangerous. So very dangerous. Luke liked steady ground. Liked knowing what to expect. With Tori, he was given none of that. Only a stirring deep inside, messing with his mind and leaving any hope at clear thought far behind.

Needing her, more than he cared to admit, he kept his hands tangled in her hair and tipped her head back. She said nothing. But the press of her body against his was all the invitation he needed.

Dropping down, he found her mouth. Slowly, first. A teasing. A quick brush that already had his blood searing. And then he needed more. So much more.

With a low, primal growl, he took her completely. Holding her captive with his fingers twined in her hair, he pressed her back against the counter.

She was his to take, in every way. The thought fueled the desire running through, pushing him to seek more. To find the completion she promised in all that she was.

With a small groan, Tori finally found the ability to move. As Luke's hands fell to her shoulders, she reached up, flattening her palms against his chest, feeling the hard crease of muscles beneath the cotton.

His hands fell lower, curling around her waist, pulling her to him until she felt his need pressing hard against her. Lighting flames to the already burning strokes of her own desire.

He pulled his mouth away, sucking in desperate breaths of air. "Have dinner with me." He found his way to the slender curve of her neck, trailing a fiery path to her collar bone. "Tomorrow night."

She could barely think. Every sense on overdrive. "Dinner?"

"Yes. With me. At my place." He dipped in for another kiss, taking every last bit she had. Leaving her sure she'd be a puddle on the floor if she hadn't been trapped between the counter and his hard, lean body.

"I want you." He found his way to the other side of her neck. Nibbled. "I want you naked...in my bed. But I don't feel right with it till we've had some kind of date between us."

"You want...oh." Her head fell back on a long sigh

as he found his way below her collar bone, teasing a line above the push of her breast. "I don't—can't think I agreed to anything with a bed."

"Details." He looked up with a smile, waving a hand in the air. "First a date. We'll take it from there."

She tried coming back down to normal thought. Knew it was important. But with the feel of him pressed against her, the heated look in his eyes staring down at her, it wasn't an easy thing to do. "I don't—"

He took her mouth again. "You don't, what?"

He wouldn't give in. She knew it. For every excuse she might come up with, he'd know the truth.

"Okay." She shook her head, forcing some strength to her weak knees. "I'll have dinner with you tomorrow night."

His answering grin was wide, close to irritating.

"But that doesn't mean," she found a trace of solid footing and pushed soft against his chest, needing the space, "that I'm going to end up in bed with you."

He took a small step back, staying close enough for her to feel the heat of him wash over her. "Like I said…details. We'll get to that after the date."

Not knowing what else to do, she shook her head at him. "Dinner." She put force into her word and gave another small shove.

With one final quick kiss, he moved away. Giving her space. Much needed breathing room. "Dinner is all I'm asking for."

There was such a sly look to him, she couldn't help but laugh.

He looked pleased by it. Taking the time to reach down and give Derby a good rub from nose to tail, he turned for the door. "I'm going to have an officer stop by tomorrow when it's daylight to take a look around the alley. I don't want you worrying if Derby lets you know he's out there."

She followed a step behind. "I'll be working. But I don't see a use for it."

"There probably isn't one." Wrapping one hand around the doorknob, he used the other to reach for her. Grabbing her wrist, he pulled her closer. "But I'll feel better having it done."

He looked down on her. The same passion from before sparked in the hazel depths of his eyes. "Seems keeping you safe keeps meaning more and more to me."

This time he was slow, gentle, as he found her mouth, sweeping her into another kiss. And then he ended it all too soon, leaving her fighting to draw stability back all over again.

"Lock the door." He let go of her wrist and pulled open the door. "And make sure you set the alarm."

She didn't have the ability to argue. Could only nod, watching him make his way into the night. Still feeling him surrounding her, she leaned a moment against the door before flipping the deadbolt and turning to the alarm.

The man was on the track to drive her crazy. She was sure of it. But first, they'd have dinner and she'd consider the options he suggested for what happened next.

****

A bit of padding, change to his hairstyle, different clothes, and he was no longer the casual tourist. Instead, he was a slightly overweight, burned-out businessman. His suit just wrinkled enough. Tie a bit undone. He was that man who'd had enough of work and barely kept going.

And he passed through Snow Ridge, making it work. No one suspected his eye was always on just one. Every move she made. Everywhere she went. Who she saw. When she saw them.

He'd spent the morning at the coffee shop, close enough to watch Precious Gems while he sipped on the brew. At the pub at the end of the lunch crowd, listening close for anything that might be said or hints that might be given.

He'd known when Seth Mundy walked up the stairs to Tori's apartment with a puppy under his arm. Had watched her open the door and welcome him in.

He'd dared his own journey up the stairs, hoping to hear something through the door. Anything that would give him a good idea of the best action to take.

Anton pulled the padding from beneath his shirt, tossing it to the chair in the corner. With tie and jacket off, he kicked his shoes by the bed then checked to make sure they'd refilled the minibar as he'd requested.

Pulling out a new bottle, he poured himself a drink, choosing to lose himself in television for the rest of the night. Propping the pillows against the headboard, he settled on the bed and grabbed the remote.

Flipping mindlessly through the channels, he allowed a moment of disappointment that he hadn't had the chance to linger longer at Tori's apartment. To find the weaknesses allowing him entry if the need came.

It was the damn dog. He must have alerted Tori. He'd barely made it up to the top of the stairs when he'd heard motion on the other side. He'd rushed, nearly run, down the stairs, putting as much distance as he could before the door opened and the dog came charging down.

And wasn't that the hell of it. He took a slow sip from his glass. From the streets of Chicago and a life filtering between glitz and glamour to murder and mayhem, and here he was, stuck in a no-nothing mountain town, running through an alley to escape a pitiful puppy.

Settling on a late-night talk show, he pushed it all from his mind for the night. Tomorrow he'd be back at it. And maybe...just maybe...he'd finally get his ticket out of here.

Chapter Twelve

"That's it, I'm letting Cade know I want a dog." On her knees in front of the counter, Cara laughed as Derby dragged his tongue up her face before nibbling at her ear.

Tori hadn't planned on bringing him down to the store. Giving him a long stretch in the alley before coming down for work, she'd hoped to use her breaks to run up and give him some loving, some play, and another bathroom break.

But Cara put a change to her plans. "He's welcome down here. No need for him to be alone when the three of us are here. Puppies, like babies, bring smiles. For us and, hopefully, any customer who might walk through the door."

And so it was, Derby found his place in Precious Gems. Tori brought down the food and bone Seth left her the night before. Cara found an old blanket from the back for his bed.

"He needs toys." Jackie bent down beside Cara, taking her share of the loving Derby handed out. "He's a playful one."

"I had him fetching my stress ball last night before bed." Tori watched as her new pup made quick friends. "And I sacrificed a sock for a good game of tug-of-war."

And then she'd spent the night fighting for space

on her bed, second-guessing her decision to let him sleep with her. Though there was no question he still had a lot of growing to do, Derby, it seemed, had already decided he was a lap dog. And he wasn't afraid to show it.

"He'll find all kinds of good toys tonight at the ranch." Cara looked at Tori, shrugging at her surprised look. "You're having dinner with my fiancé's brother. Of course I'd know about it. He's already hit Hattie up for dessert."

"You're having dinner with Luke?" Jackie pressed a hand to Derby's nose, fighting off the next onslaught of tongue licks. "You didn't say anything about it yesterday."

Deciding to join the majority, Tori eased to the floor next to the edge of the counter, giving Derby a good scratch at the ears as he jumped into her lap. "I didn't know about it then. He came by last night after Seth, kissing me senseless then deciding we needed a date before we ended up in bed together."

"What?" Cara's head snapped up as Jackie's laughter swirled around them.

Better with it today than she'd been the night before, Tori shrugged. "I'm guessing he's doing his best to be a gentleman. A bit late, if you ask me. But at least he's trying."

"Dinner with Luke. Now that's what I'm talking about." Jackie's smile was slow and smooth, enjoying the idea almost more than Tori. "And then sex. Which is always good."

"I never said I agreed to the sex part of the deal." Needing to move with the very idea of having sex with Luke, she pushed to her feet. "I agreed to a simple date.

Nothing more."

"Ah, but you're dealing with a Grady boy." Cara's smile was understanding and a bit sympathetic as she stood. "They're known for getting what they want. I should know. I've faced my own and now I'm engaged to him."

With one final kiss on the tip of Derby's nose, Jackie joined them. "And she protested as hard as you did."

"I'm not protesting. Just…being cautious." And protecting herself. Making sure, as she'd long ago learned to do, not to count on anything more than today. Because looking further into tomorrow only led to disappointment.

There was doubt in both sets of eyes looking back at her. Making a point to ignore them, Tori fussed with the invoices Cara had left on the far corner of the counter. Maybe they thought they knew better. But she was determined to keep a steady ground when it came to dealing with Luke and the temptation he offered.

"I know what she needs." Jackie came around the other side of the counter, flattening a hand against the invoices and stopping her fussing. "A session with Madame Luwiski."

"Madame, who?" Clasping her hands, Tori took a step back, resisting the urge to fumble with them more.

"Luwiski," Cara supplied, her own gaze lacking the same conviction Jackie's held. "She's our local fortune-teller, you could say. Though Jackie tends to forget the last time we met with her, we couldn't get away fast enough."

"Only because we believed her predictions were too much to be true." Jackie looked to Cara, a silent knowledge passing between them. "We know better now."

There were questions she wanted to ask but Tori took the cue and kept them silent. "I think I'll pass. Fortune-tellers aren't my sort of thing. I'm not fond of anyone trying to predict the future for me."

She saw the questioning in Cara's eyes and chose to ignore it. There was no simple way to explain it, anyhow. How did you tell somehow who never lived the experience why only the present could exist because thoughts or dreams about the future only brought heartache and a long stream of disappointment?

****

Tori had to admit it…she was putting more care and attention into her appearance than she usually did.

The jeans had been easy. She had that one pair. The perfect one, flattering her in all the right places while smoothing out the bumps.

But the shirt was a different matter.

Two already discarded on the bed, Derby giving them a good sniff, she turned back for the mirror. The light sweater was a deep sea-green, dipping low, giving a hint of cleavage while keeping the mind guessing.

Would it be too much? Too inviting?

She didn't want him thinking she'd walked in with her mind already made up. Prepared to tumble in the sheets as soon as the last bite of dinner was complete.

But she also didn't want to come off looking like a prude, discouraging even the thought of what might come.

Glancing at the clock, she knew she didn't have time to be unsure again. "What do you think?" She looked at Derby, holding out her arms. His single happy bark was enough of an answer.

The sweater decided on, she rehung the discarded shirts. She added a light spray of her favorite perfume before patting her leg, getting Derby to follow her out of the bedroom.

She went out the back, down the stairs, and into the alley, giving Derby his time before they left.

Luke had offered to pick her up but she'd declined. She had yet to drive the streets of town. To learn anything outside of where she'd gotten stuck in the snow. It was time she figured out the way of where she was and where she was headed.

Though the town was small, it still presented enough of a challenge for her to need every chance to drive herself around.

Around and out of town, she reminded herself as she called Derby, leading him through the small space between buildings. She was counting on her own sense of surroundings to remember which way to take to lead her away from the heart of town. To the ranches stretching the edges and butting up against the ski resorts.

It seemed odd, crawling into her car after so long away. Back in Chicago, it meant nothing, leaving her car untouched for days. But here, it didn't feel right knowing she'd spent more time as a passenger than a driver behind her own wheel.

She was changing that tonight. Smiling as Derby settled in the seat beside her, she turned the radio high. Music streaming from the speakers lifted her mood as she headed down Main Street.

Thinking back to the route Luke had taken, she was thankful to recognize the last stoplight before leaving town. It was just down the road now. A few miles and she'd follow the white fence and turn in at the gray-stoned gate.

"We're doing good, Derby." She reached over, rubbing her hand over his nose.

The first jolt hit before she had a chance to turn fully back to the wheel. With only one hand loosely holding on, it spun, tires following its way. Throwing both hands over the wheel, her hold desperate, she yanked away only seconds before finding herself stuck in another ditch at the side of the road.

Glancing in the rearview mirror, there was no missing the big black truck hugging her back end. The wide silver grill was a terror to see barreling down on her, getting close.

She was prepared this time. But it didn't do much good as the hit came, making her fight to stay on the road even that much worse. Her tires ducked dangerously at the edge.

Before she fully recovered, she was hit again. The wheel spun. She couldn't grasp it. Couldn't get control over the frantic thrust, shoving her over the ditch and into the wild growth beyond.

Fighting desperate to gain control, she looked up, catching the thick set of trees quickly coming close. The brakes struggled to agree with the push of her foot against the pedal. The steering wheel fought her, refusing to turn away from the impact that was coming.

Refusing to give up, she managed to slow the car, turning it as far as she could from the trees. Still, it hit the edge of the furthest trunk.

She had enough time to shove Derby down to safety before the jolt rocked through. She flew back in the seat then bounced forward in the force of reaction.

Her head hit hard against the steering wheel, giving her only a second before the black blanket fell, leaving her knowing nothing else.

Chapter Thirteen

"She'd planned on coming." Cara stood in the center of Luke's kitchen, arms weighed down by the Apple Upside Down cake Hattie sent her to deliver.

Crossing to the counter, she set the cake down and looked back at Luke standing in the middle of the floor. "She's probably just running late."

He didn't look convinced. "It's been over half an hour. She's not answering her phone."

Once a cop, always a cop. Cara shook her head. "Maybe she got lost. Why don't you go look for her? I'll stay here and watch over dinner."

"Not much to watch. Got steaks for the grill. A tossed salad in the fridge. And Hattie's scalloped potatoes on warm in the oven." He looked around as if deciding if there was anything else.

"Go." Cara stepped up, giving him a small shove. "I'll watch over things. You'll bring back Tori. And dinner will go on as planned."

Luke figured she was right. Tori had simply gotten lost on the way. She'd insisted on driving herself. "I need to learn my way around," she'd told him when he'd offered to pick her up.

Grabbing his keys from the counter where he'd tossed them as he carted in bags from the grocery store earlier, he dropped a quick kiss on Cara's cheek. "Thank you. I'll be back soon, I'm sure."

The night had begun to settle as he found his way out the front door. To be sure, he tried calling her again as he climbed in his truck. Five rings and it went to voice mail.

He didn't like that she wasn't answering her phone. That bothered him. But there were explanations and he was going to do his best not to worry…not yet.

He headed down the drive and back to the main road for the ranch. She was lost. It was the only thing that made sense. Snow Ridge might be small, but it could still hold its own complications in finding yourself from point A to point B.

Cara wouldn't lie. And Tori had manners. If she'd decided not to keep the date, she would have called to let him know.

Which meant she was somewhere between her apartment and the ranch. He just had to figure out where that somewhere was.

****

It was the nonstop licking to her face that brought her back.

Cursing the pounding against her temples, Tori forced her eyes open. Big, brown puppy eyes looked back at her. Another sloppy lick up her face helped fight away the lingering grogginess.

"Okay." She wrapped her arms around Derby, needing to keep him still. For just a minute until she had a better balance. "It's okay. I'm okay."

Her vision was blurry. Her head hurt like hell. And when she reached up, placing a hand to her forehead, the sticky warmth of blood clung to her fingers.

But she was awake. She was aware. Considering the situation, that definitely meant she was okay.

And with that came the memory of what happened. Somebody had forced her off the road. She saw it again. The big truck with the frightening grill, coming at her, refusing to give up.

Fighting back the throbbing pain in her head that spread through her limbs as she became more aware, she did her best to pull her thoughts together.

It was getting dark. Her car was far from drivable. And she was hurt at least bad enough to be bleeding. Not good odds, but ones she could work with.

Sucking in a breath, she took a moment to check Derby. Relieved he didn't show any signs of injury, she kissed the tip of his nose and set him in the passenger seat before searching for her phone.

It was nowhere to be found. She searched as much as her injuries allowed only to come up empty-handed. It was in the car. She knew it was. But wherever it had found itself after impact, it wasn't anywhere close to where she could find it.

But she couldn't just sit there and hope it magically appeared. She had to do something. If she couldn't call for help, there had to be another way.

Luke.

She thought of him as Derby inched back over, wanting to find his way back to her lap.

He'd be expecting her. Wouldn't sit back and do nothing when she didn't appear for their dinner date. He'd be out looking for her. If not now, then soon.

He'd want an explanation. Would follow his cop instinct to find an answer to why she didn't show. It was who he was. What she counted on as she pushed against the door.

It barely budged. Dragging in a harsh breath of air,

preparing for what was to come, she struck her shoulder against the edge of the door. Pain, deep bone-searing pain, shot through, leaving her lightheaded.

But the hit had done enough. With one final push, she was able to put a foot out. Waiting to catch her breath, she dared the other foot.

"Come on, Derby." She gave him a nudge, thankful when he jumped out without argument. Following, she braced her hands on the edge of the car and pushed to her feet.

And it hurt.

Fine points of fire burned against her spine and down her legs. For a moment, she was tempted to sit back down, wait in her car, and hope for the best.

But she couldn't. Not where she was, pushed deep into the trees and far enough from the road that the chance of being seen wasn't good.

The first step was hell. She whimpered, pulling Derby back to her side. He stared up at her with a curious tilt to his head. She tried a smile for him but couldn't bring it forth. The pain shooting through was too great for anything but concentrating on her next step.

Her head pounded. Every inch of her body ached. Sucking breath into her lungs was a struggle as she fought off the wave of dizziness threatening to tumble her to the ground.

The light from inside the car helped her see the ground at her feet and get a feel for where she needed to be headed. But the shadows caused by night lingered, disorienting her as she forced another step. And then another.

Derby ran off ahead then came back as if making

sure the path was clear. She stumbled and nearly fell. Crying out, she forced weak legs to carry her while fighting the black cloud collecting in the corners of her eyes.

It hurt so bad. Tears threatened to fall. It took all she had to resist the urge to give up, fall where she was, and simply let the dark take over.

The small incline to the road should have been nothing. But for her, it was agony. Piercing, screaming pain came with every step. Reaching the top, she barely held on as everything around her was spinning.

Close to dragging herself, she found her way to the side of the road. She looked one way then the next, seeing only the black night coming back at her.

But at least she'd made it here and given herself the chance to be seen.

****

Luke didn't like this. Not one bit.

He'd made a roundabout way from the ranch into town, searching for signs of Tori. He went by her apartment where her car was no longer parked in the space she'd left it last.

Still, he'd needed to check. Going back to the alley, climbing the stairs, he gave the door a hard knock. There hadn't been a sound beyond. Not a hint of movement.

He'd been tempted to find a way in and check for himself.

But he'd held back. Deciding on another drive around first before getting the spare key from Cara.

Which was where he was headed now, back to get the key. He'd traveled the roads crisscrossing through Snow Ridge and the ranches surrounding it. And still nothing. No signs of Tori or any clue as to what could have happened to her.

He'd go back to the ranch, get the key, then do another drive through back into town. And if he came up empty again, he'd give in to the worry quickly growing stronger by the minute and put in a call to the station. Get others out to help him search.

He turned out of town and aimed for the road headed for the ranch.

Thoughts of the man willing to pay to have Tori fired, of what Seth shared, had fear fighting to take hold. He knew he couldn't go there yet, but it was hard to fight. His heart pounded against his chest. His mind played terrible images of what could be.

And then she was there, caught in his headlights.

Her and the new puppy on the side of the road where he knew she hadn't been when he'd passed earlier.

Drawing close, everything in him stilled.

The headlights caught the dark stain of blood on her head. Illuminated her swaying, barely able to stay on her feet. She looked so beaten. So frighteningly pale.

He barely had the truck in park before throwing open the door and racing around the front bumper. "Tori." His voice echoed in the dark around them.

She looked up but didn't seem to truly see him. She swayed and he was there, catching her in his arms before she tumbled to the hard ground.

In what seemed to be a fight for awareness she forced her eyes to settle on him. "Luke." She struggled with it, lifting a hand to his face and flattening her palm against his cheek. "I knew you'd look for me."

And then she was gone. Deadweight in his arms as

whatever had kept her going drained away, leaving her lifeless as he held on while Derby ran frantically between his legs.

He pressed two fingers against her neck, thankful for the steady pulse beating back. His mind raced with questions even as he bundled her carefully into the passenger seat before lifting Derby and putting him in behind her.

It would take too much time calling for an ambulance. The ranch was closer. And Penny, Joe's nurse, was there. She'd provide care a lot sooner than getting her to a hospital.

His phone was to his ear as he came around the front of the truck. Cara answered quickly, listening then promising to have everything ready in the short time it would take him to get to the ranch.

Climbing in the truck and starting the engine, he ended one call to make another. This time it wasn't favors asked but orders given. Though he hated leaving the scene, his officers would be right behind him. He was making sure of it.

And taking care of Tori was his first priority.

With that thought, he tore off down the road.

"Sorry, boy," he mumbled as Derby struggled for stable footing.

Reaching over, he pressed his fingers back to Tori's neck, thankful to find a steady pulse still beating.

What the hell happened?

Through the shock of finding Tori, the questions came. He didn't see her car and figured it was deeper in the trees. But how had it gotten there? She'd driven off the side of the road once. But that was in the middle of a blizzard.

There was no snow, now. The roads were clear and dry.

With one last glance in the rearview mirror, he turned on to the road for the ranch. His officers would check it out and let him know. Whatever the reason, they'd have the answers soon enough.

Chapter Fourteen

She drifted back.

Though it hurt like hell to do, Tori opened her eyes then slammed them shut as bright light flooded in. Sucking in a deep breath, she tried again, forcing them to stay open as they adjusted to the light.

Disoriented, not sure of anything but the desperate pounding inside her head, she tried making sense of what was happening. Where she was.

Fighting back the wave of nausea pushing forth, she put her mind back, searching for an answer. She was going somewhere, wasn't she?

Yes.

She caught it there, at the back of her mind. Getting ready, climbing in her car, and heading to the ranch. She was coming to see Luke. A date. Their first.

And then—

"You're awake."

She had to move slow. The hurt was too great. Turning her head, she bit hard on her lip, fighting back a painful cry.

Luke was there, looking back at her, a gentle smile on his lips. Worry clouded his eyes. "How are you feeling?" Reaching out, he grabbed her hand, cradling it between his.

"I—" Her throat was dry, making words difficult. Doing her best not to move, she searched for something to drink. As long as it was in liquid form, she'd take it.

Luke watched the back and forth of her searching gaze. Letting go of her hand, he pushed up from the chair at the side of the bed.

A bed she knew. Realization hit as he disappeared from sight. She was back where she'd spent her first two nights in Snow Ridge. At the ranch. In Cara's old room.

Before she could make sense of it, he was back, handing her a small glass. "It's bathroom water. I hope that's okay."

She didn't care. She was desperate enough for anything.

Every muscle screamed in protest but she managed to push up and take the glass from him. Holding it to her lips, she quickly finished the water while wishing for more.

"Hold on." As if reading her mind, he took her glass, disappeared, then returned with it full again.

She drank slower this time. Worked down to sips as Luke watched her, concern clear in his hazel eyes as he waited for her to find her voice.

"Thank you." Much easier to talk now, she cradled the glass between her hands and looked up at him. Though the bone-deep aches hadn't disappeared, she found the strength to push up on the pillows and rest against the headboard. "How long have I been out?"

"About an hour." He reclaimed the chair at the bed. "I was getting ready to give you a shake to wake you up, according to Penny's directions."

"Penny?" Her mind couldn't make a connection.

Reaching over, he took the glass from her hands as she swallowed a final drink. "Joe's nurse. She took good care of you."

She fought to bring back the missing pieces. To understand why she was lying in a bed back at the ranch, in need of a nurse. "I don't understand. I can't remember much after leaving for your place."

"Derby?" She shot up, every muscle screaming loud in protest as the memory of loading him in the car returned.

Luke put a gentle hand to her shoulder, easing her down. "He's fine. Dad and Joe had him outside, last I knew. He's caught the heart of everyone here."

Relieved, she eased back again, closing her eyes against the never-ending headache. "Tell me how I got here." She opened her eyes and turned her head, catching him in a long, hard stare.

"I went looking for you when you didn't show up for dinner." He moved closer and grabbed her hand, spreading heat up her arm. "I made it to your apartment, was heading back, when I saw you and Derby on the side of the road."

She pushed her mind back, finding the first hint of memory. She saw herself standing there on the side of the road. Felt the pain taking over, pushing her to give in.

She forced back further. The climb up the embankment. Coming to in her car with Derby licking her face. "The truck." She saw it, living it again. "He came behind me. Hit me more than once until I went off the side of the road."

Luke tightened his hold. "It's what my officers determined, as well. You were hit pretty good from behind."

"Yes." Tori nodded, sucking in a harsh breath as

the motion tumbled painfully through her throbbing headache. "The grill. It was a black truck with a big grill. I kept seeing it come at me. Over and over again."

She closed her eyes against the memory, wanting it gone.

"The truck belonged to Smith Baker. He owns the local feed store and reported it missing an hour before I found you." Hating to see the worry and fear in her eyes, Luke wished for a way to make it all go away. "My officers found it about half an hour ago abandoned near one of the ski resorts."

And they would be going through every inch of it. He made sure of it. He needed something to nail the one who'd done this to Tori.

A small knock at the door stopped the roam of his thoughts. The anger that was again starting to build.

Penny's short, blond curls pushed through the door, blue eyes narrowing on the bed. "I came to check on our patient and see how she's doing."

He waved her in, reluctantly letting go of Tori as she pushed her way between them. "Hattie's got some soup made." She looked at him as she picked up Tori's hand, pressing fingers to her wrist. "Why don't you go dish her up some."

He was being kicked out. As pretty as Penny tried to make it, there was no denying the truth.

It worked for him. He'd get the soup. But first, he'd take a moment alone to sort through what was running through his head. Slipping from the bedroom, he found his way down the stairs and quietly turned away from the kitchen toward the front door.

****

Cade heard the creak of the stairs, turning in time

to watch his oldest brother quietly let himself out the front door.

Luke was stewing. Not that he could blame him with all that had happened. Sometimes, a good long time with your thoughts was what was needed to sort out the craziness.

So he waited, watching the clock while enjoying another of Hattie's wonderful yeast rolls.

The group was thick in the kitchen. Hattie. Jake and his dad. Joe and Cara. Seth. There was no reason to make everyone aware. Reaching into the fridge, he grabbed three beer bottles and shook them at Jake before heading out of the kitchen.

At the front door, he waited until his brother joined him.

"Luke's out." He opened the door, the chill from the night brushing in. "Think he's got a head-full going at the moment."

Nodding, Jake followed him out and closed the door.

Handing over one of the beers, Cade curved around the long deck, finding his brother brooding in the corner, as he expected.

Without a word, he handed a beer to Luke before twisting the top of his own. Jake made his way to the other side and together they stood there at the rail, looking over the ranch, saying nothing.

There was time, plenty of it, for Luke to work through the mess in his mind. His brothers didn't push. Didn't expect anything from him.

They stood there, drinking from their beers, watching the night dance over the ranch.

"She's doing okay." Luke finally broke the silence.

"Beaten up pretty good. But, according to Penny, nothing serious."

Not that it registered with him. In his mind, he still saw her. Bloody and pale. Lifeless in his arms.

He was a cop. He knew such things. Had long been part of it. Yet, with Tori, it was different. Hit him in a way he couldn't make sense of.

"She was definitely run off the road." Taking a long draw from his beer, he turned and rested back against the rail. "Her memory of what happened matches what my officers determined."

And it scared the hell out of him.

"You thinking it has something to do with Cara's visitor from a few days ago?" Cade matched his brother's lean against the rail.

"I can't see any other reason. It's all tied in. I know it. From that to whatever happened in her past with her parents' murder, it all has its place." Luke chased away the frustration with another drink of beer. "I just can't make the pieces fit."

"You will." Jake stared back at the house with his brothers. "It's what you do best."

Luke wished he was as confident. With walls thrown up every time he tried searching Tori's past and the inability to find the visitor who'd come into Precious Gems, it felt as if there was nothing willing to give.

"It bothers you." Cade didn't bother looking at Luke, just sipped slowly from his beer. "Like it did with Cara when she was in trouble."

"It bothers me when anyone under my watch is in trouble."

"Not in the same way." Cade pushed the truth Luke

knew existed. "Cara hit you harder because you care about her. The same can be said about Tori."

There wasn't an answer, only more silence.

Luke figured he could deny it. He might even get away with it. But what was the use? His brothers would still know the same truth he held.

"I'm about done with it." His voice was close to a growl. "These cases hitting too close when I can't do a damn thing about them. My oath is to protect and serve. So where does it take me when I can't protect those I care about?"

"It takes you right back to human." Jake nudged him. "Like the rest of us."

His only answer was a scowl. He'd get there, he was sure. But for now, doubt, anger, and frustration ruled a terrible war inside his head. And at the moment, he was on the losing end.

****

It was Seth, not Luke, bringing her a bowl of Hattie's soup.

Fighting back the pain, Tori pushed up against the headboard, offering the best smile she could manage. "I didn't know you were here."

"Cara called to let me know what happened." Careful not to push at her, he puffed the pillows behind her before setting the silver tray over her lap.

The enticing scent of onion and bacon swirled from the thick cheese soup set in front of her. Warm rolls covered a plate. Chocolate pudding tucked in the corner of the tray left a tempting promise for dessert.

"I don't think I've ever eaten as good as I have since being introduced to the ranch." She picked up her spoon, sipping slowly at the soup.

Seth looked at her, so much in his gaze, she didn't even want to try and guess what hid there. He reached over and grabbed the hand not currently pulling off the corner of a roll. "I want you to listen to me."

Not liking the sound of it, she took her time, enjoying the buttery, yeasty bite teasing her taste buds. When she looked at him, she nearly regretted it. There was so much in the pale blue eyes looking back at her. So much worry and concern, leaving her uncomfortable.

There wasn't much to the smile he tried to offer. "I think it might be a good idea for you to consider going back to Chicago."

She was shaking her head before he finished. He held up a hand, stopping her. "I love having you here and being given this chance to know my sister again. It's something I never allowed myself to think of. And now, it's all that is in my thoughts."

"But," reaching over her, he tore off his own bite from the roll, "I don't like what's happened since you got here. I keep running through my mind the warning of danger from so long ago. And I feel like I'm watching it happen right before my eyes because I didn't follow through and stay away."

She heard the guilt. Saw it in the cloudy look in his eyes. But she wasn't going to give in to it. Or allow him to do the same.

"I won't run, Seth." She tangled her fingers with his. "I don't know if what is happening now is connected to our parents' murder or not. But I'm not going to let that chase me away from what I've wanted so bad and worked so hard to find…building a relationship with my brother."

"And what if even worse happens?" He tightened his grip and looked hard into her eyes. "You're already here bruised and beaten."

"Damn it, Tori." Letting go of her hand, he pushed from the chair. Turning his back on her, he stared for several long seconds out the door leading back to the hall. "You could have been killed."

He turned back, folding tight arms over his chest. "Knowing you couldn't be a part of my life but were still alive, is one thing. But to accept the risk of not having you in my life because whoever is doing this might not have yet finished his job, is another thing, altogether."

"If you go back to Chicago, away from here and away from me, at least I'll know you're safe."

"No, you won't." She wanted to reach for him but he stood too far away. And the pain was too great to move closer. "Anything could happen to me in Chicago. I could be mugged and killed on the street. I could be hit by a car or caught in a fire. The risks and dangers are many. Just as they would be anywhere I go."

"It's not the same and you know it." He settled on the far edge of the bed, still out of reach. "Here, the danger is now. It's real. Somebody doesn't want you here. And it scares the hell out of me."

It hurt every inch of her body as she set the tray to the side, pushing closer to where her brother sat. Fighting back the pain, she rested a hand over his bent knee, matching her heavy gaze with his. "If this has anything to do with me finding you then running only means they win. And I refuse to let that happen. I won't walk away now after all it took to become a part of your life again."

He wanted to argue. She saw it. Was thankful when he didn't. Instead, he pulled in a long, harsh breath and wrapped an arm around her shoulders. "I don't like this." He drew her close, dropping a kiss on her forehead.

"If I shared my chocolate pudding would it make it better?" She rested against the crook of his arm, enjoying the moment she was never sure she'd have when she left Chicago behind.

He nudged her and she bit back the pain racing through. "It will. Only because it's Hattie's."

Doing her best to pretend it didn't hurt all over, she scooted back to the pillows propped against the headboard. It took a moment, needing to just be still, before she was able to grab the tray and move it between her and Seth.

And there, in her strangely appointed room at the ranch, she did something she never dreamed of…shared a bowl of pudding with her brother.

Chapter Fifteen

It was a couple of days late but still nice.

The weather wasn't quite warm enough to open up the floor to ceiling windows but was gentle enough for Tori to relax on Luke's amazing back porch. A glass of wine in her hand, she watched him grill their steaks.

A fire burned in the pit, just enough to chase off the mountain chill. Vivid flames of orange and red danced before her, catching her attention when she wasn't lost staring at the handsome man making her dinner.

Back from his exploring, Derby jumped in her lap. "He likes it here." She smiled at Luke as he turned back to look at them. "All this attention seems to be just fine for him."

"He's cute. That helps." Luke sharpened his gaze. "How are you doing? You feeling okay?"

She nodded. And there was no lie to it. With the pain pills Penny had given her and a couple good night's sleep, she felt a hundred times better than she had that first night.

Being restricted to bed rest for two days helped too. Cara had made it clear she was not to show her face at the shop. And Hattie let her know she wouldn't tolerate any sneaking out of bed as long as she was there to take care of her.

So, she'd been pampered and spoiled, barely

having to lift a finger for whatever she needed. And the results of it had given her the chance to get out and enjoy the date she and Luke missed.

Convinced by the look of her, he turned back to the grill to flip the steaks. "A few more minutes and we'll be ready to eat."

She already knew there was nothing she could do to help out. He'd made it clear the minute she'd walked in. Handing her a glass of wine, he led her past the already set and ready table, ordering her to do nothing but sit and enjoy the evening, which was made easy. Between the amazing wilderness and the heart-stopping handsome man grilling her dinner, she'd had plenty to enjoy.

Derby perked up as Luke stepped away from the grill, two perfect steaks centering a plate. "Dinner is ready."

The smell alone was enough to pull her from her seat. Derby jumped at her ankles, thinking he had a chance, as she followed him inside to the table. "This looks wonderful."

Balancing the plate in one hand, he pulled out a chair for her. "I can't take credit for it all." He set a steak on her plate before topping off her glass of wine. "I threw together the salad and the steaks are mine. But the scalloped potatoes and dessert are compliments of Hattie."

Claiming a place across from her, Luke gave her another long, hard stare. She did look better. There was bruising, sure to grow uglier as the days passed. And dark circles lingered under her eyes. But there was life bringing red back to her cheeks. A true smile again on her lips.

He loved looking at her. Felt like he'd never get enough of it. Bruised and beaten. Alive and thriving. It didn't matter. The sight of her was all he needed to satisfy.

"Tell me about your life back in Chicago." He waved his hand at her plate, waiting until she handed it over for a serving of potatoes.

"What do you want to know?" He caught the flicker of hesitation before she chased it away. Taking her plate back, she added salad between the potatoes and steak.

"Anything. About you." He grabbed his own helping of salad and took a slow sip from his wine. "I don't care what it is."

She cut a small piece off the corner of her steak, chewing while considering her answer. "I loved my job working with old and rare books. I had a passion for knowing the worth and importance in first editions. In rare copies. In what made one book valuable while another was merely a token item in one's collection."

"And you left that to work at Precious Gems?"

"No." She shook her head. Her gaze drifted away. "I left that to find my brother. For so long, it's been about finding him."

He tried imagining it, being separated from his brothers for so long. But the thought wasn't one he could comprehend. It existed so far outside the reality he knew.

But for Tori it was true and painful, leaving him wishing there was something he could do to ease the hurt she'd lived with. "I've been doing what I can to figure out what happened to you and Seth after your parents were murdered. The more I dig and the more I learn, things don't seem right in how they were handled."

"I've wondered before if there was more at play when my parents died." She stuck a fork in the potatoes and looked over at him. "Even as a young child, none of it made sense. Being kept from my brother, having no idea what happened to him. I can't imagine that was normal procedure, separating us the way they did."

He shook his head. "It wasn't. Somebody had a hand in it. There had to have been strings pulled somewhere. There's no other explanation."

"But why? It doesn't make sense."

Her attention drifted, staring out the windows at the darkening night. "I've never had an answer or reason, for why somebody broke into our house and murdered my parents. That whole time is like this big empty space without any substance."

Derby poked at her, and she cut off a small corner from her steak, treating him to the bite he'd been hoping for. "I used to ask, when I was younger. One foster family after another, I'd come to them with questions, asking them to find the answers for me when it came to my parents' murder. To where my brother was."

"But you never got those answers."

"I didn't." She shook her head while grabbing for her wine. "Even those who made promises to help came back with nothing in the end other than encouraging me to stop asking."

None of it fit right. Luke played over what he knew and what he continued to learn. There was something very wrong in what had happened—could very well still be happening.

"Somebody didn't want you and your brother together. They didn't want either of you asking questions." Of that much, he was sure. The barriers he'd dealt with for days left no doubt. "The question is why."

Tori didn't have the slightest idea. It was clear in her face, looking back at him. He'd find the reasons, though. Was more dedicated than ever to do just that.

Because it all tied into one. It had to be. What happened all those years ago. What happened in today's reality. Somewhere there was a connection.

And he'd be the one to find it. He swore to it. Wouldn't give up until he had it.

****

If this wasn't paradise, it was pretty close.

Sitting on the back porch with night long ago falling and a fire burning bright in the pit, Tori held another glass of wine in her hand with Luke close at her side on the outdoor couch.

It was everything she needed at the moment. Everything and more.

The aches had pretty much gone. The pain nothing more than a small rumble finding a place here and there. She'd enjoyed a wonderful dinner, followed by an amazing dessert. And was now ending the evening surrounded in the beauty of the wilderness with a handsome man at her side and an adorable puppy twisting at her ankles.

Really, at that point, what more could she ask for?

"This is beautiful." She held up her wine glass, toasting the scenery.

Luke looked at her, saying nothing as his hazel eyes dug deeper than she liked, pulling forth an awareness she was fearful to admit.

In what felt like slow motion, he leaned forward, taking her glass from her hand and setting it on the table. His gaze never wavering, he moved closer and stared as a breeze picked up, swirling around them.

"You give some good competition when it comes to beautiful."

It wasn't the kind of compliment she expected coming from him. Caught off guard, she couldn't find the words to respond. Could only stare back. Her heart pounded against her chest while her pulse caught a quicker beat.

And then his mouth was there, covering hers, pulling her slowly up and into him. There was gentle in his kiss. A slow seduction, taking over mind and body.

Curving rough palms around her cheeks, he held her there before pulling away and looking hard into her eyes.

What he sought, she couldn't say. With Derby at her feet, the breeze swaying and easing around her, she waited, knowing nothing of what ran through his mind. Only of the lingering feel of his lips on hers.

Words still didn't exist as he came back to find her mouth again. She sank into him. Every nerve ending caught on fire as the hard lines of his body brushed against hers, hinting at promises she knew she couldn't turn down.

Spearing her fingers through his dark hair, she held on. This…it was what she wanted. Hadn't been able to stop thinking about since that first brush of his lips against hers when he'd walked her home from the pub.

She'd be crazy to deny it or turn away from it. He ignited a heat she couldn't douse. Reminded her of needs unsatisfied for a very long time.

It took every bit of strength she had to pull back from the kiss. Sucking in a deep breath, she pressed a hand to his chest. "I need—"

She looked at him, forgetting everything but the heated look in his hazel eyes. "I need more." She struggled to find her voice. Some sense of clear thought. "More…from you."

Luke couldn't figure out what the hell was being said. He knew only the fierce, growing need inside. The tremble he wanted to feel again under his hold as he pulled her to him, claiming her mouth as his own.

It took every bit of concentration he had to focus on what she was saying. "More what?"

"More of this." She waved her hand between them. "More of us."

She looked away, concentrating on the dark wilderness surrounding them. "But, not here. I can't—"

She didn't have to say more. He understood. But still he wouldn't rush, no matter how desperately he wanted to. Though the thought of throwing her over his shoulder and getting her upstairs as quickly as he could jumped to attention, he knew better.

Knew she deserved better.

Gathering the hand pressed against his chest, he drew her close once more, finding her mouth for another long, tempting kiss. She sank into him, giving him all of her. It dug deep, flaring his need even more.

Easing back, loving the lost look of desire clouding her emerald eyes, he pushed to his feet. Grabbing her wine glass in one hand, he held the other out for her.

She didn't hesitate, resting her palm in his.

Urging her to her feet, he cupped a palm around

each side of her face and stared for a moment. "Are you sure?"

"I am." There wasn't doubt, only passion, in the eyes looking back at him. Pushing onto her toes, she dropped a soft kiss on his lips. "It is, after all, what you promised once we had our first date."

It was exactly what he needed to hear. Making sure Derby followed, he led her inside to all that waited for them.

****

She didn't have second thoughts.

They should have been there. From the moment they were back inside, Luke leading her through the kitchen and up the stairs, Tori expected to hear their screams.

But all she knew was need and desire as he caught her in the hallway, backing her up against the wall. "Last chance to change your mind." He nibbled his way down the slope of her neck, bringing greater life to the rush of emotions charging through.

"I won't be changing my mind." Confidence laced her words, earning a hungry growl from Luke as he backed her down the hallway and into his bedroom. His mouth trailed over bare skin as he moved, never giving her a chance to come down from the high he took her on.

She caught flashes as he continued to trail long heated kisses down her neck and over the delicate curve of her collar bone. Thick gray carpet. A wall of windows as great and brilliant as the room off the kitchen. A vaulted ceiling with bared beams crossing the wide span.

Edging her toward the massive king-size bed, he

found her mouth, taking her over completely so she knew only him and nothing more.

His hands, stable and sure, ran over her—up her arms, over her shoulders and gliding down her sides, then they slid beneath the hem of her shirt. So warm, so gentle. Resting against her ribs, he pushed higher, slipping the worn cotton up and over her head.

Tossing it carelessly to the ground, he held her, staring. His heavy gaze held the same heat as his touch sliding over her, lighting flames in its path.

"So beautiful." He folded his hands over the blue silk covering her breasts. Stepping in closer, he drew her away in another kiss leaving her weak and breathless.

She sighed into him, pressing delicate curves against hard lines. Unclasping her bra, he did away with it, tumbling bare breasts into his hungry hands.

His crisp, seductive scent surrounded her. With a low growl, he did away with the rest of her clothes and held her naked and vulnerable in front of him. When she reached for him, tugging at his shirt, he grabbed her hands. "Not yet. Only you."

The words were enough to spark something new and foreign, inside her. Where the need had burned, it now flared. Desire took a ruling step, leaving her wanting nothing but him with an intensity that terrified even as it excited.

Circling his large, rough hands around her slender wrists, he held them at her sides. With nothing more than a slight shift, he had her mouth in a soft kiss, melting her insides.

He drew in all she was. All she had to give. Building the need as he pulled more from her. Never touching but with his lips. Kicking at everything burning through, stretching her higher till she was sure she could take no more.

Breathless, he pulled back and clasped tight hands around her waist. With more force than she'd expected, he bent her back, pushing his weight against her until she gave in, falling to the bed.

He came over her, holding his weight by his elbows while spearing long fingers through her chestnut curls. "You stun me." He dropped a kiss to the curve of her shoulder before seeking lower, running his tongue over her hardened nipple. "From the moment I found you on the side of the road, you've had me caught."

She didn't know what to say. Didn't even know if she could form the words. There was so much heat rolling off him.

She should have expected no less. In the time she'd come to know him, there was no half-best in anything he did. He gave every bit of himself, no matter the situation.

And tonight, it was her…only her.

Part of it terrified her as she'd never been so needed by another. As if her very breath was a part of what burned through him, making him whole.

But the fear was nothing compared to the desire burning through. Her own need repeated his, making him the center of everything she sought. Had to have.

Pushing up, off his elbows, he hovered above. His hands fitted to her curves, over the soft round of her breasts, and down the smooth line of her stomach.

His hazel eyes, deep with the fire burning between them, caught hers, holding as his fingers brushed against the inside of her thighs, teasing only to slip away again.

She could only stare back. Not sure what to expect. Wanting the intimate touch he promised. She held her breath as he came so close, only to slide down, leaving her hungrier than she'd been.

And then he was there, fingers gently probing as his mouth fell to hers again, igniting flames through every inch of her body.

"Luke." Her voice nothing more than a harsh breath, she shifted her hips, lifting them from the bed and pushing into his probing touch. Needing more. Desperately.

Even as his mouth drifted down the slim line of her neck and over her shoulder to her hardened nipple, he watched as he built the excitement.

His eyes never strayed as she pushed into him, rubbing against the friction he created with his fingers. Diving inside her. Pulling out. Working her higher and higher until every nerve ending screamed, begging for the end.

"No." She shook her head frantically and tried closing her legs against him. "Not yet. I want you. Inside me."

Refusing to miss a beat, he used his elbow between her thighs, opening her to him again. "Soon," he promised, still watching as he drew her up, playing on everything fighting inside. "But first you. I want to watch you and see you slip away. Know I had the power to do that to you."

His words alone almost pushed her over the edge. The heat of his gaze pushed it deeper, stronger. Over an edge she never knew existed.

In those moments, as his fingers vibrated against

her, throwing her so close to losing control, his heavy gaze taking in every moment of her sensual struggle, she traveled in a world unknown. So open. Vulnerable.

And then there was no more thought. Nothing but the rolling tide taking over, pushing her into him, seeking it all. Needing every bit of what he offered.

Her head arching back, his name exploded through her as she lost control, shivering underneath the force of his unrelenting touch. Over and over her hips rose, seeking every bit of the fierce release he'd brought.

The room spun around her. She lost focus on everything but the shivers tightening her limbs, sucking the breath from her lungs.

And still she knew he watched through it all.

Knowing it made it so much more, raging through her until she collapsed under him.

She needed a moment. To breath. Find steady ground. Make sense of everything her body gave. But Luke didn't give it to her.

Sliding his hands up her arms, he caught her wrists, holding them above her head. "I need to be inside you." He dropped frantic kisses to the curve of her chin and up to her swollen lips.

Holding her captive, giving her no chance to come down from the high he'd taken her on, he pushed a knee between her legs.

She wasn't there. Couldn't be ready again after still reeling from her recent tumble. Still there was no push to stop him. She wanted him inside her as much as he wanted to be there even while every nerve begged for a moment to settle.

He was slow as he pushed in deep. Still on fire, the torrent of sensation was almost more than she could handle. For a moment, she feared she'd tumble again as the fierceness of it was too great to handle.

Buried deep inside, Luke's head fell back with a fierce growl. He didn't move, afraid if he did, he'd lose it in that first moment. She closed around him, unmoving as he held her captive with his hands around her wrists. His weight pressed her into the mattress.

Her emerald eyes, still cloudy and wet from only seconds before, looked into his. So soft. So innocent. His own desperate need reflected back at him, pushing him to let go and give in to the desire pounding against him. Demanding satisfaction.

Slow. He pushed the thought through the frantic rush drumming through his head. He wanted to savor. Wanted to enjoy every minute of having Tori in his bed, pleasure staining her cheeks, clouding her beautiful, emerald eyes.

He slid out, hovering at the edge before pushing in deeper.

A breathless gasp escaping, her head fell back, eyes glossing over.

Slow. Again he teased, burying deeper. Lowering his hands, he circled them around her hips, holding her to him. Every part of her fit as if perfectly made for him. The curves of her body. The softness surrounding him as he slowly took them higher.

She rose and fell with him, giving even as she took. It was a seductive dance he'd had with others. But none like this. None with the same intensity to the heat burning and growing between them. The same exploding need to take it all, without hesitation, until every screaming demand was satisfied.

Slow no longer registered. He wanted it all.

Wanted it now.

He dropped low, claiming a kiss. He felt the last of her control slip away. She pressed her hands to his back, holding on as wave after wave of pleasure assaulted them. She looked hard into his eyes and he felt it…the tug of something much greater than he was ready to admit.

"Luke, I—"

There was nothing more as she exploded around him. He found her lips again, capturing her and taking her hard and close as they fell together in the heated wonder waiting for them.

****

He didn't like mistakes. Had no patience for them.

No harm was to come to Tori. Not at this point. He'd been more than clear the objective was to scare only. Nothing more.

Learning of her injuries left him angry. Disgusted by the lack of accuracy he expected, he grasped tight to the phone, making his displeasure clear and leaving no room for argument or debate.

Though Anton professed his apologies, Filip was no longer certain he'd sent the best man for the job. It wasn't a normal occurrence, doubting the lack of efficiency one of his very best provided. But this one seemed to be a tripping stone, creating questions he'd never before known when it came to his trust in Anton and the success he'd secured over the years.

"The Chief of Police is already digging in areas he doesn't belong. This latest disaster will only encourage more." Filip remained stiff in his chair. The only factor saving Anton from his wrath was the previous successes he'd brought. He was a man who understood the need for second chances when they were warranted.

But there would be no more. Anton had a job. Was paid dearly for it. Another mistake would not be taken so kindly.

"I will be more careful." Anton's voice did not waver, giving no signs of fear though Filip was confident it was there. Those in his control were known to fear him. It was the way he'd created it. The very basis on which he had built the empire he enjoyed.

"You will do the job asked. Just as it is asked." Filip gave no room for anything but his demands. "I will not appreciate being disappointed another time."

Moments passed before Anton's voice, less sure this time, came across the line. "I will take care of what needs to be done."

It would do. For now. "It is what I count on." Filip didn't bother with goodbye, dropping the phone to his desk.

He'd known this wouldn't be easy. For years it had been too easy, using his power to keep Seth and Tori apart. But this one had slipped past his control through someone unknown and unexpected, giving Tori what she had sought for so long. And by the time he'd found out, it had been too late.

But he would take care of it. As he always did. There were things not to be known or remembered. Inside the mind of Tori, there was a truth she could not be allowed to recall. One he'd put so much into keeping hidden where it belonged.

She'd seen what Seth hadn't. Always held the threat of recognizing the face looking down at her as she suffered the death of her parents.

He couldn't let that come to life. And every minute

she spent with Seth was a risk of her finding the strength to face what she buried inside.

Seth had been older and wiser on that fateful night. Allowing her close to him back then and giving her a chance to talk might have very well been the end of it long ago.

Because words that might sound like nonsense to strangers could very well have made sense to her own brother. If she had shared the wrong thing or offered even the smallest hint of all she'd seen, it would have been over.

But he'd protected the truth, making difficult decisions in order to do so. After all this time, he refused to take the chance of what would come with brother and sister reunited and free to share what they knew. All they remembered.

Too much was at stake. And as much as it might pain him in the end, he would hold back nothing to keep the secret hidden.

Chapter Sixteen

Opening her eyes to the morning sun and a man sleeping in bed next to her wasn't in Tori's realm of comfort. She could count on one hand, with fingers still to spare, how often she'd faced such a situation. And not one of them ever made her feel too good.

She tried slipping quietly off the side of the bed, but before she moved more than an inch, Luke's heavy arm fell over her. "Not time to get up, yet," he mumbled half into his pillow.

She wanted to argue but decided against it. Resting back against her pillow, she did her best to ignore the heat gathering where Luke's arm rested against bare skin.

Maybe it wasn't so bad. This strange sensation of waking up with a strong, warm, male body beside her, his very touch reminding her of all they'd discovered the night before.

The first hint of morning sun peeked through the curtains. The fall of his breath brushed across her. The softness of the bed, the pillows, encouraged her to sink in and enjoy the stolen moment while she could.

And with that, she drifted back to sleep. Though she had no idea for how long. One second she was hanging on the edge of dreams. The next, a strange brush against her cheek gently pulled her back to reality.

Pushing heavy lids open, she stared into Luke's deep gaze. Propped on an elbow, he stared down on her, running a smooth, soft finger against her cheek.

He smiled, the linger of sleep adding a sexy tilt to his lips. There was a gentleness, almost vulnerability, in his first moments of being awake. It was something she never thought she'd witness in him, pushing her to want him all over again no matter how dangerous she knew it to be. "Morning." She flattened a hand to her mouth, hiding the yawn.

He didn't say a word, the look in his eyes doing it for him. She saw the lingering desire from the night before. The need again building.

He lowered and nibbled at her bottom lip. Pulling up, he stared down at her as if seeking some sort of answer to an unknown question before going back to claiming her mouth as his own.

The uncertainty fell away. It was just Luke again. As it had been the night before. His masculine scent washed over her. His weight as he rolled, pressed on top of her. The glimmer in his hazel eyes left little doubt to what he wanted.

Wrapping her arms around him, holding him close, she fell into his kiss. There were definitely advantages to waking up in bed with the man you made wild love to the night before. And this—being with Luke, the morning sun burning through the curtains, dancing over them—was definitely one of them.

She could drift away with him. Fall back into everything still simmering from the night before.

Lost in him, in the feel of his lips and body pressed against hers, it was a harsh jolt when Derby jumped on the bed. Tail wagging, tongue licking, he pushed his short nose between them.

He had priorities they couldn't ignore. Not if they wanted to avoid a mess to be cleaned up.

Groaning, Luke shifted, giving Derby room to settle between them. While Tori got the licks, he was attacked by a wagging, excited tail. "Okay." He held out his hands, protecting his face.

"So much for that." He looked over Derby's swaying butt and smiled. "How about a raincheck?"

Laughing, she nodded, rolling out from underneath Derby. "If you make coffee, I'll take him out." She searched the piles on the floor, tossing through what he'd stripped from her the night before.

She felt his eyes burning against her skin as she slipped into her clothes.

"I'll make the coffee and meet you outside." Following Derby off the side of the mattress, he found clothes for himself, catching her attention just as she'd caught his.

The thought of his promised raincheck teased at her as she stepped out of the room ahead of him. Gave her something to look forward to.

****

There was something about the morning hours on the ranch that caught Tori. Left her feeling almost weepy as she stood at the edge of the back porch, watching Derby run into the trees while waiting for her coffee.

She'd never known air so clean or crisp. Hadn't even imagined it existed after a lifetime living in the swell of big-city pollution.

Not that she was against her mornings back in Chicago. She loved them too. Watching the busy city wake up and catching the hint of the river coming in with the early breeze. Hearing the buzz of traffic gathering for rush hour before becoming a part of the swarm of bodies lining the sidewalks, heading off for the start of their day.

It was an experience of its own as well.

But here, on the ranch, it was different. Instead of rush there was peace. A slow-moving start to a new day rather than a frantic push to get it started.

It was beautiful. Quiet. Cleansing in a way she couldn't describe but felt deep down.

The light flutter of a bird hopping from tree to tree caught Derby's attention. She laughed as he yapped playfully, darting between thick trunks. Paws scraped against weathered bark as he tried, unsuccessfully, to climb up after it.

"At least somebody's enjoying their morning." Luke came up beside her, handing over a steaming ceramic mug.

The overwhelming scent washing over her left little doubt he liked his coffee strong. A sip confirmed it. "This is definitely a jolt to the system." She turned just enough to get a good look at him while keeping a careful eye on Derby.

"Sorry." He shrugged. "Been making cops brew so long, don't think to make it any other way."

"It's coffee. Can't complain." She took another sip to prove her point.

Luke looked out over the ranch and she found herself caught in the hard lines framing his profile. It was a struggle, knowing she'd tumbled into bed with a guy she barely knew.

A prude wasn't her way. But, usually, she had at

least a bit better knowledge of the men she had sex with. Though she was careful to stay clear of those seeking relationships, she did enjoy their companionship and time together.

But with Luke.

She couldn't explain it. From that first moment, seeing him through the flurry of flakes, there had been something brewing inside she didn't know. Didn't understand.

It frightened her even as it excited her.

She looked away, putting her attention back on Derby. There was no reason to make more out of things than there truly were. Sex with Luke was great. Above great. She had no problem returning to his bed. How could any sane woman have a problem with that?

If nothing else, sex with him would help keep her mind off the craziness surrounding her since she'd arrived.

"I need to get to the station soon." He gazed at her over the rim of his coffee mug. "Do you want me to take you into town? See about your rental car?"

The very thought of having to handle the mess with a rental and deal with her insurance company left her cringing. She already felt the headache threatening to take shape.

"That would be great. Thanks." It felt strange to be so casual with Luke after the night they shared. But this was exactly how she wanted it. Preferred it. Two adults who could have wild, amazing sex without letting it suggest they needed any kind of relationship between them.

Casual was good. Casual was how she liked it.

"I'd like to meet with you and Seth later." He

whistled for Derby, patting his thigh to bring him to his side. "Dinner at the pub, maybe. If it works for both of you."

Following man and dog inside, she took the last sip from her coffee before rinsing her mug in the sink. "I'll talk to Seth and let you know."

With her back against the counter, she watched him move through the kitchen. He rinsed his own mug before grabbing his badge and strapping his gun to his side.

He stopped then to look at her, long and hard. Without a word, he crossed the floor, bracing an arm on both sides of her. Curling long fingers around the edge of the counter, he pressed close.

The rough, masculine scent of him washed over her. Memories from the night before flooded through. "I plan on making good on that raincheck." He nibbled on her bottom lip, pulling a sigh from deep inside.

Moving his leg between hers, he held her trapped between the counter at her back and the hard, firm muscles sculpting his chest. Hands still at her sides, she arched her neck, staring up at him.

The look reflecting back at her was much more than she expected. The intensity simmering in the hazel depths left her breathless and unsure of what she should do.

Before she could bring clear thought to her mind, he bent down, capturing her mouth with his. Drawing on all they'd shared the night before, he tugged her with him over the edge of having no choice but to fall into him and return his kiss with the same passion brewing inside.

She sucked desperately for air when he came away,

a smug smile on his lips. "I'm finding I like this." He brushed a soft finger over her swollen lips. "Much more than I thought I would. That raincheck can't come fast enough."

Turning on his heels, he walked away, leaving Tori desperate to find stable ground.

What was that she had convinced herself?

Casual was good.

It had worked, up until the kiss. There was nothing casual about that.

Such a realization wasn't a good one.

****

He needed to get her out of his mind.

Sitting at his desk, Luke shook his head. Thoughts of Tori, naked and vulnerable underneath him, were playing havoc with his concentration, making it damn near impossible to focus on anything else.

And that wasn't good.

There was too much to be done. Too many facts he couldn't get a handle on but desperately needed to.

What was happening to Tori wasn't coincidence. He was more convinced than ever. The ties might not be there yet, but he was sure it all came back to the heartless murder of her parents.

Unfortunately, finding that connection was proving to be a challenge. For every question he had, every record he searched, there seemed to be one obstacle after another thrown in his path.

It didn't matter he wore the same badge and took the same oath, the information he sought through the precinct that had investigated the murders wasn't coming easy. Most of it wasn't coming at all.

Frustrated, he shoved up in his chair then grabbed

his phone from the corner of the desk. It was time to ask for a favor from a friend.

"Chambers." The familiar voice on the other end made him smile. Alec Chambers was an agent with the Colorado office of the FBI. He was good at what he did. If there was information to be found, he'd be the one to do it.

They'd met many years back when a kidnapping case brought him into Luke's jurisdiction. Working the case together, celebrating in the end when they found the little girl alive, formed a friendship they'd kept up through the years.

"I swear you sound older every time I call." Turning in his chair, Luke stared out the window, imagining Alec in his own office doing the same.

"Nothing old about me." There was laughter in his friend's voice. "I'm holding up about as good as ever. Actually better these days."

"I'm guessing that's due to your beautiful wife. Still can't believe you actually convinced somebody to marry you." He'd been at the wedding. Had the typical male bout of envy when introduced to his bride, Jessie.

Though an agent herself, she was more fit to join the models lining the runways in Paris and New York. It hadn't taken long, though, to realize her striking beauty was nothing compared to what she carried inside. The courage and passion that was truly her, far beyond her looks.

"Still can't believe it myself." Alec's answering laugh echoed from the other end. "Heard your brother is on the same path. Figure it will be your turn soon enough."

"Don't take bets on it. I'm perfectly happy without

the ring on my finger." Tori's face, soft and subtle after a night of making love flashed in his mind. He quickly chased it away.

"Used to say the same." There was an amused hint to Alec's voice. The sound of one who knew a secret Luke hadn't yet figured out. "So what brings your call?"

Turning back to his desk, Luke opened the file of what little he'd been able to gather about Tori's parents. "I have a favor to ask." Tapping a finger against the edge, he shook his head at the scraps of information he'd been given so far. "I've got a case I'm working on that I think has a connection to an old murder case in Chicago twenty-five years ago."

Alec listened as Luke filled him in on what little he knew about the murder of Tori's parents. The threat Seth was given to stay away from his sister. What Tori had faced since arriving in Snow Ridge.

"I feel it in my gut. There's a connection here. But I'm hitting nothing but roadblocks whenever I try looking into the old murder case. Nobody is too eager to give me any information. Instead, I keep getting the runaround."

Alec was silent for a moment, taking it all in. "You think someone's trying to keep you from digging into the case?"

"Sure as hell feels like it." Frustration returned. He fought it back, knowing it would do no good.

"So what do you need from me?"

It rubbed Luke raw, knowing he had to ask for a favor to gain information that should have been available to him as an officer of the law. "The Bureau has more reach than I do. I was hoping you could do some digging for me. See if you have any better luck."

He heard a faint flutter on the other end and knew Alec took notes as he talked. "Send me over what information you have. I'll look into it. Hopefully get you what you're looking for."

"I'd appreciate it." Luke closed the folder. "I don't have much but I'll get you what I do have."

"You do that and I'll get back to you as soon as I know something."

It helped, hearing that. With his position, Alec had a better chance of digging deeper than he could and break through some of the walls he'd been facing from the start.

There was no guarantee. But at least it was another step. One he hoped would prove to be the right one. Tori needed this solved. Ended.

He was going to do his best to give that to her.

Chapter Seventeen

"So tell me, how was it?"

Tucked away at a table near the fragrant fire inside the pub, Jackie glanced at Tori, a mischievous glimmer in her eyes.

"How was what?" Tori made room as the tawny-haired waiter set a full beer down in front of her.

Though Cara had argued, making it more than clear she expected her to take another day to recover, she hadn't won. Instead, Tori put in her time, enjoying the distraction of time spent with Jackie and Cara. And quickly agreed to share a drink at the pub before her dinner with Seth and Luke.

"How was sex with Luke?"

Reaching for her beer, Tori's hand stalled in midair. Her eyes snapped up, meeting Jackie's. "I…we—"

Curling her fingers around the handle of her mug, she took a long, stalling drink. "How did you know?"

"Ha. I knew I was right." Jackie shot a smug smile Cara's way. "I told you."

Cara gave a slight shake to her head. "And I told you, it wasn't any of our business."

"Of course it is." Jackie beamed at Tori, raising her beer in a one-sided toast. "Us three, we're friends. And friends share, especially when it comes to tumbling into bed with heart-stopping, handsome men."

"And I can't imagine any sane woman," she paused long enough to take a sip from her beer, "spending a night with one of the Grady brothers and not enjoying herself. That, alone, told me all I needed."

From her side of the table, Cara's smile held as much amusement as apology. "And it *was* a bit obvious this morning when Luke dropped you off. You had that look. The one that leaves little doubt to how you spent your night."

"A look?" Tori shook her head, trying to keep up with the two. From their knowledge of her sex life to Jackie's claim of friendship, her mind was hopping. "There's a look?"

"Of course there is." Jackie made room as her mandatory order of wings was delivered to the table. "You can't tell me you've never seen it before plastered all over your girlfriends' faces." She waved a wing at her.

"Actually." Tori sucked in a harsh breath and looked carefully at the two women sitting beside her. "I've never really been close enough to anyone to have the chance."

Jackie and Cara exchanged a look. She wondered what they thought. She'd heard the stories. Knew they'd been the best of friends since childhood. She couldn't imagine it was easy for them to understand what it was like to never have formed such a tight relationship with anyone.

"Well, now you are." Cara leaned over the table, resting a gentle hand over hers. There was a tenderness in her eyes making Tori feel uncomfortable even as it brought a strange sense of belonging.

"Yep." Jackie placed her hand over Cara's,

creating a pile of three on top of the table. "You've got us now. We don't just do close. We do, obnoxious, tell everything, spill your heart and your guts, close."

Tori didn't know what to say. Didn't know how to react to anything that had been shared since reaching the pub.

"So, with that settled," Jackie clapped her hands together and rubbed her palms. "I ask again, how was it?"

Tori couldn't help but laugh. It was just…so much. Such a different experience. One part of her wanted to run screaming. While another encouraged her to dip a toe in and give this new friendship a chance.

"It was—"

She took a slow sip of beer while she considered. "It was good," she fumbled out, unable to find a true word matching the night she'd spent wrapped in Luke's arm. Lost in everything he was. All the wonder he offered.

Jackie looked disappointed. "Just good? That's it?"

Both sets of eyes settled heavy over her. She tried not to squirm under them. Did she have that *look* again? The one that had given her away from the start?

She drew in a harsh breath. Told herself she could do this. "My brain is struggling to catch up. It's hard to come up with the right words to describe it."

"Ahhh." Cara's smile stretched from ear to ear. "I remember that feeling. Cade did the same to me. It must be a Grady brother trait. They get us so spun around, even words are forgotten."

Tori nodded. Though she was due to have dinner soon, she grabbed a wing from the center of the table, needing something to do with her hands. "I'm not one who is usually at a loss for words. Don't like it much, really. It was sex. It was good."

"No." The forgotten wing dangling from her fingers, she shook her head. "It was better than good. Much better. Still, it was just sex. A great way to release tension and work off some stress."

Finally remembering her wing, she tore off a bite. "So why the hell am I having such a hard time making sense of it?" She stuffed it in her mouth, chewing slowly.

There was a knowing look in Cara's eyes Tori wasn't sure she liked. "Because, as it took me a while to learn, there really isn't anything easy to figure out when it comes to the Grady brothers."

It wasn't an answer she wanted to hear. Tori wanted, craved, easy. She didn't want anything complicated. Didn't need to be confused or unsure when it came to Luke and whatever happened between them.

She knew enough about the story shared between Cara and Cade to know what happened between them was right. The final happy chapter in all they'd been through and struggled with.

But that wasn't the story for her and Luke. This was nothing more than a small bit of time, given to enjoy one another's company and find some relief from all that was happening.

But there would be no happily ever after for them. It wasn't a road she would even consider traveling. Getting close to someone meant losing them. She'd already had enough loss in her life. There would be no taking risks to repeat it.

****

He was drawn to her the minute he walked through the door.

Through the many heads crowding the pub, it was the gentle tumble of chestnut curls forcing Luke's attention.

He couldn't figure out what the hell it was about Tori drawing him in. She wasn't what he'd consider his type. Though he wasn't one who put much stock in believing such a thing.

But, hell, she tended to hold him off as much as she drew him in. And that alone should make her far from his type. No man liked a roller-coaster ride when it came to enjoying himself with a beautiful woman.

He preferred the smooth sailing. The knowledge that the one he was with wanted him just as much, if not more, than he wanted her.

And, with Tori, there was no way to know for sure.

Pushing his way through the crowd, he kept his eye on her. Wondered what was being said as her head dipped low around the table.

In his experience, women caught up in such deep conversation wasn't particularly a good sign. The way their minds worked was a mystery to him. But he knew well enough to know, catching them deep in talk as they were didn't always bode well for any men in their presence.

"As often as you're here, you three are doing your own fair share of keeping Jake in business." He went for casual, leaning a hip against the corner of the table. He smiled as all three eyes popped up, meeting his with the hint of one caught with their hand in the cookie jar.

Cara was the first to recover, meeting his smile with one of her own. "It's one of the benefits of owning a place so close."

"Not to mention being engaged to the owner's little brother." Recovering as well, Jackie held up her beer before tipping it back for a drink.

Only Tori seemed a bit off still. Slowly picking at a wing she held between her fingers, she did her best to pay more attention to it than Luke. Only after the stretching seconds threatened to become awkward did she force her own smile. "You're early."

"Not by much." Hooking his hand around the back of an empty chair at the neighboring table, he settled beside her. Grabbing her beer, he finished it off then waved at the bartender for another for them both.

Tori did her best to recollect herself. Having Luke appear while discussing his wonderful ways in bed wasn't exactly ideal. In fact, it was far from it, leaving her struggling to bring some sense back to her thoughts. Some order back to dealing with him.

And order was what was needed. Especially with Luke.

The beers were delivered. Conversation turned to the town, the ranch. Tori sat back from it all. Enjoyed the back and forth while forcing herself back down to an even level.

By the time Seth showed up, she was nearly there.

"I didn't realize we were having a party." Seth glanced over her shoulder as Tori pushed up from her chair to hug him.

"No party." Finishing off the last of her beer, Cara rose, nudging Jackie to do the same. "We were just leaving."

After quick hugs and knowing looks passed Tori's way, they were gone. Seth claimed the empty chair across from her and stole her still full beer for himself. "So, what's the reason for dinner?"

"I'm hoping to get a little more information." Luke pushed the empty wing basket to the edge of the table while watching for Jake to come out of the back. "Sometimes the right questions can get answers you weren't even sure you had."

Though she heard his words, Tori struggled to make sense of them. It had been fine this morning. Until his damn kiss. Until Cara and Jackie and their demanding questions about the night spent.

Now her brain was a mess. And what should have been easy and casual was threatening to become more.

Not that she would let it. Pulling up the last bit of her self-dignity, she looked straight at him, sure she gave nothing away. "What more can we tell you? My memories all come from the nightmares. There's no way to know what of it is real."

He looked at her, an expression in his hazel eyes she didn't dare try to figure out. "If it comes out to be nothing, that's fine. But there's no wrong in trying for more."

"You're digging because you believe what's happening to Tori is related to our parents' murder." The stolen beer held in his hand, Seth looked between her and Luke.

Luke didn't hesitate as he nodded before picking up his own beer, reminding Tori she was now the one doing without. "I don't doubt coincidence, but this is too much. If I had my guess, from what you've told me so far, somebody doesn't like you and your sister together."

He caught sight of Jake and waved him over.

She watched him, wondering about what he said. Could it really be that? Had someone gone so far they were willing to do whatever it took to keep her and her brother apart?

It made sense. In a sick sense of realization, she thought of all the disappointments she'd faced trying to find her brother. The feeling that someone or something was working against her as every effort came back without results.

If someone truly didn't want her with her brother, how far would they go? How many years had they been working against her?

The answers coming terrified her even as they sickened her.

She shoved it down as Jake approached their table. "How are you?" He looked over Tori carefully, sympathy and concern in his eyes.

"I'm okay." It was the truth. The aches had diminished to nothing more than small pangs rearing up, reminding her of the accident whenever she'd work her mind away from it.

"Do you need menus?" He looked at her over the others. She was the odd one out when it came to knowing her way about the pub. Still, she'd already decided what she wanted.

Joining Seth and Luke in turning them down, she put in her order for the Shepherd's Pie and another beer to replace the one Seth had taken from her.

Leaving it to the privacy of the three of them again, Jake headed off to place their orders.

"So what is it you're hoping to know?" Seth didn't waste time, leaning over the table closer to Luke. If there was more to know, he wanted it done.

"I want to try going back, rather than forward." Luke shifted, his attention shared between him and Tori. "We might find more answers."

Making way, he waited for the bartender to place a beer in front of Tori. "I want to know what you might remember in the months before your parents were murdered."

Tori was already shaking her head before he ever finished. "I was only three. I've tried, but I don't have very many memories from that time. I can remember Seth. My parents. But not much else."

"That's okay." Luke laid a hand over hers. "Seth was older. He might remember more."

Looking at the two of them, Seth did his best not to let the questions run wild. Something had changed. He knew. Could even guess what it was. What he didn't know was how to react. Or if he was allowed to.

"I have some vague memories." He reached for his beer, needing the distraction. "Not many, though. I was still pretty young, myself."

"What do you remember? About the people around you? Your day to day life?"

He drifted back. Tried to pull from some of the furthest reaches of his mind. Memories old and faded, broken up by the experience and knowledge of a small boy. "I remember them being loving parents. Not just in the thought and wishes of a boy who lost them at such a young age. But in what I can still see. Still feel inside."

He didn't like this. Going back. It should have been easier with so many years passed. But there was still hurt. Loss he wasn't sure he'd ever fully get over.

"I remember people too, lots of them. They always seemed to be around the house. Meeting with dad. Part of the dinners our mom would host."

Tori gasped, pulling the attention of the two men. "I remember." She drifted back and could see it. So clear, it shocked her.

"We were there. You and I." She waved a hand at Seth, nearly forgot Luke at her side as the images raced. "Sitting in the upper hallway. Our legs dangling between the banister."

She closed her eyes, bringing it back. "We were in our pajamas. Weren't supposed to be out of bed. But we were there, watching everybody in the great room below."

Like flipping through photos in a picture album, she went through it. One by one. Her dad, so handsome in a dark suit. His arms wrapped tight around her mom's delicate waist.

She heard the music. Smelled the distinct scent of cigar smoke in the air.

And the people. There were so many of them. Some on the couches. Others gathered around the small bar at the far end of the room. Laughter drifted up. Music softly poured through the speakers.

And then she saw him. The horror of it had her gasping for breath. Holding on, she looked at Luke. "He was there. The man I saw the night my parents were killed. The one I'm sure I should remember."

She saw the same hard-lined features. The thinning hair. The eyes, looking so hard through her as she stood there in the hallway on that fateful night.

"It was him. I'm sure of it."

Feeling sick from the memory, she sucked in deep, hard breaths, trying desperately to find steady ground again.

"Do you know who he was?" Luke turned her hand, curling her fingers with his and holding on tight.

She tried seeing him. The sight of him from that night of the dinner party to the terror of her parents' murder. His face still wasn't clear, drifting in and out of distant shadows. She should know it. That much she knew. But the harder she tried, the more it clouded, leaving her shaking her head in frustration. "No. I'm sorry."

"It's okay." Luke wanted to grab her. Hold her. Chase away the fear and pain reflecting back in her emerald eyes. If only they were alone and back in the privacy of his room. He'd fold her in his arms. Make sure she lost whatever horror lingered behind her memories.

"Do you remember the night?" Still holding tight to Tori, he looked at Seth. The answers were coming. Of that much, he was thankful. Even the tiniest detail helped.

Seth looked from him to Tori. "I don't think so. I don't know. I have memories of such nights. But I can't focus on one in particular. And I don't know who was there the night our parents were killed so I don't know a face to compare."

Luke wished for more. Was thankful for the little bit he'd been given. He ended his questions as Jake returned, arms heavy with their dinner orders. There was more to learn. Of that he was sure.

But tonight had given him something. There was a connection. Just as he'd thought. Whoever was behind it all had a history with Tori. With Seth.

Though they might not know the connection, it was there. And he'd find it. He was sure of it.

****

"I think it's best you go back to the ranch."

Standing at the bottom of the stairs leading up to her apartment, Tori did her best to sound convincing.

Luke had walked her back from the pub. Waited while she let Derby out. He'd stay for the night if she'd let him. Of that she was sure.

But him staying wasn't a good idea.

It might have been. Even something she would have been looking forward to. But the night had shown her she'd been foolish. Not only about falling into bed with him. But in believing anything between them could ever be casual. Could be carried on with no strings attached.

It was the talk with Cara and Jackie. Her own traitorous reaction when Luke had made his way to the pub.

She'd been a fool to think any of this was good. She'd been through it enough. Knew it was always best to walk away before being left.

"And why would you think that?" His look, so knowing, so tempting, was almost her undoing.

As Derby twisted his way between their legs, she steeled her spine, vowing to stay strong no matter how he argued. "Because this," she waved her hand in a circle between them, "isn't going to work."

"What is this?" Though he stood a few inches away and didn't touch her, she felt the heat of him washing over her, making her wish for more space.

"You know what *this* is." She tried holding on to the spark of anger, using it to keep her strength up.

He only smirked before moving closer.

Refusing to be dragged in, she turned her back.

Heading up the stairs, she called for Derby. His paws echoed on the stairs behind her while Luke's heavy steps did the same.

Groaning silently, she rested her hand on the knob and turned back to him. "I can make it from here."

"I'm sure you can." He pressed close, backing her into the door. "But I'm not sure if I can."

She only had a moment to register his words before his mouth found hers. The gentleness she'd known from him was gone, replaced by a desperate need that pushed at her, demanding a response.

Still, she fought. Her arms curled behind her back, hand still around the doorknob, she swore she wouldn't react. Wouldn't be dragged under.

But the feel of him pressed so close, hard lines meshing with softer curves. The taste of his lips with hers. His scent so strong, teasing her. It was near impossible to think of all the rational reasons why he should go.

Barely aware of his hand slipping past her sides and wrapping with hers around the knob, she nearly fell through when he opened the door behind her. Would have if he hadn't been holding her tight against him.

He pushed her back into the kitchen, waiting for Derby before closing it behind him. And still, his mouth took, sapping every bit of control she had left.

"This isn't leaving." She found the strength to pull back enough to look into his eyes, seeing the passion burning there.

"You're right. It isn't." He pulled her hard against him, drawing her into a long, slow kiss. "Is that what you still want me to do? Go?"

What did she want? She couldn't get her mind to

think straight. To form a thought over the desire crawling through and taking hold.

He wasn't playing fair. She felt the stir of anger but couldn't hold on to it. The heat rising, pushing her pulse to a frantic beat, left her with little will to do anything but take what he offered and get lost in it.

She didn't answer but he was already reaching behind her, locking the door.

She should argue. Damnit, she should. But it wasn't there. That need to be rid of him. To walk away from whatever it was between them before it became something she couldn't handle.

Instead, she pushed closer, rubbing where his need teased against her.

It was all he needed. With a growl, so primal it reached deep inside her, he backed her out of the kitchen and toward the bedroom.

This was a mistake. She knew it. Couldn't argue it.

Still she'd be taking it, having no strength left to demand different when her body screamed for him. For everything he'd do to her during the heart of the night.

Chapter Eighteen

He'd felt the tug deep in his gut. The one promising to stretch further, leaving him wanting even as he was satisfied.

Backing Tori against the wall as soon as he had her inside her bedroom, he took with all he had, needing every bit of her. A full surrender, giving in to the needs swirling so hot, so desperate, between them.

He should have gone. He'd admit it. When she tried brushing him back to the ranch, he should have turned on his heels and walked away without a look back.

But...damn. He couldn't do it. Not with her.

There was something there. Something dragging at him and pulling him under. Everything that was right and sensible around her became nonexistent. And it became nothing more than needing to feel and know the beauty, the fiery mystery she promised with no more than a look from her intoxicating, emerald eyes.

Running his hands down her sides, he grabbed her slender waist, holding her against him. His mouth still taking, demanding, he yanked her shirt over her head, tossing it carelessly to the ground.

Red lace held up her beautiful breasts. And he guessed, as he'd discovered the night before, her panties would match. The thought was enough for desperation to build, leaving him wanting so much more.

But not yet. First, he wanted to know, love, and cherish every inch of her. Discover what he'd missed the night before. Leave her wanting for more and never again trying to send him away.

"Luke, I—"

He waited, wondering if she'd stop him now, second thoughts getting the best of her. He'd walk away if she wanted, though it would kill him to do so.

She said nothing more. Her eyes clouded over with the desire he loved seeing in their depths. Relieved even though he hated to admit it, he unhooked her bra, adding it to where her shirt rested in a messy clump, catching her breasts in his hands. "So perfect. Just right."

He rubbed his thumbs over the hardened nipples, dragging forward a gasp from deep inside her. The sound of it pushed him to want more. Need more.

Tori felt him watching but couldn't react enough to look. Her head back, breath barely finding its way through her lungs, she could only feel. Rise higher as he dipped his head, replacing his thumbs with the slow, heated twirl of his tongue.

She wanted to push him away even as she drew him closer. It was so much. *Too much.* She shouldn't feel this. Shouldn't know such an intense need burning inside.

It was frightening. Yet she couldn't stop it. Couldn't fight back when every inch of her body screamed for more.

"I need to see you." On a harsh breath, he pulled away, tugging desperately at the button on her jeans. Freeing it, he slid the denim down before working on the red lace between her legs.

He lingered for a moment before pushing at her and lifting so he could slip it away and add it to the pile.

And then she was there. Naked and beautiful. His for the taking.

And he took.

Pushing her back against the wall, he pressed tight, letting her feel everything she was doing to him. Her head fell back, a low groan escaping as he rubbed against her. His need hers to know.

Dipping low, he found a hardened nipple, his hands roaming over the slender slope of her waist and the gentle curve of her thighs.

Afraid she'd melt to a useless puddle, she curled her fingers around his strong shoulders, holding on as he teased with mouth and hand.

Her back pressed against the wall, she could do nothing but feel. Every touch, every glide, heating her blood, leaving her weak and needy for more.

While the night before had been about exploring, tonight he simply took with a ravenous fire that burned through her. Left her heart a painful pound against her ribs. Her body throbbing every place his touch lingered.

Before she had a chance to stabilize herself, he grabbed her by the waist, lifting her from her feet. His hands curved beneath her, he held her tight as he found the bed, falling back so she settled on top of him.

It was a position she liked. For all that he held her captive while sparking fire inside, she saw her own chance now. He went to roll over. Tightening her legs at his sides, she stopped him. "My turn."

Her smile was daring. Seductive.

It was nearly Luke's undoing. Soft skin rubbing

over him. Her delicate, sweet scent teasing him. And she was all his. Here in this moment, wanting him with those seductive eyes and taunting him with her haunting beauty.

She bent low, chestnut curls fanning over his chest as soft lips trailed a slow path. Gentle hands shaped against hard lines, finding their own way.

With a low groan, he fisted his fingers around her slender shoulders, holding on with all he had. She played. She lingered. Her tongue tasting, exploring, before slowly moving lower.

When she took him in her mouth, it took everything he had not to explode. "Damnit, Tori." His fingers curled tight around her shoulders. Afraid to let go. Afraid he'd lose it all if he did.

He rose into her and she took. Hands wrapped around his waist, she moved him with her, setting the pace from slow to fast then back to slow again. Always taking. Exploring all there was while sending his pulse into frantic mode.

Through the chestnut curls falling over her face, she lifted her eyes to his while running the tip of her tongue down the length of him.

And he was done.

He didn't have the ability to form words as he yanked her up by the shoulders. He held her above him, eyes probing deep while his hands slid to her waist and he pushed inside with one swift thrust.

Tori's entire body shuddered. The breath raced from her lungs. Everything in her tightened. The movement was frightening, leaving her feeling as if she would shatter into a million pieces if she dared.

Fighting for some sort of control, she looked down

at him, finding in his clouded gaze the same struggle. His chest rose and fell underneath her as he sucked in a breath. Then he moved her. Hands around her waist lifting, he slowly pushed her back down over him.

He was taking control again. The realization forced her to find enough strength to grab his hands, folding her fingers with his and holding them at his sides. "Still my turn." Her words were breathless as she tightened, circling her hips around him.

He filled her completely, each rise bringing him deeper. She slid over him, tightening around him, using every bit of her control not to race to the explosion she longed for.

He looked at her. His hazel eyes peered deeper than she'd ever allowed another soul. She couldn't stop. Still needing to move and feel him inside her, filling her with every rise and fall of her hips.

It became almost desperate. This need to satisfy. The desire burning through, controlling every part of her.

It terrified her but there was no stopping it.

It drove through, pushing her faster. Driving her pulse into a desperate rhythm as she closed around him. Everything built, tugging her higher and higher. So close to the edge. Seeking it with an intensity ruling her.

He pulled his hand free from hers, twisting his arms around her back and throwing her down to him. Holding her there, he moved with her, matching each rising thrust. His heart pounded against her own, breath barely possible as he wound fingers through her hair, pulling her mouth to his.

And she tumbled, crying out his name against his

lips. Rising high, falling hard, as everything shattered, tumbling her over.

He pressed her closer, deepening the hold of his mouth as he followed. Pushing off the mattress, he buried deep inside as his body shook beneath her, arms crushing her to him as they slid off into a place that was all their own.

****

Seth never considered himself a fool.

Alone now at the table inside the pub, he took a long draw from his beer and looked over those still lingering, trying his best to distract his thoughts.

There was no coincidence in Luke and Tori leaving together. Yes, he'd heard the excuse about making sure she got home safe. But that was well over an hour ago and Luke's truck still sat in front of the pub.

He couldn't blame Luke. His sister was beautiful. He looked at her and saw what he still remembered of their mother. The gentle smile on her face when she'd pull him into a tight hug. The twinkle in her emerald eyes when he and Tori would cuddle up to their mother's side for a bedtime story.

To this day, he still heard her laughter, how it carried through a room, brightening it. Still saw her when she'd dress up for a date with their father. So beautiful, he'd sometimes wonder if she was real.

He missed them both. What memories he carried were reminders of all that was lost the night his parents were murdered. A happy childhood. A loving family. Security in knowing where he belonged. Who he belonged with.

And he'd been able to reclaim some of that. Not that it was ever close to what he'd known with his parents and his sister. But he'd found acceptance in a family who knew and understood. Never pushing or demanding he sacrifice his own family, his own blood, for their acceptance or love.

But Tori had never been given that. Listening to her stories of the life she had after they were separated pulled painfully at his heart. Made him curse the little boy he was who allowed others to scare him away from his own sister. Leave her to face such struggles alone.

But he was also wise enough to know that little boy couldn't have done differently. But the adult he'd become—that was a different story.

It was hard knowing Tori had spent so much time searching for him. Hadn't given up while he'd done nothing to look for her in return. To find his little sister he'd lost all those years ago.

But, no matter how old he'd become, he was still that little boy frightened by the threat given so long ago. And when he'd think of her, he'd see her in the very best of lives. A family loving and adoring her as she deserved. An amazing life he didn't want to put at risk.

Not when there was a chance doing so would bring her harm.

But he'd been so wrong. It ate at him, knowing that. But he couldn't go back. Couldn't change what he hadn't done or should have done.

He could only go forward and give Tori everything he hadn't from the past. Be the brother she deserved. The one who never stopped loving her.

Which was why he sat there brooding over his half-full beer, not liking the thought of Luke's truck still sitting in front of the pub.

Not that he didn't believe Luke was a good guy. He liked him. Respected him. But somehow none of that mattered when it came to his sister.

And how in the hell did other brothers handle this?

"Want another one?" Jake appeared at his side, nodding at the beer in his hand.

Seth considered for a moment then shook his head. "Probably best for this to be my last. Need to get myself back to the ranch."

"Surprised you didn't go with Luke and Tori." With a quick look, making sure he wasn't needed, Jake wrapped his arms around the back of an empty chair.

"Don't think those two were particularly looking for any more company."

Understanding struck in Jake's gaze. He glanced over his shoulder as if searching out Luke's truck himself. "You okay with that? Your sister? My brother?"

"Hell. I don't know." He took another long drink from his beer. "Don't know how I'm supposed to feel. Or if I even have a right to it."

Pulling out the chair, Jake eased into it and signaled the bartender for a beer of his own. "Seems to me, you feel it, you have a right to it."

Deciding if he was going to have company, he'd go for another beer after all, Seth held up two fingers for the bartender. "Yeah. Except it doesn't feel like it when you got twenty-five years in the middle of it. Don't know how much I like the idea of Luke…or anyone for that matter…with Tori. But can't decide if I'm even allowed to be the protective big brother after all these years."

"Luke's a good guy." Jake only smiled at Seth's

sharp look. "Yes. I know. I'm biased as his brother. But that doesn't change what is fact. Fact you're aware of as well."

"I like Luke. Doesn't mean I'm good with the idea of whatever it is he's starting with my sister. With all she's got going on right now, not sure she needs more added to her shoulders."

Jake waited for the bartender to set the beers between them. Thanked him. "I don't know Tori well but she strikes me as a woman who's very good at taking care of herself. I'm guessing, if Luke was too much, she'd let him know."

"The sad thing is"—Seth finished off the last drink of his beer and reached for the new one—"I don't know her that well either, right now. So all I can do is hope you're right. Still doesn't mean I have to like it."

Jake's answering smile was a bit too knowing. "No. Don't suppose it does. Though I don't have any experience to know with a life of only brothers. But, I'm guessing, Tori would find it good, knowing, even after the years apart, her brother still cared enough to worry about her."

Seth couldn't know for sure. And there seemed to be a lot of the not knowing these days.

Maybe it was the beers. Or the time spent with Tori. But tonight, he felt the twinge of loss stronger than ever before with the thought of all he and Tori had missed. This strange getting to know each other again without knowing what, if any, boundaries he might be crossing was a new reality for him.

He should have been the brother scaring her with spiders. The one carrying her inside when she'd scraped her knee. Shot dirty looks to any boy daring to date her through her teenage years.

He should have been the one to know her better than anyone. Share the kind of relationship with her Jake had with his brothers.

But somebody had taken that from him and Tori. He wanted to know why.

He wanted to know who.

****

He picked slowly at his food, nursing his way through two beers. And still, he sat near the door of the pub, watching the same table he'd watched for hours.

His laptop popped up, and Anton feigned the look of one who worked. A man sitting alone and doing nothing drew curiosity. But, in today's world, a man sitting with an open laptop beside him barely caused a second look, no matter the hours he spent.

And now was the time to be careful. He knew the police searched. Wouldn't stop till they found answers to who had forced Tori from the road.

He was good. Knew how to keep from being identified in even the most horrid of crimes. But it still was no excuse not to be cautious and keep himself as low-key and unseen as possible.

So he'd moved around his laptop with the outside look of one with a purpose. Watched the table as first the three women occupied it, their laughter drifting through the pub. The smiles on their faces gave proof Tori was beginning to form ties here in Snow Ridge.

A reality Filip would not be pleased to learn. One Anton had no intention of sharing but didn't doubt the old man would learn, regardless.

And it would be the least of Filip's worries.

Because he'd seen the rest after the two had left,

leaving Tori with her brother and the Chief. And what she'd shared earlier was nothing compared to what was growing between her and her brother—the very one Filip wanted her far away from.

There was a connection between them. One that couldn't be mistaken even by a stranger's eye. The way they moved, talked, laughed, even the looks they exchanged. There was no doubt to the blood they shared.

But there was more. The way they'd tucked their heads together to talk. The looks they shared over the table, sharing something others were no part of.

To think he could break that up wasn't something he was so sure of anymore. He'd find his way. He didn't doubt it. But with his hands tied by Filip on what he could and couldn't do to convince her to leave and the bond that was there between brother and sister, he was going to have one hell of a time finishing this job with a success.

And that didn't even bring into the equation the addition of the dark-haired, hard-as-rock, Chief of Police. Luke was his name, if he remembered right. Part of some important family in these parts.

They'd left together. Tori and the Chief. And there was no question, at least in the eyes of the Chief, what was to come once they had the rest of the night to themselves.

Anton cursed and shoved down the last of his beer.

This job was getting deeper and harder by the minute.

He'd come to this little nothing town in the middle of the Rockies and expected to glide through. Be done before he barely started.

Instead, he found himself with a hell of a lot harder of a struggle than he'd come up against back in Chicago. Back where he dealt with some of the worst of the worst.

Failure wasn't an option for his flawless record. But, damn. He sure was tempted to give up and walk away from this one. From what was turning out to be much more than he ever anticipated.

Chapter Nineteen

Two mornings in a row waking up to Luke beside her in bed.

Tori couldn't even pretend she was okay with it.

Using the excuse of coffee, she eased away from Luke's hold while he softly snored beside her. Quietly throwing on a t-shirt and sweats, she slipped from the bedroom.

She didn't want him up yet. Wasn't ready to face him.

In the kitchen, the sun barely peeking through the window, she went through the automatic steps of getting the pot brewing while her mind wandered.

She hadn't wanted him to stay. Had been set against it. The fact she'd failed in sending him away sank like a heavy rock in the pit of her stomach.

She knew her boundaries. Knew where and when to draw the lines, keeping others at a safe distance. It was something she'd perfected over the years. Foster home after foster home, never being good enough to be considered one's own, had taken its toll, leaving her feeling as if she truly didn't belong anywhere or with anyone.

But she'd toughened up. Learned to survive. And she'd done well for many years keeping the walls in place, preventing any hint of such pain or loss from becoming a part of her life again.

Until Luke.

Until those deep, hazel eyes of his. The touch of his rough hands gliding over her skin. The heat igniting every time his lips touched hers.

She wasn't, never had been, one who had men falling at her feet. But she'd had those like Luke—seeking more time from her than she was willing to give.

And she'd always stayed firm, never allowing the risk of opening herself up to the heartache and loss she'd known through childhood.

She didn't have close friends. Didn't have family. Certainly didn't have any real relationships to speak of. She had only her. Just the way she liked it.

But coming to Snow Ridge was changing that. She was rediscovering a relationship with her brother and finding friendship with Cara and Jackie.

And now…waking up twice in as many days with a man who tested every bit of her control. Left her still wanting for more even as she sat there, the coffee brewing, calling herself a fool.

She couldn't do it. The fear racing up her spine, demanding she run as far and as fast as she could, was proof enough to that.

Reaching into the cupboard she wrapped her fingers around the handle of a ceramic mug and pulled out another as she heard Luke's steps coming down the hall. They'd have coffee, sit down at the table, and she'd let him know, though the sex had been great…even better than that…it wasn't something she was willing to repeat.

****

Luke heard her get up and make her way to the

kitchen.

His first instinct had been to grab her and pull her back to him as he had the day before. He hadn't. Instead, he decided to let her go, figuring he couldn't afford another day enjoying a bit more time in bed with her no matter how badly he was tempted.

But as he walked into the kitchen and caught sight of the look coming back at him, he quickly regretted his decision.

There was nothing good to come from a woman's serious expression after a night of making love. Every reasonable, sane man knew that. Would have turned on their heels and escaped as quickly as they could.

He was tempted to do just that and ward off any chance at discussing whatever brewed inside that head of hers with an excuse of having to get to the office to take care of things.

And he would have if it had been any other woman. But with Tori, he couldn't do it.

And that alone turned his attitude sour before he heard what she had to say.

"I don't have much for food." She pushed a steaming mug into his hands without looking at him. "But I thought I could toast us some bagels for breakfast."

"You don't need to bother." He heard the surliness in his voice before she flashed her emerald eyes at him.

And damn, he didn't need to accelerate whatever it was he was sure he was in for. "But a bagel would be great. Thank you."

Though she didn't smile there was, thankfully, a dull to the fire in the look she'd turned on him.

He'd take it.

Sensing he wasn't needed, or wanted, to help her put together their breakfast, he settled at the table, watching her move from the cupboard to the refrigerator to the toaster.

And it was evil, sitting there and watching her. His need grew as the morning sun silhouetted her chestnut curls and her sweet, enticing scent surrounded him. A reminder of all he'd had only hours ago.

All, he was sure, that was about to be doused.

Two plates heavy with cream cheese smothered bagels in her hands, Tori turned back. Again without looking him in the eye, she set one plate in front of him before taking her own place where she'd left her coffee across the table.

"So tell me what it is." In no mood for waiting and guessing, he stared at her over the half bagel he lifted to his mouth.

Caught by surprise, Tori fumbled her own bagel in her hand. "*It* is nothing, really." She made a point of calming her nerves before reaching for her coffee. "Since we don't have much besides sex between us."

The flash of anger in his eyes was impossible to miss. Not that it mattered since she was certain she spoke the truth. Other than a couple of great nights in bed, they didn't have much more to claim.

And that should have made it easy. So why was she struggling to say what needed to be said?

"This," she waved a hand in the air. "Whatever it is between us. It's not me. Not something I'm comfortable with."

He looked at her, doubt heavy in his eyes. "You're not comfortable with great sex between two consenting adults?"

That wasn't it and he knew it. "It's not that." She scowled at him over the span of the table. "There's more to it with me and you. And that's not a risk I can take."

Confused, his heavy gaze searched as he took a slow, deliberate bite from his bagel. "So...when it's nothing but sex, that's okay. But even the suggestion there might be more sends you running?"

She didn't like how he put it. Deciding she'd lost her appetite for the last half of her bagel, she shoved up from her chair. "I'm not running from anything. I'm just stepping back from something I'm not comfortable with." She dumped her plate in the sink, refusing to look back at him.

"That's nothing but a prettier way of putting it." Grabbing his own plate and empty mug, he pushed his way beside her at the sink. "Either way, it's still running."

She puffed, ready to argue. She had it in her mind, everything she wanted to say. But it all went blank the minute his lips met hers, sucking every thought from her mind and leaving only heat instead.

Even with all she claimed, she couldn't stop her instant reaction. Falling into him, she opened so he could take all he sought.

Which was the problem. She did her best to remind herself of that as he pressed tight, leaving no doubt to the desire continuing to exist.

"You can try to run." He swept an arm around her waist and nipped at her bottom lip. "For an old ranch boy like me, the chase is part of the fun."

He took her again before she had a chance to respond. His mouth demanded a truth she fought to deny. She wanted to push him away. Wanted to pull him even closer.

It was a battle she hated. Was trying to do away with, if he'd let her.

Instead he took, drawing everything from her until finally stepping away, leaving her weak and unsteady on her feet. Grabbing the edge of the counter, she did her best to collect her wits back.

"I think," she sucked in a harsh breath, "you should probably go."

His answering smile held too much satisfaction for her peace of mind. Still, he didn't argue. With one last peck against her cheek and a quick goodbye pet for Derby, he found his way out the door. The answering thud of it closing behind him echoed around her.

And she couldn't even say if she'd done any good or simply created more damage.

****

He shouldn't have been smiling, nearly whistling, as he walked into the station.

The woman he'd spent two amazing nights in bed with had just tried to give him the brush off. For normal men, it would have been reason to brood over a cold beer. But for Luke, he figured he must not be a normal man because what he felt was far from brooding.

In fact, he felt energized. Ready and willing to face the challenge laid before him.

Which he wasn't convinced was a good thing. But it didn't change it.

There was something about Tori. Something that intrigued him, leaving him wanting more no matter how much he was given.

Brushing away the flakes of snow that had begun

to fall on his way in, he tugged his jacket free from his arms and swung it over a chair in his office.

Settling behind his desk, he pulled Tori's face to mind and saw the tremor in her bottom lip when he'd take her. The soft shadows in her emerald eyes when he was buried deep inside.

He heard the soft lift of her laughter. Felt the delicate wisp of her fingers against him as she talked, drawing him into whatever she had to say.

Yeah. He needed that. More than he was willing to admit yet.

She could try running. Give it her best shot. It wouldn't stop him no matter how hard she protested.

Getting his computer up and running for the day, he flipped through the reports waiting for him, checking off what needed his approval and making notes of what needed to be addressed when he spoke with his men for the day.

And always she was there.

Switching to his email, he scanned through the normal communications, printing or saving what was needed before deleting the rest.

And then he saw it…the one waiting at the bottom. It came from the very same department in Chicago he'd been trying to get answers from.

Opening it, he didn't recognize the name. It wasn't one he'd spoken to in his efforts to discover the truth. There hadn't been a reference to a Detective Olsen in what little he'd been able to learn.

But, for whatever the reason, he'd reached out to Luke. Which, in itself, with the walls he hit, was a miracle. And his message was short and to the point.

We need to talk. But not by department

communication.

He left a number for what Luke assumed was his own personal phone. Nothing more.

Forgetting about all else needing done, he grabbed his phone and hoped for the best.

****

"This should help." Coming out of the back office, Cara held up the bottle of Chardonnay she carried in one hand with two wine glasses clasped in the other.

They'd locked the doors for the day. And now a pile of boxes waited for their attention. Jackie had been shooed off to take care of her precious baby boy, leaving Tori and Cara to handle the stocking of new items.

And, yes, the wine would help, Tori decided as she stepped up, grabbing the glasses from Cara and setting them on the counter. After starting the morning the way she had with Luke, the wine was definitely a better way to end the day.

Cara poured the wine, handing one her way. "So should we unpack or gossip first?" The gleam in her eyes left little doubt where she was headed.

For a moment Tori felt the need to shut it out— shut her out. Sharing wasn't exactly her thing. She preferred long conversations with herself in the mirror. It was about all the true experience she'd had before reaching Snow Ridge.

But there was something about Cara. Something kind and caring that drew her in. She and Jackie had tested and opened up a part of her she hadn't been aware existed…a need for true friendships.

"How about both?" Checking on Derby snoozing in his bed behind the counter, Tori carried her wine glass to the pile of boxes. "I have a feeling I'll need something to do with my hands."

She didn't need any more explanation for Cara to understand. Nodding, she joined Tori at the boxes with her own wine glass. "Did you know, Cade is the most irritating man I have ever dealt with in my life?"

Without looking at Tori, she broke the seal on the first box and pulled out a set of hand-blown glass goblets. "When I first came back to Snow Ridge, after a decade away, he was the very last person I wanted anything to do with."

Tori looked at her for a moment, surprised. "I've heard enough to know your story isn't all sunshine and roses. But to see the two of you together, I'd never guess at anything too bad between you."

Cara's answering laugh filled the store. Even Derby perked up long enough to give her a look before settling back down. "Oh. We've had our bad. It might not seem like it now. But our share was there."

"And even after we worked through the bad." She pushed to her feet, carefully arranging the goblet on a shelf behind them. "I still fought him when it came to any kind of commitment between us. I was sure I was happy with nothing more than sex. I didn't need anymore."

Intrigued, Tori reached in the open box, pulling out the bowls to match the goblets. "There's nothing wrong with sex being enough."

"There isn't." Cara nodded her agreement as she took a slow, thoughtful sip from her wine. "If that's all you're sure you want and need in your life."

Though there was a moment of hesitation, Tori shoved it away as she arranged the bowls next to the goblets. "For me, that *is* all I want. All I have ever needed."

She came back to the boxes and picked up her own glass. "I've never had, or wanted, a serious relationship with anyone. Hell, even this...talking with you over a glass of wine...isn't something I've known or wanted before in my life."

"I'm good on my own." She went back to the box, tossing out the bubble wrap. "Good in living in today without having to worry about what the future might bring. Without having to worry about relationships bringing those future worries to reality."

Over the rim of her glass, Cara studied her. "It's interesting how much I lived in the past and let it shape me. And how much you, in turn, live in today and let it shape you."

Tori didn't know how to respond. Wasn't sure she should even dare. How much did you share with one you still barely knew?

"The problem we have," Cara continued without her response, "is whether we live in yesterday or today, we have to deal with a Grady brother along the way."

"They can be annoying." That much Tori could freely share.

Cara's answer was a quick laugh and a shake of her head, tossing ebony curls over her shoulders. "Yes, they can. I won't try to deny that. But—"

Tori looked at her. Knew there was more coming.

"There's a lot of good in them too. Every single one of them." One box emptied, Cara threw it aside before unsealing the next.

Tori came down beside her, resting back on her heels. "I know Luke is, overall, a good guy." She went to what she knew they'd been dancing around. "Doesn't change the fact he's also annoying. And not what I need in my life."

"So you're done with him, then?" Cara pulled out a hand-stitched quilt, shaking out the folds for a good look.

"Yes. No." Tori let out a harsh breath. "Hell, I don't know."

Amusement mixed with sympathy in the look Cara shot her way before pushing back to her feet. "Well, that sounds definite."

Deciding one glass of wine was definitely not enough for this kind of talk, Tori made her way to the bottle, topping off both their glasses. "There's no way to have definite with Luke."

Handing Cara her glass, she rested a gentle hip against one of the unopened boxes and took a slow sip from her Chardonnay. "I tried letting him know this morning whatever this is between us isn't going to work. But, I have a feeling I wasn't too convincing. I'm not even sure he understood, or at least accepted, a word I said."

"He left your head spinning, didn't he?" Cara took a sip of her own.

Thinking back to the morning in the kitchen, Tori nodded. He'd done just that. To the point, she'd stood in the same place he left her for several minutes before finally shaking her head in anger and heading off for a long, hot shower.

She'd stood under the heavy spray, cursing him and herself while wondering what, if anything, she'd accomplished. Had he heard her? Or had she just sparked some part of him, pushing him to want even more what she wasn't ready, or willing, to give?

"Is that what Cade did to you?" Though she was sure she already knew the answer, wouldn't be too eager to like it, she asked anyway.

As she expected, Cara nodded. "He did. Over and over again. Through some of the hardest, he left me wondering if I was coming or going. Made me sure I was going crazy."

Yeah. That was about the way Luke was leaving her to feel. The difference, she had no intention of going anywhere near what Cara and Cade discovered in one another. The very thought left her terrified.

Whatever it was about these Grady brothers, she wasn't sure she wanted to know or experience any more. Luke was a threat. She felt it clear to the bottom of her toes.

He had the ability, no matter how nerve-wracking it was, to tempt her places she didn't belong. It was better to stay away from him.

Any other option was too great a risk. One she wasn't willing or ready to take.

Chapter Twenty

Luke didn't figure Tori would be happy to see him the next morning. And the look of her when he walked into Precious Gems proved him right.

He might have considered giving her a bit more time to settle, but his call with Detective Olsen made that impossible.

And he was the Chief of Police, tasked with taking care of those in Snow Ridge. As well as a good friend and soon to be brother-in-law of the owner of the very store where she worked. It was ridiculous to think, or even try, to stay clear of one another.

Plus, he really liked the sight of her. Liked being around her. That wasn't something he was willing to give up. Not when he had only barely discovered such enjoyment.

At least Cara's smile was welcoming as she came out from behind the counter. "Funny." She held out her hands, drawing him in for a soft kiss on the cheek. "We both live at the ranch but I seem to see a lot more of you these days than ever before."

Her voice was low enough for only him to hear. Her gaze held a wisdom of so much more than she should know. "You're either a crazy man or a daring one."

"A bit of both." Dropping his own kiss on her delicate cheek, he moved around her, putting his attention on the one he sought.

Tori made a point of not looking at him as she concentrated on the receipts spread out before her. At her side, Jackie watched with interest sparking deep in her curious gaze.

He hitched a hip against the opposite end of the counter, waiting with every ounce of patience he could dig up for her to acknowledge him.

It didn't happen easily. It seemed, the longer he stared, the more stubborn she grew. But he refused to give up, knowing, at some point, he'd win.

Unable to take anymore, she slapped an open palm against the receipts and looked at him. "Can I help you with something?"

The fire and flash were enough to have him wanting her all over again. His hands itched to grab her and drag her up the steps to her place to find everything he'd spent the night dreaming about.

"It's more like what I can help you with." He flashed a smile, strangely pleased to see it irritated her. "Though, perhaps you'd prefer I leave the investigation into your parents' murder alone just as you expect me to leave you alone."

It was a low dig, he knew. But damn it, he wasn't a bad guy. Didn't think he was all that hard to look at. And he did take pride in treating a woman good.

But this one. You'd have thought he'd committed some terrible crime in the look she passed him. In her reluctance to even have a conversation with him. He still carried with him the feel of her pressed tightly against him. The thrill of watching as her world exploded. To think he could brush it off as nothing and simply turn his back and walk away.

It was as ridiculous as her belief she could do the same.

"What are you talking about?" The receipts completely forgotten, she leaned in closer. "Do you know more about what happened to my parents?"

The vulnerability in her eyes is what did it. Coming down from whatever crazy emotions he'd felt when walking in the door, he softened his look and laid a hand over where hers rested on the counter. "Not yet. But, hopefully, I soon will. I leave for Chicago in the morning to meet a detective who claims to have information for me he's only willing to share in person."

"I'm going with you." She came out from behind the counter. And then, as rational thought settled, looked to Cara. "Or, I'm hoping I can go with you."

Cara's answering smile was understanding as she made her way to the counter, throwing a friendly arm around Tori's waist. "You do what you have to do." No longer acknowledging Luke's presence, she looked hard at Tori. "Don't worry about anything here. We can handle it."

Coming around on the other side, Jackie held Tori in the same way. And it so quickly became a force…the three of them against all else. Coming together for one of their own. "You need to go. We'd be crap if we couldn't handle things here so you could do that."

Except they were missing one very important fact—he hadn't agreed to any of it. And as Chief, the choice was up to him. A choice he'd already put plenty of thought in to and decided it would be too much of a risk. Especially after all that had happened recently.

"I've already made the arrangements. And you

weren't included." He knew it sounded harsh. Wasn't sorry for it. He wanted her here safe, regardless of what her new-found friends decided for her.

All three sets of eyes turned on him. Harsh and angry.

It was Tori, though, who spoke for herself, jumping in before they could. "I can include myself without you." She glared at him. Seemed to gain strength from Cara and Jackie at her sides. "I know Chicago. It's my place. And I can get there as easy as you."

Sucking in a deep breath, hoping to pull everything back to reason, he dared a step closer, ignoring the triple set of disgusted gazes staring back at him. "You're safer here. I don't know what to expect. Don't know anything but somebody I've never met, never knew about, claims he has some information about what happened to your parents. I can't even know if it's true or if he has a different motive planned."

"But, yet, you're still willing to go." She looked at him hard. "Regardless of the doubt and risks involved."

"Yes. For you. Because you deserve to know the truth."

His honesty earned an easing of the harsh looks Cara and Jackie directed his way. But from Tori, there was no change.

"You're right." She stepped out of their hold and came closer. "I deserve to know the truth. I also deserve to be there if someone is finally willing to give it."

He was surprised when she reached for him, gathering his hands in hers. "You've barely started this fight. But for me, it's been a part of everything I am since I was three years old."

Cara and Jackie came up behind her, their support

still clearly with her.

"I need and deserve to be part of this." Her emerald eyes hardened, leaving no room for argument. "I know you're only trying to protect me. But what you're trying so hard to protect me from is something I've already faced and dealt with for many years. Long before you came along. I handled it then. It's an insult to suggest I can't handle it now."

And, well damn, she made sense. Had a point.

But how was a man to admit that with three women staring him down?

"I'm not convinced it's a good idea." He tried instead of giving in. "It would be safer if I went alone then came back to tell you what, if anything, I learned."

Tori said nothing, only stared. Cara's and Jackie's expression matched hers.

Well, hell. For as much as he knew he could carry it on, saving his pride wasn't worth it. And Tori made good points even though he hated to admit it. What he'd believed was the best choice, she'd proven he'd been wrong.

"I'm leaving first thing in the morning," he gave instead of argument. "And I won't be waiting around for any excuses for being late."

Tori smiled. "You won't be waiting. I promise."

He didn't figure he would. And that scared him about as much as her going along.

****

They made their way into Denver, boarded a flight, and arrived in Chicago before noon.

For Tori, she'd expected different when they'd exited the plane and made their way through the busy airport.

Chicago was home. The only one she'd known before Snow Ridge. But the longing and loss she expected didn't come as they moved out with the crowd to wait for a taxi.

"You okay?" Luke's gaze carried worry as he held the door for her.

Nodding, she slipped along the cracked plastic, making room for him to join her. Giving the driver the address for their hotel, he settled back into the seat.

On the interstate, through the crazy traffic that was so much a part of Chicago, Tori watched everything she knew and was so familiar with pass by. Her heart should be aching and calling out for what had always been home.

But, though she would always love Chicago, there was no call. No ache. Only the gentle, welcome understanding of a place that would always hold a special spot in her heart.

It didn't seem right. Didn't feel right. But still, it was there.

And so she'd accept it.

Resting back on the seat, she stole a look at Luke and wondered what ran through his head. Though it made little sense, she hoped he would find good in the place that was so much a part of her. See the beauty she'd found throughout her life in a city that was, so often, judged for the ugly rather than the good it held.

Feeling her gaze, he turned and smiled. "I was thinking, after our meeting this afternoon, you could be my tour guide. Show me all that's great about this city of yours. We only have tonight. Might as well make the most of it."

Whether he knew it or not, it was exactly what she

needed to hear. And even though she knew she was a fool for doing so, she agreed.

With a satisfied smile, he settled back for the rest of their ride. She did the same, watching through the window as so many familiar sights passed her by.

Her breath caught when the taxi turned toward a part of town she hadn't expected to find herself. Shaking her head, she turned wide eyes on Luke before turning back for the window, watching while the taxi pulled into a smooth circular drive and stopped in front of elegant, double glass doors.

They were right there. On the river. In front of one of the fancy hotels she'd only ever admired from afar. "It's not what I expected."

"Surprises are good." Paying the taxi driver, Luke waited for Tori to climb out from her side while he waved down a bellboy.

He'd admit, it was a bit much for a night. But the look on her face made all the last-minute change of plans worth it.

He'd never planned on putting this trip on the city's bill, giving him the freedom to do more once it was decided she'd be going along.

Stepping into the hotel's bright, airy atrium, he watched her, enjoying every smile. Leading the way toward the front desk, tucked away in a corner so as not to disrupt the spacious beauty welcoming guests, he wondered if the smile would continue once she learned they'd be sharing a room.

They'd shared a bed. Woken in the arms of one another. The idea of ignoring such a fact and pretending they'd each need their own rooms for this trip was too far out of his reach.

He'd heard what she'd said the other morning back in her kitchen. Didn't doubt, at that point, it was what she meant. But a man could hope.

And if it took reserving one of the smaller suites at a fancy downtown Chicago hotel to help along that hope, it was the least he could do.

She didn't protest, though her smile wavered a bit. On the elevator trip to the eleventh floor, she looked at him as if ready to say something but decided against it.

He took it as a good sign. Chose not to push it.

Then there was nothing but her smile and wonder again as they stepped inside the suite. "It's beautiful." She turned in a quick circle before looking at him. "So beautiful."

And hope kicked back in full force.

While she roamed, Luke answered the door for the bellboy. Collecting their luggage and tipping him on his way out the door, he went in search of her.

She was in the large, bright bathroom, turning circles within all the marble. "I wish we had more than a night." She looked at him resting against the door. "This room alone demands a day of pampering."

If he could give her another night, he would. Later, he promised silently. After all this chaos surrounding her was figured out.

For now, they had other plans to take care of.

And it killed him to have to remind her. "We've got only about an hour before we need to head out to keep our scheduled meeting."

He looked at the large Jacuzzi tub at his side, wishing he could take her there with the jets bubbling around them. Another time, he reminded himself. "We'll take care of our meeting. You can show me your

Chicago. And then the rest of the night is ours. Here. Where only you and I will matter."

He saw fear battle with desire. Waited. Wondered which would win.

Though hesitant, her slow smile told him all he needed to know. Daring a step closer, he pulled her close, dropping his mouth to hers.

Dragging her up and away with him, he let the hope rise even higher.

****

Their taxi dropped them off at a small dark bar just outside of Chicago.

Even for Tori, it was an area she was unfamiliar with.

Shoved in a strip mall between a dry cleaner and a Chinese restaurant, there was no flash or fashion to the place. Only the old tired look, feel, and smell of a place appealing to a select few.

Working through the dim light, they found a table near the back. "How will we know who he is?" She took a seat next to Luke, scanning the thin crowd gathered around the tables tossed recklessly through the bar.

"He said he'd find us." Luke took a slow look over their surroundings, seeming to take it all into memory.

"What can I get you?" Looking as tired and worn as the bar itself, the dark-haired waitress tossed two flimsy cocktail napkins on the table in front of them.

Realizing it would gain attention not needed, coming into the bar without ordering a drink, they both placed their orders for a beer and a glass of iced water.

And then they waited.

The waiting was hard as she stared at the front

door. She hadn't allowed herself to dwell on what this Detective Olsen might have to say. But now, there was no stopping it. No way around the nerves jumping fiercely through her gut.

After twenty-five years, was it possible someone had the answers she'd been denied for so long? Could she actually be given back a part of herself she'd lost that night long ago by learning the truth?

It was frightening to consider.

As if sensing her struggle, Luke rested a gentle hand on her leg as the waitress returned with their drinks.

"He's here." He kept his voice low so only she could hear. "He just came in."

"How do you know?" She followed the path of his gaze, catching sight of the older, stocky man at the front of the bar. "I thought you had no idea what he looks like."

Luke kept a careful eye on him as he moved through the tables. "I don't. But a cop knows a cop. Can't imagine this place draws many. So odds are—"

He trailed off as the older man's gaze met his through the murky light. He glanced from Luke to Tori and there was a moment of recognition.

He knew who she was. There was no question.

She watched him move toward them. Though he'd been the one to call the meeting, he looked less than eager. The lines around his face were hard. The gaze in his dull, brown eyes carried a hint of doubt.

He approached with an outstretched hand for Luke. "You must be Chief Grady." His shake was firm. "I'm Detective Olsen. And you must be Victoria Mundola."

His searching gaze made her uncomfortable.

Accepting his hand, she forced a smile, wondering what he was looking for as he stared at her. What answers he might have hidden away.

He took a seat beside Luke then waved down the waitress. "I know this isn't the best of places." He divided his attention between them after ordering a beer of his own. "But I didn't want to risk being seen. Too many jurisdictions crossing too many paths around here."

He thanked the waitress as she set a beer in front of him. "So, tell me, why a sudden interest in a murder case from twenty-five years ago?" Though he directed the question at Luke, his gaze rested heavy on Tori.

"There are some current incidents I believe are tied directly to it." Luke took a slow sip from his beer, watching Olsen over the rim. "In fact, I'd wager to say, they are a direct result of the case."

Olsen shook his head and looked as if he fought some inner battle. He had been the one to contact Luke to bring them here. There'd be no reason if he didn't have something to offer. Something he felt was worth taking the risk of sharing.

"I take it you're involved in these *incidents*." He looked at Tori. "Considering—"

He drifted off, stalling with a long sip from his beer.

"Considering what?" Pressing her hands flat on the table, she leaned closer. Fear and impatience warred inside. She wanted to know so much. Was afraid of what she'd learn.

"You've grown up but I remember you. It's the eyes. The same ones I remember looking back at me all those years ago." He looked as if he wanted to reach for her before quickly stuffing his hand beneath the table.

"I was new to the force, then. Still green." He turned his attention to Luke as if looking at Tori was too difficult for him. "I hadn't been part of the initial call. I didn't pick up on it till they reached the station."

He went back to his beer for another healthy drink. "Won't ever forget the moment when they brought you and your brother in." He dared only a quick glance her way. "My girl had just been born a few months earlier. So to see another little girl in such pain, it was almost more than I was prepared to handle."

"Like I said,"—he tossed a half smile Luke's way—"I was still green. Hadn't seen all the ugliness yet that comes with the job."

"What happened after you saw them being brought into the station?" Luke leaned in close, forgetting everything but the details he was being fed.

"They separated them immediately. Took Victoria into one of the interrogation rooms. Left her brother at one of the detective's desks."

He sucked in a harsh breath. "I remember asking about it. Why they separated them when it was clear they wanted to be together."

"And what were you told?" Tori tightened beside him and Luke wished for a way to ease whatever was going on inside her head as she heard the events replayed yet another time.

"I was told it wasn't my worry." Olsen glanced over his shoulder as if worried someone might be near enough to hear what he shared. "It was made clear I was to ask no questions. Only follow the orders given."

Picking up his beer, he finished it off and waved the waitress down for another. "I went to argue and was pulled away and set straight on the manner of things."

"Set straight?" Though Luke asked the question, Olsen put his attention on Tori.

There was something there. In the way he looked at her. A troubled look, speaking of regret. Of doubt. Of being forced to face an ugly truth. "You don't know Chicago without knowing our organized crime history. And twenty-five years ago, they still had their pull in many of the department's business. Not to say, they don't still have their share today. But not as it once was."

"Organized crime? You aren't suggesting my parents' death had anything to do with some kind of mob, are you?" Tori felt dizzy with it. There was no way such a thing could be true. It was the sort of stuff you watched in movies. Not learned was part of your own past.

"Not in the way you're imagining." He shook his head as another beer was placed in front of him. "It's not the flash and flare people tend to believe and see so often in movies."

He looked almost amused by it. Came close to his first smile of the night. "Make no mistake, these people are criminals. There isn't anything romantic or exciting about them. They kill, lie, steal, and cheat to get what they want. This isn't the Al Capone, Italian mob so many write into our fiction. This is the real thing."

"And how does this play into what happened to Tori?" Luke gave him a long, curious look.

Olsen looked around the bar again before coming back to the table. "Though it was never said outright, there was never a question that what was happening had orders coming down from those with dirty-hand ties within the department."

"What does that mean?" Tori looked from Luke to Olsen, wishing one of them would speak in words she understood.

Luke grabbed her hand, holding it tight. "It means, it wasn't routine procedure but was, instead, dictated directly from somebody outside the department. It means others were pulling the strings to get what they wanted in making sure you and Seth were kept apart."

"But why?" Needing something to do with her hands, she wrapped them around her beer glass. "Why would someone care enough to keep me from my brother?"

"Because you had seen too much."

The single sentence from Olsen fell like ice water over Tori. He sat so stiff, uncomfortable now, across from her. Hesitant, it seemed, to look at her.

"I heard them talk," his voice was low, nearly a whisper. "Some of the other officers around me. Somebody—whoever was pulling the strings, I'm guessing—was very afraid. Of you. Of what you saw. You were to be kept alone and isolated until it was determined what information you would share."

Tori felt sick. Pressing a flat palm to her stomach, she fought it back. Flashes from her nightmares fought their way back. She tried to think back to the frightened little girl she'd been. Imagine what it must have been like, kept away from her brother and forced to be alone so others could find what answers she held.

But she couldn't put herself there. Had no memories from anything other than the nightmares haunting her for so many years. "What would have happened if I'd shared something others didn't want me to know?"

Olsen's expression darkened, telling her all she needed to know. "After it was decided you weren't an immediate threat." He winced at the harsh tone of his words. "It was about control and making sure you wouldn't ever have a chance to remember."

"What was I supposed to remember?" There was desperation now as images flashed, dark and frightening, through her mind.

Luke reached for her, twisting his fingers with hers. As much as she hated to admit it, it helped.

"Never heard directly." Olsen shrugged, the shadows still darkening his dull eyes. "But if I had to guess…what you saw that night would have been enough to solve who killed your parents."

And now she really was going to be sick. Fighting it back, she held on with all she had, refusing to give in to the horror facing her down.

Though she knew it wouldn't sit well in her already irritated stomach, she took a slow sip from her beer, needing something to help settle the terrifying thoughts running wild.

She thought of the hazy images from her nightmares. Of the one she thought she should recognize.

It was him. She felt it deep in her bones. Figuring out who he was, why she felt she should have known him, was the key to understanding everything that had happened. From the terrible night of losing her parents to the frightening realities of the present day.

She just needed to remember. Needed to find a way to get through whatever blocks stood in her way.

If she did she might finally have the answers she

sought for so long.
Might finally have some peace.

Chapter Twenty-One

Luke worried about her. Tori felt the truth of it from the moment they left the bar.

In the back of the cab, his gaze weighed heavy on her as they set out for her promised tour of what she loved about Chicago. But, instead of seeing what passed by them out the car windows, he watched only her.

"Enough." She slammed an open palm against his thigh. "You can stare as hard as you need. You won't see any different. And you won't catch me breaking down. It's not going to happen."

He covered her hand with his own. "I'm worried about you. What you heard. What we learned. It couldn't have been easy."

"It wasn't," she admitted, knowing it was useless to lie. "At the end, I was sure I'd end up running to the bathroom to throw up. Not that I should be admitting that to you." She turned away, shaking her head.

He pressed a finger under her chin and turned her back. "I'd have been more worried if you hadn't admitted it."

Her skin burned where his finger rested. She did her best to ignore it. "I'll admit, I need to process and work through some things. But I have to allow myself to do it in bits. If I try to handle it all in full, I'll be asking for a breakdown."

"And you don't have to handle it alone." Easing her hand from his thigh, he turned it over, curling his fingers with hers. "Remember that."

She didn't want to. The look in his eyes and gentle tone of his voice was enough to cause the itch, the one pushing her to, again, end whatever this was between them before it grew out of her control.

But not tonight.

Tonight, she just wanted to forget and enjoy.

So she took him through the Chicago she knew. Away from the hot tourist spots. To everyday life where people simply lived, day to day.

She took him down the block where she'd lived before moving to Snow Ridge. Had the cab driver move slowly along the same route she'd taken every day to the bookstore she so loved.

"Mrs. Griggs won't be shutting down for another hour." She shook her head as they drove by the still brightly lit windows. "She was wonderful to work for but very firm in her ways."

There was a tinge of loss hitting as she stared out the window, reflecting back to the many nights she'd been there, closing up for the night. "Seven on the dot. Not a minute earlier and certainly not a minute later," she remembered as the driver passed by, picking up speed to keep up with traffic. "Even in the worst of storms. The slowest of days. There was no changing closing time."

"Do you miss it? Working there?"

She thought about it. Put herself back in the bookstore. She'd liked it. There was no denying it. For so long, the books had been her passion. She'd enjoyed getting to know the importance of the ones passing through the store. Helping customers find exactly what they were looking for.

It was so much a part of her. A part she would miss.

But then she thought of Precious Gems and the friendship she'd formed with Cara and Jackie. "I do. But not in the way I first thought I would."

She stared out the window as the cab driver made his way to the interstate, thinking about what she'd left and what she'd discovered. "When I first learned where Seth was and made the decision to leave everything I knew behind, it was one of the most frightening things I had ever done."

"I was sure I'd hate every bit of it. Leaving here. Starting over in Snow Ridge." She smiled, thoughts of those months leading up to her big move floating through her head. "But, I told myself it would be worth it, getting the chance to reunite with my brother. To see if there was a chance between us."

"What I didn't count on," she pulled in a deep breath, relaxing back into her seat. "Was to actually find so much I liked in Snow Ridge, outside of reuniting with my brother."

Before she could react, Luke bent forward, dropping a quick kiss on her lips. "Like the handsome Chief of Police who came to your rescue in the middle of a blizzard?"

There was such a boyish charm to his smile, she couldn't help but laugh. "Yes. Like that." She shook her head at him. "And getting the job at Precious Gems. Meeting Cara and Jackie. It's all been something I never expected."

"Better than I could have ever expected," she

added, turning to stare out the window as the cab driver wound his way through the last remains of rush-hour traffic.

Luke wanted to try a true Chicago deep-dish pizza. She wasn't going to disappoint. The place they were headed wasn't the famous and flashy so many tourists found themselves at.

It was local. A favorite among those born and bred here.

She'd made Luke call ahead since that was the way of it at Bart's. The pizza needed its time and there was no one happy there if you showed up without first placing your order.

All of it was so much a part of her. Her past. Everything she'd become over the years. This, the side of Chicago so many never saw or experienced, was who she was.

Yet, now she was becoming something different. Someone she hadn't thought existed.

Glancing at Luke. The hard lines of his face. The tumble of dark hair over his forehead. She saw the mix of where she had brought her life. The future that lingered, mixing with the past she'd been bred from.

****

"I ate too much." It was at least the third time Tori proclaimed such information since they'd left the restaurant.

Luke waited for her to enter the elevator and couldn't help but smile at her. Though he knew so much still worked through her head after all she'd learned, she'd let go, enjoying herself during dinner.

Pizza and beer. What better combination could you ask for?

Especially with a beautiful woman sitting across from you. Laughing with you. Forgetting, at least for the night, her decision to try and chase you away.

He'd seen another part of Tori here. A glimpse into who she'd been before Snow Ridge. Memories brightened her emerald eyes as she'd taken him by where she'd lived. Along the very blocks she'd once walked. Her favorite market. The park where she liked to sit on the bench to read. The Chinese restaurant that always added extra egg rolls to her order.

It was an insight to a woman who had always done everything alone. Who formed and shaped her life around relying only on the person she was and nobody else.

It was what she knew. Had known for so long. And she made it work.

Tapping his card key to the door, he held it open for her, admiring the slight sway of her backside.

She was an interesting woman.

Her independence intrigued him as much as it frustrated him. Her courage was something he found himself shaking his head in wonder at.

She had a kind, caring, heart. He'd seen proof of it. But she wasn't willing to open it up for many, keeping it carefully guarded to avoid more of the pain and loss she'd suffered as a child.

Yeah. So much to like and admire. It wasn't any wonder he found himself falling hard. No matter how much of a fool he was for doing so.

And it was that fool that drove him. He grabbed her as soon as he had the door closed, locking it tight behind them while finding her soft lips.

She didn't have a chance to react. Just the way he

wanted it.

It was good this way, catching her by surprise before she could protest. Hands cupped tight around her waist, he held her soft curves tight against him. Loved the feel of her easing into him, allowing what he sought.

He'd been afraid she might pull away. Instead, she flattened her palms against his chest, pushing even closer. Her knee found its way between his legs so she could slide with him, leaving little doubt to the heat building inside.

Groaning, he brushed back against her, making sure she had no doubt to the need drumming through as he shoved long fingers through her hair and arched her head back. For a moment, he stared into eyes clouded with desire. Then he had to take. From the curve of her collar bone to the tender spot below her ear, he trailed tiny nips up until finding her mouth once again.

Her passionate sigh washed over him, driving him higher. He needed more. Had to have it. Right there, where they stood. No matter where the bed might be or even the couch tucked cozily in a corner.

Right there. Right now.

Yanking on the hem of her shirt, he had it, and her bra, free in seconds, tossing them carelessly aside.

Caught by surprise, Tori could do nothing but stand there, hands at her side while Luke cupped her breasts, running a thumb over each hardened nipple.

Over and over, circling and teasing, watching with every flick. His gaze a storm cloud of emotion sucked her in, leaving her little space to move or breathe.

And then he was gone, the shock of it causing a chill as he fumbled with the button on her jeans, stripping her from the waist down and leaving her standing there, bare and vulnerable in front of him.

Uneasy, she folded her arms around her middle.

"No." He tugged on her hands, pulling them back to her sides. "Let me see."

His hazel eyes traveled over her. Fiery. Full of so much need and desire it frightened her. "So beautiful." His voice barely a whisper, he came back for another mind-numbing kiss. Hands roamed over bare skin, igniting a fire with every touch.

It was too much. Way too much. This was a mistake. Allowing one more night. She should have known better. Should have realized it was too hard to fight against everything he created inside.

But even as her mind roamed, her body responded. Her own need grew stronger, leaving her desperate to feel more. Thoughts no longer mattered as his hands roamed. Over curves, down slender lines. Teasing. Drawing forth the flames.

She wanted him. More than she remembered wanting anything in a very long time. Curving her hands over his shoulders, she inched him back. Just enough so she could meet his eyes and let him see what burned in her own.

"Please, Luke." She tightened her grasp, needing him to hear the desperate plea in her voice.

He grabbed her, chasing the air from her lungs as she was swung up against his muscular chest. In a few, large strides, he dumped her on the bed and stripped away his own clothes before coming down on top of her.

He waited until her eyes met his then pushed deep and hard, threatening to toss her over the edge in that first moment. There was nothing slow or gentle this time. There was only desperation, feeding them both.

Coming together, over and over again, frantic, searching for more. Always more. It rode close to crazy, what begged to explode between them.

Gazes locked, bodies rising and falling, they rode the wild wave together. Neither able to push a word, hardly a breath, past the painful throbs of their hearts beating together. The heat building and swirling between them.

Until it all exploded. A violent swirl of release, taking them both over as one.

"Luke." His name ripped free from deep inside as she twisted around him. Held on with all her strength as the world pitched and heaved, tossing them together off the highest cliff.

He held her tight as they tumbled back together, making her feel safe. Loved. Cherished.

Making her feel like she truly mattered to someone for the first time in her life.

****

He was tired of it. Tired of this whole mess.

This was so far from his normal work. From what he was good at.

Yet, here he was. Still trying. Still hoping to satisfy and bring the success expected from him.

Because of all things, the one thing Anton was not was a quitter. He'd carry out this crap for a job. Get it over with...hopefully soon. And be right back on track with what he knew. Thrived at.

Having such heavy restrictions resting on his shoulders, limiting so much of what he could do, was far from what he was good at. He preferred quick and easy. Taking a life if needed. Sparing one in the rare situations where it was necessary.

But this—

Shaking his head in frustration, he headed up the back stairs leading to Tori's apartment. She was gone. Back in Chicago, of all places. That much he'd learned from listening carefully. From being where he should without being noticed.

Perhaps coming back to find her privacy violated would do the trick, finally convince her she'd be better off if she went back to Chicago and stayed there.

It took only seconds to get through the locks. A few minutes more to silence the alarm. Dark and quiet greeted him as he closed the door behind him, allowing his eyes to adjust to what surrounded him.

There was nothing he wanted. Nothing he figured she owned worth taking. But there was plenty he could destroy. Use against her, building her fear. Making sure she felt violated was the only goal he sought.

He found his way to her bedroom and started there. Allowing the anger, he'd felt since being assigned this job to come forth he used it, letting it take control as he tore through, ripping clothes from their drawers. Dumping pictures, vases, small trinkets to the ground, relishing the sound of them shattering as they hit.

He stripped the bed of everything, throwing the mattress from its frame. Shoes flew, hit walls with punishing force, leaving holes in their wake.

In the bathroom, it took one forceful sweep of his arm to create a toxic mix as bottles of perfume and lotion crashed together, scents rising and waving around him. Cream and liquid flowed together on the linoleum floor. Shards of glass punctured the offensive puddles.

Storming down the short hall, he yanked the knife resting in its case at his waist. Wielding it like the madman he felt raging inside, he struck at the cushions of the couch centered in the family room. Stabbing again and again, drawing foam from the insides as he had, so often, drawn blood from others.

He destroyed. He ruined. Nothing was left untouched.

Books flew. Chairs hit hard to the ground.

There was not a dish to be left untouched. Each one shattered against the hard floor. Mugs and glasses joined them. What he found in the refrigerator became part of the mess.

Curtains came down. Slashed. Destroyed.

Everything he felt and carried with him as his time in Snow Ridge grew, became fuel to the fire, shoving at him even as he thought he'd done enough.

Emotion wasn't something he allowed to rule him. But tonight it felt good. A desperate relief he'd needed. Celebrated in as he left the apartment mutilated over every inch. Nothing spared. Not a single inch saved.

And even then he still had the urge to kick, hit, break, destroy. Emotions pushed hard, demanding more.

He didn't bother closing the door behind him. What was the use? Fueled by the anger and frustration he'd released, he hit every stair hard. Still seeking more. Wanting it desperately now that he'd given it the chance to escape.

Caught in it all, he didn't see her till he was nearly to the bottom stair. Barely caught in what little light there was, her dark, beady eyes centered on him as she stood in the small space between the coffee shop and Precious Gems.

"What are you doing?" Never taking her eyes off him, she fumbled frantically through her over-sized purse. "I heard you in there. It sounded like a war was taking place."

Even as she continued to search her purse, she leaned closer, getting a better look. "I don't know you. Never seen you before. You don't belong here. I know it."

He should have been able to handle it, switching quickly to the soothing, reassuring man he'd pulled forth often to dissolve a situation threatening to go bad.

But in his current state of mind, and watching as what little light there was glimmered off the phone she pulled from her purse, there was no control. Nothing inside him to handle the situation in the way it called for.

Before she got the phone to her ear, he was on her. One hand grabbed while the other curled tight around the knife he'd never put back.

She didn't have a chance to say another word. The blade, slick and sharp, ran in one quick slice over her neck. For a moment, surprise flashed in her gaze before death clouded over. As the blood flowed her phone fell, clattering at her feet before she tumbled down.

A helpless, lifeless heap becoming nothing more than an unimportant pile next to the trash.

Chapter Twenty-Two

Luke got the call as they were boarding the plane.

Everything in him tightened as his Lieutenant described the details of finding Maxine Hagdard in the alley behind Precious Gems. Her body slumped against a pile of trash waiting to be picked up.

And that was how she was finally discovered…when they'd come for the trash the next morning. Her throat slit. Eyes wide and body cold.

He knew Tori watched him, her patience tested as he continued the call while they settled in their seats. He looked at her, everything inside him dropping as he heard the rest.

For a moment he was tempted to grab her and drag her off the plane. Insist she remain in Chicago where, it seemed, she'd be safer than back in Snow Ridge.

But he didn't. Instead, he finished the call, looking away from Tori long enough to gather his own heated emotions before daring a word.

Though she fidgeted at his side, she waited patiently. "Whatever it is, I know it isn't good," she finally spoke when he looked back her way.

He hated telling her. Didn't want to be the one to put the fear in her eyes and bring her crashing back to reality.

But he had no choice. She needed to know. Needed to be prepared for what they'd face the minute they reached Snow Ridge. "Something happened last night," he gentled his voice as the plane rumbled beneath them, backing away from the terminal.

What would be worse, learning of the heartless murder of a woman she didn't know or the absolute destruction of her private space?

Start from the beginning. It was the best he could do at this point. "Somebody broke into your apartment last night. They destroyed it. From what I've been told, it's pretty bad."

Tori trembled, feeling as if she'd been punched in the gut while air was sucked harshly from her lungs. Her first thought was Derby, thankful to know he was safe with Cade and Cara. Then she thought of the place she'd begun to consider home. Had added the little extras, making it hers.

To think of someone inside, violating everything that was hers, pushed bile through her throat. Left her shaking.

"There's more." He collected her hands, holding them tight. "One of our residents, Maxine Hagdard, was lingering in the coffee shop after closing, talking endlessly, as she's known to do. When she left, she headed back to the alley, a shortcut for home she often takes."

He sucked in a harsh, angry breath and Tori knew she didn't want to hear the rest. "My officers believe she must have come across the intruder as he was leaving your apartment. She was found this morning. Her throat had been slit."

Now she really was going to be sick. Wishing she was anywhere but stuck on this plane, Tori fought it back the best she could. Sucking deep breaths through her lungs, she fought back nausea made worse as the plane sped down the runway.

She wanted to cry. Scream. Hit something.

How could this be happening? Why was it happening?

She found it so hard to wrap her mind around the idea she set it all into motion when she arrived in Snow Ridge, seeking her brother.

And again, the face from her nightmares surfaced. Taunting her.

Who was he? What memory did she have but couldn't pull forth?

She'd only been three years old. What knowledge could she possibly possess to warrant such tragedy? An innocent woman was dead. And for what? Because somewhere in the back of her mind was something she couldn't pull forth. Some answer she was expected to have. An answer she wasn't sure she'd ever known or would ever know.

****

The ride from Denver to Snow Ridge was torture.

Tori knew Cade wanted to ask questions the minute he picked them up from the airport, but Luke discouraged him.

She'd been anything but calm since learning about what happened. Had battled back the sick feeling in her gut all the way from Chicago to Denver. Still fought it as Cade turned off the interstate, bringing Snow Ridge and the ugly reality waiting for her closer.

"Cara closed the store," he informed them as he found a spot in front of Precious Gems. "Didn't keep her from being here though. She's been pacing the floors, waiting for you, since before I left."

"And Derby?" Tori had to ask. She needed to know he was okay though he'd never been at risk.

"Home with Dad and Hattie." Cade killed the engine before pushing open his door. "Being properly spoiled and loved."

It helped knowing that.

Before she could open the door for herself, Luke crawled out and opened it for her. She saw the worry, dark and stormy, in his expression. Knew, if he could, he'd keep her far away from here.

Taking her hand, he led her to the sidewalk and through the door Cade held open for them.

"Oh, Tori." Cara grabbed her, wrapping her tight in a hug. "I'm so sorry. I can't believe this has happened."

The trembling control she had over her emotions threatening to burst, she took a step back. "I can't—"

Shaking her head, she tried stuffing back all that rumbled inside. "I need to see the apartment."

Understanding the emotional ledge she hovered on, Cara left a gentle hand on her arm. "I wish you wouldn't. But I understand why you need to."

Jake, standing so quietly by the counter she hadn't noticed he was there, came around from behind Cara. "We'll go with you. No way you should see any of that on your own."

Though she was thankful to them, part of her wished to go alone. To see and react without the thought of others watching, waiting for her to crumble.

Luke stepped ahead, leading the way. He was back to Chief of Police mode. She saw it clearly as he headed, stiff and firm, up the stairs, taking in everything around him, missing nothing. Cara remained at her side as they followed, her grasp on Tori's arm growing tighter with every second drawing them closer.

Inside the door, an officer stood guard, not that Tori could figure out a reason for it to be needed now. Stepping close and lowering his head, Luke talked with him in hushed tones meant only for their ears. Nodding, the officer moved through to the kitchen, disappearing with the click of the outside door echoing back.

Tori gasped with her first step inside. If Cara hadn't been there, holding tight…

Her entire world spun as she stared at the cushions of the couch, viciously sliced to pieces, stuffing scattered everywhere. The few pictures she put up laid shattered at her feet. The coffee table upended. Lamp dangling in an awkward broken angle against the edge.

There was nothing left untouched. Everything was broken, destroyed, ruined.

"Who would do this?" Her voice barely a whisper, tears gathered in the corners of her eyes. For a moment, she wanted nothing more than to turn and run. Escape everything that had happened since she'd reached Snow Ridge. Deny it ever was a reality.

Knowing she couldn't do it. Knowing it would do no good, anyhow, she forced her feet forward, needing to see the rest.

The kitchen was just as bad. Glasses and plates shattered everywhere. Silverware tossed. Table and chairs upended, broken into pieces.

She saw rage. So much rage, and wondered why.

Shaky, tears burning, she turned reluctantly down the hall, toward her bedroom. And that's where she lost it. Not even Luke's arm coming around to hold her could prevent the tumble. She fell, an emotional puddle, to the floor, no longer able to stand up to the horror she saw.

It was so much chaos, she couldn't make sense of what scattered around her. Her bed was destroyed, blankets and sheets torn to shreds, mattress yanked from its frame, thrown against the opposite wall.

Her clothes were everywhere, ripped and torn. Her favorite robe, so loved, was nothing but strips of wasted material at her feet. The dolphin figurine she'd treasured for so many years was now nothing more than shards of glass.

Her favorite books, once cared for so lovingly, were ripped and torn to pieces, shredded papers falling throughout the room. Destroyed pillows scattered the space between bed and door. Jewelry, tossed carelessly around, littered every corner.

Her stuff. Gone. Ruined. Taken from her.

It hit hard. So hard. The life of a foster child slammed back at her with unrelenting force. She was back there, losing what she had, what was hers, for every move and every new family she was placed with.

A trash bag of clothes had been her existence through so much of her childhood. She'd sworn to never know that again. To always have that which was important to her without risk of losing it again.

And now…it was gone.

She was barely aware of Luke lifting her, holding her to his side, and leading her away from the terrible disaster. She heard the lowered voices of the others but didn't understand the words floating around.

"What the hell is going on?" It was Seth's loud, angry voice pulling her back. He stood at the end of the hall. His face a dark turbulence of emotion.

His eyes clashed with hers. So much rested in their

depths, it pulled at her insides. She saw it there, more than she ever had in the time she'd been in Snow Ridge—the love and connection of her older brother. The fear he carried as he stared at her being led down the hall by Luke and surrounded by the others.

He reached her with one large stride. Wrapping large fingers around her arms, he pulled her from Luke. "Are you okay?"

She didn't have it in her to do anything but look back at him, unable to answer. Standing in the middle of the disaster, she fumbled for what little control she'd had when she first entered.

"I think we should get her out of here." Jake pressed a gentle hand to her back, easing them back the way they had come.

They reached the stairs when Luke reached for her, grabbing her in his own protective hold. Pressing a soft hand to her cheek, he dropped a kiss to her lips. "I need to take care of things here. Jake and Cade will get you back to the ranch. I'll meet you there as soon as I can."

She could only nod, holding on tight as he claimed another kiss, tugging her up and away from the horror of it all.

Then he was gone. But she was far from alone.

****

He hated to leave her. Felt the punch of it deep in his gut.

But even more, Luke hated what he saw as he walked back through the apartment. Living with the badge, it didn't do him good to let his emotions get the best of him. Today, though, there was no getting around it.

Not as he walked through and saw the destruction

left behind. Thought about how much some spineless fool had stolen from Tori.

He wanted to punch something. Hard. Until the rage eased.

But, as his officers walked back in, he knew it wasn't a pleasure he was going to get. "Walk me through it." He looked between the two he considered some of his best. Knew he was asking for a repeat of all he'd already been told. Didn't care a bit about it.

They took him through what they had determined were the facts of the night. The break-in. The terror wielded over the apartment. The killing of an innocent bystander.

And all he could think of was what would have happened if Tori had been there. Inside the apartment, alone and defenseless, when someone with so much hatred, so much rage, had intruded on her personal space.

It was a horrific fright he couldn't allow himself to dwell on. Not if he wanted to maintain the ability to carry out this investigation.

And he would carry it out with everything he had and every resource he had available to his department. He'd find the bastard who had done this. Make him sorry for the fear he caused Tori.

Because this time, it was more than just his responsibility and loyalty to a town he'd sworn to serve and protect. It was personal as it threatened the woman he'd fallen in love with.

Chapter Twenty-Three

"I don't care about the time. She needs a toss of whiskey." Setting a glass of amber liquid in front of Tori at the kitchen table, Hattie stood above her. Arms crossed, she kept her gaze steady until Tori picked up the small glass and swallowed it down.

It was a jolt to the system, burning as it went down, chasing away the last of the haze holding on since stepping foot into her apartment.

"Good girl." Hattie dropped a soft hand to her shoulder. Taking the glass, she was back in seconds, placing a steaming mug and a cinnamon roll in front of her. "Now some coffee and food to finish it off."

Because she stood over her, Tori tore off a piece of warm roll. As always, with everything Hattie made, it was amazing. The sweet cinnamon dough played with her taste buds, helping pull her even further from the dark hole.

"See." She patted Tori's cheek, smiling with satisfaction. "There's nothing a quick shot to the gut and some good food can't help."

Tori couldn't deny her. She did feel better. Whether it was the whiskey, the cinnamon roll, or a combination of both, she felt parts of herself coming back, fighting against the ugliness she'd been lost in.

Of course, coming back meant having to deal with what she desperately wished she could forget. And there would be none of that, she knew, as she looked around the crowded kitchen table at the many worried eyes reflecting back at her.

They gathered as they had that first night she'd been on the ranch with the addition of Seth and Jackie. It felt like so long ago, almost a different life, when she'd sat here with a blizzard raging outside. So unsure if she was doing the right thing. Her worst fear being her brother turning her away.

Now she feared what she'd brought into their lives by finding him.

"So, we've got some shopping to do." Bouncing Baby Evan on her knee, Jackie smiled from across the table. "We could go later this afternoon, if you're up for it."

Confusion held for a moment before it hit her—if it hadn't been with her in her suitcase in Chicago, everything she owned was destroyed. She had nothing now other than what she could claim in one little bag packed for a night away.

The realization threatened to push her back over. Fighting it back, she followed Hattie's advice, breaking off another piece of cinnamon roll, using it to anchor her where she needed to be.

"I will need to get some basics." She didn't want to think of the toll it would take on her meager savings. But there were things that had to be.

Cara reached over the table and grabbed her hand. "I was thinking giving you an early bonus from work might be of some help. I'd planned to do it anyhow during the holidays. No reason I can't step it up earlier."

Ashamed at even the thought of it, Tori shook her

head. "No." Unable to meet the gazes around the table, she stared down into her coffee. "I'll be okay."

She heard the scrape of a chair against the kitchen floor but still didn't have it in her to look up. It wasn't until there was a slap against the table beside her she dared to glance up and right into her brother's hard gaze.

She glanced down to where his hand rested only a few inches from her plate, catching the edges of a dark-colored credit card peeking through.

Already knowing what was coming, she shook her head. "I'm fine, Seth. Really."

"I don't want to hear it," he snapped, the hard look covering his face leaving no room for argument. "You're my sister. My blood. It's about time I start taking care of my own after all these years."

She didn't want to do this. Not here. Not with so many around to witness what should be private between her and her brother. "There are other ways. Another time."

"And there is also right now. This moment." He stood firm, ignoring all else but Tori.

In the complete silence taking over, she watched his heated expression soften into one of love, regret, and loss. It tore at her. Right through the very depths of her heart.

Moving closer, he cupped a hand against her cheek, catching her by surprise. "I didn't do for you as I should have. Not as the young boy I was but as the adult I became. For that, I will always be sorry."

She couldn't find the ability for speech. Could only sit there, caught by it all.

"But you finding me gave me back the chance to

be a brother again. And whether it's all you're ready for or not, I'm no longer satisfied holding back out of fear it isn't the right thing."

He turned away and shook his head, dealing with what burned inside. When he turned back, there was a plea in his sharp gaze she couldn't deny.

"I want you to give me this." He pushed the credit card closer. "A chance to do something for you. To stand up and be the brother you deserve."

"Seth, I—"

He waved her off with a quick sweep of his hand. "I want you to do it without arguing. Because I'm selfish. Because I want to be proud of being your brother. Of stepping in and doing the right thing when it's needed."

She had no words. Caught in a tumble of emotions, she stared for a moment before pushing to her feet and wrapping tight around him.

The tears came but she did her best to hide them in the crook of his arm. "Okay." She looked up at him, biting back her pride. Her need to do it on her own.

A slow smile starting, he bent down and dropped a soft kiss on her cheek. "Thank you." His whisper was low so only she heard.

He stepped away and headed back for his place at the table. Watching him she realized, no matter what had happened since she'd reached Snow Ridge, she would never regret what she'd found.

The brother she'd only known, for so long, through her memories. The brother she would never lose again.

****

Luke turned off the road for the ranch and saw the lights of the main house shining bright. Felt the first sense of relief since he'd gotten the call.

There was always something about home. About the comfort it offered. Even on the worst of days, in the darkest of circumstances, finding his way back to the Double G always made things better.

And the thought of Tori being there helped even more.

He felt every ache through his bones as he pulled up in front of the main house. He'd pushed himself and his officers hard. Wanting and demanding answers.

Whoever was responsible for this hell would be found. He was making sure of it.

The voices floated toward him as he walked through the front door. His father, Hattie, his brothers. There was Old Joe's laughter drifting through. A softer response from Penny.

But he didn't hear what he craved. The soft rise and fall of Tori's voice. That slight, but still there, accent she brought with her. The higher tilt to her tone when she was excited. The cautious drawl she picked up when uncomfortable or nervous.

The very things he now found himself needing to hear. Be a part of.

And there was disappointment when he didn't find her as he made his way into the kitchen.

"She's off shopping." Reading his mind, Jake slapped a hand to his back. "With Jackie and Cara. Who knows when those three will be back."

Luke refused to feel disappointed. He wasn't *that* bad off. At least, he didn't want to believe he was.

"Dad and Old Joe grilled up some ribs." Cade nudged his way past, a full plate in one hand and beer bottle in the other. "Jake and I were just headed out to the back deck to enjoy. Want to join us?"

What he really wanted was to go home, take a long, hot shower, and wash away the hell of the day. But even as he thought it, his stomach rumbled, leaving little doubt there were other priorities to tend to first. Especially since he hadn't eaten since breakfast back in Chicago.

Had it really just been that morning? It seemed like worlds away now.

Piling his plate with ribs, Hattie's famous potato salad, and more than his fair share of cornbread, he grabbed his own beer from the fridge before following his brothers out.

They settled at the outdoor table. Fall in full force, the evening air was brisk. A slight breeze rustled through from the mountain tops.

Like old times, he thought, as he popped the top from his beer. The three of them caring nothing about the cold. Leaving the others to the warmth inside while they snuck out together.

It wasn't so often anymore they had these chances. They'd learned to enjoy them, now, when they came.

And things would change even more in a few months once Cade and Cara were married. And then with Tori.

His thoughts came to a quick halt. Was he actually thinking in such long terms when it came to his relationship with her? Daring to put marriage out there as an option?

"Any news about what happened?" Jake lifted a rib to his lips, digging in with the delight of a child.

Clearing away where his thoughts had been headed, Luke took a slow sip from his beer before going after the food on his plate. "Nothing. Or, at least nothing more than we already knew."

"Wish Cara would keep the store closed longer." The protective streak he was known for creeping forward, Cade sent a frustrated look Luke's way. "Can't say I like the idea of her being there while this guy is around. Brings about old fears that haven't yet gone away."

Luke understood. He was having a hard time fighting back the memory of what had happened to Cara not too long ago as this new threat faced Tori. "I'll have a patrol drive by as often as possible. But don't go telling Cara about it or she'll have my backside." He picked up a rib, waving it at his brother.

"Thanks." Cade toasted him with his beer bottle. "And my lips are sealed."

"What about Tori?" Jake shared a look between his brothers. "She can't go back to her apartment. I can't imagine her ever wanting to go back there after what she saw today."

"She won't be." There wasn't room for question in Luke's firm voice.

"Nope." Cade shot a wink Jake's way. "She'll be tucked away nice and safe at Luke's place. Just where he wants her."

Across from Luke, his brothers laughed, enjoying themselves way too much. He shot a look at Cade, both of them knowing he had his own ammunition, if needed, to pull out. And Jake.

Well, there was still hope.

"She know this yet?" Quieting his laughter, Jake forked up a generous bite of potato salad. "That you've pretty much moved her in?"

The look on Luke's face was all they needed to know.

"Wish I could be there." Cade nudged Jake. "A fly on the wall to see how well that goes over."

"Just because you came close to having to bring Cara to the house kicking and screaming doesn't mean the rest of us suffer your shortcomings." Casual, and a bit snarky, Luke pulled off a slice of meat from his rib, enjoying it with slow satisfaction.

It was as it had always been, loving his brothers with the ability to poke at them. It's what they did. If they didn't have each other to keep them in line, who would they have?

"Yeah well, still wish I could be there to see it. She seems to be a pretty good match to Cara with her stubbornness which means it could be a good show."

"And proves again why I'm proud to be single." Jake raised his beer to his brothers, smirking at them over the rim.

Luke ignored him as ideas ran through his head. There was no telling how Tori would take it, staying with him. But that didn't mean he couldn't try to pave the way beforehand. Make it easier when it did come down to it.

"I'll be back." Grabbing his phone from his waist, he pushed up from his chair, moving to the corner of the porch.

He'd make a quick call. Put some things in motion.

****

Shopping with Cara and Jackie should be considered an Olympic event.

Tori looked at the pile of bags shoved beside her in the back of Cara's car and shook her head. How she'd ended up buying so much, she still wasn't sure. What had started out to replace the essentials quickly became so much more.

It was Seth's fault, she decided, as they turned onto the ranch. He'd set his expectations before they'd left and Jackie and Cara had been more than willing to oblige.

Exhausted now, with more than she'd ever imagined she needed, she rested her head against the seat, watching the freshly-painted white fence pass by.

The main house, full of light and life, rolled away. "Where are we going?" She pulled up and shot a curious glance at Cara's back.

"I've been given instructions to drop you, and all your wonderful new purchases, off at Luke's place." Cara spared her a glance over her shoulder.

Tori felt a flick of irritation, wondering at the fact it was nothing more. She knew what he was up to. Should be mad he was making decisions for her without a thought to ask first.

But the reality was, she'd already thought about where she'd stay for the night. The apartment was out of the question. She couldn't imagine ever staying there again. And she'd considered renting a hotel room while they'd been in town. But she hadn't done it. Hadn't even come close.

Because she'd known Luke would insist she stay with him. If not at his place then the main house. And she'd admitted it was what she wanted. Though the truth of it was hard to accept.

With Luke, she felt safe, secure. All the horrors she'd faced lately dimmed when he was at her side. Getting too close to him, she knew, was dangerous. But right now, she simply couldn't find the desire to do anything about it.

Right now, what she wanted was Luke.

And then, there he was as if drawn from her thoughts. Dark hair tumbling above those deep hazel eyes of his. Hard, muscled body, still dark and sun-kissed even with the change of seasons.

He'd showered. She saw it in the damp strands curling around his ears. Jeans hugged his hips. A soft cotton tee stretched over his chest.

Her heart did a jolt as Cara pulled to a stop.

He was there before she got the door open, eyes popping wide at the pile of bags she began tugging at. "What did you three do, buy out every store?"

"We came close." Cara climbed from the driver's seat, grabbing at her own share of the bags.

Between the three of them, arms heavy, they hauled her new purchases through the front door.

"We can leave them here for now." Luke dumped his load on the couch, stepping aside so Tori and Cara could do the same. "Do you want a drink before you go?"

Cara shook her head. "I've got to get Jackie home and get back to your brother before he sends out a search party."

Flashing a knowing smile, she wrapped Tori in a hug. "If you need to take tomorrow off, don't hesitate to let me know. It can't be easy, having to go back there, after what happened."

Images of the destruction jumped to life. Chasing them back, refusing to allow them to haunt her, she squeezed Cara's hand. "Thanks, but I'll be okay. No use letting them win by being chased away from the store I love. I'll be there, as usual, ready to go."

"All right. I'll see you tomorrow." A hug for Luke and she was gone.

"So, are you going to let me have it?" Ignoring the pile of bags, Luke crossed his arms over his chest, easing a hip against the corner of the couch. "Having Cara bring you here?"

"It's tempting." Stepping closer, her smile was slow and easy. "But, I figure, since this is exactly where I want to be, not much I can use against you. Kind of ends the fight before it gets started."

His answering smile beamed from ear to ear. Reaching out, curling big hands around her arms, he drew her to him. "Well, that's much better than I'd have guessed." He dropped a soft kiss on her lips. "Much, much better."

As always when he was close, a tingle of awareness started through her limbs. Melting into him, she laced her fingers behind his neck. "Happy I could oblige." She eased his mouth down to hers, heat spiking as the next kiss sank deeper, drawing her up and away into all his touch promised.

Yes. This was what she wanted. Needed. After all that had happened, the strength and security Luke offered made it easy to put all else out of her mind for brief moments in time and enjoy what she found caught in his arms.

Knowing, deep down, it was wrong, didn't possess the power needed to chase her away. So she stayed, enjoyed, until Luke slowly broke the kiss and stepped back.

For a moment he simply stood there, staring at her, before gathering his senses back. "So, all this." He swept a hand over the pile of bags. "The guest room is ready. We can move it up and get you settled. Or—"

There was a mischievous glimmer in his hazel eyes. "We could save the trouble and land it in my room to start with since that's where I plan on having you, as often as I can, while you're here."

She couldn't help the bubble of laughter. It felt good after the way her day had started. "Are you sure you have enough room for it all?"

"Now that I can't guarantee." He dropped one more quick kiss to her lips before reaching down for the bags. "But, for you, I'll sure give it my best shot."

****

He didn't like to travel. Preferred to have others do what needed to be done while he remained in the comfort of what he knew. Had known since bringing his new bride from Romania to create a life here in the states.

Scotch waved in its glass as Filip turned his chair and stared out over the river. He'd been so young and unknowing those first moments he'd spent in Chicago. A young man sure he'd find the streets of gold in this great country. With a little hard work, he'd build a good life for himself and his love.

And he had worked. His first year had been nothing but sweat and labor. He'd hauled crates heavier than him from the ships. Come home smelling like lake and fish and the burning smoke that clung to the air.

And his sweet Amelia would hold him in her arms. Love him even when he smelled bad enough to chase away the worst of bums. So, because of her, he'd get up the next morning, doing it all over again. Whatever it took to give her the life she deserved.

He'd have stayed at it he thought as he watched tourists and locals mingle on the sidewalk below. Right there in all that muck and grime. Day in and day out. Earning his way. Providing for his beautiful bride.

But opportunity had come for him through another who broke his back every day at his side. He knew the right people. The jobs they needed satisfied. And soon, Filip found himself working for one of the most powerful families in Chicago.

A glimmer of happiness sparked as he remembered the first time he'd been able to buy diamonds for Amelia. They'd been so small. Little studs for her delicate ears. The satisfaction of seeing the happiness in her eyes was the push he needed.

Taking a slow sip from his scotch, he looked around his office. The dark wood. Thick, smooth leather. It was a small part of all the luxury he'd achieved. Starting from the bottom and working his way up until the day he sat as the one in charge. The one feared. Respected. Giving the orders rather than receiving them.

His only regret was Amelia was no longer with him to enjoy it.

But those thoughts were for another day. Tonight there were other things requiring his attention.

Like the hard-hit reality he'd be leaving his beloved Chicago for a small, nothing, mountain town he'd hoped to avoid.

Because he'd trusted the wrong one to do what needed to be done, leaving him no choice but to go and finally take care of what should have been ended years ago. No matter how much it ached him to accept what it was he had to do.

Chapter Twenty-Four

"Are you sure you really want to do this?" Her words heavy with doubt, Cara shook her head at Tori from the opposite side of the counter. "What happened wasn't your fault. You shouldn't be carrying this on your shoulders."

"It's something I have to do." Tori looked at Cara and wondered how to make her understand.

In the days that had passed since she'd come back from Chicago, saw the disaster of her apartment, and learned of the murder of an innocent bystander, she'd reflected through more emotions than she cared to admit.

But one stayed steady and true, refusing to be chased or explained away.

She needed to do something for the woman who'd been murdered because of the intrusion into her apartment. She couldn't sit back and pretend it never happened. Refuse to accept someone's life was terribly cut short because of the evil in her own life.

"Luke said the woman, Maxine, who was murdered, it was just her and her older sister, who passed away last year." The sadness of it had been hard to hear. "I know her parish is planning for, and covering the cost of her funeral. But I still need to know if there is something I can do. Some way to pay my respects after what happened."

"But what happened wasn't because of you." Cara reached across the counter, resting a gentle hand over hers. "I understand the need to do something. And I'll go with you to see Father Frances, just as I said I would. But I worry about you. I don't want you feeling responsible for what happened to Maxine."

"I don't." Tori looked Cara in the eye and saw the doubt. "Okay. I'm trying my hardest not to. But it doesn't change wanting to do something for her. I'd like to hope I'd feel the same way simply out of kindness."

Silent for only a moment, Cara nodded, squeezing her hand. "Okay."

Letting go, she bent down to drop a quick pat to Derby's head as he danced between her legs. "We'll close up, take this one here to Hattie, and put her on puppy duty. Then we'll head over to Saint Mary's and have a talk with Father Frances."

"Thank you." Releasing the breath she hadn't been aware she held, Tori was grateful she wouldn't have to go alone. She'd have done it, if it needed to be, but felt better knowing it wasn't a reality.

She didn't want Luke to know what she was doing. Had purposely kept it from him, sensing he wouldn't take kindly to it. It was better he knew after she'd gone, when there was nothing he could do to change it.

****

If there was one thing Tori had come to know since arriving in Snow Ridge, it was the amazing smells that always drifted from Hattie's kitchen. Morning, noon or night, the delicious aromas lured, enticing the senses.

Even Derby had grown wise to the treats waiting for him, heading directly for the kitchen the minute they walked through the door.

"She stocked up on his treats this morning." Cara leaned in as they headed down the hall, her voice barely above a whisper. "Don't go letting her know I told you, though. Hattie's always liked us to believe the family pets were a nuisance under her feet. Of course, we knew better."

As if on cue, Hattie's voice drifted back as Derby entered the kitchen. "There you are, looking just as cute as ever."

Entering a step behind, Tori and Cara paused in the entry as Hattie crouched low to give Derby a good, long scratch between his ears. "Suppose you'll be wanting one of your treats." With her hands gently curved beneath him, she raised his nose to hers. "Seems to me, you've come to think I'm made of those things."

Shaking her head, a gentle smile on her lips, she straightened, catching sight of Cara and Tori watching her. "Comes running in here like he owns the place." She tried a scowl but it didn't do much good on a face already softened.

Reaching into the cupboard, she pulled out a tub of the bacon treats he'd come to love, palming one in her hand. "Takes up space in my kitchen I don't have to spare, keeping these things around for him."

She held it out for Derby. And though she tried hiding it, there was no missing the sparkle in her eyes as he happily took it, thanking her with a long, slobbery kiss along her fingers.

Choosing to remain silent, Cara led the way into the kitchen. Opening the fridge, she grabbed a water bottle for herself and Tori. "We shouldn't be long." She uncapped the top of her own, taking a long, slow drink.

"Thank you for doing this," Tori added, grabbing the bottle Cara held out for her. "I know puppy sitting isn't exactly a glamorous job."

"Done enough sitting in my lifetime. Children and puppies alike. Figure I can handle this one just as well." With another quick rub between the ears and a quick glance at Cara and Tori, daring them to respond, Hattie flipped the lever on the sink.

Soaping her hands and rinsing them under the water, she looked back over her shoulder. "Where is it you two are headed?"

Tori caught Cara's hesitation and wondered about it. "I'm going with Tori to Saint Mary's to talk to Father Frances." She pulled a towel from the rung of the stove, handing it to Hattie.

"And you're thinking that's a good idea?" Slow as she worked the towel between her hands, Hattie's stare was hard.

"Don't see any reason why not."

Tori didn't understand the looks between them. But there was something there. Of that, she had no doubt.

Replacing the towel, Hattie stepped closer, cupping her hand against Cara's cheek. "I won't be telling you what to do. I know how much you hate that. I'll just say be careful."

With a soft smile, Cara leaned in, dropping a kiss on Hattie's age-worn cheek. "I'll be okay. I promise."

She turned to Tori, her smile widening. "You ready?"

Tori wasn't sure what she was. Curious...she knew that much. And not so confident now she should have asked Cara to come along. There was something she didn't know. Something warning against Cara visiting the church with her. "Maybe I should just go."

"Of course not." Looping her arm through Tori's, Cara led her from the kitchen and back down the hall. "You shouldn't be doing this alone."

"But—"

Tori glanced over her shoulder back to the kitchen. "Why doesn't Hattie want you to go?"

"Because she worries too much." Opening the front door and stepping out into the chilly evening, Cara pulled in a long breath. "Which, I admit, she has a right to."

Leading the way to her car, she waited till they were both tucked away inside before continuing. "You've heard the bits and pieces about what happened not too long ago here in Snow Ridge. The ranch hand who was kidnapping, torturing, and killing women."

Tori had heard enough to know Cara, herself, was part of the horror. That she'd almost lost her own life at the hands of the one who had murdered two other women before he'd gotten his hands on her.

"I know that I can't possibly imagine how you made it through that." Tori looked at Cara as she pulled away from the main house and started for the main road. "If that were me, I'd have been a lump of uselessness in the corner."

Cara's laugh was quick. "No, you wouldn't. You've already proven otherwise in dealing with what you're going through now. It's amazing the strength we find when we have no other choice."

Tori settled back against the seat and thought about what Cara said. "I think a lot of it has to do with the people around me. If I'd been back in Chicago, alone like I was, I don't think I'd be handling this so well. It makes a difference to have all of you. To know I don't stand alone."

Cara pressed a hand to her leg. "Nobody should have to be alone. Especially not when going through what you are."

She turned back and sat for a moment in silence before releasing a long sigh. "I was lucky to have many of the same wonderful people there for me, as well. Sometimes I need to remind myself of that. Like with Hattie and her worry."

"She didn't want you going with me. That much was clear."

"No. She didn't." Cara slowed for the turn leading them back into town. "It has nothing to do with you, causing her worry. It's my returning to Saint Mary's."

"Back when I was going through my own nightmare, there was a connection to Saint Mary's." Though Cara kept her gaze aimed straight ahead, there was no missing the tightening of her spine. The dark shadow crossing through her expression. "It wasn't a pretty one. A crucifix had been stolen from Father Frances and used in the worst of ways with the second woman who was murdered."

"Oh, Cara, I didn't know." Guilt now rising, Tori considered having her turn around and forget about the whole thing. "Why didn't you tell me when I asked you to go along?"

"Because it wasn't the crucifix, the church, or Father Frances responsible for what happened." She turned a block away from Main Street, pulling up against the curb. "If I were to stay away from everything associated with what happened, I'd never be able to walk back into my own store. Or even the ranch.

I'd be nothing more than a sorry sight, locked inside four walls with nowhere to go."

Opening the door, she climbed out and waited for Tori on the sidewalk.

"If you have the courage to do this for a woman you never even knew," she continued once Tori joined her. "I can definitely find my own to walk back in those doors and face whatever I find."

****

Tori had vague, fleeting memories of church.

It seemed every foster family she was placed with had practiced a different sort of religion. From Baptist to Protestant to Catholic.

But her memories, she decided, had played with her and her visions of the Pastors and Priests she remembered. Because sitting there in the office of Father Frances, staring at him from the opposite side of his desk, she saw nothing like what those memories carried.

There was something intriguing about him. He was young—or at least younger than she'd imagined him—with a certain vital quality, leaving one wondering what he was doing under the oath of celibacy.

Which that thought alone was sure to condemn her to an uncomfortable afterlife.

But really, how was a woman to ignore the dark fall of hair over a handsome face. The charm in his smile. Sparkle in his emerald eyes.

"I'm so sorry for all you've gone through." He leaned over his desk and held out a hand.

Scooting forward in her chair, she reached out her own, letting him fold it into the warmth of his palm. He at least had the look about him. That deep, thoughtful expression she'd always associated with those who stood behind the pulpit. As if they were forever contemplating the life they knew with the afterlife they promised.

"But I don't feel it's right for you to burden yourself with an obligation to do more for Maxine than offer your prayers for a soul who has found her way home."

He looked from her to Cara and then back. "Of the greatest things you could do for her, out of your heart with love and not your mind with guilt, is to be here for her services. Take part in honoring a wonderful woman who left us too early, as they all seem to do."

She'd hoped for more. Needed more to ease the gnawing inside. But she also knew it was time to admit there'd be nothing else coming. Not from Father Frances, at least.

"I'll be here," she promised with a nod of her head. Not that a funeral was what she looked forward to. "And if there is anything else I can do, please let me know."

She pushed to her feet as Father Frances rose behind his desk, Cara doing the same at her side. He came around and took her hand. "Maxine would appreciate knowing the kindness and concern you've shown."

His gaze lingered a moment more before turning for Cara. "I was surprised and pleased to see you." He took her hand in the one that had held Tori's. "I've thought of you often. Wondered how you were."

"I'm okay, Father. Better than okay."

"I'm so pleased to hear that. I've worried about you since that first time you sat in my office. Hoped things had gotten better." His charming smile reached his eyes.

"They have. Much better."

With a quick, brisk nod, he let go of Cara and turned his attention back to Tori. "So, I will look forward to seeing you tomorrow. Services for Maxine are at three."

"I'll be here," Tori promised again. "It's the least I can do."

Saying their goodbyes, Cara slung her arm through Tori's, leading them from the office and back through the church. "You're a good person, Tori." She stopped for a moment, her smile sincere. "Not everyone would be willing to do what you are doing for a complete stranger."

"I don't feel like she's a complete stranger." Tori's voice softened with emotion. "I know it makes no sense. I never knew her. I only know what she looks like because I insisted Luke show me a picture."

Needing to move, she encouraged them on, repeating their steps down the long, dark hallway toward the front of the church. "But, in my life, I've known the murder of three people now, somehow tied to me. Nothing can ever, or will ever, match what it was like to lose my parents in such a way. Their murder is something I have come to accept I will grieve every day of my life."

She paused before taking the final step leading them outside. "But, even with Maxine, there's something there. Nothing anywhere as close to the heartache I suffered when I lost my parents. But enough, knowing it tied back to me, to be unable to simply turn my back and walk away without another thought. So, I'll be here tomorrow. And I'll honor her life. Because it's the least I can do."

Cara's answering hug came quick and unexpected. "You don't have to come alone." She pulled back with a smile. "I'll come with you."

"You don't have to do that."

"I know I don't. But I want to." Cara set a hand to one of the heavy wooden doors and pushed. "It's the least I can do. For you. And Maxine."

The evening sun poured over them as they stepped outside, casting a hint of glare as they caught sight of who waited for them at the curb.

"Looks like Hattie talked." Cara's look was a bit of amusement mixed with caution as she hooked her arm with Tori's.

The setting sun danced over their hard-carved faces. Twin hazel eyes watched their every step. There was no question of their relation or the interest they carried for the two women coming their way.

For a moment, Tori wanted to simply stop where she was and take it in. Two of the three Grady brothers, so handsome, so strong and vital, leaning against the side of Luke's truck and watching them with intent heavy in their gazes and something even stronger in their heated expressions.

And one of them was all for her. She wasn't the one on the outside looking in this time around. She was part of it, drawing her own fair share of attention from an amazing, handsome man who wasn't afraid to show how much he wanted her.

Where there was fear there was also thrill.

"So, how did you convince Hattie to tattle on us?" Reaching Cade first, Cara pushed on to her toes, dropping a soft kiss on his lips.

"That would be my doing." Wrapping an arm around Tori's slender waist, Luke pulled her close for a kiss of his own, surprising her. "And there was no convincing or tattling involved. I went to the main house looking for Tori. Hattie told me where she was."

Cara cocked her head and looked hard at Cade, knowing him all too well. "And you?"

He shrugged, doing his best to plaster a look of innocence on his face. "I just came along for the ride."

He wasn't believed but before anyone could argue, Luke waved to the back of his truck. "We picked up some beer and a few bottles of wine. Jake's on his way to my place with food from the pub. Figured we could make a night of it."

Something was up. Tori felt it. With a look at Cara, she saw the same suspicion reflected back at her. They hadn't asked a single question about why they were there. Seemed all too eager, though, to get them away.

"I'll take you back to the ranch." Luke opened the passenger door. "Cade can ride with Cara."

Tori and Cara shared another look, both doubtful and curious. But they didn't argue. Agreeing, without words, to wait and see.

Chapter Twenty-Five

"I told my cooks to get creative." Sliding a stack of cardboard boxes onto the table, Jake took the beer Luke held out for him. "Been working on a pizza dough with Guinness in it. Had them use the recipe and make us their version of an Irish pizza. We've got four different kinds to try."

Cade opened the top box, scents so tempting they teased the stomach. "So we get to be your guinea pigs." He pulled out a slice.

"What else is family for?" Jake spread the boxes across the table, opening each one.

Stepping up behind him, Luke dumped a pile of paper plates between them. "Are we deciding what hits the menu?" Grabbing a piece from the center box, he dropped it on his plate.

Taking his own piece, Jake nodded. "I'll run a couple as a special for the start of tourist season and see how they do. If they're a hit, I'll make them permanent."

Behind them, Tori and Cara watched, shaking their heads. The three Grady Brothers, so strong, so potent in their very existence, grabbing pizza with their beers, their movements so similar to one another. The very way about them leaving no doubt to the blood linking them.

"Is it any wonder why we love them." Cara

winked, sipping from her glass of wine.

The mention of love stumbled Tori back. Sucking in a long breath, she reminded herself it was just an offhand term Cara had chosen to use.

For her and Luke, love wasn't involved. Of that she was sure.

But the thought of it, for the first time, tempted her. Spending so much time watching Cara and Cade together. The secret looks between them. Their need to touch, be close. How could one not secretly desire that for themselves?

It wasn't for her. That she knew. But it didn't stop the desire to experience such a love just once in her life.

Too cold to be outside with the dark settling and a storm threatening, Luke grabbed Cara's glass of wine, waited for her to choose her pizza, then led the way to the table. If they couldn't be outside, where he preferred it most, they'd at least have the big windows surrounding them.

The talk was quick, voices tumbling one over another, as pizza disappeared, and another run was made to the refrigerator for more beers.

Grabbing the wine bottle Cara and Tori were quickly working their way through on the way back to the table, Cade topped them both off. "So, how did it go with Father Frances, today?" Finally breaking through the topic they'd ignored earlier, he kept a close eye on Cara as he took his seat.

"It was okay." She looked at Tori before turning back to Cade. "We're going to Maxine's funeral tomorrow."

There was a sudden hush as Cade and Luke stared at one another across the table.

"And what's that for?" Cara nudged Cade while shooting a hard look at Luke.

Beside her, Tori felt Luke stiffen as if preparing for a fight. On the opposite side, Jake gave a low whistle under his breath before taking a long, slow draw from his beer.

"Is someone going to speak?" Cara's heated, frustrated gaze passed over all three brothers.

Dropping a hand to Tori's leg underneath the table, Luke looked at them. "I've been probing deeper, since our meeting with Olsen back in Chicago, into the theory your parents' murder might be connected with organized crime in some way."

He looked only at her then, his hazel eyes deep with worry. "I don't like where it's headed." His hand resting on her leg squeezed. "If Olsen was right, and more powerful forces were involved, then what you're facing is much more than we imagined."

If he could, Luke would keep Tori at his side at all times. Fear grew greater with every little bit he learned. And all he wanted was to keep her close and safe.

He'd never truly understood Cade's protective nature over Cara until now. He'd believed himself to be better. A bigger man than that. But as the threats against her continued to mount, he realized the truth of it was so much different than what he'd once believed.

Because the very idea of her being harmed in any way was almost too much to handle. And it stopped mattering to him about being the one who respected her right and ability to take care of herself. Becoming, instead, only about his desperate need to keep her safe at any cost.

And if that made him as bad as he'd once believed

Cade to be, he'd take it.

Just as he was about to take what he knew would be a far from favorable reaction from Tori. He'd seen it enough in Cara and knew to be prepared for it. "I'm thinking it's time we take some more productive steps in keeping you safe."

"What kind of steps?" Caution already lingering in her voice, Tori lifted her wine glass to her lips and took a sip, watching him over the rim.

Luke glanced at his brothers, knowing they were prepared for what was to come. "I think it's best if you weren't out alone anymore. If one of us can't be with you," he nodded toward Jake and Cade, "then I want one of my officers with you."

The silence fell quick and hard.

While Cara glared at him from across the table, Tori, wine glass still grasped in her hand, simply stared. After a moment, she shook her head and took another slow sip before carefully setting it on the table.

"Is that the true reason why you and Cade showed up at the church?" She looked from him to Cade and then back. "To start this protection of yours?"

He could have lied and given another excuse, but what was the use? "When I got to the main house and discovered you weren't there, I shared my concerns with Cade. We both decided it was best to go to the church."

From the corner of his eye, he caught Cara turning her deadly stare Cade's way. Silently apologizing to his little brother, he kept his own gaze steady with Tori. "There isn't anything good going on here. I wish I could say different. Wish I could believe different. But from the little we continue to learn and dig up, my gut tells me the danger is greater than we imagined."

Her expression turned thoughtful rather than angry. For that, he was thankful. "It's been twenty-five years since my parents' murder. I have never felt threatened by any kind of danger in all that time."

She held up her hand when he opened his mouth to respond. "I know it's different now. I'm not foolish enough not to understand what's changed."

"But," she finished off the last sip of wine and drew in a careful breath. "I'm still not willing to give up my freedom because of what happened in the past. I don't want to let whoever it is win by becoming the victim."

Tori looked around the table, all eyes resting on her. Shaking off the strange feeling it created, she rested on Luke. Dropping a hand over where his own continued to linger on her leg, she offered what she hoped was a convincing smile. "Most of my life has been about taking care of myself. I'm not ready to change that."

"No one's asking you to change it. Just be safe about it." Frustration rang clear in his voice.

And there was something else. Fear. She saw it in his eyes as they held hers. It surprised her. Of all she'd come to know and learn about him, seeing such an emotion reflected back wasn't something she'd prepared for.

"I am being safe, the best I can." Turning her hand, she curled her fingers with his. "If I'm not at work with Cara and Jackie, I'm with you. And if I'm not with you, I'm with Seth. Or at the main house with Hattie."

She smiled, gentle and slow, hoping he'd understand. "I rarely even drive that nice rental car I was so happy to find. It seems, every time I need to go somewhere, there's somebody there taking me."

"This is already a big change for me." She looked around the table at all the faces that had become so much a part of her life. So much different than what she'd ever expected. "So many times, I find it hard to grasp how quickly I went from being alone to having my life so full of people."

"I'm thankful for it." She squeezed her hand around Luke's. "I truly am."

"But I'm asking you," she stared hard into his hazel eyes, shrinking the world down so only the two of them existed. "Please don't force even more. Don't place the restrictions that I can't even turn around without someone there to look after me. I promise to be aware. To keep myself with others as often as I can."

Luke leaned forward, dropping a gentle kiss against her lips. He was listening, hearing her. Knowing that helped. "I can't handle strangers in uniforms lurking around. I can't be good with expecting to let my every move be known. To give up that much freedom. I can be careful. I can accept that I'm safer with others. But I can't give my entire life over and lose everything I have ever known."

He wanted to argue. She saw it. Knew it. It felt like every breath around the table stopped, waiting for his response.

It wasn't easy. Silently, Luke cursed, fighting between holding her close and shaking her until reality settled.

Needing a distraction, he pushed up from his chair, grabbing a beer for himself and another bottle of wine for Tori and Cara.

Filling both their glasses, he settled back down beside Tori. "We'll go to the funeral with you and Cara tomorrow." He looked at Cade and Jake, receiving nods in agreement. "You promise to be aware of where you are and who's around you no matter the situation?"

Though it was weak, Tori nodded, grabbing for her refilled wine glass. "I promise. Though you need to know, I have lunch planned with Seth tomorrow before the funeral. I don't plan on canceling it or letting you tag along. We need some time alone. I'm not willing to give in on that."

"I wouldn't expect you to." Understanding the need for siblings to have their own time, Luke released the worry still collecting.

And there were advantages to being Chief of Police. He could add the extra uniforms without pushing them on her, setting patrols around Precious Gems, the ranch, and wherever else Tori might frequent.

Knowing that eased some of his fears. He wouldn't close her in and force protection she didn't want. But he'd do what he could from his end to protect her. To keep her safe until he had all this craziness figured out.

Without another word, he tugged gently, bringing her close. Caring nothing about the others who watched, he captured her mouth for a slow kiss that had her sighing softly. "Lunch and the funeral tomorrow." He shoved his hands through her long chestnut hair, holding her there. "We'll figure the rest out after that."

She nodded, falling into another kiss as he swept his lips over hers again.

****

She couldn't be sure if it was the wine or Luke's

constant touch. Maybe it was a bit of both.

The tension that had come so quick with Luke's words faded to nothing more than a distant thought to be collected later.

Sitting at the table, conversation picking up again, beer and wine enjoyed, Tori slipped into enjoying every moment while acutely aware of the handsome man sitting at her side.

Feeling the bit of tipsy caused by finishing her third glass of wine, she took advantage of the block of the table, running gentle fingers up the inside curve of Luke's leg.

She teased. Enjoyed it. Even more when Luke's heated gaze shot her way. Stroking up, back down. Getting close but never there. Always coming back toward his knee only to slide up again.

Caught in a swirl of alcohol and attraction, she kept a polite smile on her face. Holding up her end of the conversation, she relished in the bit of secret she carried on as her fingers glided slowly, teasing for what she hoped would come.

"Think I'll play it safe," Jake pushed his last empty beer out of the way, "and stay the night at the main house tonight."

Luke did his best to hear his brother's words over the blood roaring through his ears. Tori wasn't playing fair. His need burned through, threatening to burst.

"Suppose it is about time to call it a night." Finishing off the last of his own beer, Cade grabbed Jake's empty bottle and pushed up from the table, tossing them in the trash.

Luke didn't think he'd ever been so happy to have his brothers leave. Not even on that long-ago teenage night, skinny-dipping with Marsha Plummet in the river when he was nearly caught by the two of them.

The desperation he'd felt then was nothing compared to what raced through him now as Tori's fingers continued to tease. Coming so close…oh, so close…only to drift away again, killing him with every stroke.

Though his brothers showed no signs, there was knowledge in Cara's eyes as she pushed up from the table. "Yes. I think it's time for us to head back to the main house."

Even as she came around the table, closer to where he continued to sit, fearful of what might be seen if he rose, Tori continued her torment. It wasn't until Cara came close to standing beside them that she dropped her hand and stood from her seat.

"Thank you for going with me today." Tori wrapped her in a tight hug while Luke continued to suffer in his seat, letting the seconds pass before feeling the confidence to move from the protection of the table.

Even then it was risky, made worse by Tori's seductive look catching him over the curve of Cara's shoulder. Pulling away, she found her place between Cara and Cade, walking with them from the kitchen to the front door.

Luke watched as her backside swayed seductively. Need, desperate and hot, speared through his blood.

"Looks like you'll be enjoying your night." Jake's large hand slapped his back, reminding him he wasn't alone. His gaze, too, followed after Tori.

Elbowing his brother's attention away, Luke sent him a scowl. "Better than yours."

And the need for it became almost too much.

Resisting the urge to shove his brother toward the front door with the others, Luke chose to follow beside him, every step feeling slower than the next.

His eyes caught Tori's again, coming through the front room. Desire flamed, hot and potent. He was sure he'd never wanted her more than he did at that very moment.

As she stood at the open door with Cara and Cade, she looked back, a flicker of her tongue against rosy lips.

That was it. What little patience he clung to snapped. Walking quicker, hoping to encourage Jake to do the same, he was at the door in seconds, fighting off every urge to grab Tori right there and then.

What Jake had figured out, Cade caught on. While Cara did her best to usher them both out the door, his brothers took great enjoyment in lingering until Luke felt the urge to punch them both.

This was not fun. Far from enjoyable.

He needed...wanted. Soon, very soon, there would be no stopping him.

Though it was only seconds, it felt like hours as Cara finally got them out the door and down the drive to their cars. While he hovered at the door, Tori stepped out onto the front porch, waving them off.

The minute she turned, he grabbed her and yanked her inside. Slamming the door behind them, taking the second needed to flip the lock, he shoved her against the hard wall.

He didn't give the chance for a word, or even a breath, before taking her. His lips were desperate, angry as they clashed with hers, feeling as if his life depended on the need to feel her, taste her.

Which it did. He was sure of it. The heat boiling inside. The need thrashing through. It was enough to kill even the sanest, calmest of men if not satisfied.

She poured into him. Hands lifting, curling tight around his shoulders, she held on as he lifted her from her feet. There was nothing soft or seductive about them. Only an animal-like need to take all they could.

He stripped her of her clothes as he moved her toward the front room. He wasn't foolish enough to believe they'd have a chance at making it upstairs to the bedroom. That required time he wasn't willing to give.

She slid, slow and smooth, down the length of him as he released her long enough to rid himself of his own clothing. Then it was just them. Skin to skin. Fire striking with every touch, every brush against one another.

He couldn't handle foreplay. Couldn't give another second before burying deep inside her. Falling back onto the thick, oversized chair angled at the fireplace, he took her down on top of him. Entered her with one swift jolt of everything burning through.

"Oh. Luke. God." Her head fell back on a long, heavy sigh. Chestnut curls tumbled over bare shoulders. Slender legs clutched around him. He heard the frantic beat of her heart, matching his own. Felt the harsh breaths shoving through her lungs, shaking her tender body.

This woman, discovered during a blizzard, was turning out to be so much more than he ever imagined. More than what he'd known in his past. Thought he might ever know for his future.

She was everything. So much a part of him already, he couldn't look toward another day without her.

The knowledge of it, the heart-hitting reality, thrust at him hard.

She was his. Of that, he had no doubt. His in every way.

He needed just her. Every feel. Every touch.

So close to losing it right there with the thoughts, the sensations, and the desire raging through, he closed hard hands around her waist, holding her still.

"Slow." He pushed up, dropping a kiss to her lips and across the smooth line of her jaw.

With the force of his grasp, he guided her. Raising her slowly, bringing her down, full and deep, until he filled her completely.

The sensation was almost more than Tori could handle. Over and over again, he pulled her up then back down, slowly building what raged inside and teasing the desperate release she knew they both sought.

"Oh...Tori." His head fell back, dark hair falling over the back of the chair as she worked herself free from his hold, setting her own pace.

There was power in knowing what she did to him. Excitement in the ripple of muscles she felt underneath her. A shudder ripping through as he fought to control what barreled through.

She buried him deep. The air sucked from her lungs as he filled her, leaving her unable to move. He looked at her, his own turmoil flashing in his hazel eyes.

Time stopped. The matching pound of their hearts was the only sound.

Afraid she might lose it right there in that moment, she slid up slowly. Hands tucked behind her back, she touched only where she joined him.

She came down then rose up again, steady with the seduction racing through. The heat grew, taking over. He filled her. So deep. So full. Left her breathless with every move. Desperate to find the final tumble hovering so close. The need to take all she could sizzled through, leaving her blood pounding through her veins.

Oh God. She wanted. So much. All of it.

"Damnit, Tori." Luke's harsh growl broke through. Rising, he curled long arms around her, pulling her hard against him. Soft curves held tight against firm muscle.

Taking control, holding her still, he moved deep inside. The pace no longer slow, he was frantic as he desperately sought what pulsed between them, needing to end the torture.

Her soft lips found his, taking him in as he took her. A gasp…wide emerald eyes clashing with his. And then he watched as she tumbled over, shaking under his hold. Closing tight around him, she took him with her.

Her name was a hungry, fierce growl as he exploded. Over and over, he buried himself inside her, taking every bit to savor. To draw him through until there was nothing left.

Collapsing on top of him, she rested her head in the crook between his shoulder and neck, saying nothing as she fought to catch her breath.

With his arms still closed around her, he drew in the scent of her. The feel of her. Just like this, he could stay forever. Knew there'd never be another who fit him as she did.

****

There were things to be done. To be taken care of.

He had no desire to be here longer than necessary. Found irritation that it had come to the point where he'd had no choice but to come.

The night was heavy by the time they reached the hotel. Waiting for his driver, Perry, to come around for the door, Filip stared blindly through the windows, wondering what the light of day would shed on this small mountain town.

There was the chill of snow in the air. It brushed over him as the door opened and he stepped out onto the sidewalk. He waved Perry away as he made a move to join him at the front doors.

There would be no audience for this. Only him.

He knew the room he sought. Had no need for the front desk. He didn't bother staying low key and unseen by those he passed. There would be no more than a day here for him. By the time the thought settled to seek him, he'd be safely back in Chicago without any threat.

The elevator doors slid open. Others joined him as he entered. An elderly couple, looking at one another with the love of the young, brought a flash of memory. Of his own sweet Amelia. Of the heart she still owned.

No time for such thoughts now, though. Distractions would only delay his time here. Something he wasn't willing to accept.

The elevator stopped at the floor he needed. Leaving the lovebirds to their privacy, he made his way down the hall and dropped a quick, brisk knock against the heavy, wooden door.

He'd hadn't been expected. Surprise and shock were clear in Anton's eyes as he pulled the door open. Stepping back for Filip to enter, he quietly closed the door behind him.

He opened his mouth to question him but before a word escaped, Filip pulled gun and silencer from the back of his waistband and took aim.

It took only one quick, efficient shot. Anton tumbled at his feet, eyes wide from the last moment of shock he knew before life drained from him.

For a moment, Filip felt pity for the one who'd given so many successes in his time. It was sad to know the loss of one who'd satisfied so many of his requests.

But too many mistakes had been made. Mistakes that could not be forgotten or ignored.

Pity gone, leaving nothing but cold acceptance, he turned away from the dead man at his feet. Grabbing the Do Not Disturb sign, he hung it from the knob and quietly closed the door, slipping into the hallway.

Chapter Twenty-Six

Luke wasn't ready to let Tori go.

As she stirred in his arms, he tightened his hold. "Not yet." His voice nothing more than a harsh whisper, he held her to the chair.

She cuddled back into him. Chestnut curls spread over his chest. Soft breath fanned over bare skin. He knew her to be strong in all she'd faced. But here, in his arms, she felt so fragile.

Not that he'd say such to her. He knew better.

Keeping her tight against him, he found his way to his feet. He wanted her again. But not here.

He wanted her in bed. Spread out beneath him. Long and seductive as he took her.

She clung to him. Wrapping long legs around his waist, she rested her head against his shoulder as he flipped off lights left on earlier while finding his way up the stairs.

At the open door of his bedroom, he paused. Needing to taste, unable to wait even a few seconds more to get her to bed, he bent low and found her soft, inviting lips, savoring the soft purr she responded with.

Testing his skill and agility, he kept his mouth with hers as he made his way to the bed.

Gently, he took her down with him, finally letting his hold up as she came down on the soft mattress. Emerald eyes stared up at him, full of all that fired inside of her.

She trusted him, there in that moment. He saw it in her gaze. Felt the jolt of awareness singe through. For all that she demanded she do on her own, here she gave of herself, opening up in ways she kept so protected in her day to day life.

He wanted that look forever. Wanted to know it in and out of his bed. The realization, the force of it, was nearly his undoing.

Needing to feel, taste, know, he bent low, trailing his mouth over the delicate edge of her chin and down the slender line of her neck. He wanted slow. Seductive. Drawing out what he'd come to realize meant so much.

A soft touch against her breast, barely a tease to bare skin, had her sucking in a breath. His mouth tasted while his hands roamed.

Tori rose into him. Arching off the mattress, she deepened the touch and feel of him loving her.

Her blood thickened as he took her with only mouth and hand, lavishing his magical touch over every inch of her. Missing nothing. Taking her in and drawing her up until she was sure she floated on nothing more than a simple cloud above the bed.

"So beautiful," he whispered, coming back to her. Finding her mouth, taking her in a kiss holding so much, he drew her emotions from the furthest reaches of her soul.

It was—she didn't even have a word for it.

Lifting her hands, she tangled them through his hair. "I need you." She tugged on him, pulling him away to look into his hazel eyes. "Please."

His hands continued to roam. His smile was slow and seductive as he stared down on her.

Everything inside burned for him. She needed him more than she remembered ever needing anything before in life. Fingers still twisted in his dark hair, she brought him back for another kiss. Giving all she had inside, she hoped he felt what she couldn't yet say.

He drew them higher. Away from everything except the feel of their bodies pressed together. The heat that gathered and built between them.

With a press between her knees, she parted for him. He eased over her, cradling her cheeks between his hands and watching as he sank deep inside.

She rose. Closed around him.

She wanted this to last forever. This moment. The here and now. One with Luke in every way. The feel of him pouring through her senses, bringing him even closer.

He rushed nothing, slowly rising before returning to fill her once again.

Tears collected at the corners of her eyes. Her heart swelled for every second his gaze locked with hers as he moved with her, creating everything that was so perfect between them.

She felt the rise. The need growing, stronger and stronger with every stroke. Every touch. Every look.

She touched with hands, body, eyes, as she drifted higher and higher, watching, intrigued by the raw passion reflecting in the dark shadows of his eyes. In the quakes she felt rumble through him for every time they met.

And then there was nothing but sensation surrounding her, leaving all else behind. Rising and falling with Luke, every inch of her was on fire, desperately needing release.

He buried himself deep inside, staring hard into her eyes. "I love you."

And with that, he tumbled over, taking her with him.

****

The first hints of sun poured through the slit in the curtains, rousing Tori from sleep.

Her first thought was of Derby, knowing there would be no lingering if he was ready to go out.

But there was no Derby, she remembered, still half caught in sleep. He'd stayed the night at the main house.

She had more time for sleep. The joyful thought had her snuggling deeper into the heavy comforter. She turned, brushing against the hard lines of Luke's chest. The warmth of his skin chased up her arm.

Never in her life did she believe she'd find comfort in waking up to a man in bed with her. Especially not as one morning had stretched on to two and more.

He'd told her he loved her. The memory returned as she cuddled against him, finding a peace there she was coming to count on way too much.

In her mind, his voice continued to echo as she remembered the words slipping from him. Part of her wanted to deny them. To excuse them away as nothing more than being caught up in the heat and excitement of what they shared.

But she knew better. Knew Luke better. Such words were not something he'd toss so carelessly, not even in the throes of sex, no matter how amazing or great it might be.

Though she'd hoped for more sleep, it slipped away as her mind wandered, playing with the idea of

Luke's love. What it meant. To her. To him. To what she knew of her life and how she'd always lived it.

Did she love him? The question filtered through her thoughts. How could she know? She had nothing to base it on. No true experience to tell her one way or another.

The love she knew was lost so many years ago. Before she was old enough to recognize it for what it was. Her life had been about avoiding it. Resisting it at all costs. How was she to know now if what she felt for Luke was true? If it was love or merely infatuation with something so new and foreign in her life?

He shifted beneath her. Pushing up onto an elbow, she gazed down on him.

"Morning." His early morning drawl still held the thick hint of sleep. He rose, curled an arm around the back of her head, and brought her to him for a slow kiss.

There was no stopping her eager response as she sank into him, enjoying the touch of him against her. She was quickly coming to learn, more than the nights of sex—as amazing as it was—it was these few stolen moments in the morning that lingered with her. Lifted her.

He brushed gentle fingers down the ripple of her spine, deepening the kiss until they were both lost in it.

She could stay there forever, right in that moment. The morning sun sliding over them. The warmth of their bodies surrounding them. A soft, slow kiss welcoming them to the new day.

Letting out a reluctant sigh when he pulled away, she did her best to ignore the fact they both had places they needed to be.

Still they lingered, neither eager to leave the heat and comfort of each other. Luke hitched a finger under her chin, bringing her face back to his. "We should get up." He dropped another kiss. "Though I'd much rather spend the day in bed with you."

"If only we could." Tori's answering sigh was long and wistful. She thought of work. Her lunch with her brother. Maxine's funeral.

"Another day," she promised with a smile.

He didn't respond, only stared at her. His hazel eyes darkened with whatever thoughts ran through his mind. "We could have plenty of those days," he ran a finger down the line of her cheek, "if you agreed to marry me."

It took a moment for the hit to make its mark.

"What?" She shot up, taking the comforter with her, holding it above the swell of her breasts. "There's no need to talk of marriage. None."

Fear was a cold chill racing through. Chasing it away, she sought to grab on to the anger finding its way. The heat of it felt much better.

The slight tilt of a smile on his face made it even stronger. He reached for her again but she brushed him away, scooting back on the mattress, out of reach.

"Knew you wouldn't take that one lightly." Pushing up, caring nothing about covering himself, he sat a few inches away. Naked, bronzed skin skimming over hard muscle, he tempted her in the most unfair of ways.

"Of course I wouldn't." She shoved a handful of hair back from her face. "How in the world could I? I laid there," she waved an errant hand where they had been so close only seconds before, "going through my mind what it meant when you told me you loved me. And before I can even get my mind around that, you throw marriage at me."

Shoving off the bed, she stood, glaring down at him. "I told you before, I don't do this." She waved an arm carelessly in the air. "Any kind of commitment, and especially not marriage, isn't something I want in my life."

He grabbed her around the wrist before she could walk away. "I love you." His hazel eye burned with the truth of his words. "I hope, someday, to marry you. But—"

He tightened his grasp as she tried pulling away. "I'm not about to battle it with you. If this, what we have right now, is all you can do, then I'll take it. As long as I have you in my life, the rest can wait."

He released her. She didn't have a response, her mind refusing to function with the thoughts tossing around inside. Sucking in her breath and turning her back on him and all he'd offered, she forced her legs to keep her upright as she made her way for the bathroom.

She may have closed the door harder than she needed to. Set the shower higher than she normally would. But there was a burn inside. One she needed to break free from before it pushed her to make the kind of mistakes she couldn't turn back from.

****

Sometimes a woman just knew.

Standing behind the counter, watching as Tori reorganized the same shelf for the third time, Cara shook her head.

"Got any idea what that's about?" Joining her behind the counter, Jackie gave a jerk of her head in

Tori's direction.

"My guess...Luke." Careful not to trip over Derby where he slept on his bed, Cara came out from behind the counter.

"Moving them around a million times over isn't going to help whatever's bothering you." She laid a gentle hand over Tori's, stopping her before she got started on her fourth attempt at rearranging.

With a long, heavy breath, Tori nodded, moving away from the shelf. "Suppose you're right."

Tossing an arm around her shoulders, Cara moved her further away before she was tempted to go at it again.

"So, what did he do?" Jackie stuck an elbow against the counter as they came closer and rested her chin in her palm.

There was only a moment of hesitation before Tori shook her head. "Last night he tells me he loves me. This morning he starts talking about marriage."

She sank into the empty stool behind the counter and gave Derby an absent scratch behind the ears as he jumped to her lap. "Then he ends it with declaring, if I don't want those things yet, he'll wait, just to have me as part of his life."

"Evil man." Jackie couldn't help the short burst of laughter.

Shooting her a dirty look, Cara went around to where Tori sat, looking so lost and confused.

"Do you love him?" She rested an understanding hand over Tori's shoulder.

"That's the hell of it. I don't know." Tori's shoulders slumped under Cara's hold. "I've never come close to being in love with anyone. Or being loved back. And it's not like they have a chart to follow—if you have these feelings, your hearts already gone. If you have these other feelings—just keep on walking."

Cara couldn't help her own bit of laughter. "Suppose that would make it easier."

Tori's smile wasn't much but it was something when she glanced up. "Sure would for me, especially now."

From behind the counter, Jackie pulled out three water bottles and brought them over. "This kind of talk calls for a drink." She handed one to Cara and to Tori. "But, since it's too early for that, this will have to do."

Twisting the cap on her own, she took a drink, looking at Tori over the top edge. "So tell me, this thing with you and Luke, whatever it might be, when you give your goodbyes in the morning, are you done with him or stuck thinking about him as the day goes on."

He constantly irritated her thoughts. Tori couldn't deny it. "I don't like it. But he's there, no matter how hard I try chasing him away." She opened her own water bottle and took a long sip. The cool liquid helped ease what burned inside.

"And he has a knack for annoying me when I'm with him or away from him. Has this way that just seems to sink in deep, taking its bites."

The look Cara and Jackie exchanged wasn't one Tori liked. "Love is supposed to be something a lot easier than this," she defended, wishing she believed it as much as she hoped they'd confirm it. "Not that I've ever cared to find out. It's never been worth my effort. You go long enough without it, you soon learn how little it really can mean in your life."

"Are you trying to convince us or yourself?"

Though a knowing smile still lingered on her face, Cara's voice was gentle and understanding.

"Hell, I don't know." Agitated now, Tori pushed up from the stool. Her water bottle collapsing under the force of her hold, she paced back and forth between the counter and the window. "He could have kept his mouth shut. Said nothing about love, and worse, marriage. Then I wouldn't be here looking like a fool, feeling as if I'm acting like a child, trying to figure it out."

And now she was sounding irrational to top it off. Like a spoiled little girl who didn't get her way. "Sorry." Shaking off the emotions threatening to overwhelm, she rejoined Cara and Jackie at the counter.

"Love can drive you crazy, can't it?" Jackie slung an easy arm around her shoulders and gave a tug.

There was no use denying what Tori knew, had just proven with her outburst. "Yes. It can."

Feeling drained, she returned to the stool, slumping into it. "Not that I enjoy admitting it."

"Love isn't always fun." Cara patted her knee while encouraging her to drink more of her water. "But, in the end, it's worth it."

Tori wasn't convinced of that yet. Hell, she wasn't convinced of anything at the moment. Other than the fact her choice to come to Snow Ridge had completely turned the life she knew upside down.

****

"You look like hell." Sipping from the one beer he allowed himself for lunch, Seth stared over the rim at his sister.

"It was a long morning." Not daring alcohol with the emotions churning inside, Tori sipped at a glass of iced tea before taking another bite of her stew.

"And you've got a longer day yet." Taking a bite from his own bowl, Seth shook his head. "Are you sure you want to go to this funeral. Everyone would understand if you changed your mind."

She hadn't wanted to go from the start but that was beside the point. "I have to go. It's only right."

"I don't like it." Reaching across the table, he rested a hand over hers. "You being out and about with all that is going on. If I had my way, you'd be safe and sound back at the ranch. Moonshine or the Double G, I don't really care."

She groaned, not ready to have this argument again. "Now you're starting to sound like Luke."

"I happen to agree with him." Pulling his hand away, he reached for his beer. "Told him as much this morning when I met with him."

"You met with Luke? Why?" She pushed her bowl out of the way, having no interest in food. Memories of the morning swept back, dragging with them all she'd done her best to forget since her talk with Cara and Jackie.

"Because I care about you. Because I want to know what the hell is going on with the investigation." He lowered his voice, his eyes heavy as they stared at her from across the table. "Because it scares the hell out of me to think something might happen to you. That I might lose you just as I got you back."

Her throat thickened. Reaching for her tea, she took a long, slow swallow, chasing back the threat of tears.

How in the world had she come into all of this? From barely allowing herself to dream of a relationship with her brother and living a life that was her own without others to so much more. *So many more.* From her brother to Luke, even Cara and Jackie. It didn't seem possible.

And she wasn't sure what to do with it. How to handle or accept it all. First instinct was always to run. To end it before it could be ended on her.

But, for the first time in her life, taking flight didn't feel right.

And what that said about where she was proved a bit too frightening to dwell on at the moment.

"I'll be okay." It was all she knew to say.

He wasn't convinced. Far from it. Still, Seth chose to keep his arguments silent. She had enough to battle at the moment. He didn't need to be adding to it.

Plus, he trusted Luke. Knew that look he saw in the chief's eyes when talk of Tori came up. He loved her. As much as Seth struggled to know how to deal with such a fact, there was no denying it. And loving her meant protecting her with all he had.

For his worries, that helped. So much.

"Eat." He pushed her bowl back. "You've got a long enough afternoon ahead of you without trying to face it on an empty stomach."

His stare was hard, unrelenting, until she picked up her spoon and took another bite. Satisfied, he did the same and silently chose to let stress and worry go for a few moments of enjoying the time he'd been given with his sister.

Chapter Twenty-Seven

The snow that had been threatening finally found its way. Small flakes fell over those who strode slowly into the church.

There were so many. Standing on the sidewalk watching it all, Tori was surprised by the amount of bodies pushing their way inside.

"Small town." Cara threw an arm around her shoulders. "Don't have to personally know her to feel it's right to be here."

Tori looked around her at the others who had come. Her brother. Luke and his brothers. Cara and Jackie. Would they have come regardless?

She figured it was an answer she didn't need to know.

As one, they joined the crowd working their way inside. Luke grabbed her hand, holding it tight. Looking up at him, she wondered what ran through his mind. Did he think back to last night? To the way they ended the morning?

While her mind wrestled with everything said, he seemed so calm. So easy with the two of them together as if nothing had come to change things between them.

Had they not been headed in for the solemn goodbye of another, she might have stopped him where they were, demanding answers to the confusion, anger, and uncertainty brewing inside.

But, as it was, she had no choice but to wait until a better time presented itself.

They thinned out to make it through the heavy doors, stopping long enough to add their names to the leather-bound book waiting on the other side before finding their way to the pews.

The chill from outside drifted in as so many entered. A heavy, somber mood hovered as Amazing Grace drifted from an unseen organ. From where she sat, Tori saw the dark mahogany coffin, the top section propped open as people slowly strode by.

"Where are you going?" Luke grabbed her hand as she pushed to her feet.

"I need to see." She nodded toward the altar where the coffin rested below.

"What's the use of it?" He didn't let go, holding her where she was. "You're already doing for her by being here."

Over the broad width of his shoulder, Tori looked to Cara and Jackie for support. Where he wouldn't understand, she knew they would.

"We'll go together." Standing, Cara put an arm around her shoulders and sent a look at Luke, stopping whatever further arguments he might have.

Jackie found her way to the other side, forcing Luke to drop his hold. Twining her arm through Tori's, she and Cara led her to the aisle while the sound of the men following came up from behind. With a glance over her shoulder, she saw only Seth left, saving their places along the long, wooden pew.

"Thank you." She looked between Jackie and Cara.

"Not something I'd be choosing to do in your situation." Jackie tightened her hold as they made their way through those around them. "But, if it's something you need, we'll get it done."

The brothers only a few steps behind, they found their way to the growing line waiting to pay their final respects. Drawing closer, Tori stepped free from Cara and Jackie, needing the distance though she couldn't explain why.

Sensing her need, they hung back, giving her space.

She wasn't sure why she did this. Why she was hesitant now that she was there. It settled with her, as she came to the head of the coffin, that she'd never seen Maxine in life, only through a single picture.

This would be her first and only time to take in the face of a woman who lost her life because of the horror haunting Tori's.

She looked peaceful, at ease in her rest. Her dress was a deep, ivy green, contrasting against pale skin wrinkled by age and whitened by death.

Even in death, the kindness in her face showed through. It was round and soft with short gray hair permed tight around it, bringing forth images of a Grandmother in the kitchen making cookies for her sweet little ones or sitting on the couch with them gathered on her lap, reading a story.

She didn't have grandchildren. That much Tori knew. But that was what she saw as she stared down on the innocent woman who had lost in the worst of ways.

A tear escaped. And then another. She mourned for this woman she never knew. Hurt for whatever family, loved ones, she'd left behind.

It was odd. She'd built a life of no connections so she'd be free of the pain of loss. Yet, here she stood, feeling that pain for someone she had never crossed paths with.

"There now child." A gentle arm slipped around her shoulders. "She's moved on to a better place. One full of joys we could never imagine here among the living."

The voice wasn't one she knew. Swiping at her tears, Tori turned her head, staring into a set of violet eyes unlike anything she'd seen before. They seemed to reach out and pull her into whatever secrets dwelled within her mesmerizing gaze.

Long, gold hoops danced in her ears. Jeweled rings glimmered from the fingers resting against the curve of her shoulder.

She had only a moment to feel uneasy before Cara and Jackie were there, working their way between Tori and the stranger at her side. With both their arms protectively around her waist, they stepped her back, away from the coffin, and out of the hold of the other woman.

She turned, stepping away from the coffin as well. A smile of recognition grew on her face as her eyes passed over Cara and Jackie at Tori's side.

"So, you do well." She went to reach for Cara, dropping her hand back to her side when Cara took a step back. "I heard about the evil." Sadness filled her violet eyes. "Was relieved to learn you hadn't been lost to it."

Confused, Tori could only pass her gaze between them. What was she missing? She had a sense of others gathering and glanced back to see Luke and his brothers coming up behind them.

Reaching out, Cade drew Cara back against his

chest, wrapping protective arms around her. "I hope you aren't planning on offering my fiancé another of your readings, Madame Luwiski."

The name sounded familiar. Tori went back in her mind, doing her best to remember where she'd heard it before.

"I'm not here for readings." She shook her head, long, thick auburn hair falling over her shoulders. "This is a day to honor those who have passed from this world into the other. To wish them peace and joy on their travels."

"Which is why the tears are only for us, child. The living are the ones left to suffer as those who have passed find so much better." Reaching out, she grabbed Tori's hand, cradling it between her own.

The look in Madame Luwiski's eyes changed, darkened, as her hold tightened. "Oh my." Her breasts rose harsh under the low cut of her dress.

Tori wasn't sure what to think. She tried pulling her hand away but Madame Luwiski only held on tighter. "You must be careful." Her voice lowered to nothing but a rumbling whisper.

Tori didn't understand. Was pretty sure she didn't want to. With another tug, harder this time, she pulled her hand free and took a step back, finding herself coming up hard against Luke's broad chest.

She was thankful for the comfort of it as Madame Luwiski continued staring through those violet eyes of hers. A dark shadow lingered in her expression that had been so open and gentle only minutes before.

"You have darkness hovering close. You must listen." She moved forward, stopping as Jackie moved from Tori's side, preventing her from getting closer.

"Please." Desperation filled her eyes. "I felt it when I took your hand. Something is lurking, very close. So close. You must be careful."

The words fell like heavy stones. Tori backed even further into Luke, fighting the urge to turn and run.

Feeling her tremble, he shifted so he stood between Tori and Madame Luwiski. "I think it's best we get back to our seats." Wrapping her tight to him, he eased her away.

She didn't argue as he guided her, holding tight to her hand as they squeezed back across the pew where Seth waited.

"Somebody please explain what just happened." She sucked in a harsh breath, hoping to chase away the lingering chill.

Cara settled beside her, resting a hand against her leg. "You've just met Snow Ridge's personal psychic."

Memory struck. "The one you suggested I visit?" Tori leaned forward, her gaze passing by Cara, resting on Jackie. "That's what you wanted?"

"No. Not that." Jackie shook her head. "She used to be something fun Cara and I shared. It never meant anything. Not really."

"Until the Spring Festival." Cara closed her eyes as if remembering it. "Scared the hell out of me with her predictions of evil coming into my life."

And she'd been right. Tori knew the rest of what they weren't saying. Evil had come to Cara. In the worst of ways.

And now—

"*You have darkness hovering close*."

The words echoed inside her head. Sent a chill racing up her spine. With all that happened up until this point she feared, more than ever, whatever the darkness was waiting for her.

****

Luke's frustration simmered just below the surface.

Father Frances' voice rose and fell yet all he heard were the words of Madame Luwiski. All he felt was the delicate warmth of Tori close at his side.

He wanted to grab her and drag her from the church. Back to the ranch. To his place. Where he could bundle her up and keep her safe until this horror was over. Until he caught the bastard behind it.

He'd get her to see the truth of needing to do more, he decided as Father Frances sprinkled Holy Water over the coffin, his voice low in the prayer for absolution. This funeral she'd insisted on was all but over now. He'd given her what she'd needed to be here and pay her respects.

But that would have to be the end of it. Madame Luwiski's warning put a fear in him, changing the promises he'd made. If she didn't agree to protection, he'd force it on her. Taking her anger, her wrath, as long as it meant keeping her alive.

He wouldn't lose her now. Couldn't lose her. Even a lifetime of facing her hatred of him would be better than no lifetime at all.

As the organ began to play and the coffin was carried away, he stood with the rest, his decision made. He reached for her hand, planning on holding her tight until he had her safely back at the ranch.

The ringing of his phone changed his plans.

Glancing down at the familiar number, he knew it wasn't a call he could ignore. He hated leaving Tori for even a second.

"Make sure you stay close with your sister." He dropped a heavy hand over Seth's shoulder. "I'll meet you outside."

He didn't have to wait for the nod. Seth would take care of Tori. There was no doubt or question in his mind.

The phone already to his ear as he pushed out the heavy doors, he no longer heard the music behind him, only the familiar voice of Alec coming through with the answers he had asked for.

****

Tori wondered about Luke, watching as he disappeared out the doors. He hadn't said a word to her before grabbing his phone. He'd said something to Seth, though, in the seconds before he left.

Stepping closer, Seth settled an arm over her shoulders. "You know how it is." He pulled her into a quick hug. "Duty calls."

She knew but still wondered.

It was the nerves picking up strength and mingling with Madame Luwiski's frightening prediction. With the funeral and the threat continuing to hover, day after day, it was getting so damn close to pushing her past the breaking point. Away from the sanity she desperately clung to.

Sucking it in, something she seemed to be doing more and more these days, she waited as over-crowded pews emptied into the aisle, following the coffin through the doors.

Stepping aside so the others could go ahead, Seth linked an arm through Tori's. There were so many bodies pressed together, moving through the aisle, it was impossible to stay together.

315

She lost track of Cara and Cade as they pressed together into the mass of people. Even Jackie and Jake as they found their own chance to escape the pew a few steps behind.

Seth held tight as he found a gap for them to squeeze through. They were pushed from behind as more found their way into the aisle, the heavy double doors ahead promising an escape.

Tori felt the impatient press against her back. Was tempted to turn back with a reminder she couldn't move any faster than the person ahead of her. But this was a church. A funeral they were leaving. Snapping at others on the way out wasn't exactly the thing to do.

Still, did they have to be so close? She swore she could feel their breath against the back of her neck. The toe of their shoes nearly grabbing her heels.

"I doubt this church has ever held so many." Seth did his best to keep them going. "Not even for Christmas or Easter can I imagine it being this full or crazy."

It surprised him, really, how many had come to pay their respects. He'd known Maxine had been a local. Liked by many. But it seemed as if the whole town had found their way to the church.

Inching forward, he wondered how many had come simply for the horror of how she died. The shock of such ugliness again settling over Snow Ridge when they had yet to recover from the evil they'd faced only months before.

Perhaps this was the healing the town had needed. A way to stand as one and let it be known they wouldn't be broken.

He couldn't know for sure. All his mind was sure

of was the relief he sought once they made it through the doors. And they were close now. Slow step by slow step, they drew near.

They made it, a single step outside, when he was tugged on. "You didn't tell me you would be here." A slight pout to her red lips, Misty Sanders looked up at him with her dreamy, blue eyes. The very ones he'd lost himself in only a few nights before.

He hadn't imagined there was any kind of commitment between them requiring him to let her know he'd planned to attend the funeral. But, by the look on her face, he'd obviously thought wrong.

"It wasn't part of my plans until late yesterday." He tried moving her along with him, but she stayed planted where she was, pulling him closer.

There was no stopping it, with the shove from behind and the sudden change to Misty's side, he lost hold of Tori. Couldn't get a chance to grab at her again.

He wouldn't worry, he promised as he caught sight of her moving with the rush down the stairs. With this many people around, only a fool would try something. She'd catch up with the others only a bit ahead of her and wait for him to catch up.

Which he would do just as soon as he let Misty have her pout.

****

Tori barely managed a glance back as Seth's hold slid away. The force from behind was still powerful and unrelenting.

But she saw enough of the pretty blonde he turned to speak with. Enough to wonder about the story between them.

And then they were gone as she was shoved from

behind. Careful not to trip down the stairs, she bit back the angry words lingering.

Ahead she saw Jackie and Jake joining Cara and Cade on the sidewalk. Keeping her focus on them, she waited for the crowd to thin out as bodies spread over the church grounds.

From behind, again, she was hit. But this time with more force, causing her to stumble forward. A hand fell to her arm, steadying her.

"Careful." She didn't recognize the voice but was thankful for the help in keeping her on her feet.

But as she tried to turn and move her arm from his hold, he tightened, continuing to push her forward. "You'd be wise to say nothing." The voice came now as nothing but a harsh whisper against her ear. "Unless you're wanting harm to come to your new friends."

She looked back at those gathered on the sidewalk. Wondered about Luke. Thought of Seth behind her. "What do you want?" Her voice matched the same whisper.

"Just to talk." She was eased toward the far end of the crowds. To the thick set of Evergreens lining the church property.

She didn't believe him for a minute. There were plenty around. All she had to do was scream. That would be all it would take.

As if a part of her thoughts, a firm hand clamped over her mouth as she was pulled deeper into the trees. "I don't wish to hurt you. Please do not push me to that point."

The hand pushed tight, leaving her gasping for breath. She tried fighting it, shaking her head fiercely from side to side. But it was no use. The grasp over her was too strong. Too intent on keeping her silent.

And now she was out of sight of the others. But there was another, she noticed, coming out of the trees only a few steps away. For a moment relief swelled. Then she saw the look in his dark eyes and the gun cradled against his thigh.

He wasn't there for good.

She had nothing. No way to fight the one who held her from behind. The other with the weapon she had a feeling he wouldn't be shy to use.

"No need to worry." The voice from behind fell low and harsh against her ear. "Perry has no reason to harm you. He is only here to make sure we get away without incident."

And so they hurried her. One from behind, the other at her side, forcing her down the line of trees and toward the back of the church. Though it eased some, allowing her easier breaths, the hand continued to hold tight over her mouth.

Her heart beat a frantic pace against her ribs as fear became overwhelming. With all the push and shove after the service and so many bodies so close together, nobody would have noticed what happened or realized she was being torn away.

And once they did…her pulse jumped at the long, black car waiting in the alley…it would be too late.

The one with the gun stepped off ahead, opening the back door.

"We're going to take a ride." The voice from behind rose a bit as the threat of being overheard disappeared. "Again, I have no desire to see you harmed unless you leave me no choice."

She was shoved in the car, hand removed from her

mouth and door slammed tight before she had a chance to utter a sound. The one with the gun stood there, staring down at her through the window as the opposite door opened.

And then, there he was. The one who'd taken her.

As he came into view her blood froze. Her heart stopped.

The face. She knew it. Felt the chill of it.

It was the face of her nightmares.

Chapter Twenty-Eight

Luke stood a few steps down the sidewalk, away from the crowds flooding from the church. Phone to his ear, he kept a steady gaze on those gathering in groups after the funeral, waiting for the familiar face he sought.

"When you told me you were hitting walls, I didn't imagine how damn thick they were." Alec's voice held a ring of frustration as it traveled through the phone. "I had to resort to threats of sending agents down there to do some looking on their own."

Luke waited, knowing there was more. His eyes scanned the crowd for the long flow of chestnut hair he knew so well.

There was a long heavy sigh on the other end of the phone. "You aren't going to like what I've learned. I have a feeling, even with what you might have imagined, it comes nowhere close to the truth."

That got his attention. "What do you know?"

He listened as Alec laid it out for him. Every detail he'd learned. The dark truths, hidden for so long.

From those in uniform who'd known, from the start, who'd been responsible for the murder of Tori's parents. To the cover-up that followed.

It was an ugly reality. But he'd been prepared for it. Knew there wasn't anything good that had happened the night Tori so tragically lost her parents. He handled it, accepted it, until Alec's final share of information.

Anger and disbelief seethed through his blood as he heard the truth of who was behind such a horror against Tori.

How could he? The thought ran harsh through his mind, playing over and over again. Of all things he'd expected, this was not it.

His fear for Tori burning stronger, he ended the call, rushing back toward the crowd gathered in front of the church. He caught sight of his brothers with Cara and Jackie, gathered together on the sidewalk.

He didn't bother with a greeting, fear leading the way. "Where's Tori?'

"Haven't seen her." Jake shrugged, no sign of the worry Luke had running wild inside. "It was hell getting out of the church. We were separated coming out of the pew. She and Seth were a bit behind us. They're probably caught up back there somewhere."

Turning, Luke looked over the many still hovered around, searching desperately for the familiar, beautiful face. The emerald eyes always sparkling with emotion. The full mouth so perfect when pulled into a smile.

But, even as he moved deeper in, elbowing past those gathered to chat and share memories of the deceased, he saw no sign of her. Near the doors, he caught sight of Seth. Head bowed deep, he was caught in conversation with a well-endowed, currently pouty-lipped blond.

It took only a few long strides to reach him. "Where's Tori?"

Caught in mid-sentence, Seth looked away from the blond, a look of surprise covering his face. "I'm guessing she's met up with the others by now. I got held up." He spared a glance to his side. "But that was the way she was headed."

Fear spiked as Luke took another look around. "She isn't with them. They haven't seen her since before you left the church."

Worry shadowed Seth's gaze as he forgot the woman at his side and turned with Luke, scanning the crowd. "She has to be here. There was nowhere else for her to go."

"I was sure she'd be safe with all these people around." Guilt took root in the dark rumble of Seth's voice. "It was just to the sidewalk where the others waited."

There was not a bit of this Luke liked. Pushing through others, not giving a damn about manners or apologies, he frantically searched. Needing a glimpse of her. Praying for one.

"What's going on?" Cade was at his side as the heavy weight of realization settled, nearly choking him.

It was Seth who answered as Luke fought to form words over the lump caught hard in his throat. "We can't find Tori."

"How's that possible? Weren't you with her?"

Luke waved his hand before Seth had a chance to respond. "It doesn't matter." He fought back his own irrational anger at Seth, knowing it wouldn't do any good. "What matters is finding her."

"We don't know for certain anything has happened to her." There was a trace of hope lingering in Seth's gaze as he continued to search. "Maybe she went back into the church to use the bathroom. Or didn't see the others on the sidewalk and is somewhere looking for them."

Luke only shook his head as he grabbed his phone

and pressed it to his ear. He'd call in every damn officer he had if that's what it took to find her. Unlike Seth, he had no trace of hope to hold on to. He knew. His gut screamed it.

Tori was gone.

He thought of what Alec told him, dread hitting hard. "Your sister's gone." His voice and gaze were hard as he turned on Seth. "And it's your grandfather who has her."

****

She'd never known such fear. This was her nightmare, come to life. Shoving back against the door, as far from him as she could get, Tori fumbled for the door handle. Needing escape. Craving it as desperately as a breath through her lungs.

"You'll find Perry has already engaged the locks." He made no move to get closer, only watched from his side of the car.

She felt the movement beneath her as Perry pulled away from the curb, starting down the deserted street. Tearing her gaze from his, from those eyes that had haunted her for so long, she stared out the window and prayed for someone to come around the back of the church and see them before it was too late.

But there was no one to be seen.

How long would it take them? When would they know she was gone and nowhere to be found? The answers were too frightening to think of.

"I had hoped this would have ended different." The deep voice from the other side of the car brushed a chill over her skin. "I sent one who I believed to be my best to take care of things. Unfortunately, he failed."

"You sent—"

Tori shook her head, trying to make sense of it all. "The one who tried to get me fired, ran me off the road, destroyed my apartment, murdered an innocent woman…that was *your* doing?"

Anger lit in with the fear. As much as she wanted space between them another part of her wished for the ability to strike out and cause him pain.

Because it wasn't just the memories of what had happened since she'd come to Snow Ridge coming to her. But the memories of her parents' murder haunting her. And that was the worst of it. Seeing his face. Bringing back with it the images of the night her parents died. Knowing he was there and a part of it.

She wanted to make him pay.

"I've only done what I must." His voice drifted as the car turned, picking up speed. "As I have since you were a small girl."

And there it was. The truth she already knew. "It was you. You were there the night my parents died."

"It was an unfortunate situation."

"An unfortunate situation?" She wanted to surge at him and claw him with all the pain raging inside. Anger tampered the fear. Left her wanting revenge more than escape. "Is that what you call the murder of two innocent people?"

He didn't respond immediately. Instead, he shifted to stare a moment out the window. "Innocent is not a word I would use for your father." He turned back, an emotion in his eyes she was afraid to know. "But for your mother, yes."

"Why?" She felt the pain of it in her heart. The continued ache of a loss she'd never recovered from. "Why my parents? Why them?"

Brushing angrily at the tears escaping, she pulled back with her strength, refusing to let any sign of weakness shimmer through. She needed answers. Deserved them. And then she would find a way to get as far away as possible. Even if it meant leaping from a moving car.

"Your father once worked for me. Because it was your mother he married, I placed him high in his position. He wanted for nothing. I gave all I could. For them and for you and your brother."

He sucked in a harsh breath and, for a moment, drifted away. "I loved you. All of you. It was in me to give you the very best. I agreed with the marriage, though your father had never been part of the family we kept close. I'd believed he would do only good where I placed him."

He made no sense, talking of love in the murder of her parents. Who was he? What did any of what he had to say do with what happened all those years ago?

"But, your father, he did not have the heart for it." His gaze held steady with hers. Even as she wanted to look away, she couldn't. "My business began to wear on him and his true cowardliness came through. He wanted out. And when I wouldn't allow it, he resorted to threats of going to the authorities, ruining everything I had worked so hard for."

There was anger. She felt it in the space between them. "Your business, it's not legal?" It was more statement than question, remembering what she'd learned in Chicago.

"Some may see it that way." His shrug of the shoulders held no care for what others saw.

They picked up more speed. Glancing out the

window, Tori saw they'd reached the highway leading away from Snow Ridge. Fear caught back up, reminding her what she faced. As much as she thrived for answers so long denied, she needed to find a way out of this. A way, she prayed, that spared her life.

But first, she had to know. "Is that why my father was murdered? Because he threatened to go to the authorities?"

There wasn't an ounce of remorse in the hard eyes looking at her. "He left me no choice. What I have built is more to me than any fondness I might have once felt for him."

"And my mother?" Her words choked over the lump in her throat. She saw it as if in the nightmare again. Sitting on the bed watching her mother, so wanting to be like her. Only to, minutes later, watch as the last moments of her life drained away.

Surprise hit as she saw sadness reflected back at her. "Your mother is my greatest regret. She, as well as you and your brother, were not to be hurt. Had she not put herself in the position she had and taken a bullet meant for her husband, I never would have lost her."

"You lost her?" Tori's voice rose high in the car. Her hands bunched into fists as she fought back the bile rising in her throat. "How dare you."

"I dare because she was mine. Just as you are."

Her head spinning, she fought for even breath. Nothing made sense. Not a bit of it. "What the hell do you mean...she was yours?"

"I mean it as I said it. She was mine." Though he didn't move, he seemed to reach out to her. Tori stuck her back closer to the door. "She was my only child. My daughter."

"No." Shaking her head, she denied the reality of his words. He lied. He had to. Because if there was truth in it…the horrid connection left a violent, acrid taste in her mouth.

If it was truth, she'd just met the grandfather she'd never known she had.

Chapter Twenty-Nine

Luke barked orders, leaving no room for argument or debate. They'd asked questions of everyone. And yet only one thought she might have seen a man and woman step through the thick mash of trees lining the church. But, even with that, she couldn't be sure.

The only thing anyone could be sure of was Tori was gone. She wasn't in the bathroom, as Seth had suggested. Or anywhere around the church. She'd disappeared. And somehow, only one person might or might not have seen her.

The anger, fueled by raw fear, threatened to take control. Only the training he'd known and the life he'd lived behind the badge kept him up. Kept him going when his strongest urge was to search for Tori himself without care to the risk of it.

The storm, teasing through the day, opened up. Soft flakes fell thick as his officers began closing up around the church, urging away those who didn't need to be there and secluding off areas they saw as relevant for another look.

Not that they'd find anything. Luke knew it just as they did.

"We can't stand here and do nothing." At his side, Seth's fear and worry rolled off him in hot, violent waves. "If this man you claim is my grandfather has her then who knows what in the hell he has in mind. He's already proven he's capable of having his own daughter murdered. Do you think he's going to give one damn about Tori?"

Luke understood the anger vibrating in his words but knew better than to react to it. "We're standing here but we're far from doing nothing. One of the best of the FBI has already tracked your grandfather's movements."

He blocked out horrifying images of Tori, frightened and vulnerable at the hands of a man who'd already proven he had no loyalty for the blood of his family. "And we're still tracking him, using every resource we have to find him."

"And if you're too late?" What had been defiance in Seth's gaze simmered into fear.

"We won't be." Luke fought back his own fear. "We can't be."

****

She was going to be sick. She was sure of it.

Tori couldn't find a word or clear thought to bring her back from the spiraling emotions taking control. They sucked on her, drawing her down, until she was sure there was no way to claw herself back up to any sense of reality. Any hold on the truth she'd learned and the threat she knew she faced.

Her grandfather. The idea didn't seem real, so impossible to grasp.

She stole another glance, as she had done many times in the silence that lingered since his declaration. How could it be? *How could he be?*

She thought of her mother. Saw her there, as she always did in her nightmares, bleeding and dying while he watched.

"Did you care at all?" The question came before she could stop it. "Watching my mother...*your daughter*...die. Did you even give a damn?"

His movements were slow as he turned to look at her. There was something in his eyes—a sadness that sickened her. How could he carry any emotion after what he had done?

"I loved your mother." His voice drummed low through the confines of the car. "She was my only child. A part of me and my greatest love...your grandmother. But you don't climb the way to success, as I have, without understanding sacrifices must come."

"Sacrifices? Is that what she was to you?'

Unable to stand another moment looking at him, she turned to the window, staring out at the last of Snow Ridge quickly slipping by. "And Seth and I? What were we? Disposable nuisances to get rid of?"

"You're talking foolish, now. I loved the both of you. You, too, are part of me, just as your mother. I never wanted you to see what you did. One of my greatest regrets is what you saw. I've wished many times I could change it."

His heavy, tired sigh brought her attention back. He stared straight ahead now, seeming to see more than just the inside of the car. "I've often thought of how different it would have been, taking you and Seth home with me and raising you after your parents' death. But that was not a choice to be made. Not once you had seen me."

He turned back, his dark eyes searching as if trying to see through her. "I'd have given you a good life...the best life. Like your mother, you would have wanted for nothing. Your happiness would have been my duty to deliver."

"But life plays unfair games." He shook his head as if hating his own words. "And times can call for survival over all else. Which was the choice I had to make that night, knowing you saw me and understanding the terrible risk if you remembered what was buried inside. I did what I had to in letting you and your brother go. Doing what I could to keep you separated on the chance, together, there might be the push for you to understand what you saw."

"I grew up alone." Though the sadness clenched as it always did, there was less force to it. "You destroyed my family. Left me to suffer without one for my entire childhood. All for your sick sense of survival."

The anger growing inside was hot, sparking greater as he showed no emotion to the truth of her words, only a cold indifference, leaving no doubt to how little he was truly capable of feeling.

She saw it in his eyes. The sick knowledge that he'd take before ever being expected to give. That's why her mother had died. Why she'd been forced to give up a childhood to loneliness.

To him, it was no more than the cost of what had to be done. Just as it would be again. She wasn't naïve enough to believe he planned on letting her walk away from all she'd learned. He'd shared the truth because, for him, her fate had already been decided.

And it was one that matched her mother's.

****

"How in the hell could you not remember you had a grandfather?" Luke's angry words shook through the police cruiser. He knew it wasn't fair, taking his anger out on Seth. But he needed a release before he exploded with the worry and fear tearing through.

Though it had only been thirty minutes since Tori disappeared, it felt like hours passed before they had information to follow.

And he owed Alec another big one for dragging up what would have taken him and his department twice as long to find. Poking through the walls and protections put up, they'd been able to track Tori's Grandfather from Chicago to Snow Ridge.

He wasn't a man who bothered with simple civilian transportation. The private plane that had brought him here waited at a small airfield only an hour away from Snow Ridge.

He had men on it. Just as he had others following behind, tracking what would have been his best route. There were plenty of badges ready and willing to act for Tori's safety. Yet it still did nothing to ease the gnawing fear tearing through his gut.

"You'd have been old enough to remember him." Luke spared Seth a glance as the sirens allowed him his furious speed down the highway.

He never should have allowed him to come along. It wasn't safe. But Seth refused to back down. Sank low enough to use Luke's own loyalty to his brothers as justification to thrust a civilian where he didn't belong.

And there, watching him, waiting for an answer, Luke saw it—the pain and fear burning in his gaze just as it would have been if it were one of his own brothers at risk. Time and separation didn't matter. The blood holding them together was all that burned through Seth now.

"I would have been lots of things." He didn't come back with the same anger Luke had thrown at him. His tone carried a somber note. One of sadness and grief. "Most of all, a young boy who had lost everything he knew. His parents. His baby sister. I may not have seen their murder, as Tori did. But I saw them there, lying in the hallway, bloody and lifeless. I watched the end of their lives through the eyes of a little boy who didn't yet understand what it meant."

And now he felt like a complete jerk as Seth turned, staring out the window at his side. "All I knew from that point, all I grew up with, was the knowledge that I had no family other than Tori. And, to keep her safe, I had to pretend she didn't exist."

It had torn at Tori too. The forced separation their own grandfather had put on them. She'd been denied what family she'd had. Still lived, to this day, with the reality of that.

It wasn't a matter of her having to tell him. Luke understood her fear to get close and offer her heart to others stemmed from that night long ago. A night she'd lost so much more than most could ever imagine.

"You'll have her back." He spared Seth a glance as he shot through traffic. "Your grandfather has caused enough damage. It's time we put a stop to it."

He needed to believe his own words, just as he hoped Seth believed them. There was no room for doubt. Not when it came to Tori and the hold she had, would always have, over his heart.

He couldn't lose that. And he'd make damn sure neither Seth nor Tori had to lose what they had found, either.

****

"Where are we going?"

There was no longer a sign of Snow Ridge, leaving

Tori lost. She only knew one thing, she had to get away. Somehow, she needed to escape the car, her grandfather, and whatever terrible fate waited for her.

Not knowing where she was, feeling as lost as she had the first night she'd made it to Snow Ridge, didn't help the nerves building, fierce and stubborn, inside. But it wouldn't hold her back. Wouldn't stop her once she found a way to run.

"I have a plane waiting for me. I'll be going back to Chicago now that I've had a chance to speak with you." He looked at her with those hard eyes of his. There was nothing there. No love one would expect from a grandfather. No remorse for what he had done or the childhood he'd left her with. There was only cold acceptance reflecting back at her, chasing a chill up her spine. "Perry will be making sure you're taken care of."

Brittle dread hit like shards of ice to the skin. "Take care of me how? You claimed you had no intention of harming me."

"I did." His answering nod was slow, thoughtful. "But minds can be changed, as mine has. With the information I've given, I don't see it in my best interest to take the risk of you repeating what you know. As I said, I don't take risks against what I've worked so hard to build."

Fighting back the bile rising in her throat, she reminded herself she'd already known the answer. From the moment she realized who he was, she'd had no question her fate was already sealed.

But she'd hoped. Somewhere deep inside, she'd hoped. It was a terrible clutch to the heart to know her own grandfather could so casually do away with those he was meant to love and treasure above all else.

Fear surged, clutching at her and dragging air from her lungs while sending an icy chill up her spine.

Needing something, anything, to hold on to as she fought the feeling of drowning in what was to come, she stared out at the flakes, falling heavier now.

She thought of the blizzard. Of being stuck on the side of the road. She thought of Luke, so strong and forceful standing there in the sheet of white. His slow, easy smile. The glimpse of something sexy and willful in those hazel eyes.

He'd been her start in Snow Ridge. There through every step, refusing to leave her side even when she'd done her best to shove him away.

As they picked up speed down the unknown road, she put her mind back to that first night in the pub when her brother had walked in. When she'd known he was hers. The one she'd searched so long and hard for.

Her fear eased a notch as she saw Derby. His constantly wagging tail. His happy bounce when she returned home from work. Her brother had given her that. A small, yet quickly growing, bundle of energy bringing smiles even in the hardest of times.

So much, she thought, as she refused the urge to steal another glance at the hard, cold man sitting beside her. So much she had discovered the moment she'd found her way to Snow Ridge.

She hadn't truly known friendship until here. Hadn't realized, as a woman, what she'd missed living without other females who were close and able to understand those things men could never work through in their mind.

Cara and Jackie had given her something she hadn't been aware she was missing—the easy comfort and solid foundation of true friends.

In such a short amount of time, Snow Ridge had snuck in and become so much a part of her life. Become her home. She had a dog, brother, friends and a man who wanted to make her his wife.

And now, in the push of losing it all, along with her life, she didn't feel the rush to run from it. But instead to find a way to run back to it. To escape the fate her grandfather had planned and find her way back to what waited for her.

She'd found family again. Made a home for herself that involved so much more than she imagined possible. She couldn't lose it. Couldn't allow her grandfather to again destroy what she held dear in her life.

The need for Snow Ridge, for all it held, burned strong. For a moment she considered taking her chances by opening the door and throwing herself out without a care about the speed they traveled down the lonely road.

But then what? Injured on the side of the road with no one around to help wasn't going to get her anywhere except back inside the car.

She'd have to wait until they reached wherever it was her grandfather's plane waited. There had to be an opportunity then. Some way to run before her planned fate had a chance to be carried out.

She'd wait. She'd prepare. Confident in her resolve to fight with all she had. Hold on to what she'd found the moment life brought her to Snow Ridge.

Chapter Thirty

"We have officers at the airport." The nasal bite of his deputy's voice poured through the phone as Luke sped down the mountain highway. "They're staying low key. Don't want to scare them off before we get a chance."

Adrenaline shot frantic through his veins. Every passing minute felt like hours. He was less than half an hour behind the officers already at the airport, yet it felt as if he'd never get there.

"As soon as there's a sign of them, let me know. They are not to get on that plane." The fear of what might be planned grasped hard. He would not lose Tori. Not now. He wanted a life with her. And though she might not be there yet, he was hanging on until she figured it out for herself. He'd found his other half and be-damned if he'd let it go.

"What happens if you're wrong and my grandfather isn't headed for the airport." Stress and worry dragging hard on Seth, he turned haunted eyes on Luke, desperate for answers he couldn't give.

"We can't be. We won't be."

It had to be that simple. Luke wasn't prepared to accept any different. He'd worn the uniform and badge for longer than he cared to count sometimes, but he'd never faced this. Not even when Cara had been missing. Even the hard, painful hit of that hadn't pushed this deep, leaving him with a bone-chilling fear he couldn't shake free from.

He wouldn't let it rule, though. Couldn't afford to. Tori deserved the cop he was. The one who'd sworn to serve and protect. Who knew better than to let his emotions have a say when they threatened to shadow over hard-earned instincts.

Instincts that would bring Tori out of this alive.

Picking up speed, thankful the snow had not yet begun to stick, he wondered how close he might be behind them. Were they around the next bend or pulling into the airport?

He hated not knowing. Wished there was a better way to get a lock on their location.

The vibrating ring of his phone had him steadying the steering wheel with one hand and bringing the phone to his ear with the other. The more he listened, the more the fear grew. He felt Seth's curious gaze burn into his side. Knew the tone in his voice did nothing to ease the worries he battled.

Pushing back the urge to give his phone a good, long hurl, Luke dropped it to the center console. Taking a moment, he eased back his own emotions before answering the questions he felt simmering through Seth.

"Dispatch caught a call as we were leaving the church." He sucked in a harsh breath and fought back the urge to push the car even faster. His speed already hovered on the side of dangerous down the highway with its sharp turns and bends.

"Damn." He slammed an angry hand against the steering wheel. "They found a body inside one of the hotel rooms. There was a do not disturb sign on the door but they went in anyway. Don't know why. Doesn't matter."

There was a growl in his voice. Luke knew it but couldn't stop it. This new info lashed at him. Brought desperate to a new meaning as he flew toward the airport, a million prayers tumbling through his mind. "My officers haven't had much time to process the scene but they don't figure he's been dead more than a day. One bullet. Clean shot."

"You think my grandfather had something to do with it." It was a statement, not a question, coming from Seth.

"I'd bet my life on it. Your grandfather hasn't been here for what's happened to Tori. Everything points to the fact he never stepped foot in Snow Ridge until yesterday."

Bits and pieces worked through Luke's mind like a puzzle to be solved. "But *somebody* has been here. Somebody has been terrorizing your sister since the moment she reached Snow Ridge."

"You think the dead guy is the same one who has been putting Tori through so much?" Seth came to attention with the thought. "It fits." Luke hated to think it but the truth was there in the facts. "Perhaps he didn't do the right thing or took too long to get the right thing done. Who knows what the hell a mind like his thinks. But I'd bet anything, taking care of him, and of Tori, is what brought your grandfather to Snow Ridge."

"And he doesn't plan on leaving till both are done," Seth finished up on a dark, ominous note, leaving Luke unable to deny such a frightening fact.

****

Tori tossed her frantic thoughts aside as the car

slowed to turn off the highway they'd traveled for what felt like an eternity.

Long, low buildings hovered against the edge of the skinny dirt road. Coming around a bend, she spotted the tower with long stretches of asphalt spread out beneath it.

The airport. Her heart leapt painfully with the realization they'd reached their destination. What happened next? Her grandfather had made it clear this was the end of his ride. But what about hers? Where exactly was Perry to take her? What were the final plans?

Not that she planned to let a one of them slide by easily. She had a fight in her. She planned to use it with every chance she had. If she was destined to find a fate the same as her parents, she sure as hell wasn't going to go at it without hitting back.

She heard the shuffling beside her and tried to ignore it, keeping her attention firmly on what passed by outside the window.

"I truly do dislike how this must end." The deep rumble of her grandfather's voice brushed chills over her. "I truly would have enjoyed having a chance to know you in my life rather than sitting back and watching from afar.

"You have your mother's looks." There was softness in his words, but Tori refused to be swayed. "Her stubbornness, too, I've come to realize."

"Why are you pretending to care?" The question was lightning quick, anger and disbelief fueling the force of it. "Just stop now. I don't care to hear anymore."

He didn't argue. Didn't utter another word.

Thankful, Tori put her mind back to her surroundings. To the very desperate need to save her life.

It was Luke she saw there in her mind, as she fought desperately for some way to escape her fate. His hazel eyes capturing hers. The rough fall of his voice. The ease in those strong hands of his gliding over her.

As hard as she'd fought it and as much as she'd tried to deny it, she'd fallen in love with him. And not in a gentle, easy kind of way, either. It was a full on tumble.

And now...

No. She wouldn't let herself travel down a road with no solutions. There had to be a way. She'd find it somehow.

The tower drew closer as they continued down the dirt road edging the runways. She saw it then, blending with the flakes of snow picking up strength, a sleek white jet idling at the far end. Her grandfather's plane. They'd reached the end.

A chill raced down her spine, leaving the sour taste of fear in her mouth. Seconds felt like hours as she stared hard through the window, seeing the waiting plane as her final fate, holding life and death in the hazy puffs pushing through the cold air.

They slowed, pulling off the dirt road for the far edge of the runway. The storm kicked up with more force. Large flakes fell around the car as it stopped between the waiting plane and the tower.

"I am sorry for this." Her grandfather passed a long look over her as he waited for Perry to come around and open the door.

She barely heard him, her mind coming around to what was about to happen. If there was a chance to be had, this was it. It was risky. There wasn't much to give her hope. But she had to take what she could.

Perry circled the front bumper and headed for her grandfather. He'd have to disengage the locks. There was no other choice. And when he did...if she was quick enough.

Careful in her movements, she trailed her fingers gently over the tufted leather covering the inside of the doors. Seeing by touch, afraid to give herself away, her hand slid across the smooth hook of the door handle.

Her grandfather noticed nothing as he tugged on the cuffs of his jacket, preparing for his rush through the snow to reach the plane. Surprised he couldn't hear the pounding of her heart, she forced her breaths to slow.

Steady, she reminded herself as she waited for the right moment.

Watching Perry come around to the door, she heard the soft click as he disengaged the locks. She cracked her door with her grandfather's, hiding the sound within his. But she made no move. Gave no hint of what she planned.

With one last look her way, he slid smoothly from his seat and pushed to his feet outside the car. It was then she moved, as Perry stepped aside to let him by, distracted for that one moment she needed.

She stumbled in her rush to get out of the car, praying for her wobbly legs and weak knees to hold her as she ran. She didn't know where she was going. What she would do next. She only knew to escape as fast as she could.

There was a rumble of shouts from behind. More, she was sure, than just her grandfather and Perry. Still, she couldn't take the risk of looking back and losing those precious seconds. What happened behind didn't matter. It was what was in front of her she needed to see.

Her heart thundered in her ears. Her lungs ached for every breath. She heard more shouts and the heavy fall of boots against ground. But still, she refused to look back.

Heavy flakes danced around her. The cold seeped through. Soon, the sounds from behind filtered away as her mind swirled. As the only sound she heard was the frantic rush of her pulse. Ahead, past the runways, she saw the thick stretch of trees. If she could make it there and lose herself in the thick branches she might have a chance.

The thought pushed her faster. Not much further. If she just kept—

She yelled in surprise and pain as something closed around her wrist, yanking hard. Tripping over her own two feet, she would have fallen on her face if not for the vicious hold on her arm, dragging her like a rag doll.

For a moment, she had a flash of a familiar face before her arm was twisted behind her, biting through her shoulder.

"You aren't going anywhere." Perry yanked her against him. Her entire world shifted, threatening to throw her over, as the cold press of a gun dug deep into flesh against her temple.

****

"Hell." Luke barely had the car shoved into park before flying out of it.

He'd seen it, coming around the bend in the road, Tori running like fire over the runways. His men surrounded her grandfather while another man burst around them, caring nothing for the guns quickly trained on him.

He knew, as they did, there would be no shots fired. Not when there was a risk of hitting Tori.

She was fast, but not enough. Luke saw red when the man grabbed her and yanked her against him. And his heart stopped as he thrust a gun against the side of her head.

"Stay back," he barked as Seth's heavy footfalls echoed behind him.

"Like hell. He has my sister." Fear and anger rumbled dangerously through Seth's voice. He pushed by, nearly made it past Luke's reach before he was able to grab him and pull him back.

As much as he hated to, he stopped, forcing Seth to do the same. "Listen to me." He gave a shake, grabbing Seth's attention. "I need to be able to do everything within my power and experience to save your sister. But if you go in there half-cocked, getting in the way, you only risk putting her in more danger."

He didn't like it. Luke saw it clearly in his eyes burning with rage. But he didn't have time to stand there and try to convince him. He could only hope Seth understood.

His boots pounded hard against the asphalt as he made a direct line for his officers standing with their guns trained on the man holding Tori. He let out a quick sigh of relief when there was no sound of following footsteps behind him.

He watched Tori as he moved, every bit of him reaching out to her, wishing for a way to reassure her. To let her know he'd give his own life before allowing her to lose her own.

It took everything in him, every bit of training, not to run off half-cocked himself and barrel after the bastard who held a gun to her head. Beat him until he was nothing more than a bloody puddle on the ground at his feet.

"Back off or she's done." The deep, low voice pierced the eerie silence hovering in the space between the man, Tori, and his officers. As if needing to prove his point, he yanked hard on Tori, causing a yelp of pain.

It tore through Luke, destroying everything inside of him. "Let's all calm down, here." He clutched desperately to his training as his eyes met Tori's frightened gaze.

There was so much there. So much reaching out to him. He nearly stumbled from the weight of it. Ached, painfully, for another chance to hold her and tell her he loved her.

But not now. What she needed from him to keep her alive was every deep instinct, experience, and knowledge he carried with him.

"Name's Perry Bogdan." Newell, one of his officers with nearly as much time on the force as Luke, offered what information he had. "Seems to be the do-all for our man, Pavenco." He pointed back to where they had Tori's grandfather surrounded.

Luke didn't bother to look. His attention was only for Tori. "Perry, I'm Chief Grady. I'd like to work with you so that we all come out of this unharmed."

His answering laugh was dark, frightening. "You're nothing but a small town wanna-be with your badge and gun. Don't bother with the textbook negotiating. Wasting your time is all it is."

"Only one way this is going to end." He took a step back, dragging Tori with him. "You're going to let myself and my boss go." He twisted the gun away from Tori's head long enough to wave it toward her grandfather. "Or this one here." He slammed it hard back to her temple. "Will be meeting the fate planned for her."

It was anger pushing at Luke as he grabbed for his gun. Terror that had him putting pressure against the trigger. He was a rancher in his blood, a cop on top of that. He was a good shot. Always had been. All he needed was the chance to show itself.

"That's not going to happen." With only his eyes, he tried reaching out to Tori. He needed her to move. Just enough to get a good shot.

"And the way I see it, you do anything to harm her." He jerked his head at Tori. "You give me all the reason in the world to make sure you won't be enjoying your own fate."

Though he shook inside, he held his gun steady.

"So, as long as I keep her alive, I live." There was a dark glimmer in Perry's eyes. He took another step back then another as his tight hold took Tori with him.

He wanted the trees. The safety of them. Luke couldn't let it happen. If he made it there it was as good as over for Tori.

****

No. This was not going to be the end.

It was Luke she concentrated on, not the one holding a gun to her head. In him, she found what she needed. Through the love in his gaze, strength came, taking over.

Damn if she was going to let someone take that from her. She'd lost enough. Faced too many long, lonely years in Chicago. This was hers now. All she'd discovered in Snow Ridge. She refused to let it go.

He was dragging her back. For the trees, she realized, remembering what she'd run for. And she was his shield, carefully placed between him and the line of officers staring him down.

They couldn't do a thing. She saw it, even in Luke's steady gaze. They couldn't risk a shot when it might hit her. Wouldn't take such a chance until they had no other choice.

And that other choice, in every way she played it through her head, didn't fare well for her.

It was up to her.

Keeping her gaze locked with Luke's, drawing courage there, she didn't take time to second-guess. It was now or never.

With that thought, she put all her force into her free arm, jabbing back with her elbow and landing square in his gut, just as she'd hoped.

As his surprised curse erupted behind her, she kicked back with the heel of her shoe, lodging it firmly against his shin while throwing her head back. The crack of bone slamming against bone rocked through her. But she barely had time to register the pain as his hold on her arm loosened.

Her shoulder screaming for mercy, she yanked with everything she had inside. Tears from the pain burned her eyes. His hold broke and she stumbled back.

Through blurry vision, she caught the barrel of the gun centered on her. "Bitch," he growled, his finger coming back against the trigger.

She heard the crack, the pop of it. Smelled the acrid stench surround her. Yet still, she stood.

It was Perry who tumbled hard and fast to the ground. A stain of dark red spread like a fungus over his chest.

Too stunned to do anything but stand and stare, she only had a moment to catch the flurry of movement through the corner of her eye before she was grabbed, yanked off her feet, and hurried away.

"Are you okay?" Setting Tori back to her feet, Luke couldn't find it in him to let go. His arms tight, he held her against him, wondering if he'd ever be able to set her free again.

He felt the shakes and drew back enough to catch the tears beginning to well in her eyes. As the adrenaline wore off, reality set in. He'd seen it many times through his career. But watching Tori struggle with it tore at his heart. Left an empty, hollow feeling inside, knowing there was nothing he could do for her other than give her the time to let it out.

As controlled chaos broke out around him, he stayed with Tori, letting his officers handle what needed to be done as tears flowed, staining his shirt and striking at his heart.

Chapter Thirty-One

She ached from the top of her head to the tips of her toes. If it wasn't for Luke refusing to let go, she wasn't sure she'd stay on her own two feet.

Her shoulder and arm throbbed. The back of her head, where she'd cracked it against Perry, was a constant pounding, snaking its way to a terrible pulse at her temples.

But she was alive. The thought helped push back on the pain.

"Oh. Thank God." Seth reached for her the minute she drew close, pulling her from Luke's arms and gathering her in his own. "I thought—"

He shook his head, chasing away whatever ran through his head. "Doesn't matter. I'm just glad you're okay. I don't think I could have lived through losing you a second time."

She clung to him the same as he did her. Tears threatened again as she held on. Snow fell around them. The cold settled. And neither of them cared.

The wild mix of emotions began to settle, but only for a moment. Still tight in Seth's arms, she glanced over his shoulder. Watched as two in crisp, blue uniforms led her grandfather away from the car that had brought them there.

He turned, his eyes catching hers, sucking the breath from her lungs. She shivered with the thought, of all that were there, he was the only one who would have wished for her death at Perry's hands. Had originally planned it to be that way.

"Hey." Seth tightened his hold as Tori began to shake. "You okay?"

She didn't answer, only pulled away from him.

Anger burning fresh and wild inside, she didn't consider what she was doing. Couldn't even say, for sure, what it was.

Her feet led the way. Wide, determined steps moved her quickly over the length of the runway.

Images, like a slide-show, played through her mind. From the past, the present. Her mother, so beautiful. So kind and tender. She was there again, sitting on the edge of the bed, watching her get ready for her night out.

Whether from dream or reality, she was again that little girl, so mystified by her. So in awe of how perfect she was. Though she had no real memories of it, she felt her love, even now.

The echo of following steps drifted from behind. She ignored them. That fateful night was back. The blood, the fear, the tears. The heart-wrenching loss playing such a hand in the rest of her life.

And the years she'd been alone. So empty and cold in a life with no family to speak of. The years of thinking about Seth, searching for him only to come up with nothing.

He took that from her. In his greed, he'd stolen so much.

Pain and loss swirled heavy, burning through so that she simmered heat even with the cold of the snow falling around her. It drove her, near desperate, toward her grandfather. Needing what, she didn't know. But there was something. It crawled from deep inside, determined to be released.

Because he'd almost taken it all again—everything she'd found to create family once more in her life.

He looked up as she came close, a cold, slow smile lengthening his lips. The officers on either side of him looked past her to Luke.

She wondered if he'd stop her, giving the signal for her to be held back while her grandfather was taken away. But whatever sign they received had them stopping where they were, waiting for her.

Still, with no thought to what she was doing, she came to within only a foot of her grandfather and looked at him with eyes fueled dark by the anger boiling inside.

She felt the protection of both Seth and Luke hovering behind her. The curious eyes of the officers standing in front of her. And the cold indifference from her grandfather as he stared at her.

"Is there more you feel needs to be said?" He quirked a thick brow and looked from her to Seth. Though she was confident he knew it was his grandson, he showed no signs of it. Nothing but the same emotionless man she'd come to understand was the core of who he truly was.

And she had nothing left to say. Not a single word. What she had were disgust and rage. An ugly acceptance of who he was. A realization she was finished letting him and what he had done control her life for another second.

But, for one brief moment, she wanted him to know…just know.

And it was there before she thought twice about it. Balling her fist, she struck out with everything she had inside. With the force of her parent's death, the loss of her brother for so many long years, and the fear of losing all she'd found.

It was there, in that flash of a moment, as her fist lodged quick and hard against his nose. Bone cracking against bone. The force of it, the pure anger exploding in that one punch shook through her.

She didn't bother waiting for his reaction though there was a small part of her finding satisfaction in the blood she knew she'd drawn. Feeling the stares of everyone landing heavy on her, she turned on her heels and looked at Luke.

"Let's go home."

****

Sitting in the cozy, family warmth of the kitchen in the main house, Tori did her best to grasp what ran through her head.

It seemed like a lifetime ago, rather than hours, since waking up in Luke's arms and having him throw marriage out between them. In some ways, it felt as if the woman that morning was so different than the one sitting there now. At his side. Finding comfort, love, and a deep sense of knowing where she belonged.

They'd fussed and worried over her. They'd come together, each one of them, to make sure she was okay the moment Luke walked her through the door after his mandatory visit to the hospital.

Just to make sure, he'd pushed, refusing to give an inch. So she'd gone, fighting back the suggestion she spend the night. Her injuries were minor. A pulled shoulder. One hell of a good bump on the back of her head. Bruised knuckles from the tangle she'd taken with her grandfather's nose. They'd prescribed pain killers, advised plenty of rest, and that was good enough for her.

And then she'd walked into this big, rumbling, wonderful house to find a kitchen full of those she'd come to know, care for, and love.

Hattie had fussed. It wouldn't be her if she didn't. There'd been so much tenderness in her gaze as she rested a hand against her cheek, staring for a moment with the concern and love of a fretful mother.

Healing with food, as she knew best, she settled Tori at the table, placing a bowl of chili and a plate of cornbread in front of her.

"You'll eat and you'll feel better." She dropped a soft kiss on the top of Tori's head, nearly bringing her to tears.

And so it went from there, reminding her of the first night she'd spent here with snow falling outside the windows and warm comfort simmering within.

There were tears in Cara's eyes when she came around behind Tori to hug her. "Don't ever scare me like that again." She gently nudged her side.

Jake forgot about her injured shoulder, grabbing her in a hold so tight she nearly lost her breath from it even as she fought back the bite of pain shooting through.

This had once frightened her. The thought grabbed as she nipped carefully at her chili before grabbing a small chunk from the cornbread. That first night she'd sat here, with the same people around the table, watching them and wondering at what they were.

She didn't understand a bit of it and was so out of

her element she nearly itched deep with it.

But that had changed. They had changed it for her. Tonight, after all she'd been through, come to know and realize, she was part of who they were. As much family as the others gathered around the table with lively conversation and laughter heating the room better than any fire ever could.

"You okay?" Luke rested a hand along her thigh under the table and squeezed.

She turned to look at him, wondering if he could see through her gaze all that was rolling about inside. "I am. I'm better than okay."

She was perfect, if the truth were to be told. In that moment, that time, she realized she'd finally found home.

****

Luke wasn't sure he'd ever be able to shake the fear again.

The image of a gun to the side of Tori's head was one he'd live with forever. Even now, as he glanced at her sitting soft and quiet beside him inside the truck, the punch of it took a mighty swing.

The idea he might lose her, in the very worst of ways, stole every bit of strength he had. Left him as close to weak and helpless as he could get.

She'd worked her way not only into his life but into the deepest reaches of his heart. To places he knew would hold her forever.

He'd told her he'd wait. Just that morning, he'd made the promise. But he wasn't so sure anymore if he could survive it.

He needed her. More than the next breath he drew through his lungs. But to admit it, he knew, would only send her running.

"It was good to be with everyone." Tori's voice was a gentle breeze through the cab of the truck as he pulled up in front of the house. "But I'm glad to be home."

Home.

The word caught on him. Created a strange tightening in his throat.

Yes. That was what he wanted. This house he had built as his escape. His own slice of heaven. He wanted, more than anything, for it to be the home he shared with her. She'd stayed because of the threat hovering over her. But now that it was gone.

He couldn't imagine her leaving.

Unable to wait another minute, Derby darted from the truck as soon as Luke had the door open.

Tori watched him for a minute. Laughed at the sight of him running circles through the snow-covered yard as his puppy yap echoed in the quiet night.

This was life. The kind worth fighting for.

A tender smile on her lips, she opened her own door, following Derby into the gentle fall of snow. She knew what she wanted. Better than she ever had before. And it was right here in front of her.

Waiting for Luke to come around the front of the truck and join her, she slipped her hand easily into his. They moved up the path toward the house. At the steps leading to the deck, she stopped and turned back, staring over the snowy night settling around the ranch.

"It's beautiful here." A soft sigh escaped as she edged softly against Luke's side. "I didn't really see it at first. Not for what it truly was. But now, I can't imagine ever finding a place like this if I were to search my entire life."

Luke looked at her but said nothing.

Finally noticing nobody was calling him inside, Derby turned away from whatever he chased and ran over to plop down at Tori's feet. He stared up at them, eager excitement shining in his dark eyes.

He'd known from the start, Tori thought, bending to pat his head. Derby had known where home was before she'd ever given it consideration.

"When I first came to Snow Ridge, I didn't have thoughts to what I would do outside of taking it one day at a time. But somewhere, in the back of my mind, I always believed I would return to Chicago and continue my life there as I had for so many years."

Straightening, she turned to Luke. "I never counted on you, though." A smile tugged at the corners of her mouth. "From that first day, on the side of the road in the blizzard, to this very morning, asking me to marry you, I've done nothing but stumble and fumble my way through."

"Everything I thought I wanted and was satisfied with," tears gathered in her eyes as she looked at him, "you challenged. And with nothing more than a look or touch. All those words meant something, but they failed in comparison to the feel of you when you'd hold me. When you'd wrap around me and make me feel as if I was the safest, most loved woman in the world."

And then they came, as much as she'd hoped they wouldn't. One tear then another softly slid down her cheek. With the pad of his thumb, Luke brushed one away then bent to drop a kiss where it had rested.

Caught in his gaze, staring at him through the moisture blurring her eyes, she lost the words she was sharing. Forgot what it was she was trying to make sure he knew.

It had seemed so important only seconds before. So much she wanted him to understand. About her. About where she had come from. Where he had taken her.

But as he brushed another tear away and dropped a kiss on her lips, she realized there was only one thing she could say that mattered.

"I love you." She grabbed his hand, holding it tight against her heart so he could feel its pounding. The rhythm beating for him. "I want to spend my life with you."

Drawing back from her and dropping his hands to her shoulders, Luke held her out, looking at her with so much love in his hazel eyes. "Is that a yes to marrying me?"

Through her tears came the smile. "It is."

Wrapping arms around her, he lifted her from her feet, finding her mouth for a kiss promising his love.

Tori melted under the force of it. Her tears still fell. Her heart beat hard. She gasped for breath when he pulled away, needing a moment to steady herself.

"I've been so busy running from my fear of what the future might hold." She slowly slid back to her feet, putting everything she felt, every bit of love inside, into the words coming from her heart. "I forgot that what really matters is everything we can have today."

A word about the author...

Cassandra Bella is an author of Romance Suspense novels and has been writing for as long as she can remember, and for as long as she's been letting others know. She completed her first book, *Dear Diary*, in her grandmother's family room on a manual typewriter at the age of 12—that manuscript still holds a place of honor in her home.

With Italian and Irish heritage, Cassandra was an only child who still managed to grow up in a large family and all the craziness that goes with it. Those unique, sometimes complicated, bonds often reflect in her writing. And growing up a Cop's Brat, spending many childhood days running around the police department, she draws on that experience now with many of her heroes who are also protectors of the law.

Cassandra was born and raised in Colorado, and currently lives there with her husband, who was her high school sweetheart, and with their children and grandchildren.

Visit her at:

http://cassandrabella.com